Also by Doug Richardson

Lucky Dey Thrillers
> *99 Percent Kill*
> *Reaper*
> *American Bang*
> *The Night is Never Black*
> *Hip Slick and Dead*

Other Fiction
> *The Safety Expert*
> *Dark Horse*
> *True Believers*

Nonfiction
> *The Smoking Gun: True Stories from Hollywood's Screenwriting Trenches*

A LUCKY DEY THRILLER

DOUG RICHARDSON

BLOOD MONEY

los angeles

This is a work of fiction. Names, characters, places, and incidents either are the product of the author's imagination or are used fictitiously. Any resemblance to actual events, locales, organizations, or persons, living or dead, is entirely coincidental and beyond the intent of either the author or the publisher.

Velvet Elvis Entertainment
6038 Tampa Avenue
Suite 366
Tarzana, California 91356

Cover photo by Tono Balaguer/Shutterstock.com

Cover design by Karen Richardson

More information at http://www.dougrichardson.com

ISBN: 978-0-9964563-8-8

For my loving mother,
Barbara Richardson

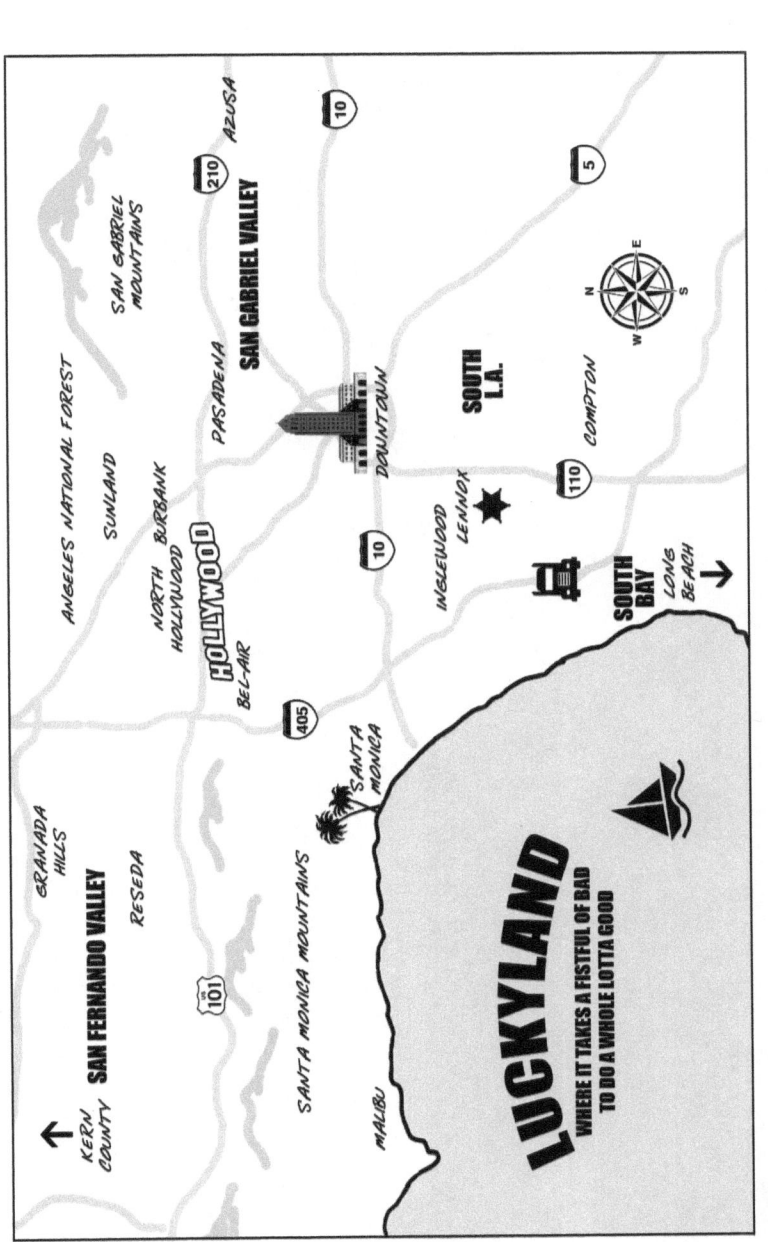

Monday

1

Somewhere in Kern County, California.

Beemer cursed.

Two words. Two syllables. A mental rim shot inside Greg Beem's skull. The simple phrase was perfectly descriptive, and summed up just about every seminal moment of the Beemer's twenty-nine years. The curse described a moment that was, in truth, formative. Beemer could catalog his life with his very own cursed moments.

I wet the bed.

The gun went off.

She's really pregnant?

My parachute didn't open.

That knife was sharper than I thought.

The bitch actually left me.

I really didn't mean to burn the house down.

Beemer's most recent cursed moment began at 3:16 a.m. on August 6. Beemer remembered the time because, for some unknown reason, his eyes had flicked to the digital clock display on the dashboard of the Peterbilt tandem axle tractor rig. He was alone and behind the wheel of this beautiful piece of machinery. Nearly brand spanking new. Gray leather seats in the forward cab with a comfy sleeper bed behind. The dash was equally monochrome with an array of digital gauges and switches. The steering wheel was wrapped like the grip of a $400 tennis racket. But the interior was just the icing on a very masculine cake.

Beemer had actually fallen in love the moment he first set his eyes on her. The truck was glossy black with matte airfoils. Big-ass stainless wheels. Twin chrome exhaust stacks flanking the cab. And towing a forty-foot refrigerated trailer that was as dark as a moonless night. Damn, she was pretty. A gearhead's wet dream. Too bad she was stolen. If he could have bought her, Beemer might have considered changing his vocation to that of a long-haul truck driver.

Beemer clutched, downshifting to slow his heavy load without having to jam on the air brakes. He felt the forty-seven thousand pounds of refrigerated trailer he was towing push from behind, as if it had a mind of its own, willfully nudging the man to ignore the warning, hit the gas, and damn the consequences.

The warning: a Kern County sheriff's deputy a hundred yards ahead, astride the yellow center strip of Highway 395, waving both arms over his head in an international sign of distress. Beemer wished he could count the number of times one of his cursed moments had begun with this kind of signal. In the deputy's hand was a high-intensity flashlight, the beam igniting the big rig's windshield, directing the driver to pull over. Beemer slowed and clicked on his high beams. The blast from the big rig's lights revealed the scene beyond the deputy. A single Kern County sheriff's unit parked at an angle across the southbound lane. Driver's door and trunk lid open. And twenty yards further, an overturned Porsche Cayenne SUV. White. By the looks of the deformed body and black road char, the SUV seemed to have taken a few tumbles before coming to rest on the shoulder. The windows were either blown out or spider-webbed so badly they had turned nearly opaque. Totaled. A $70,000 brain fart. A certain cursed moment for the owner or, more likely, the leasing company.

Not to mention the driver and passenger.

Beemer clutched again, releasing the gears, and eased his foot onto the air brakes. Ten sets of brake shoes uniformly pinched ten oversized ceramic disks. Once again, he could feel his cargo shoving the cab from behind. Controlled inertia. Forty-seven thousand pounds of restrained energy came slowly to a safe stop.

"Step out of the cab, please," said the deputy, his voice muffled by the tractor rig's safety glass.

Beemer rolled down the window. As the deputy circled round and through the headlight beams, Beemer clocked the cop as young. Twenty-three years old tops. Maybe five-foot-eight. Shiny black hair, matted down across his forehead by a flop sweat. The deputy's face was pale, nearly colorless in the dimness.

"Sir?" said the deputy. "I need your assistance. Need you to climb out and set up flares to your rear in order to control traffic."

"What traffic?" said Beemer. Monotone. Still, he thought the delivery sounded a little like he thought it was a joke.

"I got accident victims…" The deputy bit his lip in frustration. What cool he had left was slipping away. "Goddammit, mister. I need your help!"

Mister? The poor deputy couldn't see past the fog on his own lenses. Beemer wasn't much older than him. Wiser? Most likely. Experienced too. Worldly. And practiced in the art of covering his ass—not to mention his precious assets, all presently behind him in a stolen refrigerated trailer rig.

"All right," said Beemer. "I'm on it."

"Got the flares in the trunk here."

"Right. So what the hell happened?"

The deputy heard the question but didn't answer. Not that Beemer needed to know. He could guess some of it. The Porsche SUV had soared past the eighteen-wheeler not fifteen minutes earlier. Beemer had glanced down as he sped down the adjacent lane. He thought he'd seen a blonde behind the wheel. As for a passenger, he couldn't make out if it was a man or woman. All Beemer had seen was the glowing ember of a lit cigarette, followed by sparks as the dumb-ass flicked the butt out the window. It was August. Hot. Drier than a dead gnat. Though this was the high desert, there were roadside grasses that could easily ignite. A fire would draw attention. Attention was exactly what Beemer wanted to avoid. Driving the rig at a safe sixty-two miles an hour, he figured the Porsche Cayenne and its two passengers were traveling something near eighty-five miles per hour. Its red tail lights had disappeared into the night.

"You know how to light these?" asked the deputy, passing off a bundle of road flares.

"Sure," said Beemer. By now, he was close enough to see the front left portion of the sheriff's unit. The bumper was badly deformed and the headlight was dangling by a pair of wires. Beemer could see paint transfers. White. Instantly, Beemer was revising the story in his head. At first, he had thought the speeding Porsche had lost control and flipped. The deputy was probably in the area and had stumbled across the accident scene. But the damage to the patrol car added a new wrinkle. Somehow, the deputy's vehicle and the SUV had traded paint in some kind of collision. This would explain the young deputy's demeanor. The sweat and fogged glasses. The panicked tone.

This was definitely one of those cursed moments. A flash in time shared by both the deputy and the big rig driver. Only the poor deputy clearly hadn't recognized the importance of seeing the moment for what it was. Adrenaline had already pumped though his bloodstream, crossing the cerebral cortex, cementing the time and place of the incident in his memory for as long as he would live. But adrenaline can have dangerous side effects: impaired judgment and problem solving. Stab a competitive chess player with a syringe full of adrenaline before a critical move and watch his ability to plan ahead turn to mush. The key, Beemer knew, was to identify the cursed moment at the precise moment at which it begins to unfold. Training had taught him as much. Not to mention all the government-issued therapy. Awareness stems the adrenaline push and leaves the critical thinking lobes of the brain unaffected. The chess game can continue.

Beemer scratched the top of the first flare. Sparks. Then a familiar blaze of red-dyed flame. His thoughts were clear and unmuddled.

The deputy had surely called for assistance. EMS, a sheriff's backup, Highway Patrol. Because of the obvious contact between the sheriff's vehicle and the Porsche SUV, an internal investigation would follow, making the big rig driver a witness. They would take his statements there at the scene with follow-up interviews at a later appointed date. Beemer would be asked to give personal information such as his identification, current address, and occupation. At some point he would be asked to explain what the hell he was doing driving an eighteen-wheel refrigerator rig southbound on Highway 395.

This was too much information for Beemer to give. He had known it well before he applied the air brakes to stop. He also had known that he wouldn't have the time to give it. He was on a schedule. And there was no place for this sort of delay.

So how much time did Beemer have until assistance arrived? Ten minutes? Five? Two, even?

The young deputy was on his knees, reaching into the SUV in an effort to help the passengers inside. As Beemer walked closer, he heard whimpering. He didn't know if it was the blonde woman he'd spied from his truck's perch or her cigarette-flicking, potential fire-starting companion. And it didn't really matter a whit to him. Beemer had only moments to execute his chess move and put this event in his rearview mirror.

The red glow of the flare lit Beemer's measured footsteps as he closed the gap between himself and the deputy, who was nearly prone, with his shoulders wedged inside the turtled SUV. Beemer keyed on the holstered pistol on the deputy's hip. A standard Glock 19.

"Shit!" yelled the deputy, wriggling from the SUV's passenger window. This is when he noticed the red glow of flare. He snapped his head toward the blazing stick. So bright he had to shade his eyes. "What the hell are you doing? You're supposed to place flares—"

The deputy saw his own gun in the hand of the big rig driver, thus experiencing his second cursed moment of the night.

"Aw, fuck!" said the deputy.

"Stealin' my favorite curse, brother," said Beemer, squeezing the light trigger. The Glock gave a slight jolt and punched a neat hole through the deputy's skull. As the deputy's chest heaved one last time, his silvery name tag glinted in the flare's light. Beemer wasn't sure why—whether it was curiosity or habit—he leaned forward to note the name etched in black. A. Dey.

"Okay. So you seen it, Beems," he said as if to cue himself to carry on. Next, he followed the smell of gasoline, dripping from a crack below the SUV's right rear fender. Beemer stepped back, preparing to toss the flare into the growing puddle when he heard a woman's voice.

"Help me…"

The voice was slight, barely above a whisper, yet distinctively feminine.

"Please…"

"Yeah," said Beemer, keeping the adrenaline from crossing his cerebral cortex. He was still in control. Still thinking with clarity. Impulses in check. With that, he let go of the flare, tossing it square into the gasoline puddle. In a combustive flash, the SUV was fully engulfed in flames. A pyre that could be seen for miles. If there were helicopters in the area, it would be a beacon calling for help. No time to waste. Get back to the rig.

If Beemer heard the woman screaming from inside the burning SUV, he would be able to dismiss it into a remote corner of his memory. Cataloged with all the other cries he'd heard in his twenty-nine years.

Beemer climbed back into the tractor rig. As he restarted the diesel engine, he reminded himself that his thirtieth birthday needed to be a real humdinger. A go-hard, envelope-pushing night of partying. Preferably at some faraway island resort. He'd open a tab at the bar and invite all comers. Men *and* women. Preferably strangers because they would be easier to get along with and so much more appreciative of all the free food and liquor. They wouldn't even need to know his name, but would be grateful to the sandy-haired surfing vagabond who had just turned thirty.

The sudden urge for a cigarette came about the same time the flaming SUV disappeared from Beemer's rear mirror. With his fingertips, he felt just below the shoulder joint of his left arm. Under his polo shirt was the familiar relief of a nicotine patch. Beemer was calculating when he had last replaced the patch when a northbound car surged past. The headlights appeared from around a corner, quickly switching from high beams to low. Beemer couldn't make the model or year. All he could tell was that it was gray in color. Nondescript as hell. American? Korean? Japanese? Most affordable cars looked the same nowadays. Especially when blasting by at seventy miles per hour. A solo driver, Beemer reasoned. A driver who would, in moments, be a witness. The driver would soon come upon the burning SUV. After the initial shock, the solo driver would fumble for a mobile phone and dial 911. It didn't matter to Beemer how long would it take the emergency operator to marry the report from the driver with the call for assistance from the sheriff's deputy. Events were unfolding in their natural order. By the time the driver was officially interviewed, would he even remember having passed a southbound big rig barely a mile from the crime scene? Affirmative or otherwise, Beemer would be near his destination of Long Beach, California, by then. Once there, his precious cargo would be transferred into a refrigerated shipping container and set on a journey halfway around the world.

2

Lucky Dey had never ever gotten used to it. Of the thousands of times he had been awakened by a telephone, it had always been with a start. As if jolted by a billion volts. It was in his DNA. His father was a heavy sleeper. The same went for his granddad. Sleeping had always come easily to Lucky. Rest his head, close his eyes, and slumber would be summoned. Anytime, anyplace. It was one of his gifts. He was a veritable Superman of sleep. But if Superman had kryptonite, Lucky Dey had the telephone. Whether it was the classic jangle of bells or some smartphone electronica or the gentlest of musical ringtones, Lucky would still feel the surge of juice and wake with a jump. So why not turn off the phone? asked one of many girlfriends who had witnessed Lucky's bad waking habit. Simple. Lucky was a cop. He was often on call. And until a mad scientist could implant a waking node in his brain to gently tickle him when he was needed, he would have to suffer the goddamn telephone.

"This is Lucky," he croaked, clearing his throat only after he had answered. It was dark, but morning. He knew that much. It had been a.m. when he had closed his eyes. There's no way Lucky could have slept through the day into night. Nobody ever left him alone that long.

"Captain needs you," said the voice, which Lucky guessed was Chelsea's, the part-time secretary, part-time 911 operator. Her voice was slightly throaty, with the occasional excited squeak at the high end when she finally got a joke. Very sexy. But also very married, like so many East Kern County women. So many of them were freshly scrubbed, earthy, and real. Nothing at all like the ladies from down Los Angeles way. Kern County women wore their lack of sophistication like their denim. Tight and without labels.

"Goin' on, Chelsea?" asked Lucky, fishing around his night-stand for the familiar feel of an Excedrin bottle. He snapped the lid with his thumb and dry-swallowed two capsules. The headache hadn't landed yet. But Lucky knew it would eventually arrive and settle near the base of his skull, as it did most every day. "Chelsea?"

There was a pause at the other end of the line. Either that or Lucky had fallen back asleep. He opened his eyes, swept his apart-ment bedroom for light, landing on his television screen, where the DirecTV logo bounced from edge to edge like an old Atari video game. To his left was the bathroom where the door was cracked, leaving a slice of incandescent light to bisect the small space.

"Chelsea?"

"It's Tony," said Chelsea, her voice cracking abnormally.

Ah, hell, thought Lucky. Of course she was calling about Tony, his half brother younger by eleven years. Since Tony was four, Lucky had joked that his little bro was an accident-prone mini-me. Little Tony Tumbles, the family poster child for ambulatory care. The list of Tony's accidental injuries could fill an orthopedics man-ual. When the Dey family lived in San Pedro, there had been a local orthopedics practice comprised of five partners. And by the time he was a high school sophomore, Tony was on a first-name basis with every last one of those docs.

But young Tony, fully intent on following his big brother into all adventures, including the Los Angeles County Sheriff's Department, kept seeking more thrills. Motorcycles. Football. Even base jumping. Each extreme activity had ended in a bone-breaking dust-up that left Tony radiating with permanent pins and screws deep beneath his flesh.

"What's he done this time?" asked Lucky. He was sitting up now. That thin band of light from the cracked bathroom door touched his bare torso, revealing a landscape of scars. Bullet wounds. Stitches.

"They did everything for him."

"Who did everything? Wait. Did you say *for* him? Or *to* him?"

"I'm so sorry, Lucky. Tony didn't make it."

"What?"

"I'm sorry."

"Sorry for...my brother Tony?"

"Yes. Tony. Something happened out on 395."

"He was in a car accident?"

"I don't know. It's a mess out there—"

"And Tony is on the scene or at the hospital?"

There was a pause again on the other end of the phone. Lucky could hear Chelsea breathing. Or was it the buzzing in his skull? He could sense that the oncoming hangover was in a foot race with his daily headache.

"Lucky?" asked a new voice. Masculine with an edge of FM radio circa 1977 in it.

"Cappy?" guessed Lucky.

"Chelsea's all broken up about this. She's not sure you heard her right."

"My nimrod brother got into somethin' out on 395. Just wanna know where he is so I can bang his head."

"And you heard the part where she said Tony didn't make it?"

The tingling started just below Lucky's ankles, slowly tracing upward along the architecture of his nervous system. As if portions of him were suddenly dying on a cellular level. Then came the déjà vu. From when Lucky was a young L.A. sheriff's deputy stationed at Lennox. A member of the Trace Street Crips had found his way into the station lunchroom and dropped a shot of cyanide into an Igloo cooler of lemonade. Lucky recalled his mental state when it had been radioed Lennox-wide that the poison had been discovered. He had guzzled from the cooler of lemonade earlier. And though the cyanide had not yet showed any negative affects in Lucky, the news that he might be on a countdown with death caused him the very sensation he was feeling now while seated at the edge of his bed, phone to his ear, his "Cappy" making sure his top detective was clear on the inference.

"Your brother is dead, Lucky. Medics didn't have a chance. He died along with the other two."

Other two? Weren't we talking about my brother? The sick sensation coursing inside Lucky stopped at his ears, burning them hot until they stung.

"Tony, he's…I heard you…I heard you…" stammered Lucky, trying to keep from throwing up in his mouth. He swallowed, then spat words out loud enough to split his own skull, "Whadda you mean…Drew? What the fuck happened?"

"Still sorting it out," said Captain Edward Andrews. "Got three vics. Possible TC between Tony's unit and the civilian. A car fire. One maybe witness—"

"So he died in a wreck?"

"No. Shot in the head. We think the perp set the fire after," said the captain. "Listen, Luck—"

"On my way in."

"I don't need you today. Just need you to—"

Lucky snapped the phone cord from the wall, effectively ending the call. For a matter of minutes, he sat at the edge of bed, nearly motionless, barely breathing, infected with a form of living rigor mortis. If in the future some shrink would have the chance to ask Lucky when the precise moment was that he had lost his last true connection to humankind, he'd have to say it had been then in that little stucco shithole. Number 112. Ridgecrest Palms Apartments.

"What fuckin' palms?" Lucky had wise-assed on the first day he had moved from his Venice Beach shag palace to the little cookie-cutter one-bedroom apartment. For six months he had shared the space with his little brother who slept on the futon. That was until Tony hooked up with a divorcee who owned a nail salon and moved in with her. Lucky had imagined he would look for a condo or maybe even a house. Invest in his new hometown. Finally possess that government tax deduction called a mortgage payment. That was five damn years ago. And the only stake he had made in Ridgecrest life was the detective job and a twenty-three-foot Centurian Enzo ski boat that hadn't left dry dock in fifteen months.

Now his brother was dead. The weight of it was overwhelming on so many levels that somewhere inside Lucky a switch flipped that sent him into a remote functioning mode, without which he wouldn't have been able to shower or dress. He did, however, have trouble finding his gun. The apartment didn't rack up a square footage larger than that of a single-wide trailer and was choked with unfolded laundry, cardboard boxes piled three and four high from items never unpacked from the L.A. move, a big-screen TV perched atop the dining table, swap meet art purchased for the house he had never shopped for, water skis, and wake boards. In other words, the space was merely a crash pad furnished with good intentions and no follow-through.

Lucky found his gun atop the cabinet just above the toilet. It was a reissue Colt model 1911, locked and loaded with a fat bullet in the chamber. Not exactly regulation for an off-duty cop, but what good was a *pistola* that wasn't ready to rumble? Lucky stuffed the weapon between his belt and the small of his back, slung on an antique high school letterman jacket, and walked out into the dawn without locking the door behind him.

It would be the last time Lucky ever saw the place.

3

Interstate 5. Four miles south of Valencia.

The tractor-trailer rig was on the downslope, pointed due south, its big wheels rotating forward a few feet at a time before stopping again. This was the usual morning commuter traffic where thousands upon thousands of vehicles converge into the San Fernando Valley section of the City of Los Angeles. Beemer could see the heat rising from the valley floor, adding to the mirage effect of the morning light glinting off the arcing rows of windows and paint jobs from all those Sunday car washes. Why the hell did this site remind him of Fallujah? Sure, there were similar heat signatures. The desert light. But nothing else. Still, Fallujah kept flooding back to him.

Beemer checked his instruments. Slightly less than a quarter of a tank of diesel. According to the GPS, plenty of fuel to get him the final fifty-seven miles to Long Beach. It was 7:58 a.m.

Temperature outside: ninety-one degrees.

Temperature inside the cab: a comfortable seventy degrees.

Temperature inside the trailer: twenty-five degrees and holding.

When Beemer picked up the goods the night before, he hadn't quite anticipated the bone-numbing chill. He cursed himself for not bringing winter gloves. They hadn't been on his to-do list. How the hell could he have left gloves off his list? He had arranged everything else. The refrigerated tractor-trailer rig. The forged shipper's manifest in case he got stopped at a weigh station. Properly faked IDs. Credit cards. Of course, he had a mask and guns for the heist itself. Just in case. Not that he had anticipated trouble. He had bought and paid for all the vault security codes.

He checked his face in the mirror. Particularly curious about the tip of his square nose. It was pink and freckled just the way it always was. No discoloration. Nor did his ears appear to look anything but slightly undersized and exposed by a haircut that purposefully resembled that of a Japanese manga cartoon. Dyed as black as the rented eighteen-wheeler. During the robbery, he had stuffed his hair under a woolen cap.

The warehouse itself was part of a loose collection of industrial buildings, not quite defined as an organized "park," but more as an evolved locale on the edge of the city in the shadow of the mountains. There was a two-lane road that split a mile-long corridor of manufacturing and warehousing businesses—each two-acre plot surrounded by cyclone fencing topped with razor wire. Most exterior advertising was limited to simple signage by each gate. Casing the target, Beemer had practically memorized the order of businesses, most of which began with "Reno."

Reno Industrial Business Machines.

Reno-Tahoe Kitchen and Bath Supply.

Reno Farm Equipment Repair and Service.

Reno and Sons Tire and Retread.

Third on the left after the second stop sign was a low-slung corrugated structure and a smaller annex with heavy ventilation. The sign at the gate was equally mysterious. Just a placard with the capitalized initials "C.B.P., INC." It was still early enough in the evening that the gate had not yet been closed. Nobody paid any attention to the big rig making a careful turn through.

The parking area was empty, lit only by two flanking street lamps at either corner. Another single light splashed across the warehouse's blank office entrance. Beemer kept the truck in a low gear, carefully riding the accelerator as he kept the semi to the left, drawing a wide circle around to the loading dock at the rear. Next came the hard part: maneuvering the trailer portion of the rig as he backed it up to the bumpers. This was a skill Beemer didn't possess. In Iraq, he had driven enough heavy equipment to fake operating just about any kind of vehicle. But putting a tractor rig into reverse and steering a levered fifty-three-foot trailer square up to a pitch-black platform? That wasn't something Beemer had practiced, nor had he ever been too concerned about it prior to the actual night. He kept his eyes on his side-view mirrors, doing his best to gauge distances with only a pair of back-up bulbs to guide the way. Finally, he felt the bump. A slightly metallic thud, sounding that the eagle had landed.

Beemer felt his heart up-shift with excitement. This is when he needed to be extra efficient. It was going to be one man, one warehouse, and one trailer with over three thousand cubic feet of freezer to load. He rolled up the trailer flap and then the warehouse door. Keyed in the code to the outer magnetic doors and entered the freezer unit. The temperature dropped forty degrees in a single second. Refrigerator temp. Beemer wasn't yet in the freezer. He searched for the door marked "C Closet," pulled on the lever, and released a steam of utter cold. The freezer was fifteen degrees Fahrenheit, frosty white at the fringes, and forty feet deep in wax-coated cardboard cartons, each the size of a large microwave. He looked left, read the label on the first carton, yanked it off the top, and removed the lid. Inside were frozen pint bags, neatly stacked, each stuffed full of a frozen liquid that resembled crushed corn. Yellowish and marbled and labeled with precision. Measured in mils. Recommended storage temp. Date packaged. The industry called this product by its initials: FFP.

Fresh Frozen Plasma.

Beemer recalled how he had laughed the first time he had heard of the newish blood product. It reminded him of the ads on television for frozen vegetables purchased from the Piggly Wiggly. But the importance and value of frozen blood products quickly took on a serious tone. Frozen blood products like plasma and red cell concentrate were in high demand in the war-ravaged Middle East. These were life-saving interventions. A must for trauma surgery. And in a part of the world where massive blood loss was fast becoming one of the top causes of death, frozen blood products were nearly worth their weight in silver.

Using a hand truck, Beemer stacked and rolled the cartons from the freezer to the parked trailer. He lost count as to how many trips it took to fill the trailer. All he could think about was why the hell he hadn't thought to bring gloves. He griped at himself with every step. Into the freezer for more cartons, load, then roll to the refrigerated freezer trailer. No time for his fingers to thaw before careening back into the biting cold. He worried about frostbite every time he gripped the hand truck. But he was more worried about the timing. He made the choice to forgo searching for a pair of mittens—forgo comfort—for what he had prided in himself since dropping out of Stanislaus Community College for what he thought was going to be a career in the United States Marines: mad efficiency in everything he did.

In under two hours and in a freezing sweat, Beemer had loaded the trailer rig with so much fresh frozen plasma and red blood cells that the rear bumper had dropped a full seventeen inches closer to the pavement. Beemer had only estimated the weight, hoping greed wouldn't put him over the forty-eight-thousand-pound road limit. The excitement of finishing the job, wiping down the surfaces he had touched, rolling and locking down the trailer door, then slipping back into the confines of the tractor's cab was cause for an adrenaline push into Beemer's bloodstream. The momentary high that came with the change in brain chemistry was welcome, not to mention a-okay. This wasn't an *aw, fuck* moment. There were no surprises but for his frozen hands. Perfect mental acuity wasn't required to put the semi-rig into a forward gear and roll back out onto the two-lane. With that, the black-as-night truck trundled into the high desert air, well camouflaged by the darkness, the GPS plotting an uninterrupted passage to Southern California.

Some of Beemer's fingers tingled. The pinky and ring finger of his right hand and the ring, middle, and index fingers of his left. He couldn't decide if it was a tingling or a burning sensation, both being potential signs of frostbite. He had cranked the heat in the semi's cab and made sure the windows were rolled up tight to guard against the symptoms he was feeling. The bad fingers appeared reddish but for the very tips which turned a whitish gray when he gently pressed them against the steering wheel.

Twelve hours later, Beemer had barely made a decent getaway. The digital clock read 8:17 a.m. Since he had last checked the time, he had rolled off only 2.6 miles. He surmised there must be some sort of accident somewhere, clogging the delicate condition of Los Angeles commuter traffic. All it took was a single fender bender in the wrong lane at the wrong moment to stop up miles upon miles of freeway like a root-infected septic line. For a minute or so he tried to imagine the severity of the accident. One car? Two? Three? Maybe a chain reaction pileup? Beemer hadn't a clue. The only thing he knew for sure was that somebody else was experiencing their very own cursed moment.

"Hello?" Beemer answered by rote. He hadn't really heard the mobile phone ring as much as he had felt the vibration from inside his shirt pocket. And knowing California's laws about driving while talking on a cell phone, Beemer made sure to uncoil the hands-free cord and insert the bud in his ear before accepting the call.

"It's Rey," said the caller. "Just checking to see if we're all good."

"Clean so far," fibbed Beemer. "Taking in traffic and all that shit."

"It's our version of weather," said Rey. "What we talk about here. Where are you?"

"Uh…" Beemer looked around. "Southbound 5 at just about the 210 freeway."

"Lemme guess. Clean sailing 'til you hit Valencia."

"Somebody knows their traffic."

"Born and raised, buddy."

"Thought you were born in Guatemala."

"That's my older brother. He got to swim the Rio Grande with my mom. I started out my life at County USC."

"Glad we got that worked out," said Beemer, allowing the tone in his voice to make the point that he was already bored with the conversation.

"Whatever, right?" continued Rey. "By my clock, you're about two, two and a half hours from touchdown."

"My GPS says only forty-eight miles."

"Rush hour, man. Nothin' you can do."

"What about another route?"

"Won't matter, really. It's all inbound. You're swimming upstream in the rat race."

"Swell," said Beemer, instantly imagining an Alaskan snow wedge welded to the front of his stolen semi-rig. How far would he get if he hit the gas and moved all the lesser vehicles out of the way like chunks of road ice?

"No worries," said Rey. "I'm here. My brother's guys are all down and waiting to expedite."

"Right," said Beemer, not telling Rey he was going to have to refill his diesel tanks. Better Rey knew only what he needed. Primarily, Beemer's ETA. And that wasn't going to be for at least a couple more hours. "Call you when I'm closer."

"You got it, pard."

Beemer clicked off the call, wishing he had stayed on long enough to finish with an acerbic blast like, "Hey. And don't call me 'pard.'" Nobody was ever Beemer's "pard" or partner. Beemer made simple and clear agreements and stuck to them. He expected those with whom he had made the agreements to hold to their end of the deal and understand the consequences to be suffered for failing to do as much.

Fatigue began to set in. He had been behind the wheel for nearly twelve straight hours. His body wanted him to find a spot to pull over, roll up the windows, and escape into the bunk behind his seat. A little more than two hours until the hand-off. After which Beemer could roll himself into the nearest hotel and, a hot shower and a couple of Ambien later, fall into at least nine hours of dead man's sleep.

4

Ridgecrest City Hall and Sheriff's Substation. 8:28 a.m.

It was like walking on eggshells. The normally upbeat sheriff's office had turned darkly somber. Like an angry blanket had been dropped over the entire building. Word of the young deputy's death spread wildly through the glass and tile postmodern building. The emotional wound was fresh on nearly every face, from the parking attendants to the vice mayor. All were stunned and eager to hear more. It was still too soon for real grief to have settled in.

Outside the captain's office, a small crowd had gathered. Deputies, on duty and off, along with a scattering of civilian personnel, milled about, barely communicating, awaiting news and further instruction. The office blinds were squeezed shut.

There were four people in Captain Andrews' office: the captain himself, Undersheriff Shepherd Van Pelt, Duty Sergeant Ron Mayfair…and Lucky Dey, sitting in the captain's desk chair, rolled all the way back against a corner shelf unit chock-full of labeled binders. Lucky appeared to need more space than the small office provided. Instinctively, the other three kept what distance they could in the cramped room.

"We can see the tags there on the SUV," said the captain as they reviewed the black and white dash cam video from Anthony Dey's sheriff's vehicle. "Registered to Patrick Watts, CPA. Don't know if he's one of the vics in the car or just the name on the registration. Still checking on that."

The captain's computer screen was turned sideways in order for Lucky to squarely see the video replay. And though Lucky was mostly stoic as he watched frame after frame of the dash cam footage, his hands gripped the armrests as if hanging on for dear life.

The grainy image was from a slightly wide perspective, shot from a tiny lens mounted on the rearview mirror. The stiff suspension of the vehicle broadcast every bump and ripple in the road. At screen center, pictured through the windshield, was the speeding Porsche Cayenne SUV, occasionally drifting across the center line before jerking back into the right lane. The telltale sign of a drunk driver. The reflections from the sheriff's cruiser's lighting array pulsated across the hood. Then the cruiser began to accelerate to close the gap between the two cars.

"Not too close, T," mumbled Lucky, as if anticipating the immediate danger. "Fuck, they don't see him—"

Lucky cut his own words as a nightmare moment unfolded on the computer screen. Upon being lit up with those blazing red and blue xenons, drivers under the influence have been known to panic and sometimes over-apply their brakes. Cops are trained to hang back a safe distance to avoid a sudden collision. According to the dash cam, Deputy Tony Dey's training momentarily escaped him. The acceleration of the police cruiser. The sudden recognition by the drunk driver and the SUV he was chasing suddenly slowed, its brake lights flaring. The framing of the mounted camera dipped downward in a sure sign that the doomed young deputy had applied his own brakes, sending the front end of the sheriff's cruiser closer to the pavement. Then came the brief shudder of locked tires chattering across the pavement, followed by the inevitable collision. What followed was a staccato of video frames with plastic lens casings shattering and scattering into the night, dust from the road shoulder spewing from the cruiser's undercarriage in a breathy plume, and the faint picture of the luxury SUV sparking ahead as it tumbled over the pavement. Three and a half crumpled turns before it finally came to rest.

"Christ almighty," breathed the undersheriff.

More video followed. The cruiser shot ahead, skidding to a stop only yards from the wreck. There was a slight movement as the vehicle unweighted.

"Okay," said the captain.

"'Kay. Freeze right there," said Ron Mayfair. "Here's where he gets out. Now you'd think he'd be running up to check for survivors."

Ron Mayfair keyed the video to freeze. Pictured was a partial view of the Porsche SUV as it had come to a stop on its crushed roof. The headlights of the police cruiser as they reflected off the shiny white surface of the SUV created a hot spot in the center of the screen, blowing out the video's definition.

"Can anybody tell if the victims are responsive at this point?" asked the captain.

"Just play the goddamn vid," said Lucky.

Ron Mayfair didn't wait for a nod from the captain or the undersheriff before rekeying the video back into play mode.

"We have audio?" asked the undersheriff.

"Not yet," said the duty sergeant. "Dunno if it's a glitch in the transfer or if it's just not there at all."

"Where the hell's my deputy?" asked the undersheriff. "Two vics in the car and he still hasn't even checked them yet?"

"There's why," said Lucky.

"There's what?" asked the undersheriff. He couldn't see the light shifting at the upper left-hand corner of the screen.

"Second set of headlights," pointed Lucky. "See there? That's Tony's shadow. Probably flagging it down."

The captain leaned closer to the screen. He saw the slightest shadow crossing the wreck, back and forth.

"Can't be certain," said the captain.

Once again, the duty sergeant stopped the video, then tried to frame it backwards and forwards to isolate the moving shadows.

"Restart the video, will ya?" urged Lucky.

"Just wanna confirm—"

"Stop the video again and I'll twist your fingers off at the knuckle," said Lucky, his voice a whisper above a growl.

"Right," said Ron Mayfair, restarting the video.

The headlights' reflection on the left-hand side of the screen slowly increased in intensity until it leveled off. The haunting forty-eight seconds that followed seemed to last an hour to most in the room. All but for Lucky. It would later play in his head in a mix of speed and slo-mo. Fast-forwarding and reversing, playing over and over and over with zero satisfaction.

"There he is," barked the undersheriff in a moment of excitement.

Yes. There was Deputy Tony Dey, sneaking in from the left edge of the frame on his knees, flashlight in hand, at last attending to the crash victims. The undersheriff's brief thrill was stunted by the sudden ignition of a flare off-camera, followed by the entrance of a baseball-capped figure standing over the prone deputy. The figure, whose features were bleached unrecognizable from the brightness of the flare, was seen slowly bending at the waist and easily unholstering the young deputy's Glock.

"Fuck no," said the captain.

Lucky merely leaned forward, steeled for what he knew was about to happen on the computer screen. He saw his brother's face turn innocently toward the figure. The pyrotechnic mix of the flare's chemicals—potassium nitrate with magnesium—flushed Tony's face white in an angelic glow. Then came the single frame of muzzle flash, and Tony's neck flexing with a deathly spasm.

The room was silent. As if all air had been sucked backward through the air conditioning vents. All that was left to watch was the off-camera ignition of the gasoline leaking from the SUV—

assumedly from the flare—and the following conflagration. The
heat signature was so hot on the Kelvin scale that the only detailed
information left on the digital video was contained in the far corners of the frame. Whatever vehicle Tony had flagged, whatever
vehicle carried the cold murderer, was utterly unseen.

"Okay," said the captain, hoping to break the silence gently.
"Our one witness is a farm veterinarian. He was northbound on
his way to some kinda horse thing. 'Bout five minutes before he
showed up on our crime scene, he passes a southbound vehicle.
Best recollection is that it was some kinda big rig. Tractor-trailer or
moving truck. Passed in a flash, so…"

"Right," said the duty sergeant. "So we also got this from a
gas 'n' gulp in Adelanto." He slipped the DVD into the tray and
waited for the computer to recognize it. Shortly, another video
played. The screen was divided into four equal quadrants, each
pixelated rectangle assigned to a different exterior camera for the
open-all-night filling station/mini mart. Ron Mayfair got instructions for the correct time code from the Post-it note attached to
the jewel case. He entered in the numbers and the DVD instantly
skipped to the correct hour, minute, and second.

Lucky leaned forward, as did the other three men. For eleven
seconds there were the same four images. Two views of the gas
pumps, one of the entry to the mini-mart, and a fourth, wider shot
that included a seventy-yard stretch of Highway 395. It may have
well been a frozen image but for the time code ticking off in a box
at the bottom of the screen.

Then it happened. Movement. Headlights entered the top left
frame of the wide shot, followed by the outline of an eighteen-
wheeled truck rolling smoothly through.

"Freeze it!" said Lucky.

The duty sergeant's fingers weren't fast enough. The semi rig
had cleared the frame before he was able to stop the image. Then
his nerves took over and he skipped the video backwards a full
minute and eight seconds. Lucky wasn't moving, still leaning forward in the chair. But the way the sergeant worked the keyboard

and mouse, Lucky might as well have been standing, imposing himself right on top of the nerve-wracked man.

"No worries," said Ron Mayfair. "I got this."

And he did, slowly rolling the video forward until, once again, that semi-rig appeared in the upper left of the security cam quadrant. Next, as the image was advanced frame by frame, the eighteen-wheeler reached an area where the spill from the filling station's lighting painted the vehicle with maximum definition. Yet the maximum wasn't quite optimum. There wasn't enough information on the video to identify a license tag or any distinguishable features of the driver. The best anybody could deduce was that the tractor was a new model Peterbilt painted black with chrome trim. And because the equally black trailer sported its own topside compressor unit, it was probably refrigerated.

Lucky was on his feet with his car keys jangling, swinging on his San Pedro High School letterman jacket. Black and gold. On the back was a faded pirate emblem embroidered into the wool that was thinning like the owner's hair.

"Whoa, now," said the captain. "Where you think you're going?"

"That truck's got a five hour jump on me," announced Lucky, not a decibel of nonsense in his voice.

"First off. This isn't your deal. It's your brother and we're awful sorry. But ten'll getcha fifty that truck's not even in Kern County no more."

"No shit?" said Lucky. "That's some kick-ass detective work. Must be why they made you cappy."

"Luck—"

"Truck's goin' to L.A. or further south. If it goes into Mexico, I'm on its ass."

"Gotta say no, Lucky."

"So, say 'no.' Won't make a difference. I'm going." Lucky's hand was already on the door handle.

"That was an order from your captain," said the undersheriff.

Did Lucky hear him? Probably. But he didn't respond to the

calls after him. The small pond of hangers-on outside the captain's office parted as Lucky made the short distance to the exit. He knew nobody had the stones to chase after him. These were Ridgecrest folk. Cops, for sure. Good cops, even. But they hadn't seen what Lucky had seen, done what Lucky had done, or experienced the violence Lucky was capable of imparting without so much as a second thought. The most the captain would or could do was order a sheriff's unit to follow Lucky as far as possible and make certain he didn't do anything that would cause embarrassment to the department.

Lucky climbed into his 2011 Dodge Charger, which quickly became a metallic gray streak, busting past ninety miles an hour down Highway 395. He didn't stop or blink as he blew through the crime scene. By the time he picked up the southbound Route 14 at Rancho Seco, Lucky had lost his ground tail. All that was left to record his progress was the county sheriff's air support helicopter, which, despite its cruising altitude of fifteen hundred feet, reported back to the Ridgecrest captain that Lucky's car was moving like a Ginsu knife through fresh yellowtail. The captain thought of alerting California Highway Patrol. But what exactly would he say to them? To pretty please watch out for his runaway detective with a lead foot? As far as the captain was concerned, Lucky careening south meant he was headed home. Where the hell else should Lucky go after losing his last living relative?

All in all, it took Lucky less than ninety minutes to cross the demarcation line between Kern County and his old stomping grounds, Los Angeles County. Home of the Los Angeles County Sheriff's Department. Nine thousand deputy cops strong, covering 4,083 square miles of all kinds of badass. Indeed, Lucky was going home.

5

Downtown Los Angeles.

Modern news in America seems to run at two speeds. There's the normal and relatively quick twenty-four hour cycle, fed by both cable news and the advent of so many vehicles in the field with on-camera reporters, all designed to give the illusion of "happening now" to the viewers. Television generally sets the pace, leaving print media, both internet and conventional, and let's not forget the blogosphere, to follow with the detail and depth that the TV news bytes were incapable of imparting.

That is speed number one.

Speed number two is, at a glance, no different from speed number one. Same networks, news outlets, reporters, remote camera trucks, microwave dishes, internet. What sets speed number two apart from speed number one is the addition of one extra component. Celebrity. Adding the "famous" ingredient to the news recipe is like putting a fuel injector on the average internal combustion engine. Celebrity is all it takes to supercharge the speed at which a news story travels through all wires, cables, internet carriers, and broadcast frequencies. Celebrity not only determines how fast a story breaks, but also which organization breaks it.

In the case of young Pepper Ellis? Her story broke on TMZ.

Within moments of identifying the registered owner of the Porsche SUV, Kern Sheriff's Department left a message on CPA Patrick Watt's office voicemail, kindly asking him to return their call. When his office assistant retrieved the message shortly after her arrival at work, she was quick to relay the message to her boss, who was inbound to his West Los Angeles office from the Pacific Palisades. He asked his assistant to dial for him and, while he was stuck in traffic on Sunset, Patrick Watts was given just a few of the details of the accident and crime. After he overcame the initial shock from the bad news, he informed the Kern County Sheriff's Department that though his name was registered on the lease, the true owner of the Porsche was a business management client of his. Actress Pepper Ellis. Though the Sheriff's Department couldn't confirm that Pepper Ellis was the driver of the Porsche SUV before the local coroner had received dental records and DNA, they were able to tell the accountant that there were two deceased people in the car. One man and one woman.

As Patrick Watts and the representative from Kern County Sheriff's Department continued to exchange pertinent information, the accountant's assistant sat gobsmacked, silent, and still connected to the call via her muted headset. Before her boss had hung up, she was able to transmit the tragic news via instant message to three of her best friends. One of those friends possessed a Twitter account. Then faster than somebody could say 4G, in one hundred and forty characters or less, the Twitterverse was informed…

Nickelodeon star Pepper Ellis has died in a car accident near Ridgecrest, California.

* * *

"Ah, shit!" said Assistant United States Attorney Graham McDonald. He was looking for his glasses on the nightstand of room 1046 in the downtown Los Angeles Biltmore Hotel.

"What's that?" asked a woman's voice from the bathroom.

"What's that girl's name? Pippa Ellis? Pepper—"

"Not a clue what you're saying," she said.

Graham sat up in bed, fixed his glasses to his face, but instead of returning his attention to the television, caught a glimpse of himself in the wall-mounted mirror behind the credenza. His curly hair was badly tousled and there were red creases across his face from one of the bed pillows.

"Pepper Ellis," said Graham, repeating what he heard again from the television.

The KTLA morning news team was reporting the presumed death of Pepper Ellis. They had no sources other than the celebrity gossip website, TMZ. So, in essence, the KTLA morning crew was reporting the report. Not exactly journalism. But it was a celebrity story. Rocket fuel had just been injected into the news machine.

"Who's Pepper Ellis?" the woman asked as she crossed naked in front of the TV. Her name was Lilly Zoller, and she was carrying a portable blow dryer. Lilly plugged the blow dryer into the outlet nearest the mirror and began blasting hot air through her inky black hair. Through the mirror, she could see what Graham was more interested in—this Pepper-whatever-her-name-is or Lilly's tool-and-dye-cut rump. Lilly was proud as hell of her thirty-eight-year-old body. She was tanning-booth brown from head to toe with a healthy minimum of body fat.

And Graham wasn't looking at her. He was glued to the TV.

"Did you eat paint chips as a child?" asked Lilly.

"Did I what?"

"I asked you who was this Pepper blah, blah, blah."

"Yeah, I heard you. Can I listen to this, please?"

Lilly turned to face her Department of Justice fuck-buddy,

giving him her full-frontal best. But Graham barely glanced her way.

"My baby girl's gonna be really upset," said Graham.

"Your daughter knows this Pepper Whosit?"

"Ellis. Pepper Ellis. And no. It's like they're friends. She just watches her every day on TV."

"Okay. She's on TV. Why should anyone give a shit?" asked Lilly, returning to the mirror and her hair.

"'Cause she's dead," said Graham. "Least that's what they think. Car accident up north."

"Tragic."

"Damn straight it is. This is a sweet girl. Has this show on Nick about this girl from the city who—"

"Nick? Is that a channel?"

"Nickelodeon. It's a cable channel for kids."

"So this Pepper Lala is pretty famous?"

"Suppose, yeah."

Lilly took her naked body to the bathroom for a brief pee. Her voice echoed as she called out.

"Was she driving?"

"They didn't say. Wait…Holy shit."

"Did I ever tell you that your vocabulary is stimulating?"

"There was a sheriff's deputy killed too."

"In the accident?"

"No. They got a source that says there was possible foul play."

Lilly returned from the bathroom and began slipping into the clothes she had shown up in. Simple black cocktail dress. Stilettos. From the room phone she connected with the valet and asked for a cab. Next, she would elevator down, slip through the lobby, and take the three-minute cab ride to her downtown loft.

"What kind of foul play?"

"They're not sayin' it, but yeah. It was murder."

"And where'd this happen?" asked Lilly, sounding mildly interested in the story for the first time.

"Dunno. Where's Kern County?" asked Graham. He was a

visiting New Yorker. What he knew or cared about Southern California could be learned on a postcard.

"North of here. Bumfuck Bakersfield, then east to Nevada," said the Los Angeles native. Lilly had little use for any part of the state that didn't have a Starbucks or Coffee Bean and Tea Leaf within jogging distance. "Some lucky county DA's gonna get himself a—"

"Or herself."

"It's all Mayberry up that way. No such thing as women DAs," corrected Lilly. "What I was saying is that they may get themselves a celebrity case. National attention. Book deals. It's lottery time for Harvey Hillbilly, DA."

"Sounds like a TV show."

"Exactly," said Lilly, leaning over and kissing Graham on top of his nappy head. "Regards to the wife and kids."

"Do you have to do that?" asked Graham, perturbed.

"What? Kiss you goodbye?" teased Lilly.

"You're a real bitch."

"Meaner than I look too," winked Lilly from the door. "Next time."

Lilly let the door shut behind her. Click-clack. And that fast, she forgot Graham Whatshisname, the assistant US Attorney from Albany. Maybe he would call her when he next visited their Los Angeles office. Maybe he wouldn't. Lilly didn't give a rip. She had had her night of fun, left the married man with a proper tease and the memory of her steely body and what tricks it could do.

What she couldn't forget was that name. Pepper Ellis. She was certain she had never heard the name before that moment in the hotel room. And while waiting for the elevator to arrive, the name bounced around in her skull. It couldn't be a real name. Pepper Ellis. Not even a stage name, for that matter. The name sounded like a made-up name she would have read in her preteen years. Like some young, fictional heroine. *Another Pepper Ellis Mystery!*

Lilly's cab was stuck in some poorly timed rush-hour construction traffic. *Damn*, she wondered. *What city idiot ordered this clusterfuck?* If she wasn't in her stilettos, she would have tossed a ten spot at the cabby and hoofed it home. She fired up her smartphone and, instead of reading through her litany of emails, Googled two words: Pepper Ellis. Up came a Wikipedia page, Nickelodeon links, fan pages, and photos. Pepper Ellis was a pretty little girl. Sure, her Wikipedia page informed readers that she had just turned seventeen, but by the look of most of her images, the child actress could easily have passed for fourteen or fifteen. There were a couple of movie premiere pictures that tried to reveal Pepper's more mature side, showing her wearing sophisticated dresses and makeup. Immediately, Lilly was reminded of JonBenét Ramsey, the murdered five-year-old beauty contestant from Colorado. The story was a sensation occupying the national zeitgeist for months on end, propelled mostly by photos and videos of a little girl dressed and made-up as a showgirl, prancing up and down a pageant runway.

Then it hit her again. That tingle of jealousy she had felt back in the hotel room when she was lampooning some imagined country-music-loving DA from Kern County. She momentarily regretted following the federal path in the US Attorney's office. She had once fantasized about prosecuting high profile villains like John Gotti, Ted Kaczynski, or Timothy McVeigh.

No such luck.

Since September 11, 2001, nearly all terrorist cases came under the auspices of the military tribunal established at Guantanamo Bay. That left the US Attorney's office's present caseload chock-full of boring, sexless, faceless corporate criminals and Wall Street con men. What Lilly Zoller wouldn't have given to try a scandalous murder case.

But this murder was in Kern County. Far, far away from federal jurisdiction. Yet she was asking herself questions. What was this young actress doing in Kern County? Was she from the area? If not, was she passing through? And if passing through, from where was she driving? Was the crime drug related? Kern County wasn't too far from the California/Nevada state line. Had drugs crossed the state line? Was Pepper Ellis induced to cross the state line against her will?

The potential violation of federal statutes began to add up in Lilly's mind like a grocery list. And if there were such violations, the feds would have the authority to swoop in and big dog the local rabble into taking second position on the headline-making case.

Lilly speed-dialed a number on her smartphone.

"Owen? It's Lilly," she said on the FBI man's voicemail. "Want you to pull up everything you can find out on this Pepper Ellis thing. And I mean *everything*. I'll be in the office in an hour."

Lilly clicked off, then rested her head on the seat back. Despite her excitement at the prospect of striking career pay dirt, she found her eyelids slamming shut in need of a nap.

"Damn," she said aloud. "I need a goddamn quad latte."

6

Long Beach.

Rey Palomino let his eyes rest on the skyline of the Long Beach Harbor. Every time he tried to count the number of ship-to-shore cranes he would get distracted by the intensity of the heat. *Damn*, he thought. *10:00 a.m. and it's ninety degrees in Long Beach?* The one day he had the opportunity to leave the Valley and come to the harbor was this rarer than rare day devoid of any breezes. Onshore or offshore. Any wind to cool his Guatemalan face would have been as welcome as rain. Instead, he just stood in the blistering sun and waited without seeking cover. This was because Rey wanted to be the very first person Greg Beem saw when rolling his precious cargo into the shipping yard. He didn't want to risk anybody speaking before him. He didn't want to risk Beemer's wrath, about which he had heard plenty from his recently deceased son. Rey had some bad news. Temporary bad news concerning an unforeseen delay. But to some people, bad news is bad news and their reactions could be volatile.

As a custom pool contractor, delivering news of unforeseen delays came with the territory. Rey couldn't remember a job that had ended in a timely manner. Part of the game was massaging the clients, explaining why that big hole in their backyard wasn't yet the inviting, glistening pool of cool water that they had been promised.

"Yo, Rey Baby!" yelled the yard foreman. "Where's your dude?"

Rey pointed at his watch, shrugged, and smiled despite the annoying jab. He had been called Rey Baby for as long as he could remember being Heber Palomino's younger brother. The nickname was designed to remind Rey of his place in the family. Always the child in need of care.

From a macro position, delays in his business could usually be blamed on the client. Usually, homeowners or real estate speculators had blown most of their wad on the house, whether in upgrades or from ground-up construction. Sure, they had always planned for a backyard pool. But by the time they got around to bidding it out to contractors, they were usually looking for lowball bids and the promise of a speedy job. This often led to delays, because for the pool contractors to make a profit they needed to keep their crews small and the jobs coming. This would always spread Rey thin, leading to missed deadlines and a constant tap dance to keep the clients from suing.

Only the delay he needed to explain to Beemer had nothing to do with the client and everything to do with his nickname. Rey Baby.

Most of the roughly two acres the Palomino Shipping Company occupied on the inner harbor was used for storing and processing refrigerated containers. There was a small parking lot for employees fronting West Pier D Street. The extra-wide entrance to the lot was used by truckers delivering or retrieving their loads.

Rey leaned against the rear bumper of his twin cab Toyota pickup, facing the entrance and craving an ice cream cone. Soft-serve vanilla. Just one of those mini cones from McDonald's. Only one hundred and fifty calories. A practically guilt-free treat for Rey, a serial dieter. Not that he was obese. Or even fat. Rey just felt he was caught in a constant battle between his beer-sized gut and his bad drive-thru habits.

The sun was beating on him, and felt as if it had suddenly moved closer to the earth, raising the temperature ten full degrees. Standing smack under the sun like some dumb-ass cow, Rey wondered if his brain was damaged from the heat after thirty years of living and working outdoors, sweat-drained, often dehydrated, and so rarely seeking shade.

With that, Rey rotated around to the driver's side door of his twin cab pickup. The chrome door handle was so hot it stung his fingers, a sharp reminder that he had made a smart decision to seek the coolness of his truck. He keyed the ignition, felt the engine rumble to life, and positioned the air conditioning vents to blow at his face. There was an initial blast of hot air, followed by a stream of refreshing cold. He cursed himself for waiting so damn long.

"So who's Rey Baby?"

The voice startled Rey so much that he made an audible *whoop*. An electric-like jolt ran through him.

"Jesus," said Rey.

Rey's eyes glimpsed a man in his rearview mirror. Baseball cap and glasses. As he began to swivel.

"Don't turn around. Eyes in front."

"I'm Rey Palomino," said Rey, hoping the stranger was the guest he was expecting.

"I know who you are. You're Rey Baby."

"Can I help you?" asked Rey, trying to peel both the fear and threat from his voice.

"Why not? Got me a truck and I got a load. Just wanted a look around to see if it's safe to bring it in."

"Are you Greg Beem?" Rey asked.

"Everybody calls me Beemer."

Rey's shoulders sagged in relief. He exhaled audibly through his mouth.

"Scared the shit outta me," said Rey.

"Don't ask me to apologize," said Beemer. "Can't be too careful."

"Danny said you were thorough," said Rey, purposefully referring to his dead son. Not as much for sympathy but for the mere familiarity. He wanted Beemer to feel safe with him.

"Danny was a good egg. Got dealt a bad hand. Sorry for your loss."

"Appreciate it," said Rey.

"So?"

"Right. So where's your truck?"

"Close," said Beemer. "And you're ready for it, right?"

Rey swallowed then slowly turned to face the rear. He always wanted to be eye to eye with the client when he delivered bad news. Rey would concentrate on keeping eye contact to best convey how genuine he was.

"Told you don't turn around," said Beemer. "Got trouble with simple instructions?"

"No, no. I'm cool."

"Now, I asked are you ready for my load?"

Without the opportunity to look at Beemer directly, Rey felt as if he were delivering the bad news over the phone. A chickenshit move. Rey may have possessed a few passive aggressive tendencies, but chickenshit wasn't one of them.

"Listen," said Rey. "It's set. Ready to go. All I need is my brother."

"So where's your brother?"

"Cabo," said Rey, almost swallowing his answer.

"Cabo. As in fuckin' Mexico? Really?"

"Not my fault. He promised to be here. Double-checked with him—"

"Not your fault?"

Rey felt a cold gun muzzle against his neck. The seat leather squeaked as Beemer drew nearer, filling the rearview mirror. As he regripped the gun, the tendons on his wrist worked under his skin like piano strings. A small tattoo rippled. Red circle around an A. Rey paid it no mind.

"I made the deal with you or your brother?" asked Beemer.

"Made it with me," said Rey.

"So it would be reasonable for me to expect you to deliver? Yeah?"

"Yes, but—"

"Shut up," said Beemer. "I'm sitting on over forty thousand pounds of product. Made a deal with you to get it shipped because your dead son said his dad could get this kinda shit done."

"And I can. Tomorrow."

"I'm here today."

"So am I," said Rey, bravely. "I'm as pissed as you. It's my older brother's shipping business and he said he'd be here to get it done."

"In the meantime, what am I supposed to do with my load?"

"I got a place. All worked out."

"Oh, you do? Worked out like today was worked out?" Beemer pushed that pistol muzzle deeper into Rey's flesh. He hoped to leave a mark.

"Not like today. Like I said. I'm here. I'm taking responsibility. I've built a plan B to accommodate this bump in the road."

"I wanna talk to your brother."

"I get it. But he won't talk to you. That's his deal with me. That's his deniability. You call him, he'll leave us both in a twist."

"Even if I got a gun to your head?"

"I'm the little brother. And he doesn't give a shit."

"Rey Baby."

"Rey Baby. Yeah. That's the way it is."

"How long?"

"Twenty-four to forty-eight hours. Tops."

Beemer withdrew the weapon, returning to the rear seat. Rey quietly exhaled, but heard the crinkling of paper being unfolded.

"Mayako," read Beemer. "Mayako Inoue. Is that her name?"

It was as if all the saliva in Rey's mouth evaporated. Bringing up enough spit to wipe his sunglasses would have been impossible.

"Asked you a question," said Beemer.

"May," spoke Rey. "She likes people to call her that."

"Lives with you in Granada Hills," continued Beemer. "Not

married but who cares anymore, right? Works as a surgical nurse at Encino-Tarzana Hospital. Parents are Yokira and Shunju. They live in Monterey Park. Mayako has two sisters—"

"I get it."

"The fuck you do. And don't interrupt me," said Beemer, his heart rate barely a blip above fifty-eight beats per minute. "Okay. Sisters Sachi and Kinumi, both married, both with children. Got their addresses, their kids' schools, blah, blah, blah. Since dear little Danny's dead, this shit's where I get my leverage. You get me?"

"Yeah."

"So I'm not telling you shit other than this. I'll be taking me and my load someplace you don't know about. What time is it?"

"'Bout 10:40," Rey answered.

"There it is, then. Tomorrow. Same time. If your brother's not ready to ship my container, then somebody you know…"

Beemer let the threat hang. He didn't have to sell it. The words sold themselves.

"I'm with ya," said Rey, trying like hell to let some of the tension out of the cab. "No worries. And you won't have to do anything rash. I'll make it happen."

"Danny told you about me?"

"Yeah."

"Then you know I'm not someone to mess with."

"Right, right. Got it—"

The rear door popped open, causing a sudden exchange of air. The cool escaped with Beemer while a few extra degrees of heat were sucked back into the cab. Beemer didn't bother shutting the door. He used the rear bumper as a hoist and nimbly climbed over the double cinder-block wall that separated the yard from the boulevard. In a breath he was gone.

"Jesus," said Rey aloud. The personal audio surprised him, followed by a serious chill tracing his spine and spreading outward. It had been more than a decade since Rey had felt true fear. Back then he had almost soiled himself at the point of a machete wielded by a Mexican bricklayer who wanted to get paid. Now, behind the wheel of his truck, Rey didn't want to chance a repeat performance. He reached backward, pulled the rear door closed, shifted the pickup into drive, and accelerated out of the yard. All thoughts about cooling off with one hundred and fifty calories of a McDonald's soft-serve ice cream cone purged from his consciousness.

7

South Pasadena.

"Who the hell is Lydia Gonzalez?" boomed Lucky Dey.

This is when Lydia Gonzalez decided, if she could have been anywhere else, she would have either been in the bleachers at one of her son Travis's Little League games—or at the stick of an AS350 helo. The European-built helicopter was the newest in the LAPD's growing air support fleet. On a flat trajectory at sea level, it could top 180 miles per hour. But lower the nose and tilt forty degrees and the single engine workhorse could brush two hundred miles per hour while dropping from its ceiling of five thousand feet to a floor of five hundred feet. At peak speed, a simple touch of the stick to the left or right—along with some deft pedal work—the chopper could bank so hard and so accurately, both pilot and observer could pull three Gs. It was a better ride than any roller coaster at Six Flags. Like a Lotus Esprit with rotors, she imagined.

"Lydia…Gonzalez?"

Lydia—called Gonzo since she was six years old—was parked at a Coffee Bean and Tea Leaf café in South Pasadena. At a tiny table under a big window fronting the sidewalk, she sipped a large soy-sugar-free-caffeine-free-no-whip-ice-blended mocha. Her former partner, Romeo, used to call the drink a No-Fun-Ice-Blended. He also told her it was so un-coplike to be caught drinking something so wuss-worthy. She'd say, "It's 'cause I'm a chick, asshole."

Gonzo liked reminding fellow cops that she was a "chick." Especially when she was wearing her trademark leather jacket, jeans, and boots, standing over six feet. She liked when her words didn't fit the picture others had of her. Contradictions were sweet.

"Are you Lydia?" asked Lucky loudly to a professional-looking woman hunched over her notebook, ear buds stuffed deep into the canals of her ears.

"I'm Detective Gonzalez," said Gonzo, three yards behind Lucky. She didn't stand. Just stretched her long arm toward him with an open hand. "Everybody calls me Gonzo."

"You're her?"

"I'm me. Yeah. And you're Lucas Dey from Kern?"

"Lucky."

He shook Gonzo's hand, but didn't sit.

"Lucky," she repeated. "Nice meeting you."

"Yeah, sure," said Lucky. "So let's go, okay?"

"Go where?"

"Lennox," said Lucky. "Detoured all the way over here to pick you up. So here I am. Let's go."

"*The* Lennox Station? As in L.A. Sheriff's?"

"I'm in a hurry. I got hook-ups down there that are waiting on me."

"Slow down. I'm LAPD. You asked us for assistance."

"I didn't ask for shit. My cappy made the request. I made the concession. Here I am." Lucky gestured toward the door. "So if you don't mind, I'm parked in a red."

"You didn't request LAPD?"

"What I said. Is there gonna be a problem? Because if there's a problem, I'm gone."

"You got a captain. I got a supervisor," said Gonzo, flashing her mobile phone. "And he didn't say nuts about working jointly with L.A. Sheriff's."

Lucky gave Gonzo none of the usual eyerolls she had become accustomed to receiving from fellow cops when she dug in her feet over directives or protocol. Nor did he waste another breath arguing. He just shot toward the door and was on the sidewalk before Gonzo should so much as speed dial.

"Really?" said Gonzo, quick to realize that the deputy from Kern County whom she was ordered to assist was mere seconds from being vapor. "Wait!"

Lucky already had the Charger in reverse when he heard Gonzo pounding on the passenger window.

"Yo!" she shouted through the tinted glass.

Lucky reached across, unhitching the door and giving it a shove toward her. Gonzo climbed in, her cell phone stuck to her ear. Lucky didn't wait for her to buckle her seat belt before accelerating the car onto the crowded avenue. Gonzo cradled the phone with her shoulder while wrestling with the seat belt. The tensioners in the retractor mechanism didn't want to release the belt.

"Can you at least wait for me to put on my belt?"

"LAPD wears seat belts? Shit."

Gonzo clicked the tongue into the clasp just as someone at the downtown C.C.L. office finally answered the phone.

"It's Gonzalez. Can I talk to Mitch?"

This is when she felt all eight cylinders kick. The Dodge surged. Ahead, the stoplight turned crimson. Undeterred, Lucky maneuvered the car through the intersection before cross traffic could get off the line. Out of the corner of her eye, Gonzo caught the flash of the automated red light cam as it snapped digital evidence of the infraction.

"Well, please have Mitch call me ASAP regarding our guest from Kern. Thanks." Gonzo clicked off, but didn't pocket the phone.

"Guest, huh?" said Lucky.

"Would you prefer something else?"

"Do you have anything for me?"

"Anything as in?"

"Look, sister. If LAPD wants to babysit me, whatever. I don't care. You a detective?"

"I am."

"So whadda you detect?"

"About your tractor-trailer rig?" Gonzo caught Lucky's look as he waited for her to continue. "Other than what we got from you guys? Black semi with trailer. Refrigerated. No reports. No traffic cites. We copied your BOLO to Highway Patrol and other cities. L.A. Sheriff's, of course."

"That it?"

"What I got. For now."

"Southbound fridge rig. Where's it goin'? Markets?"

"Truck that big? Woulda had markings, right? Like Ralph's or Safeway. Chains do their own trucking. Deliver their own refrigerated goods."

Lucky continued glancing over to her. Was he testing her? She tried to suppress flashbacks from her training days.

"Who says it's got any goods at all?" Gonzo continued. "Could be stolen. Headed to Mexico."

"And you know Mexico, yeah? You got people down there?"

Gonzo stared a brief hole through Lucky.

"I'm from Alhambra, dickhead."

"Didn't ask where you were from. Asked if you had people south of the border."

"Because I'm Hispanic?"

"Because you brought it up. I didn't bring it up. Heard myself when I was talking and I for sure didn't bring it up."

"Right," said Gonzo.

Gonzo hoped Lucky was busting her balls. Only there wasn't the slightest hint of humor creased anywhere on his face.

"You crackin' on me?" asked Gonzo. "Or you just a cracker from Kern?"

Nothing. Not the slightest reaction echoed back Gonzo's way.

"Ooooooooohkay," continued Gonzo. "So this big rig? What's the interest?"

"Not the truck," said Lucky. "The driver."

"And what's Kern want with him?"

"Not Kern," said Lucky. "Me."

"This *is* official police business…?" wondered Gonzo aloud, sounding a hell of a lot more suspicious than she meant to. Though suspicious she was.

"Gunned down a deputy," answered Lucky. "'Bout eight hours ago."

"Oh, man," said Gonzo. "Deputy survived, I hope." Gonzo asked, but expected the worst. Whoever this Lucky guy was, he revealed little. Nor could Gonzo see past the black wraparound Oakleys that pinched his shaved head. *Gangbanger style*, she thought. Except, if Lucky had been a cholo, she would have been able to see tattoos unspooling up his neck from underneath his fitted polo.

She briefly lowered her sunglasses, looking over the lenses to get a better peek at a small scallop behind Lucky's right ear. A scar. Gonzo recognized all the indications of a healed bullet wound. Damn. Maybe that's why they call him Lucky.

"Gotta ask," said Gonzo. "Were you and the injured deputy close?"

"Deputy's dead. And yeah. We're pretty close," said Lucky. His present-tense usage of *we're* didn't go unnoticed.

Lucky spun his wheel a hard right off of Fair Oaks, hard-circling the car onto the short freeway on-ramp to the southbound 110, Los Angeles's oldest and original superhighway. Gonzo mapped the route to Lennox in her head. Southbound 110 about eight miles, through downtown Los Angeles, west on the San

Bernardino Freeway for eleven miles, then south on the 405 to Inglewood Boulevard. Only Gonzo was imagining the route as seen from the cockpit of an LAPD Air Support chopper. The city below, a complex grid of north- and south-running streets and boulevards, divided by subdivisions, some incorporated cities, low-slung mountain ranges, oil fields, golf courses, parks, iconic real estate, concrete river washes…and money. But man oh man. It all looked so much better—and far more manageable—from one thousand feet up.

8

South L.A.

Time: 11:58 a.m.
Outside temperature: 101 degrees Fahrenheit.
Cabin temperature: 72 degrees.
Container temperature: 15 degrees and steady.
Heart rate: 90 BPM.

Beemer removed his index and middle finger from the pressure point just above his carotid artery. This was proof beyond the sweat that had broken out over every millimeter of his body...proof that Beemer's galvanized emotional cage had been breached. Something subconscious had escaped and infected his central nervous system. His cool had officially vanished. Combine that with being seated at the controls of a rolling, refrigerated behemoth. Beemer was driving in circles, currently eastbound on the 105 freeway. All he had to do was jerk the wheel to his left and whichever compact, fuel-saving little vehicle was in his way would be crunched under his wheels. Certain havoc would ensue. Maybe even a traffic pileup. Potential fatalities. It would be news.

The blood stirred inside Beemer, making for what he called an *aw, fuck cocktail*. He knew nothing positive or profitable ever came from the concoction. Reason needed to trump his lizard-brain instincts before all his plans came crashing down around him.

Ahead was the South Wilmington exit. Beemer wheeled the big rig down the sloping ramp. He quickly zeroed in on a nearby shopping center that included a Food 4 Less, a Rite-Aid, and a General Discount. There was generous parking with a wide loading lane that cut behind the businesses, shadowed by the elevated freeway. It wasn't perfect but it would do for an hour or two. And once Beemer had parked the semi tight to the railing behind General Discount, he set the parking brake, but left the engine idling to power the refrigeration compressors.

Beemer climbed down from the truck. Because he was soaked in perspiration, his skin couldn't yet calculate the heat. All he was craving at that moment was for his boots to be touching the ground…and a cigarette.

Screw the damn nicotine patch, screamed Beemer at himself from inside his skull. He wanted a damn smoke. He could have easily circled around the front of the complex, entered the Rite-Aid, plunked down a double sawbuck in exchange for a pack of Marlboros and a disposable lighter. But that was too far to go when Beemer could see a pair of black men hanging around the loading dock. One man was stocky with half a head of salt and pepper hair and a cardinal-red shirt, stained, with General Discount silk-screened across the back. The other man wore a similar shirt and was young enough to be the older man's teenage boy. Both men wore OSHA-approved back support belts.

"Hey, dude," said Beemer loudly, not caring which man responded. "Got any smokes?"

But Beemer could barely hear himself, let alone the men on the dock. He was smack in the middle of an acoustic nightmare.

Every time a big truck or semi rolled across the concrete span, the sound waves reflected off the flatly squared stucco buildings and got trapped again by the underside of the freeway.

The elder man gave Beemer a quick once-over, then flicked his eyes beyond to the idling big rig. He cupped his right hand behind his ear in a gesture for Beemer to speak up.

"Asked if you got some smokes?" Beemer gestured back to the elder man, manipulating his index and middle finger in a scissoring motion.

"Got somethin' on there for us?" the younger shouted back.

"Hell no," said Beemer, moving close enough so he wouldn't have to shout. "I'm way over my hours. So ripped I missed my exit. No, I'm just cravin', know what I mean?"

As Beemer walked even closer and rolled up his sleeve to show his nicotine patch, his sweat-matted hair alerted the elder. Because the elder had once been an addict, he knew the signs of speed and crank abuse and instantly felt sorry for Beemer. He reached into his pocket and offered the truck driver an unfiltered Carlton.

"Yes," smiled Beemer. "Thank you, sirrrrrr."

The elder squatted on the loading dock, handed Beemer the cigarette and his lighter. It was Beemer's first draw of sweet tobacco in six long months. The smoke expanded into his lungs and was released back into the atmosphere through his nostrils and mouth.

"Man, that's good," said Beemer.

"Whatcha haulin'?" asked the younger man.

Strangely, Beemer considered answering with the facts. He was carting frozen blood product headed to a Middle Eastern middle man in the UAE. Payment for which would be a flat million US dollars wired to an offshore account in Belize that he'd easily set up on the internet. Something inside Beemer laughed at the prospect of seeing the old man's reaction to the truth.

"Frozen meat," lied Beemer.

"No shit? Like hamburgers an' shit?"

Beemer took another drag on the cigarette, exhaling as he nodded.

"Makes me hungry," said the younger man, who turned to

the elder. "Whadda you say, pops. We grabbin' some burgers for lunch?"

"Don't you got somethin' to do?" reminded the elder, without even looking directly at him. He shook the pack and offered another cigarette to Beemer. "One for the road, right?"

"Don't mind if I do," said Beemer, who slipped the extra smoke into his shirt pocket. Then he snapped a five-dollar bill between his fingers. "For your troubles."

"Naw," said the elder. "I used to long haul. Way back before they had all them rules about hours on, hours off."

"That right?" asked Beemer. "How'd you do it?"

"How'd you think we did it? Find the guy at the truck stop who was sellin' speed. Black Beauties. Man, that shit'd make you grind yer teeth down to yer gums then ask for more."

"Black Beauties? What's that? Like Dexedrine?" the kid asked.

"You got it," grinned the elder.

The loading dock was mostly shaded by the elevated freeway. A mild breeze kicked up, mixing the smoky air with the aroma of spent gasoline and diesel. For Beemer it was almost intoxicating as he sat on the dock, feet dangling, trading war stories with the elder, who, as it turned out, had served in Gulf War I at the helm of a M1 Abrams tank. The elder claimed to have been haunted by not being able to take the fight all the way to Baghdad and Saddam Hussein. He expressed jealousy that Beemer had seen the Iraqi capitol, tasted it, and wrecked its palaces. The pair of men shared nearly all the elder's cigarettes and even his brown bag lunch of twin peanut butter and banana sandwiches and pork rinds. Ever grateful for the food, company, and conversation, Beemer hoofed around to the front of the complex and the Rite-Aid. There he plunked down a hundred-dollar bill for a carton of Carlton cigarettes and a six pack of orange Gatorade. All of it for the kind elder, who had happily promised to keep an eye on Beemer's idling semi.

Then Beemer got a lousy feeling. A pit in his stomach kind of rot that, seconds after, he would explain away to himself as indigestion from those greasy pork rinds. Still, he decided to shortcut his way back to his big rig by leaving through the back of the Rite-

Aid. Before anybody in the storage room thought to stop him or ask why a customer was exiting out the rear, Beemer was out the back door, down the steps, and onto that blacktop strip that ran behind the complex.

The big rig, still idling, was being looked over by four young black men. White T-shirts, black Dickies shorts sagging off their asses. Do-rags for headwear. Beemer cataloged them as gang-bangers.

It was the younger black man in the silk-screened General Discount shirt who alerted the crew to Beemer's return. He stood atop the loading dock, skinny arm stretched toward the blacktop strip, two fingers splitting his mouth to let loose a shrill whistle. The piercing sound was instantly crushed by the din from the overpass as another eighteen-wheeler engaged its engine brake, making a belching sound akin to a .50-caliber machine gun—the Jake Brake. That was what truckers called the compression release engine brake. Originally built by Jacobs Vehicle Systems, the Jacob Engine Brake is a device mounted on the valve train of a diesel engine that mechanically actuates the combustion chamber exhaust valve. When the valve is forced open, the sudden release of compressed air creates the ear-blasting staccato sound.

Oh, how Beemer loved that sound.

Beemer stood stock still as fingers were pointed at him. He did this until he could feel his heart slowing. The key here was to make sure this was somebody else's *aw, fuck* moment. And not his.

"Your truck, motherfucker?" expressed the obvious leader of the crew. Beemer noticed the sneakers first. White basketballers, laces loosened. He instantly ranked the hoodlum as Motherfucker #1. He quickly shortened it to MF #1. Why? Because the more Beemer slowed his heart, the less effort he cared to expend on disposable humans.

"I asked you a fuckin' question!" shouted MF #1.

"Yeah," said Beemer. "My truck."

This is when Beemer saw the pistol coming out from underneath MF #1's bleached T-shirt. Even at the 115-foot difference between him and the crew boss, Beemer recognized the make and model before the muzzle was level. Glock 27, .40 caliber. Small, standard nine-cartridge capacity plus one in the pipe. Easily concealed, easier to shoot.

"Well, we gots some hungry friends," said MF #1.

"Yeah," said Motherfucker #2. "And they all likes the red meat!"

MF #2 stood slightly taller than his number one compadre, thinner even at his elongated, alien-like neck. After laughing at his own line, he climbed back up on the bumper of the refrigerated trailer, yanking rhythmically on the locked handle as if to make a point.

"Don't want your wheels," said MF #1. "Just unlock an' leave the trailer. We all do the rest."

"Right…okay," said Beemer. He left the bag of cigarettes and Gatorade on the blacktop, held his hands out to his sides, palms open in submission. "Lock's in the cab. Requires a code."

"So gimme the goddamn code, motherfucker."

"Thumbprint too," said Beemer, holding up his opposing digit in a simple thumbs-up gesture. Beemer nodded toward the cab and slowly began to walk forward as if prepared to execute anything MF #1 asked. He let his eyes flit to the other two gang members, quickly tagged MF #3 and MF #4. They were both seated on the guardrail between the blacktop strip and the weed-covered berm, beyond which was the undeveloped and graffiti-stained freeway under-strata. Presumably, this is where the gangbangers appeared from after receiving a text from the younger General Discount dock worker.

The elder was in the shade of the warehouse's open door, uncomfortably standing with his arms hanging limply to the side, his face full of resignation and disappointment.

"Your smokes are in the bag," said Beemer with a head feint to what he had left behind on the blacktop.

"Shut the fuck up and get with the thumb shit!" said MF #1.

Beemer nodded and continued walking toward the big rig, palms raised higher with every careful step. As he closed the gap on MF #1, he made sure to clock the man's pupils for any kind of drug interaction. Anything narcotic was a concern. As were potential tremors that might cause an adrenaline-spiked spasm in the banger's trigger finger. Beemer had seen enough of that. Soldiers of all stripes, jacked on everything from crack to cold medicine, their weapons innocently leveled on Iraqi prisoners. Suddenly, there would be a lone crack, a fine spray of blood in the air, followed by the knees of a prisoner buckling as he fell dead or wounded to the sand. Sure as shit, it was always an accident. The soldier would practically drop his weapon in fright at what he had unforgivably accomplished. Yessir. That was an *aw, fuck* moment if there ever was one. And he was going to deliver MF #1 his own *aw, fuck* moment.

As Beemer glided past the Glock's muzzle, he heard those white basketball sneakers shuffle and follow close behind. All he had to do was a quick one-eighty, snatch the pistol from MF #1's sweaty grip, and proceed to pistol-whip the banger until he wet himself. Beemer possessed both the training and the skill, not to mention the experience. He gave himself a 99-percent chance of success. But would it be as personally satisfying to himself as it would be memorable for MF #1? It would certainly qualify as an *aw, fuck* moment. But hardly the *aw, fuck* Beemer's ego wanted to impart on the do-ragged prick holding the Glock aimed between his shoulder blades.

Beemer was reaching for the chrome grab handle, ready to pull himself up into the cab, when he felt the Glock's muzzle press against his spine. The L4 vertebrae, Beemer reckoned, just south of his L2 and L3, fused together thanks to a munitions misfire. The army docs had told him he was lucky his entire spine hadn't shattered from the concussion instead of just enduring that penny-sized piece of steaming shrapnel lodged in his back, melting away half of the crucial disk.

"So what the fuck kinda lock needs a secret fuckin' thumb-print?" asked MF #1. "What's really in there?"

"Just meat," said Beemer, halfway into the cab, pausing and hoping to hell he hadn't erred in not disarming the gunman when he had the chance.

"Bullshit."

"Ain't the cargo, friend. It's the truck. Some weeks it's meat. Others it's refrigerated industrial parts. Me? I just drive."

The gun muzzle twisted against Beemer's back. MF #1's brain had just switched into indecision mode.

"What the fuck?" shouted MF #2, still hanging off the trailer's bumper.

"Look, dude," said Beemer, his face half turned to the banger. "It's all insured. And I don't give a shit what you do with it. You want me to tell the cops I went in for smokes and a dump and came out and the trailer was empty? Fine by me. I still get paid. You and your friends get to eat steak. Everybody's good."

"Then what the fuck you waiting for?" said MF #1. "Do your thumb thing!"

"All right, then," said Beemer, climbing into the cab. The seat gave a leather squeak as he settled behind the wheel. He retrieved his iPhone from the dash, waved it at MF #1, then bent at the waist to reach under the seat. "Watch this, dude. Latest technology."

"Stop, motherfucker!"

"Whoa, whoa," said Beemer, freezing. "I'm stopped, I'm stopped!"

"What you got there?"

"Connector," said Beemer, revealing a white Apple pin-out coupler and cord laced innocently in his fingers. "Just gotta plug it in."

Beemer didn't wait for permission. He plugged in the iPhone and quickly opened the lock/unlock application so he could show it to MF #1.

"Nifty app," said Beemer. "You got an iPhone?"

"Samsung, motherfucker!" said MF #1, incredulous.

Beemer punched up a code on the iPhone's touch screen. The image flashed to an icon waiting for a thumbprint. Oh, how he loved this application. Wished to hell he had had such a tool in Iraq when handling demolitions details. Beemer's biggest fear after setting the protocols for the demo—be it disposing of munitions or wiring up a car for a CIA assassination—had been the potential for tampering to the trigger mechanism. Had Beemer been supplied with an iPhone and the ten-dollar app, arming and disarming devices would have been as safe as playing a round of Angry Birds.

"There we go," said Beemer after applying his thumb to the touch screen and the icon had flashed green. "Open 'er up."

"SPEEDY!" barked MF #1, ostensibly revealing MF #2's street name. "Try it!"

"NOTHIN'," shouted back MF #2, only to have his voice drowned out by another overhead trucker applying a noisy Jake Brake.

Bbbbbrrrrraaaaapppppp!

MF #2 had given the trailer's latch two hard pulls, kicked the door, and pulled at it yet again to no avail.

"You hear that? Shit didn't work," said MF #1.

"S'awright," said Beemer, clearing the app, restarting the code sequence, and reapplying his thumb when prompted. The display flashed green again. "'Kay. Try it again."

MF #1 waved his gun toward the back of the rig. Beemer could feel the rig rocking slightly as the hood on the rear bumper continued to try the latch to the trailer doors without success.

"Nothin', motherfucker!" spat MF #1. He stepped up onto the running board, switched the pistol to his left hand, and wrapped his right tightly around the grab handle to steady himself.

"Wait, wait," begged Beemer. "Gotta be the connection." He twisted over and traced the slight cord into the center console. "Wait. Think I see the problem. Yeah, yeah. Okay. Try it again."

"Try again," shouted MF #1.

"Again?" asked MF #2, steamed, sweaty, but still standing on the rear bumper.

"What? Like you didn't hear me?"

"I'll try, but I don't think shit's changed."

The slender banger on the trailer's bumper slid back along the four-inch ledge, grabbed the handle, and gave it a solid yank.

"Fuckin' nothin'!" shouted MF #2, slapping the door panel in frustration.

The leader of the gang—a.k.a. Motherfucker #1—was quickly elevating from annoyed to flat-out cap-banging mad. He was considering popping the cracker truck driver right then and there out of nothing more than ghetto spite.

"I know that look," said Beemer in an audible whisper.

The gangbanger with the pistol had erred, allowing himself to become distracted by his number two. And in that nanosecond of time when he was considering unloading the Glock's clip into Beemer's body, he had gone from control to...

"Aw, fuck," said the gangbanger without a synapse of thought.

"Exactly," returned Beemer, pushing the fat barrel of a sawed-off shotgun closer to MF #1's face. A modified Benelli M4 with a pistol grip. The very same weapon he had hauled up and down every street and back alley of Fallujah.

Beemer was prepared to explain the simple yet clarifying beauty of the *aw, fuck* moment. That somehow in those rare, adrenalized snippets of time, true human character is tested and formed. But that was before Beemer heard it. The Jake Brake. Another trucker, throwing open the valves of his massive diesel engine, thus temporarily choking the engine of fuel in order to slow the load and save his conventional brakes. The blast of noise through that loading strip was like an ocean wave, building toward a peak before being sucked back into the deep. It was a snap decision by Beemer, and not particularly well thought out. More opportunity-driven than anything else. An impulse.

The braking sound climaxed at near 132 decibels.

Bbbbbrrrrraaaaappppp!

Nobody heard the shotgun fire. The din was so loud, such a stress on the auditory nerves, the action played out like a movie gone silent. A puff of smoke. A twitch in MF #1's neck. The basic G forces as his muscles gave way. The heavy sack-like way his body folded onto the pavement. The red mist that hung in the air until it was whisked away on a gust of hot wind.

When the sound of the passing big rig dissolved, Beemer swung from the cab, jacking another shell into the chamber before his feet landed next to MF #1's body. The rest was pretty expected. The gangbangers scattered back behind the trailer, tripping over the guardrail and scratching their way up and over the berm like rats under a million-watt Klieg light. Both the younger and elder remained frozen in the shade of the loading dock, seemingly stuck somewhere between their flight or fight responses. At least, that could be said for the younger.

"I know where you work, which means I know where you live, your family lives, and your friends," said Beemer, already regretting his poor decision. Then he turned the shotgun on the elder. "Same goes for you, ol' man. Only I'm gonna figure you're not dumb enough to have had any skin in this bullshit."

The elder nodded. Was it approval or mere understanding? Beemer didn't stick around to find out. He pocketed the empty shotgun casing, returned to the cab of his tractor rig, revved the engine, geared the beast into first gear, and rolled. Cool. Like Steve McQueen. At least that was the picture he was able to project.

Underneath Beemer's skin he was fist-pounding the steering wheel, screaming out loud, and cursing himself with curdled invectives. In the snap of a finger, he'd turned the gangbanger's *aw, fuck* moment into his own self-loathing revelation. Once again, his impulses had gotten the better of him. The idiot inside of him— the bastard with whom he'd wrestled his entire life—had found a way out of his psyche's cell.

My idiot, said Beemer to himself, attempting to take ownership of the personal demon. He wheeled the big rig up the freeway on-ramp, carefully checking his mirrors for law enforcement or revenge-minded gang members coordinating their bloody reprisal. All the while, he could feel his idiot friend looking for a place to relax within his core. He'd spent a lifetime learning to put a lid on the naughty bastard. Years of his prepubescent youth had been dedicated to understanding the urge to unleash the chaos. He'd even once told a therapist that his biggest nightmare was having his parents lock him in a room with nothing but a single red button that, if triggered, would launch an array of nuclear missiles that would arc into the atmosphere before an eventual descent to destroy the earth. The temptation to press the red button would eventually become so overwhelming for the boy that he'd have no choice but to choose to end the world.

It was the Marines that gave Beemer the eventual discipline to put a muzzle on his impulses. The structure and regimen of military life placed a positive spin on the young man's future. And with every ounce of confidence that grew within him, the idiot's voice turned fainter and fainter. For a while, it was so buried that Beemer had forgotten he'd ever had an issue.

Then came Fallujah.

9

Lennox.

The new Lennox station—redubbed the Los Angeles County Sheriff's South Station since it moved two blocks from Lennox Boulevard to Imperial Highway—served the county's southeast side from the edge of Los Angeles International Airport, north through Inglewood, sweeping in an arc across Hawthorne into Compton. Despite its change of location and Southwestern-style stucco and tile roof—not altogether different in architecture from half the territory's strip malls—it was still notorious Lennox, populated and operated by a collection of high-crime cowboys, a.k.a., the Lennox Lawmen.

Like most LAPD cops, Gonzo had heard plenty about Lennox. It was considered a "fast" station, a high-test culture of crime, caffeination, and skull-cracking. According to LAPD mythology, Lennox and its sister stations, Century and Compton, engaged in equal parts street justice and equal parts modern urban police work the general public expected from its law officers.

The last fifteen minutes of the ride had been shared in silence, but for the blue streak of cursing Lucky had unleashed when he'd slowed to turn into the entrance to the old Lennox station. There, he had discovered ten-foot-high chain-link circling the shuttered little workhorse of a building. Two minutes later, they were winding around behind the "new" station. Lucky had barely backed into a handicapped space nearest the tinted automatic doors at the rear of the building when he'd set the parking brake and exited the vehicle. The engine was left on, Gonzo figured, to keep her comfortable and air-conditioned. Was it a subtle effort by Lucky to keep Gonzo in the car? Or could it have been the unconscious act of a gentleman wanting to keep his passenger comfortable?

Gonzo didn't hang on the question for too long, taking more interest in the three sheriffs who had met Lucky practically the instant he'd slipped from the car. Lucky was greeted with hugs, handshakes, and consoling backslaps by the trio, each garbed in detectives' street clothes, weapons, and sheriffs' badges fixed to their belts. The display was informative to Gonzo. This Kern County cop was more than buddies with the Lennox deputies. The body language, the direct eye contact, the hushed speaking style, plus the quick and conspiratorial proximity to each other spoke volumes to Gonzo. The four-man gathering that formed in the ten square yards of shade on the other side of the gas pumps was the kind of man-huddle reserved for cops who have shared more than coffee. These were the kind of cops who'd shared each other's lives and secrets. Cops who had spilled blood with each other and for each other.

"Holy shit," said Gonzo to herself, as if wisdom were being imparted from her soul. "Lucky's from Lennox."

This is when Gonzo crawled out from her air-conditioned cocoon, shut the door loud enough to get a glance of attention, and began the twenty-step trek to the shade near the gas pumps. Her boots clicked against the concrete in a gait that sounded more womanly than kick-ass cop.

"I'll be with you in a minute," said Lucky, holding up a stalling palm.

"You're not Kern, are you?" said Gonzo, seeking confirmation. "You're goddamn local."

"Who's that?" asked Detective Lopes, the runt of the litter. Lopes had short curly brown hair, thick eyebrows, and a cop mustachio circa 1982.

"Her?" Gonzo overheard Lucky say to the three sheriff's detectives gathered on the other side of the station's gas pumps. "She's supposed to be some LAPD detective."

"Why the fuck?" asked the hulking man, later to be introduced to Gonzo as Sergeant "Flip" Bledsoe.

"Dunno," said Lucky. "Babysitter. Tour guide. Thinks I'm some shit-kicker from Kern."

None of the slurs surprised Gonzo. She'd heard plenty in her career. "So which is it?" asked Gonzo, unfazed, arms akimbo.

"We're in the middle of somethin'," said Lucky. "You mind?"

"Don't pull this shit," said Gonzo. "You think this is the first time I've gotten the 'deputy two-step'?"

"Lady? You're in Lennox," reminded Bledsoe. "This is County property. And we'd greatly appreciate it if you'd get back in Lucky's car."

"You some kinda club? Or are you cops?" suggested Gonzo, giving up no ground whatsoever.

All pupils narrowed on Lucky. As if the inference was that the next move was clearly his to make.

"I didn't tell her," said Lucky. He shook his head and looked at the ground. "She don't know."

"What don't I know?" pushed Gonzo.

"S'okay?" asked the big man. Lucky nodded. Sergeant Bledsoe put a gargantuan hand on Lucky's shoulder, squeezed with affection, then approached Gonzo. He gently offered an ushering hand, leading Gonzo from the gas pumps to a corner near a line of unoccupied sheriffs' cruisers parked bumper to bumper.

"Awright," said Bledsoe. "You're sorta right. He's a Kern County detective. But he used to be here. With us at Lennox."

"Okay, I get it," said Gonzo. "So what's the big deal?"

"Deputy that was murdered this mornin'? Was Lucky's little brother, Tony."

It's true that cops feel more for other cops than they do citizens. They are brothers in arms. Sheriffs or police, when an officer goes down, cops take that stuff personally. Family, though, is altogether different. Lucky had said he was close to the murdered deputy. Just not how close.

Hearing that it was Lucky's little brother who had been executed only hours earlier left Gonzo with a wisp of cold at the back of her neck. She felt the short hairs on the base of her scalp go wet as if ice were dripping down her spine.

"'Kay," said Gonzo. "I get what this is about."

"Not sure you do. Or even I do, for that matter," said Bledsoe. "Unless you've had a brother or sister murdered like that."

"You're right and I'm sorry," said Gonzo. "All my boss told me was there was this sheriff's deputy on his way down from Kern. Please give him an LAPD in any way you can."

"Copy that. But as you can see, Luck's got plenty of assist from his Lennox brothers."

"Fine by me," said Gonzo, feeling dismissed. She could tell she wasn't wanted. And maybe not needed. "All I need is the a-okay from my super and a ride back to Pasadena and I'm all good."

"See what I can do," said Bledsoe.

While Gonzo watched Bledsoe return to Lucky and his brothers in arms, she pressed the last number dialed on her mobile phone.

"Yeah. It's Gonzo. Mitch get back yet?" said Gonzo, referring to her immediate supervisor, Mitchell Blunt of the Community Relations Office—or CRO—of the LAPD.

"Gonzo," popped Mitchell's voice, the volume suddenly intensified. "Where are you?"

"Lennox Station."

"Sheriff's?"

"The very same."

"What's going on down there?"

"Some kinda reunion," said Gonzo. "I'll explain—"

"L.A. Sheriff's know about the FBI?"

"What about 'em?"

"Just came across. Think the feds may be looking for the same black big rig."

Gonzo listened to the rest, remaining visibly stoic while scrawling mental notes. She tabled her initial agenda to ask permission to turn over her chaperone duties to Los Angeles Sheriffs, then stuffed the phone into the front pocket of her skintight jeans. As she re-approached the county quartet, she silently rehearsed what she was going to say next. She decided to go with the tried and true.

"So whadda you wanna hear?" Gonzo began. "The good news or the bad news?"

It was Bledsoe who was first to cop a changed attitude. The helpful friend-of-the-bereaved act dropped to reveal a hulking man, willing to resign his words in exchange for the easy intimidation of his size. Especially against a woman. Bledsoe's barrel chest flexed above his even more impressive belly. Gonzo was already preparing to retreat a defensive step when Lucky hooked Bledsoe's arm.

"Wanna hear it," said Lucky.

"We had an agreement that she was gonna step off," said Bledsoe.

"The good news," said Lucky, ignoring his beefy pal.

"You mind?" said Gonzo, her eyes unwavering from Bledsoe's until he backed off. As tall and broad shouldered as Gonzo was, it still didn't seem to forestall badge-heavy males from muscling up on her. A few of those alpha males had crossed that delicate line, only to find themselves on their butts looking up at Gonzo from the ground. In those moments, she was grateful for all her martial arts instructors. From those who had trained her in Tae Kwon Do as a child to her present sensei, Lujan, a specialist in Krav Maga, the Israeli military's form of hand-to-hand combat.

The way Gonzo framed it, big ol' Bledsoe had just dodged an embarrassing bullet.

"The good news," repeated Gonzo. "FBI appears to be looking for your big rig. Thinks they got tags too."

"What's the FBI want with the rig?" asked Lucky.

"Something about a burglary in Reno. Biological materials. Crossing state lines."

"Biological?" asked Lopes. "Like terrorist shit?"

"Blood products," said Gonzo. "Thus the refrigerated truck. Stolen truck, by the way."

"What's anybody want a truckload of blood for?"

Lucky shook his head. The muscles in his jaw tightened, creating dimples in his unshaven cheeks.

"Bad news?" Lucky asked.

"Right," said Gonzo. "Since your boss requested assistance from LAPD…my orders are to stick with you while outside your jurisdiction."

"Told you Luck had all the help he needed." Bledsoe puffed out that ridiculous chest of his.

"Not my call," shrugged Gonzo.

"Whatever," said Lucky, a weird calmness governing his voice. "Just don't get in the way, yeah?"

"Get in the way of what?" asked Gonzo. "FBI's on the job. Next move is to hook up with them."

"The FBI?" said Lucky. "They can suck my white dick."

TMZ began as an acronym for the Thirty Mile Zone. The origins of the term can be traced back to Hollywood in the 1960s. If a production was to film beyond thirty miles from its respective studio, the various talent unions—primarily the Screen Actors Guild—categorized the shoot as "on location" and thus required per diems plus other travel and/or overnight expenses be paid to their various members.

But there's another meaning.

Predating even the invention of the Thirty Mile Zone, Hollywood had another old saying: It's not adultery if you're on location.

Whoever started that line should have copyrighted it and

collected royalties. In the sixties, when the unions outlined the Thirty Mile Zone—or TMZ—serial cheaters began using the cipher as a shorthand excuse for their transgressions.

"So, aren't you worried your wife's gonna find out that you had an affair with that actress?"

"What affair? We were TMZ in Santa Barbara."

In 2005, TMZ.com debuted, taking its name from the obvious sleaze Hollywood had come to associate with the old union acronym. What began as just another celebrity gossip site—albeit financed by media stalwarts Warner Brothers/AOL, Inc.—soon blew up to rival the National Enquirer for dominance in tabloid fodder. Add to that the emergence of streaming cell phone picture and video technology, TMZ distributed an up-to-the-moment product unrivaled by its competitors. From Mel Gibson's racial rants to Lindsay Lohan's indiscretion of the week to Michael Jackson's untimely death, TMZ was first and fastest to deliver the dirt.

On that Monday morning in August, TMZ churned out a new headline every hour:

NICKELODEON STAR PEPPER ELLIS IN CAR ACCIDENT!

PEPPER ELLIS KILLED IN CAR WRECK!

PEPPER'S NICK CASTMATES IN SHOCK!

*GRISLY ACCIDENT PICS: PE'S BODY
AND BOYFRIEND BURNED!*

BOYFRIEND BEHIND THE WHEEL OF PEPPER'S CAR!

*IT WAS MURDER! PEPPER'S DEATH
LISTED AS HOMICIDE!*

"Holy crap. There's already video of Pepper *gambling* in South Lake!"

Jenna Mantz let her fingernails tap the top of the plastic mouse.

Fifteen taps and then a click on the refresh button. The computer screen briefly flashed, then reloaded the TMZ.com home page.

"Thought she was just seventeen," said Dulaney Little, his short legs crossed, sports coat unbuttoned, and arms stretching out each way across the top of the sofa. Dulaney may have been small in stature and slightly overweight, but he insisted on taking up the space of a big man.

"Seventeen, yeah. But celebrities, you know?"

"What don't I know? She's seventeen. You gotta be twenty-one to gamble. And casinos don't wanna lose their license."

"It's on TMZ," pointed out Jenna. "Pepper is with her boyfriend, throwing dice at a craps table."

TMZ's most recent boffo post was video stolen by a Harrah's Casino insider, emailed to TMZ in the flick of an eyelash, and uploaded with a headline within minutes of the act. The video was grainy but in color, collected from a ceiling-mounted security camera. It showed the diminutive, seventeen-year-old Pepper Ellis in a virginal white cocktail dress, tossing dice amidst a crowd of gambling admirers. Next to Pepper was her much taller boyfriend costumed in slacker T-shirt and jeans.

"Lookit that douchebag boyfriend," said Jenna. "She's dressed like she's all that—and he's like he doesn't give a shit."

"Who's gambling. Him or her?"

"Suppose he is. And he was twenty-one too. But is she allowed to touch the dice?"

"Dunno," said Dulaney. "Not up on my Nevada gaming laws."

"You really never heard of her before?"

"Nope. Never."

"God. And you're not even *that* old."

"Thanks, Jen," said Dulaney, with a slightly feigned indifference.

"Well, you don't look that old, I mean."

"'Cause I'm black."

"I didn't say that."

"I know you didn't," said Dulaney. "A lotta black people with extra dark skin look younger than they are."

"So you're saying you're older."

"I'm forty-five," said Dulaney.

"You are not."

"Why would I lie about being *older*?"

"Good point," said Jenna. "Damn, Dulaney. You're a sexy old man."

For Jenna, the flirt was on and Dulaney knew it. But the married FBI man with four children couldn't see himself crossing the fidelity line with his boss's twenty-six-year-old assistant. Not that Jenna wasn't attractive. The petite brunette was a bona fide former Laker Girl who hadn't lost a step. After hours or when the boss wasn't around, Jenna had been known to demonstrate gymnastic flips down the US Attorney's office corridors on little more than a dare. *Very flexible*, thought Dulaney—along with every other heterosexual male who might happen upon the twelfth floor of the Spring Street US Courthouse.

"All right, Dulaney," said Lilly Zoller, returning from the ladies' room. She was still drying her hands on a paper towel that she left balled up atop Jenna's desk. "Where were we?"

"The murder," said Dulaney, on his feet and fully engaged the moment Lilly stepped back in.

"Triple murder," reminded Lilly, leading the way back into her austere office. Over a simple monochrome couch were frameless black-and-white art photos in a uniform row. Opposite was a giant whiteboard with cases listed, numbered, and divided by colored marker. Between was an uncluttered government-issued desk backed up against a tinted, floor-to-ceiling window overlooking the famed downtown four-level freeway interchange.

"Okay. Three murders," continued Dulaney, who took up his former pose on Lilly's office sofa. He left the door open. "Three murders in Kern County. Not federal jurisdiction."

"We already established that the big rig was carrying stolen goods from Nevada. The murders were committed while in the act of breaking federal law."

"Getting a little reverb from both local and the home office."

"Screw local. So what's the issue with your boys?"

"You know. Optics."

"How it looks?"

"Celebrity case. They think you might be bending jurisdiction to make a coupla headlines."

"As if all the bureau does is chase terrorists? Puh-lease." Lilly dropped into a blue leather desk chair with a back so high it framed her entire head like the ridiculous collars of a Lewis Carroll queen.

"How it looks. Just sayin'."

"Stolen biological materials crossing state lines? Sounds like a homeland security issue to me."

"Blood products."

"What for?"

"For a party with all his vampire friends. What do I know?" said Dulaney, his blood pressure slightly rising. "We got the make on the truck, the rental company, the perp's picture and ID—albeit probably an alias and a disguise—and we've released the info to all local agencies."

"And?" Lilly asked, expectant.

"And what else is the bureau supposed to do?"

Lilly opened the top desk drawer, slipped her finger under the top panel, and pressed a button. Magically, the door to her office slowly swung shut with a soft but distinct click. Oh, Lilly loved the button. She'd discovered it after having moved into the office reluctantly after losing the political battle for the much larger suite at the northeast corner of the floor. The button was remotely connected to an electromagnet mounted as a doorstop. When activated, the electromagnet held tight to a strip of metal screwed to the bottom of the door. The button in Lilly's desk drawer merely turned off the connection, releasing the door, which, powered by a piston-driven mechanism, would shut in a ghostly manner.

"Question for you, Agent Little," said Lilly.

"Sure."

"You like your job?"

"Twenty years in. I better like it."

"I'll rephrase," continued Lilly. "Do you like your assignment with the US Attorney's office in Los Angeles? Flexible hours?

Comfy office? No real shoe leather? Hardly ever have to pick up a lunch tab or cocktails because everybody you encounter's either a judge or a lawyer and they figure with a government salary and all those kids, you couldn't possibly afford—"

"I get it," Dulaney interrupted.

"Rhetorical question. No need to answer."

"What do you need, Lilly?" asked Dulaney.

"Love when a man asks me that," giggled Lilly. She stepped around from behind her desk, smoothing out the creases in her navy pencil skirt. "Need you to leak something to one of your blogger pals. The unsub in the Kern murders is suspected in the theft of a large truckload of biological materials. Get it out there with the video of him renting the eighteen-wheeler. See what comes back."

"We say 'biological,' everybody else is gonna say 'terrorist.' DC's gonna want to know why we leaked to some blogger before we talked to them."

"DC's a twenty-four-hour turnaround. By the time they wanna know more, we'll have our unsub."

"You're gambling."

"Hell, yeah," said Lilly, her mouth spreading into a grin that appeared more sexual than satisfied. It was her eyes, though, that gave her away. At the mere mention of the word *gambling*, Dulaney clocked the widening of Lilly's eyes and a slight dilation of her pupils. It was a classic addict's response to a simple stimulus. Lilly's secret groove wasn't narcotic or alcohol. She was hooked on a chemical produced beneath her own devilish skin. Dopamine. Possibly the most dangerous drug on the planet, producing a pleasurable feeling that is often associated with risk.

Dulaney didn't say goodbye to Jenna Mantz. He stepped from Lilly's office, left the door open, strode the three quick steps by the assistant's desk, and vanished into the main corridor. All Jenna caught of Dulaney was a flash of his hard-set jaw as he smoked past her. He must have been pissed off, Jenna decided. Not that it surprised her any. Lilly was known to have that kind of effect on colleagues, underlings, and even her bosses. Jenna would forever remember the day she had interviewed for the job. Lilly was at her desk, elbows propped and fingers interlaced as if in prayer. Then without blinking, she'd stated her management philosophy: "There's three ways to do something around here. The right way. The wrong way. And my way."

It wasn't the first nor the second time Jenna had heard the instruction-slash-witticism. The first time was out of the mouth of her stepfather. The second time was during a weigh-in with her Laker Girl director-cum-squad-mum. And Jenna had hated both of them.

10

Long Beach.

"I'll hold for him, okay?" said Rey to his brother's office assistant. "Got nothin' else to do but wait."

Rey pulled the Bluetooth earbud from his ear, shook off the sweat that had collected on the tiny speaker, then placed it in his other ear. Ah, yes. He could hear the ghastly elevator music far better without the gurgling of moisture between his ear drum and the connection to the Palomino Shipping Company.

To the limp beat of a Muzak version of "Every Little Thing She Does is Magic," Rey dug his right heel into a patch of dry earth and began redrawing the outline of the pool he would build next. Yes, there was a schematic already drawn and engineered by another pool company who, unfortunately for the homeowner, pretty much doubled their initial construction estimate after completing the design. The annoyed homeowner fired the pool company but kept the plans and shopped for lower bids. As usual, Rey's bid was the lowest and offered the most. Plus, the clients were really charmed by the former car mechanic turned pool artiste. Rey was a true raconteur full of adventurous stories from putting out oil fires in Kuwait to racing Porsches from Santa Barbara to Monterey.

Rey stopped sketching in the dirt, took a few steps back to measure the shape with his eye, erased twenty feet of his heel trail, and began to redraw the lines. The pool he pictured was a good bit larger than the plans called for and would cost the client more than his original bid. Some would call this tactic a bait and switch. Rey didn't look at it that way. He was improving on the design and delivering the homeowner a far more spectacular product than had been imagined. Usually, this would require a significant amount of massaging on the contractor's part, and possibly a couple of steak dinners. In the end, though, the client would most surely thank Rey for the final product.

"I'm his brother and I *need* to talk to him," pressed Rey when the snotty assistant claimed to be unable to connect with his brother, Heber. "He's got a goddamn satphone on that million-dollar tub of his."

"Maybe he doesn't want to talk to you," said the assistant, suggesting she knew more than she was letting on.

"Tell my brother if he doesn't get on the fucking phone right now I'm gonna start composing a letter to the ITC and copy the Department of Commerce and the IRS."

"Hold, please," she said.

Rey took the moment to shake the dirt out of his right sneaker, returned the shoe to his foot, and continued sketching the outline of the pool. Rey wanted each pool to fit into the landscape as if it had been formed before the house was built. Custom pools were time consuming and from a business standpoint, Rey's approach didn't make much sense. His was hardly the kind of work expected from the lowest bidder. But finances were never Rey's best suit. Otherwise, why would he have agreed to arrange an illegal shipment of some unknown frozen product to the Middle East?

"What the fuck, Rey?!" shouted Heber into his satphone.

"Didn't you say you'd be back yesterday?"

"So I changed my goddamn mind," said Heber without easing back on his acerbic tone. "Do I need my little brother's permission to stay a few extra days?"

"When we have business plans? Yeah."

"What business plans?"

"Shipping business. What the hell else?"

"Shipping is my business. Your business is pools. Am I missing something?"

"Can't believe you forgot about it," said Rey. "We talked about a customer of mine that needed a container shipped."

"You're shittin' me. Was I drinkin' when we talked?"

"You didn't sound like it. You gave me a dollar figure. Said you wrote down the date."

"Blank, brother. Don't remember a damn thing."

"Swell."

"Whatever. If I said I'd put this container to sea, then that's what I'll do. Where and when?"

"Was supposed to be today!"

"Well, we both know that's not gonna happen," laughed Heber.

"No shit," said Rey, trying to sound equally amused. "But this customer is on a timetable. He's gotta ship tomorrow, latest."

"No can do."

"Don't say that."

"Can't ship it if I'm not there. You need a favor? You got somethin' that's gotta be walked around customs? I'm the one who does it and nobody else."

"Then get on a plane."

"Yeah, right."

"I'm serious."

"Fish are biting down here. Not comin' back 'til I'm ready and that's it."

"That doesn't work for me or my customer."

"Hey!" barked Heber. "Who's doin' who a fuckin' favor?"

"You. But you were supposed to do me the favor *today*."

"So says you. I don't remember a goddamn thing about it.

Because I'm your brother and I love you, I'll do the favor. But not 'til Thursday, earliest."

The sweat had, once again, collected in Rey's ear. His brother's spiky voice was beginning to sound as if he were speaking from underwater. That and the acid in his stomach was starting to bubble up and beg for a tab of Prilosec.

"Hey, Rey. You still there?"

"Yeah."

"Make Thursday work, okay? I'll be there and all will be good."

"And if I'm dead by Thursday?" asked Rey.

"Yeah, right. Call me Wednesday night and we'll make it work," laughed Heber. "'Make it work.' Ain't that what that gay guy on the cable show says? 'Make it work'?"

"Wouldn't know," lied Rey in a self-flagellating monotone.

There was a beeping sound when the satphone disconnected, followed by the click of Heber's assistant ending the conference connection. The call was officially over.

Rey stood in the middle of that patch of flaky Reseda, California, soil, his ears filled with sweat and his right sneaker full of sand. He couldn't yet process the call or the ramifications. He thought of pressing redial on his mobile and starting the process all over again—for all he knew he could be dead by Thursday.

Maybe he didn't want to press his older brother on the issue for fear of discovering that family truly didn't matter to Heber… that his untimely end would prove inconsequential in the Lord's grand scheme of things. The thought was too great to ponder given that Rey hadn't yet even partially processed the death of his only son, Daniel.

Present calculation proved impossible.

So, Rey finished sketching the outline of the custom pool, shook the dirt from his shoe, rattled off a string of Spanish instructions for the longtime Mexican employee he lovingly called Gordo—or Fat Man—to stake out the perimeter so the client could see the space that would eventually become a beautiful custom pool.

That was, of course, if Rey lived long enough to finish it.

11

Downtown.

"Now what?" asked Gonzo.

"We wait for the call," said Lucky.

"What if they don't get it?"

"They'll get it. They're my boys."

The unlikely duo was parked on Spring Street in downtown Los Angeles, a mere half block from the federal courthouse. As heat records were crushed all over the Southwest, downtown was no exception. The sun was straight up and unfiltered through the surrounding skyscrapers. And the tinted windows of Lucky's Dodge Charger were no match for the rays that penetrated the car despite the air conditioning being switched to nearly full arctic blast.

"You know," said Gonzo. "My office is, like, walking distance. It's air conditioned. Comfortable—"

"Sounds nice. You wanna hoof it there and call today a date, then swell."

"You're saying that because you know I can't."

"Am I?"

It was one of the rare moments in the past few hours that Lucky actually looked at Gonzo. Right through his dark wraparounds, past her aviators, and to the back of her optical receptors. Lucky's was a dead stare. Motionless. As if he could wait a lifetime for a response.

"Look," Gonzo began, risking the moment. "I'm sorry about your brother. I didn't know—"

"Told ya, did they?" said Lucky of his Lennox brethren.

"'Course they did," said Gonzo. "They care."

"S'pose they do," said Lucky. He turned off that intimidating stare, emptying his gaze back onto the lunchtime traffic.

"Mind if I ask you—"

"I mind if you breathe, okay?" interrupted Lucky. "But since I can't stop you from that, what's it matter if you ask *anything*?"

Normally, Gonzo would have given as good as she got. She enjoyed trading barbs. As a woman cop, she'd been around the block long enough to be accustomed to wearing a target on her back. She prided herself on her ability to dish the trash talk—in good humor or otherwise—right back at the direction it came from. But this time, she was staked out with a cop who was grieving his dead younger brother. That and Lucky was probably still in some sort of shock, running only on sheer will or adrenaline.

"Why Kern County?"

Lucky considered not answering the question. His mouth formed something of an astringent smirk.

"You mean why Kern over some other sunny locale?" Lucky said, trying to rephrase the question into something he'd like to answer. "Shit. You didn't even ask the question you wanted to ask."

Gonzo didn't rise to the bait.

"Why did I leave Lennox?"

"I can think of a few answers there," said Gonzo, letting her glibness slip.

"LAPD, man. Not a glimmer about the South Sheriffs."

"Let's not go there," said Gonzo, not caring to open that bottomless pit of conflict between the L.A. County Sheriff's and the LAPD. Google "Pandora's Box" and she would probably find video of a sheriff and a LAPD cop squaring up in a bloody octagon.

"'Kay. So I don't know shit about South Sheriffs," continued Gonzo. "Why Kern County over Orange County or Ventura?"

"Somethin' wrong with Kern?" asked Lucky, his tone utterly rhetorical. "Had a bad experience that way? Got pulled over and mistaken for a farm worker?"

"So you think that's funny?"

"Naw. Not to you."

"And what's that supposed to mean?"

Lucky just shook his head, letting the faintest smile slip. No teeth. Just one edge of his lips was slightly upturned. He kept his gaze aimed at the street.

Gonzo folded her arms across her chest, deciding it worthless to continue the conversation. She'd be better off calculating the money the city was paying her to babysit the asshole. Whether he was grieving or not, she'd come to the conclusion that Lucky Dey was definitely an asshole.

"Wasn't me who picked Kern," said Lucky, sounding distant despite the short space between himself and Gonzo. "Tony... He, uh...couldn't make it with L.A. County. Tried and tried but couldn't pass the exam. And me? S'pose I thought that was best for him. You know, that he'd quit trying to be a cop."

Over the blast of the air conditioner, Gonzo did her damned best to read the amount of pain in Lucky's vocal inflections. The more Lucky spoke, the thinner his voice became.

"Next thing I knew he'd made an application with Kern. Didn't know anybody up there but I asked around. Got some names. Put in a good word, you know?"

"That's sweet," said Gonzo. "You were taking care of him by moving up there."

"Didn't have a choice, really. Kern pretty much said they wouldn't have him unless I came along as part of the package."

Then she heard it. The tiniest crack in Lucky's voice.

"Some job I did taking care of him." Lucky's jaw muscles tightened and flexed. The light sheen of sweat that covered his stubble revealed the hefty mandible muscle bulging beneath his cheek.

Beads of perspiration were breaking out all over him. His skin itched. He shifted uncomfortably in his seat, unconsciously scratching at his shoulders and thighs. Gonzo observed him. She was detached. She had little in the way of feelings for him. Perhaps some empathy for having just lost his little brother. Even so, she remained defensively detached.

Sweat must have been running down Lucky's lower legs because eventually he reached below the steering wheel and rolled up his left pant leg for a quick rub down. This is when Gonzo saw the tattoo. It was five-and-a-half inches long, inked on the inside of his calf. The image was of the grim reaper, fabled scythe in one hand and a handgun in the other. At the bottom was a scroll with the number fifty-two. And as quickly as Gonzo saw the tattoo, it was hidden again by the denim pants leg.

Lucky's cell phone trilled with an uncustomized tone. The noise was a loud, electronic sample of an old-fashioned bell ringer. It was startling and clattered against Gonzo's eardrums.

"Yeah," answered Lucky before the phone was even to his ear. He listened a beat then repeated the name as if he expected Gonzo to write it down. "Lilly Zoller…And she's what? An assistant US Attorney? Yeah, whatever. I'll call you back."

Lucky clicked off and popped his car door.

"Where we goin'?"

"Some lady fed is pushing this thing. See what she knows."

Gonzo trailed Lucky across Spring Street and through the revolving doors of the courthouse building. The usual security precautions manned by federal deputies were set up in the lobby. Metal detectors and ID checks. There were two lines. One for civilians—most of whom were employees or grand jurors—and another for badge-carrying authorities. Both Lucky and Gonzo supplied their badges and weapons, explained that they had no appointment, waited fifteen minutes to be cleared, and passed through to the elevator bank. For the first time in hours, Gonzo felt less anxious. The feds inside that marble building were taking over the case. Whatever further assistance Lucky needed would come from agents of the FBI. But her feelings of comfort were extinguished when she recalled Lucky's spunky little ditty from when they were standing outside the Lennox station: "The FBI can suck my white dick."

She didn't have to ask what the comment was about. Gonzo could guess. Plenty of L.A. detectives—Sheriff's and LAPD—held some form of grudge against the feds, having been at one time or another on the bottom end of an investigative monkey pile. Federal authorities were well known for throwing the considerable weight of Uncle Sam around local municipalities without much care for the consequences. That and cops who carried US government badges often treated city cops with the same indifference they reserved for common house flies.

The elevator doors opened.

"After you," said Lucky with a hint of mockery, his open hand guiding her.

"Whatever," mumbled Gonzo, taking her place inside.

Lucky followed her into the lift, pressing the twelfth floor and door-close buttons, respectively. The set of doors was sliding shut when an arm shot between them, triggering the motion sensor. The doors clutched and reopened to reveal a sharp-dressed woman who was often described by fellow lawyers as a tight package.

"Sorry," said Lilly Zoller with a minimum of eye contact. She pressed the button for the eleventh floor, swiveled to face outward, and waited for the doors to close again.

The trio rode in seconds of silence as the car accelerated then eased to a stop at the fifth floor. When the doors were supposed to open, they remained closed. The elevator sat motionless, its passengers expecting little delay.

Gonzo flicked her eyes to the button pad. Every button was brightly lit. Still the car didn't move.

With her thumb, Lilly pressed the eleventh floor button again. When nothing appeared to happen, she used the knuckle of her index finger to punch the button in an annoyed triplicate.

"So what's that mean when all the lights are on?" asked Gonzo.

Lucky reached around the petite attorney. He uttered a faint "Excuse me" as he worked both the door-open and door-close buttons.

"Fucking hell," said Lilly, bumping the side of her Jimmy Choo heels into the door, careful not to scuff the finish. "Of all the times."

"Happens a lot, huh?" asked Gonzo.

Lilly lifted her eyes up and to the side, taking instant stock of the gladiator-sized LAPD detective in cowboy boots and leather jacket. Her mouth twisted into a dismissive smirk—as if to say, "It's sweltering outside yet you're wearing that getup?"

"Government buildings," said Lilly, twisting her head to get a better look at Lucky. It was instinct the way she answered questions—ignoring the questioner and directing her response to the nearest alpha male. It was her way of establishing her place in the social pecking order. "Always the last to get serviced."

Lilly gave Lucky a double once-over. Shaved head to his Haix duty boots and back again. But the man showed an utter lack of interest in Lilly, which, to her, was odd. The man was obviously a cop and wore no wedding ring. And married or not, all male cops were dogs, always on the prowl for a taste of honey.

"What do you think?" addressed Lilly to Lucky. "Will we get out of this alive?"

"We'll survive," said Lucky, still focused on the panel. He pulled the red emergency button, expecting to hear the familiar jangle of alarm bells. Instead, the elevator shook ever so slightly, followed by an audible electronic hum.

"That doesn't sound good," said Lilly, hardly nervous, but willing to play at being meek to garner a reaction from the man standing only inches from her.

"You work here?" asked Lucky.

"Yes."

"Then you'd best dial somebody and see if they can get the maintenance super on this."

"Good idea. Got a cell phone?"

Gonzo was already holding out her cell phone for Lilly to borrow. Yet Lilly waited for Lucky to withdraw his from his front jeans pocket.

"Thanks," said Lilly.

The mobile device he handed Lilly wasn't by any means new or the latest in super-fast smartphones. It was worn from abuse and scratched and the hinge squeaked when Lilly flipped it open. Nonetheless, when the phone came to life, the tiny screen lit up with a digital photo of the cop with a shorter, younger version of himself. A brother, Lilly decided. Both men sported wide grins as if sharing some kind of wicked secret.

"Hey," said Lilly after dialing her office. "I'm stuck in one of the elevators. Wanna get someone on it?"

With the phone flipped back shut, Lilly returned it to Lucky.

"So where you boys from?" asked Lilly. The slight toward Gonzo was unmistakable.

"Excuse me?" piped Gonzo.

"Sorry," lied Lilly. "I meant cops."

"I'm LAPD," said Gonzo without a lick of humor. "He's—"

The interruption was a loud *ka-shung!* The elevator gave a minor jolt, then once again began traveling upward.

"You must really rate around here," said Lucky.

"You have no idea," grinned Lilly.

"S'pose I don't," said Lucky, revealing the faintest smile, though not exactly genuine.

"Nice being marooned with you," said Lilly as the doors to the eleventh floor opened. "Bye."

Neither Lucky nor Gonzo felt the need to reciprocate the verbal so-long. But for entirely different reasons. Lilly spun on a heel and stepped out, the automated doors closing behind her with a hiss.

The ride to the next floor took five smooth seconds with Lucky, once again, leading the way into the corridor and hunting down an office nameplate.

"We're looking for Deputy US Attorney Lillian Zoller," said Lucky without an inkling that they'd just shared more than a moment with Lilly in the elevator.

"Thought we were dealing with the FBI," said Gonzo.

"Told you. The FBI can suck my…"

Lucky was standing in front of an office door, next to which was a simple plate screwed to the wall, reading:

1208
Lillian Zoller
Deputy United States Attorney

A twist of the doorknob and Lucky was through the door, catching Lilly's assistant, Jenna, sucking back the leftover broth from her microwaved Cup Noodles lunch.

"Are you Lillian?" asked Lucky.

"Sorry," said Jenna, scrambling for her napkin. "Lilly's not in. Are you on her appointment sheet?"

"No," said Lucky, showing his badge. "I'm from Kern County Sheriff's."

"Oh, my God," said Jenna. "The Pepper Ellis case, right?"

"No," said Lucky. "The Anthony Dey case. You know, the dead deputy up in Kern County?"

"Right, right," said Jenna. "Same thing. It's just that—"

"What about Pepper Ellis?" asked Gonzo, well aware of the teen queen's TV show. That's because her twelve-year-old son, Travis, watched too damn much TV when he wasn't playing too damn much Xbox.

"You're from Kern and you don't know?"

"I'm from LAPD," said Gonzo. "He's from Kern. And it was *his* brother who was murdered."

Lucky snapped a don't-speak-unless-I-tell-you-to look dead

at Gonzo. His eyes were unblinking, cocked and loaded with an unmitigated threat.

"Oh, Lord," said Jenna. "I'm so sorry."

"Well, if it's none of your business, then you don't have to be sorry," said Lucky.

Jenna bit her lip and composed herself, then dug deep to find her most professional character.

"Officer?" began Jenna, hoping Lucky would finish her sentence.

"Detective Dey."

"Of course, if there's anything this office can do..."

"So you guys *are* on this, yeah?"

"Just what the FBI reports to us—"

"Why I'm here. FBI gets involved, it's usually 'cause they think they're ahead of the curve. Just trying to get a jump here."

"We've, uh...this office?" continued Jenna. "We refer all investigation inquiries to the FBI. I'm sure if you need assistance they'll be—"

"If I wanted to talk to the FBI I'd be in Westwood," said Lucky, referring to the Bureau's Los Angeles offices inside the Federal Building some fourteen miles due west down Wilshire Boulevard. "My guy at County said the person to talk to was Lillian Zoller. That she was runnin' the investigation."

"Honestly," defended Jenna. "This is the US Attorney's office. We don't investigate crimes. We prosecute them."

"Just tell me when she's gonna be back."

"Could be ten minutes. Could be after lunch. I'm sure—"

"How's this? Got her number? Tell her I'm here."

"Detective. Without an appointment..."

"You're right. I can wait. Couch here looks comfy enough."

"Of course, you're welcome to. But I can't promise she'll see you."

"Because why?"

"Because she's a deputy US Attorney and doesn't have to?" said Jenna in a tiny voice. That question mark at the end of Jenna's sentence had a pleading quality to it. Lucky was making the former Laker-Girl-slash-underling feel more than uncomfortable.

"Maybe…" added Jenna.

"Maybe?"

"There's an FBI liaison who works out of a satellite office in this building. Special Agent Dulaney Little." Jenna began searching through a disorderly top drawer to find a card.

"And if I don't wanna talk to the FBI?" asked Lucky. "If I choose to wait for your boss?"

"Probably a waste of time," said Jenna, at last coming up with one of Dulaney Little's government-issued calling cards. "'Cause Lilly'll just tell you the same thing. Talk to the FBI."

Gonzo was silently goading Lucky to utter his anti-federale credo, "the FBI can suck my white dick." But he showed unexpected restraint and chose to forgo the elevator for seven floors of metal stairs. Gonzo trailed again, this time stopping to check texts on her phone. She knew the dangers of driving and texting. Walking and texting was practically as dangerous. Years back, Gonzo and her son had nearly been killed when her boy had followed her into a busy Simi Valley intersection. She had been reading an email from her attorney, sadly informing her that her permanent disability claim had been rejected by the LAPD.

The stairs switched back downward. While Gonzo stopped to read an email twice forwarded—once from robbery homicide and again from her supervisor—she listened to the heavy clanging of Lucky's boots covering the stairs. One floor down…Two floors down…Then the squeak of a heavy fire door opening. Once the email was read, Gonzo started her own descent, counted off the two floors, and stepped into the fifth-floor corridor, fully expecting to find Lucky impatiently waiting. Instead, Gonzo found a hallway as equally sterile as the others, devoid of humanity, and deadly quiet.

"Shit," uttered Gonzo, half suspecting she'd been ditched by her Kern County charge. Then again, maybe she hadn't counted Lucky's footfalls well enough as he charged ahead of her. She upped her pace, sneaking innocent peeks through whichever office doors were propped open. The corridor turned at the elevator bank, then dead-ended at a pair of restrooms. She figured he was taking a leak. She twisted the knob to the men's room until she heard the latch release, and pushed it open five inches.

"Detective?" asked Gonzo, not certain she'd spoken loud enough. She pressed the door harder, widening the opening. "Yo. Dey!"

"No detectives in here," said the voice, deepened by the hardscape acoustics.

Gonzo was preparing an apology when she heard the sharp sound of fingers snapping. She turned to see Lucky leaning from a nearby office door, quietly beckoning her.

"Hurry," mouthed Lucky.

"Where'd you go?" asked Gonzo.

"Shhhh. Just stand here at the door and tell me if he's coming."

"Tell you *who's* coming?"

"FBI guy."

"Why?"

"Stop askin' and keep yours eyes open," said Lucky, leaving Gonzo to pull sentry duty at the threshold.

Gonzo scanned both ways, then shoved the door wider to get a look inside. She'd seen closets bigger. Four walls, no windows, a bulletin corkboard on a large easel, a collage of framed family photos hung under a smoke detector, and a cluttered tank desk so broad and cumbersome she wondered how the hell the movers could have gotten it through the door.

Lucky was behind the desk, flipping over papers, reading handwritten notes.

"Sweet," said Gonzo. "Nothing like a warrantless search to give me an appetite."

"FBI property," said Lucky. "I'm a taxpayer. So it's my property too."

"Just outta curiosity," asked Gonzo, "what's an FBI guy look like?"

"Building fulla lawyers," said Lucky, not looking up from his snooping. "Look for a guy in a cheap suit."

"Family pics are your three o'clock."

Lucky twisted ninety degrees to his left, sighting down the photo collage.

"Male usual," said Lucky.

"Tell me you didn't just say that."

"Offended? How's this? He's FBI. Stands for Fuckin' Black Investigator."

"Know what? I'm trying real hard to feel sorry for you. You know, your brother and all. But the racial stuff, I can't—"

"Aw, hell!" Lucky found the fed's BlackBerry underneath a legal pad chock-full of red-penned doodles.

"So he left his phone."

"No. He's *on* the phone. Blue light means—"

"Bluetooth. Crap. Gotta be really close."

"Probably in the shitter. You run block. I'll meet you in front."

"We're both going…Now!"

"Not yet. And he's three seconds from dropping a call."

Before Gonzo could think to argue, Lucky had popped the battery out of the back of the FBI man's mobile phone and was photographing the electronic serial information with his own cell.

"God, you're somethin'," pissed Gonzo, fed up with Lucky's antics.

"Still standing there?"

No. Gonzo had already broken away and was charging back down the hall on a scud path toward the men's room. She had no clue what she was about to say or do. She only knew she had about twelve strides and forty feet to come up with something.

Special Agent Dulaney Little was like most men suffering from ulcerative colitis. With his prescription and a nearby toilet, he was a-okay. Perfectly normal. He'd become so accustomed to his condition that he had started a practice of dialing and receiving calls from his porcelain throne. It bothered nobody but his wife of twenty-one years, Shanti, who was more than annoyed by what she considered a disgusting habit. That and the man seemed to always be holding conference calls from one of the only two bathrooms in their small yet busy Reseda home.

Where Shanti had it right was the dollar factor. Since Dulaney discovered the joy of multitasking from the nearest commode, he had dunked two BlackBerries at a replacement cost of more than $200 per device. It was Shanti's idea to buy him the Bluetooth earpiece, thus freeing her husband of further cell phone fumbles. So used to using the wireless earbud—and so powerful the connection—Special Agent Dulaney Little would simply get up from his desk and continue his conversation as he strolled to the men's room, closed and locked the stall door, and carried on without missing a beat. His nifty Bluetooth repeater even had a mute button, which he employed when it was time to flush, leaving the person at the other end of the call without a hint of suspicion that the FBI man had all the while been evacuating his bowels.

"Detective?" asked the voice from the door.

"No detective in here," answered Dulaney from inside the stall.

"Who's that?" asked Shanti. Dulaney's wife was in her car, connected to her husband via her own hands-free device while hurrying home with a carload of groceries before beginning her school pickup routine. As it worked out, the Mister and Missus Little had four children attending four different schools, miles and miles apart, which made for hectic days and significant gasoline bills.

"Dunno. Someone lookin' for somebody else," answered Dulaney.

"You're on the toilet, aren't you?"

"Don't start."

"And that was a woman in the men's room?"

"Don't think she came in. Just cracked the door and called out for some guy who's not here."

"Uh huh," said Shanti, busting her husband's balls.

"You were saying?"

"My car just kicked over two hundred thousand miles."

"New benchmark."

"Said we get a new one at one fifty."

The discussion continued on down a familiar road with talk of finances, property taxes, retirement and college funds, and a conclusion to revisit the Shanti-needs-a-new-car subject twenty-five thousand miles further down the proverbial road. And at the rate Shanti racked up miles, that twenty-five thousand miles would take less than nine months.

Dulaney washed his hands in the sink. As he dried them, he examined himself in the bathroom mirror. The collar of his dress shirt was showing years of wear, fraying with a fine fuzz near the points. The third lousy shirt he'd noticed in a week. He tried to convince himself his tie looked new.

Then there were the gray hairs. A year earlier, those telltale signs of age that had begun to appear above his ears had turned into a bumper crop highlighting his entire scalp. It occurred to him that this could be why men shave their heads—to cheat a younger look. He wondered if he should surprise his family or just color it with Grecian Formula.

Decisions, decisions. Dulaney rolled his eyes at himself in the mirror, then headed for the door. No sooner had he swung it open than he found himself face-to-face with a six-foot Hispanic Amazon. *Kinda hot* was his first instinctive thought.

"There another guy in there?" pressed Gonzo.

"Your detective friend?" asked Dulaney, recognizing Gonzo's voice from her first syllable.

"Not my friend. But he owes me an explanation."

"Sorry. Nobody in there."

"But he *was* in there, right?"

"Not in the past…" Dulaney checked his watch. "Ten minutes?"

"He ask you to cover for him?"

"Miss, I…"

"Detective," corrected Gonzo.

"You too. So you're looking for your detective partner?"

"You're covering for him," accused Gonzo, trying to keep him on his heels. But inside her head, she was counting off the seconds she was buying Lucky. She hoped like hell he'd gotten out of the fed's office and was heading down the stairs.

"Special Agent Dulaney Little." The FBI man introduced himself, offering his open palm. "I washed, by the way."

"Are you being weird on me?"

"No. I just—"

"The men's room. Show me it's empty," said Gonzo.

"You're serious?"

"Just show me he's not in there."

"Take a look yourself."

"Right. So now you're inviting me into the men's room?"

"I didn't say that. You don't believe me..." Dulaney put his hands up in confused surrender. "Look. Don't know you. Don't know who you're looking for. Don't care, either. Now, if you'll please excuse me."

The stalling game was over. But for drawing her weapon or grappling Dulaney down to the industrial-grade carpet, Gonzo was fresh out of ideas of how to keep him from returning to his closet of an office. Gonzo kept up the ruse by entering the men's room on her own, briefly stopping inside to castigate herself for playing a part in the con. She counted to ten, turned a one-eighty, then headed back toward the elevator bank. She didn't so much as glance away from her heading when striding past Dulaney's office. Best she could garner from her periphery vision was the door was closed. Inside of which, Special Agent Dulaney Little was likely hiding from that crazy lady cop. When she arrived at the elevators, Gonzo triple-pounded the down button, yelled "C'mon, c'mon" within her own skull. And after an eternity of thirty seconds, the car arrived with a benign ding.

"That was so many kinds of stupid, it's not even worth counting!" shouted Gonzo, slamming the passenger door of Lucky's Charger.

"Guess that makes you an expert," said Lucky, turning the air conditioning fan to high and aiming the center vent directly into his face.

"How do you go from first wanting to talk to the FBI? Then since he's not in his office, picking over his desk for God knows what?"

"Didn't wanna talk to the FBI. Wanted to talk to the US Attorney. The FBI can—"

"Can suck my you know what." Gonzo was ready to surrender. She was downtown and a short walk to the subway that would deliver her back to Pasadena and her car. "What the hell am I doing here?"

"Hell if I know."

Gonzo was more than tempted to call her boss again and further explain the situation all the way down to the dirty deed perpetrated against the FBI man. She wagered against herself, betting it would be a fifty-fifty proposition whether her supervisor would allow her to cut loose or order her to arrest Lucky on felony tampering and trespassing charges. Gonzo reckoned she would be better off bolting and taking the rest of the day to concoct a reasonable excuse for ignoring the directive to assist the bereaved Kern County detective.

Then again, there was that email pushed to her from robbery/homicide.

"So while you were exercising your hate-on for all things FBI," shifted Gonzo. She gestured with her phone. "I got this BOLO."

"Yeah?"

"Shooting in Lynwood. Everything sounds gang related except for this one witness said something about a black-on-black refrigerator truck."

"My truck?"

"You're looking for a black semi," shrugged Gonzo. "You get anything better outta that office snoop?"

"Enough, okay?" defended Lucky. "You seem like a smart enough chick to know fed policy is never to share shit with local unless they absolutely have to."

"You wanna get to this bad guy before the feds do. That what this is about, right?"

Lucky smirked, dropped the Charger into gear, and lurched the vehicle into traffic.

12

Burbank.

Twenty hours, eleven minutes, and twenty-three seconds, twenty-four seconds, twenty-five...

Beemer couldn't stop himself from obsessively counting off the time since he had initiated his one-man blood heist. He had first calculated a maximum of twelve hours from the Reno break-in to shipping out of the Port of Long Beach. He had prepared a small paper sack full of cash for Rey Palomino to split with his accommodating older brother in exchange for shipping the frozen blood products under the guise of exported frozen corn.

Twenty hours, twelve minutes, forty-two seconds...

The clock would continue ticking in Beemer's head. And he knew it wouldn't stop until his cargo was loaded and steaming for the Panama Canal. All because of dead Danny's dear daddy—Rey Palomino, the cool pool guy. Beemer remembered the stories that

the sunny young Danny would tell of his father. All those sum-
mers sweating it out on his father's pool construction sites. Racing
vintage Porsches on the weekends. Oh, how that boy idolized his
pops.

Twenty hours, fifteen minutes, zero seconds.

Beemer pushed Danny Palomino aside and rewound his brain
back to the afternoon. The idiotic mistake he had made in Lynwood and that extremely dead Motherfucker #1.

After Beemer had put the incident in his rearview mirror, he
had started driving a new loop until he had cleared the stickiness
out of his brain. The first leg was the 405 freeway north, through
where it splits Westwood and UCLA from the city of Santa Monica, over the Sepulveda Pass and into the San Fernando Valley.
At the crest, where the busy artery descends into the suburban
mecca, Beemer could see the waves of heat reflecting off the valley
floor, obscuring the pristine visibility of a nearly smog-free day.
Instantly, the temperature outside the semi rose fifteen notches to
109 degrees Fahrenheit.

The further Beemer drove, the easier it became to shake off his
idiot and that momentary loss of impulse control. With every mile,
a new plan formed. The first part involved evasion. Authorities
would soon be pulling over and inspecting every black refrigerator
truck from Boise to San Diego. Had his cargo been offloaded at
the time agreed upon by Rey Palomino, the rig would have been
ditched and Beemer would have been feet up in business class on
an aircraft destined for Shannon, Ireland. An old cousin of his was
getting married in Galway. And what better way to get lost after a
successful heist than grabbing hard onto the tail of a drunken Irish
wedding?

Interstate 118—a.k.a. the Ronald Reagan Freeway. By the
time the vet had made the eastbound turn, his clarity of purpose
was returning. He would need to stash the eighteen-wheeler and
cargo for some sixteen hours. And as sweet as that black-on-black
eighteen-wheeler looked at first sight, it was surely easy to spot
from the air. And the LAPD had helicopters in the sky 24/7. So
as Beemer kept snug to the right lane of the freeway, he imagined

how large a structure he would need to hide the air-conditioned behemoth. His eyes were flicking to the corners of his windshield, looking for police or news choppers. That's when it caught his eye. A thick-bellied aircraft amusingly painted to appear like Sea World's famed killer whale, Shamu. The Boeing 737 with the clever advertising was on approach to the nearby Bob Hope/Burbank Airport.

Because nobody cared to live right next to a noisy airport, most surrounding properties were usually dedicated to warehousing and manufacturing. And in this summer of the never-ending recession Beemer reasoned there had to be mucho empty space where he could set the brakes to the rig, power down the diesel engine, and get himself some much-needed REM sleep. But not before some Mexican food and a margarita. He could all but taste the salted rim of the glass just thinking about the chilled tequila concoction. The concept of reward came to mind. A brief, but deserving, recreational dash before bedding himself down. For Beemer, whether bunked in the cramped space of the semi's sleeper or lying in a high-desert saddle, M16A4 rifle for a companion under a blanket of stars, a few hours of sleep would always bring him greater clarity and purpose.

In the eighty-five minutes of driving in counterclockwise revolutions around the industrial streets outlying the Burbank airport, Beemer surveyed a number of potential properties for his overnight stay. Warehouses mostly with tall cyclone fences topped with rusty razor wire, with empty parking lots and untended weeds growing wild through cracks in the asphalt. The building owners may as well have hung out neon signs reading "nobody's home."

Around the corner from a sex toy shop and at the end of a side street, which appeared nearly as derelict as the buildings that occupied it, stood a compound that dated back to the 1930s, when the San Fernando Valley was nothing but farms and fruit orchards. There were three warehouses of varying size, but similar shape—each with a long arching roof and concrete ramps leading to inviting loading areas. Beemer recognized it as a former fruit-packing plant, not unlike those he'd grown up around in

Northern California, where a high schooler looking for spending money could easily get hired for six summer weeks to sort plums from peaches.

The lock was easily beaten with a pair of heavy-duty bolt cutters. The gate rolled open and shut with minimum hassle. As for security of the buildings themselves, Beemer was pleased to find the largest of the trio wasn't defended by so much as a chain. The single yawning door was counterweighted and slid aside with far less effort than expected. Moments later, the big rig was parked inside and gently idling in order to continue powering the refrigeration unit. All Beemer needed now was food, about ten gallons of diesel, and rest.

He dressed himself to better resemble a homeless man, including mismatched shoes and a woolen cap made to look extra dingy by rubbing it in dirt and spent motor oil. With that, he limped from the old compound and sought out a car to steal. Preferably an older-model Honda. That would be the easiest. When he was just fifteen, he had gotten so expert at beating Civics' entry and starter systems that he used to take bets that if he didn't boost the car in under sixty seconds he would buy the beer.

And the Beemer, as his pals called him, never bought the beer.

Less than an hour later, he was seated atop a barstool inside a local Mexican eatery called Don Diego's. He'd already ordered the classic number two on the menu—two chicken enchiladas topped with sour cream, beans and rice on the side. While he waited for his meal to arrive, he sipped on a frozen margarita while his right hand dipped into the basket of warmed, crispy tortilla chips.

A television in dire need of replacement was hanging in a high corner behind the bar. It was an older, tube-style set with a rotary channel changer tuned to cable channel 3. The color was skewed and the picture slightly distorted with video noise. But the sound was bright and easily cut through the clatter of voices, canned Tejano music, and a bartender-in-training washing glasses. It was the local news hour. And the lead story was the horrific murder of young TV star Pepper Ellis.

Pepper Ellis? Who the hell is Pepper Ellis?

Beemer's interest was instantly piqued. He leaned closer. Sure, the broadcast mentioned Kern County and the dead sheriff's deputy. But the gist of the story was about the underage actress, her older male companion, and their Lake Tahoe exploits prior to her early-morning demise. The Local 7 news broadcast had waxy reporters in Tahoe, Bakersfield, and Beverly Hills, each propped up in front of a camera cabled to a nearby microwave truck. Beemer pegged the blonde reporting from Kern County as a pixie with a nose job. A certifiable spinner, in his estimation. She was probably standing atop a milk crate just to make her look taller on TV. How important she appeared—and probably felt to her toes—as every word uttered from her lipsticked mouth was broadcast live to the news-gobbling masses. As far as the investigation went, the Kern County Sheriff's Department was giving up little other than very general descriptions of the suspect and the big black rig he was allegedly driving. Beemer guessed they had nothing and that he was way ahead of the curve.

Whatever small comfort Beemer received from the TV cutie with the nose job cracked when the anchor, an even blonder news babe from behind a prop desk, imparted some breaking news that the almighty FBI had inserted itself into the investigation. Of course, the Bureau had no comment on their interest in the murders. But Beemer knew. The FBI was on to the robbery in Reno. That, coupled with the crime in Kern County, made for an interstate crime. The Feds were now involved. Police agencies across the state were certain to be on alert. Manpower increased.

Beemer's face felt flush and red with heat. If he could have gotten away with it, he would have poured his entire margarita over his head to cool off. His eyes swirled around the old restaurant as if searching for an answer. Somehow he keyed on the tinsel and garland hanging everywhere. It was as if the restaurant owner had half an idea to make every day feel like Christmas, then gave up once they had run out of materials.

He was tired, but sleep would have to wait. Lists were forming inside Beemer's head. More boxes to check off before the next day's final push to ship his cargo.

13

Bel-Air.

"Comin' to you in three," said the news director's voice over Saji Shahin's IFB.

"Copy that," said Saji, checking her hair in the tiny four-inch monitor she used as a mirror. She readjusted her foot mark six inches to her left, hoping her ink-black hair would better pick up the kick light behind her. Officially, it was supposed to be a daylight news shot. But the Bel-Air driveway next to which she stood was blocked by huge stands of shrubbery and trees, all manicured to match the symmetry of the Gothic gate that protected the mansion beyond.

"Better," said Saji, nodding to her cameraman that she had found her spot.

"Okay," the news director said in Saji's ear. "Cameron's gonna throw it to you as soon as we come back from commercial. How long's the package?"

"Forty-six seconds," Saji answered.

"'Kay. Give you fifteen for the setup and another twenty for the wraparound."

"Sounds good."

"Comin' in sixty," said Adam, Saji's cameraman-slash-sound-man-slash-boy-Friday. His blazing white teeth were in sharp contrast to the darkness of his skin and matching dreadlocks.

Saji, a stop-and-stare news beauty, flipped her notebook open. Read and reread her bullet points while forming her mouth and tongue into a quick set of vocal gymnastics. She didn't want to get stuck on her Rs like she had nary an hour ago when the five o'clock news team cut to her live shot.

"Right Ricky Roberts rode a rocking racehorse," repeated Saji to herself, working over her Rs until they sounded closer to neutral than mid-Atlantic, where the Persian-American girl was born and raised. "Right Ricky Roberts rode a rocking racehorse."

"Anything new since we did this an hour ago?" asked the news director through Saji's earpiece.

"Nope. Still no sign of her pops," said Saji.

"Maybe we'll get lucky and he'll show during the live shot," added Adam.

"Better not lock it off, then," winked Saji, commenting on Adam's habit of locking off the video camera fixed to the tripod's swiveling head to save the strain on his lower back. This also allowed Adam to attend to both the broadcast's sound quality and tweak the lighting to best flatter his on-camera crush.

"Thirty seconds," said Adam.

Saji had a habit in the ticking seconds before the camera's red light switched on. She would look away from the lens and focus her eyes on a distant object. For the naturally farsighted woman, it provided a restful, nerve-easing respite before she was broadcast live to half a million TVs. Any facial tic, flub, or tongue-tangle would not only be exposed live to the viewing public, but would remain forever a searchable fail blog on the internet.

As Saji counted down to zero in her head, she set her eyes past the row of news trucks, each with a custom paint job to reflect its respective broadcast station, microwave mast at full attention. Beyond the hubbub came a deep blue Mercedes S Class crawling up the sweeping drive. Not that a luxury car was anything out of the ordinary. This was Bel-Air, California. Zip code to old movie stars and hedge-fund billionaires. It was as if a collective alarm had gone off inside every reporter's and photographer's brain. This was the car. And inside the car was the man they all wanted to talk to.

The electric motors hummed as the mansion's huge gate began to fold inward. Four suited security guards, all of them beefed up like offensive linemen stuffed in Armani, jogged through the crack.

"Adam!" barked Saji, jumping off her mark, hoping to set herself in a live shot as the Mercedes rolled through the gate. Cameramen and reporters converged. But Saji had both position and the live audience. She counted down to zero and, "Cameron? At this very moment, Conrad Ellis is returning to his Bel-Air home after, presumably, helicoptering to and from Kern County to see the remains of his only daughter, Pepper Ellis. As you can see, a lot of the media have gathered, hoping to get some sort of word with the car-dealer-turned-entertainment-mogul."

The chauffeur-driven car eased into the driveway, careful not to so much as nudge a single of the swarming photographers.

Saji bent a little at the waist and rapped on the tinted rear window.

"Mr. Ellis," asked Saji, playing entirely to the camera. "Would you like to make a statement? Mr. Ellis, please?"

A security guard blocked Saji's path. He was using his size to peel away the crowding throng before the luxury car slipped through and the gates closed. But that was all right by Saji. She hadn't expected an interview or even a statement. It was nothing more than great live news television. And she had been damn lucky that her news director had thrown the shot to her at the actual moment her subject arrived.

"Shit!" cried Adam.

"So we still await some kind of official statement," continued

Saji, "from Conrad Ellis or, for that matter, any spokesman from the Ellis fam—"

"We're out," said Adam.

Saji touched her IFB. There was no sound whatsoever coming through her earpiece.

"Whadda you mean, we're out?"

"They cut back to the studio before I got the head unlocked."

"You didn't get it?" asked Saji, incredulous. "You were still locked off?"

Adam shrugged, those dreadlocks bouncing on his shoulders.

"Got some audio," said Adam.

"Goddammit!" barked Saji.

"Hey!" shouted a fellow newsie. "Think you're the only live shot?"

"Sorry, sorry," said Adam, raising a hand and apologizing for Saji.

"Oh. You apologize to them but not me?"

"Saj. Really sorry. We'll get him next time."

"You made me look like an idiot," said Saji, tossing Adam the mic, then trudging off to the microwave truck, where she could review the embarrassing footage.

Safely inside the gates of his property, Conrad Ellis—or Connie to his friends—stepped directly from his car and through the front door of his mansion. A butler was waiting to take his jacket and offer his sincerest condolences. Conrad barely acknowledged the servant with a nod while keeping his eyes straight ahead as if in search of his next business acquisition. He turned left when he felt the first antique rug underfoot, then quickly recollected that his library room was in the opposite direction. The confusion wasn't just that of a grieving father attempting to navigate while in a state of shock. The house was brand new to Conrad. He had purchased the nouveau goth property and all its unconventional furnishings in a foreclosure auction only weeks earlier and had barely moved in. The previous owner, an eccentric movie actor, had spent years and millions of dollars renovating the historic house into a permanent Halloween haunt, only to find that his business manager had robbed him silly and left him bankrupt.

"Connie," said Garvin, rising from his seat and making both hands available in case Conrad needed a hug. He didn't. Conrad, a certified germophobe, kept his hands to his sides as he made his way over to the desk, sat briskly, and searched the top drawer for a bottle of Purell. None was found.

Garvin Van Der Berk, the famed Hollywood security guru, was plenty used to dealing with odd personalities. His job wasn't to judge the client. His was to provide defense against potential threats…and a discreet offense against supposed enemies.

"What can I do for you?" asked Garvin.

"Like the security," said Conrad. "That was good. Helpful. Appreciated."

"They're yours until you say otherwise."

"My little girl," said Conrad in an abbreviated, staccato style that fit his short, sharp, but powerful look, "she's dead. No mistake. It was her in the car. Boyfriend dead too. Didn't like him, so…"

"What about her mother? Is there anything—"

"On some safari thing. We've sent word. She can arrange her own security."

"Of course."

"What do you know?" asked Conrad. "About the thing."

"The accident?"

"Not an accident at all."

"You're right. Triple murder. Poor choice of words, sir."

"All I got was what was on the radio," said Conrad. "Shit kickers up in bumfuck? Didn't tell me anything. More worried about their dead deputy. 'Deputy?' I wanted to say. 'What about my precious? Did you even know who she is? She's got two million Twitter followers. How many that dead deputy got?'"

"Exactly," answered Garvin.

"So?"

Garvin quietly swallowed. He hadn't yet been engaged to investigate anything. His initial task had only been to create a security buffer between the businessman and the rattlesnake press.

"It's early yet," danced Garvin. "But the initial report is that the FBI is involved. That tells us there's most likely an interstate connection."

"Pepper was in Tahoe."

"Which could mean they have evidence that she was followed across state lines."

"Stalker thing."

"A possibility. Now, sir. Before I continue my investigation," said Garvin. "You need to tell me just what kind of result you're looking for."

"Result?"

"Or outcome."

The client slumped back in his oversized leather desk chair. His balding skull sank into the cushion. His stubby fingers gripped the armrests until his knuckles turned white with balled-up tension. Garvin observed a man used to being in complete control. A man who solved his own problems with the snap of his fingers. Rapier quick. Decisive to a fault. Self-made and self-loving and his own best friend. Garvin concluded that Conrad Ellis was a man who only acknowledged outcomes in his own favor.

"My daughter is dead," said Conrad. "How do I square that?"

"You can't, sir."

"Bullshit."

"Sir?"

"Whoever this is," said Conrad. "He hurt me. So I get to hurt him. It's only right."

"So you'd like the assailant hurt—"

"No. I want to hurt him. I pay. I get to hurt him. Me. I want to peel his skin."

"Sir—"

"You asked what I wanted. So there it is."

"Yes, sir. There it is."

"That means we need to get to him. Before the cops. Before the FBI, yeah?"

"Theoretically."

"And you can do this?"

Garvin nodded, not caring to answer or confirm verbally. It was one thing arranging to have somebody investigated, wire tapped, blackmailed, injured. Even killed. There were plenty of competent players in L.A. The right amount of cash delivered to a certain party could often obtain a positive result. Garvin's specialty was smashing the kneecaps of men who stalked female celebrities. But this wasn't close to that kind of gig. Conrad Ellis, in his moment of shock and/or grief, wanted some unholy retribution. He wanted to bring the pain up close and personal.

Garvin knew only one answer for his clients.

"As you wish, sir," he said, knowing that even the richest and most powerful, despite their grandiose talk, usually balk well short of getting their hands dirty. That put the odds on Garvin. He would make investigative headway, see how close he could appear to getting a result, but in the end, would most likely be forced to punt whatever he uncovered to the authorities. That would keep both himself and his client out of jail.

Until then, Garvin would do what he did best. Bill for copious hours served.

14

Lynwood.

While the Los Angeles County Sheriff's Department was established in 1850, the *city* of Los Angeles managed to survive without its own police department until 1869. Six officers were hired and led by City Marshal William C. Warren, who served in a dual capacity as both tax collector and dog catcher. While the mandate for the sheriff's department was the general law and order of the entire county, the city police focused on collecting fines and fees, without which the cops wouldn't have ever been paid. Therefore it might easily be assumed that from the beginning, sheriff's deputies looked down their noses at their lesser brethren. A natural and sometimes healthy rivalry developed.

A century and a half later, the friction remained. Some antagonism was natural. And some of it was good-natured. But some of the conflict bordered on criminal. Over time, those former fee collectors dressed in deep navy blue had become glamorized in fiction and movies and television shows. All while sheriffs toiled in relative public obscurity. To the LAPD, sheriff's deputies were the underclass of police down to their green and tan uniforms—which better resembled togs worn by park rangers than the clothes worn by world-class cops.

"Do the math," said Lucky. "L.A. Sheriff's got four times the manpower, covers more badass territory than the PD, and we operate with ten times the autonomy."

"I'm not exactly arguing with you," said Gonzo in a massive understatement. She hadn't uttered a word in ten minutes. Whatever argument in play was between Lucky and Lucky.

"Just sayin'," said Lucky. "Trying to make polite conversation."

If she hadn't already been exhausted by the situation, Gonzo would have let out a belly laugh. But so far she had found absolutely nothing polite about Lucky. Take away the grief and the fatigue, Lucky was less human and more like a force of nature. Gonzo's keen survival instincts always told her to steer clear of such dangerous personalities. Cops like him spent every waking hour on the prowl for trouble. Be it criminals or women. Case in point: after a brief visit to the Lynwood crime scene, where Lucky damned all normal protocol for visiting officers and conducted his own brief witness interviews, he had driven two blocks and set his parking brake some fifty yards down the street from a catering truck—or roach coach—surrounded by a smattering of local color supping on carne asada and machaca burritos. This is what cops called fishing. An experienced cop would sit and watch, all the while profiling each customer based on style of dress, behavior, or groupings. Once the cop identified his target, he would stalk him until he became isolated, then make a move.

"You've had a rotten day," said Gonzo, trying to let both herself and Lucky off the conversational hook. "Don't feel like you have to chat me up."

"What?" asked Lucky. "You don't like conversation?"

"I'm just sayin'—"

"Look. It's either you talkin' or some asshole on the radio," said Lucky. "I need the distraction right now. Otherwise I'm gonna put my fist through the windshield."

"Copy that," said Gonzo.

And Lucky wasn't lying. Denial was morphing into anger. Soon, he'd be able to taste another man's blood in his mouth. Lucky briefly shut his eyes in an attempt to purge the photo-like images of his smiling younger brother that played across the windshield in a dim mental slideshow.

"What about you?" asked Lucky.

"Yeah? What about me?"

"Been a cop long?"

"Long enough."

"How long is enough?"

"Thirteen…no. Fourteen years."

"Respectable, I guess."

"You guess?"

"Yeah. I guess," said Lucky. "I don't know where you've been. What you did to get here."

"Like sittin' here with you is some kinda upgrade?" said Gonzo, possibly too glib, yet she was becoming less concerned about seeming insensitive in the presence of a cop whose dear brother was less than twenty-four hours murdered.

"Like, you're a woman."

"Last time I checked."

"What I'm sayin' is that I meet a guy cop," explained Lucky, "it's a helluva lot easier to figure out what kinda guy he is. Qualitatively."

"There's a big word."

"Hey. Whether you liked it or not, bar was lowered for you. From the academy to all the way up the line."

"Wow," said Gonzo, feigning true surprise. "You actually went there."

"You sayin' I'm wrong?"

"If you hadn't noticed, I'm not sayin' much of anything."

"Hey. I asked. You wanna give me a buncha two-, three-word answers, then I got the right to fill in the blanks."

"County sheriffs, man," said Gonzo, shaking her head in mock disbelief. "Aren't you the poster child."

"I'm a poster child?" barked Lucky. "Me? Look at you. Female. Ethnic. Lesbian—"

"The hell?" angered Gonzo. "You don't know shit."

"So maybe you're not a dyke. Whatever. But I bet there's not a race or gender card that you haven't pulled. Bet you know the whole minority, the-world-is-biased-against-me play-book by memory. I'm right, yeah."

Gonzo swallowed hard. Was Lucky that much of an asshole? Or was he baiting her out of boredom?

"You know what?" said Gonzo, summoning what she feared was her last molecule of patience. "I've been on the job almost fifteen years. I'm comfortable with where I'm at. I'm not a rookie and you are not my training officer."

"Your TO?" asked Lucky. "If I was your TO I'd tell you to shut your fuckin' eyes and describe homeys one through three, all waitin' on their taquitos."

Gonzo snapped her attention back to the roach coach. Sure enough, standing at the concession window were three young black men. Each was uniformed as an affiliated Blood in oversized white T-shirts, shorts or baggy pants with the right leg rolled up to the calf, hat tilted starboard, basketball sneaks with red shoelaces. While Lucky had been shoving Gonzo back on her mental heels, he hadn't missed a trick.

With his cell phone in hand, Lucky hit a speed-dial number.

"Three candidates," Lucky said into the phone. "Gonna let 'em get their fiesta on before we jam 'em."

"Nothin' like no probable cause," said Gonzo.

"Watch and learn how the sheriffs do it."

With the slightest shake of her head, Gonzo clamped her mouth closed and set her jaw on shut-the-hell-up. She silently observed the targets pay for their hot food wrapped in aluminum foil then cross the street back to their wheels, a custom-painted blue Camry with wide chrome rims and run-flat tires.

Lucky eased the Charger into a U-turn from his curbside spot and set his heading eastbound on El Segundo Boulevard, keeping his eyes glued to the Camry in his rearview mirror. Gonzo lowered her window and finger-tipped the passenger side-view mirror until she had her own bead on the target. She watched the Camry easing in behind them, headlights switched on while silhouetted against a blistering red sunset. The driver and two passengers appeared equally engaged in their takeaway meals, unsuspecting that they were under surveillance.

"At the stoplight, boys," said Lucky into his phone.

Gonzo flicked her eyes ahead. The next stoplight was shifting from yellow to red. As Lucky braked, the Charger's taillights flared and ignited two of the gang members inside the Camry. *Baby faces*, thought Gonzo. The eldest of the pair couldn't have been more than seventeen years old.

"Heard this Sheriff's versus LAPD story once," said Gonzo, involuntarily needing to ease up on the tension. "Maybe you can tell me if it's true."

"Where are you guys?" asked Lucky into his telephone.

"Normandie," said Lopes over the tinny little speaker. "At your two o'clock."

Pulled up against the curb on the cross street were Lopes and Bledsoe, the bigger man stuffed behind the wheel of a maroon Chrysler 300.

"Drive-by homicide with a lotta bodies. Big mess," continued Gonzo. "Bad boys on the run in a car. LAPD with air support, pretty much herds the pair all the way to Compton just so sheriffs are forced to make the arrests and follow up with a dead-end investigation."

"Sounds kinda familiar," said Lucky.

"So the sheriffs down in Compton get all pissed off. The way they retaliate is to roll an ice cream truck up to a Crip party, load it full of unarmed gang members, then make a heading for South Central. PD territory, right? Drive around 'til they find a Blood party. Leave their cargo to fend for themselves in Bloodville. Hightail it back to Compton."

Gonzo watched Lucky's eyes perform a four-point ballet, first sliding sideways her direction, then checking in with Bledsoe and Lopes in the Chrysler 300, a shift forward to the stoplight as it switched from red to green, then finally resting in his rearview mirror on the three targets in the Camry.

"Wasn't an ice cream truck," said Lucky, easing his foot from the brake to the accelerator. "Just three black-and-white units was all it took."

"So it wasn't even twenty-five bangers."

"Oh, it was at least that many," said Lucky. "Maybe more. Sheriffs hooked 'em up with zip ties then stacked 'em like cord wood in the back seats."

"Wasn't Compton, was it?" asked Gonzo. "Was Lennox. Was you and your pals."

As if on cue, Lucky's pals, Bledsoe and Lopes, turned off of Normandie and slipped in behind the three Bloods in the Camry.

"You knew it was Lennox before you asked," suggested Lucky. "Yeah. You did."

Once again, Gonzo turned silent. She was finding herself having trouble staying in the present. Images of young black men, cuffed and loaded one on top of another like wooden planks stacked in the back of a sheriff's vehicle, glued in her mind like photos of tortured prisoners in Iraq's Abu Ghraib.

The Bloods in the Camry turned right onto a street flanked by shaggy palm trees and three-story apartment buildings faced in different shades of pinkish stucco.

"They've turned," said Gonzo.

"Yeah," said Lucky, well ahead of her. Through his rearview mirror he had watched the target car followed by Bledsoe and Lopes in the big Chrysler exit the boulevard. He then twisted the wheel counterclockwise, throwing the Charger into a U-turn so tight the tire rubber chirped in what sounded like eighth notes.

Without thinking, Gonzo's right hand moved to her waistband, her fingers instinctively tracing the hard-leather edge of her holster to the safety on her Beretta pistol. The fine hairs on her forearms were at attention. Something was about to happen.

And whatever *it* was, Gonzo's sixth sense wanted to make sure *it* didn't happen to her.

"Wanna clue me in?" asked Gonzo.

"Watch, learn, enjoy the show."

"Gladly be a witness to the crime you're about to commit."

"You can video this for all I care."

"Great idea. I can post it on YouTube so cops all over the world can see how L.A. sheriffs do business."

Lucky gassed the Charger up the residential street, quickly making up the distance between himself and the Chrysler. What followed was a maneuver so practiced it almost seemed choreographed. When he had pulled the Charger up within mere yards of the Chrysler, Bledsoe lowered his pedal, wheeled left, and accelerated around the Camry and its unsuspecting occupants. As soon as Bledsoe had taken position two car-lengths in front of the Camry he hit his brakes. This caused an instant chain reaction. The Camry braked hard, as did the Charger, Lucky slowing his front bumper only inches from his target.

The gangbangers in the Camry were trapped. Caught unaware and licking hot sauce off their digits. The initial shock of being boxed in had the trio barking at each other and spilling what was left of their meals as they dove under the seats for weapons. Then they got a look at their pursuers. Two middle-aged crackers and a wetback. All five-oh. Plus some mixed-race Amazon with a fro, recording the event on her smartphone.

Lucky tapped one-two-three on the rear windshield with the muzzle of his pistol.

"FACEDOWN ON THE STREET!" he yelled.

Practically in unison, three doors of the Camry popped open and the three young Bloods crawled out. Compliant to a fault. Ready to accept just about anything the plain-clothed sheriff's deputies had to dish out.

"Here's what's gonna happen," announced Lucky. "We're gonna look through your car. We're gonna find shit you don't want us to find. And it *will* fuck up the rest of your day."

Gonzo kept moving to her left in a continuous wide orbit, recording the event. As big Bledsoe entered her frame of reference, he queried, "Why don't you put that away, sister."

"Not ever," said Gonzo, making sure to keep Lucky at the center of her attention.

"But guess what?" continued Lucky. "My day has already been so fucked up that it might fuck up the rest of my life. So I don't wanna hear no sour grapes. I'm gonna ask and you're gonna tell me. Do I have your attention?"

All three gangbangers nodded their heads while keeping their faces to the asphalt.

"Okay. So here's what I wanna know. Six hours ago one of your blood brothers got his face blown off by a shotgun. I don't care what he was doing. Don't care if he did or didn't deserve it. I just want the man behind the trigger. Somebody saw that bastard and I need a description. I know about the truck. I know it's big and black like every one of your dicks when you don't have my boot up your ass. I don't want you. I want him. If you got his name, that's what I want. If he's got a Minnie Mouse tat and a bad case of acne, I wanna know about that. So. I'm gonna stop talkin' and you're gonna start. If I don't hear something I like, that's when your day turns shitty."

Lucky leaned against the Camry, hands on his hips, elbows sharpened.

It was just starting to get dark. A buzz sounded as the sodium-vapor streetlamp arching overhead began to wake up, just like the neighborhood itself. As each second ticked off inside Lucky's head, more spectators appeared on balconies and in doorways and on porch stoops. The cops were putting on a show. And the three most sympathetic characters were prostrate on the ground. Black youths. Gang affiliated. But the zip code assured that no matter how righteous the cops might have been, they were the antagonists in the play. And it was only a matter of moments before the spectators became participants.

The air felt electrified and prickly on the back of Gonzo's neck.

This was the kind of circumstance that could quickly become unglued. The LAPD would have called for backup—cops need assistance. There was nothing that tossed cold water on a potentially violent situation better than flooding a neighborhood with a dozen black-and-whites plus a police helicopter loudly disturbing the air from above. Gonzo would have touched her weapon if she hadn't remembered that she had already done that before exiting Lucky's Charger. She was fully prepared to drop her smartphone and draw.

"Lucky?" said Lopes, keenly aware of the increasing number of local residents creeping closer to the scene. Nine spectators had multiplied faster than melanoma cells. The detective made a mental estimate north of twenty witnesses. Each stoic and black. In a matter of moments, those numbers would double again. Next would come the taunts. It wouldn't take but a heartbeat for the cul-de-sac to explode into violence.

"Indians are getting restless, Luck," warned Bledsoe.

"These boys wanna talk to me. I can tell," said Lucky, crouching between the pair of prostrate gangbangers who had climbed from the right side of the vehicle. This is when Lucky's voice dropped an octave, turning soft. Almost plaintive. "Before this bad guy took out one of yours? He took out one of mine. So you need to look at me as somethin' other than the cop that jammed you. You need to look at me like the angry motherfucker who wants nothin' more than to disembowel this evil prick."

"What's dat?" asked the youngest of the crew, a sixteen-year-old so slight of build that even when lying flat on the ground, his shoulder bones poked out like knives underneath his T-shirt. "What's *disembowel* mean?"

Lucky smiled. Pleased. It was the very first smile Gonzo had witnessed from the bereaved brother.

"To disembowel…" said Lucky, "is to cut a man so that he watches his own guts spill out of his body before he dies."

A schoolboy's giggle escaped from the young gang member.

"That's some slick shit," said the teenager.

The following laughter was contagious. The gangbangers, still lying flat on the ground, were first to bust loose with guffaws. Joined by Lucky, then Bledsoe and Lopes. Guns found their holsters. Gonzo discovered an ending to her cell phone video.

It was as if the air's density had miraculously thinned into something more breathable. Gonzo let her lungs fill with nerve-cleansing oxygen. The crowd thinned and the sun fell below the horizon. A breeze came that was slight, but enough to cool the sweat on the back of Gonzo's neck. Thoughts of a shower slipped into her mind. A cool spray of water and a bottle of jasmine-scented body wash would surely feel heavenly. How soon that was going to happen for her was anybody's guess.

15

Granada Hills.

At one point, Rey Palomino had zero ambition in the pool construction business. His father's dream was for Rey to stay in school and become an engineer. And for some time, that was Rey's plan too. A former illegal immigrant and day laborer, Rey's father had built a career as a warehouse supervisor upon earning his hard-won citizenship. He toiled to pay college tuitions for both Heber and Rey. And while the elder brother graduated with a bachelor's degree in business, the younger didn't make it through his sophomore year at Cal State Northridge. Rey had temporarily taken over a part-time pool cleaning route for a grade school friend who had gone on a surfing sabbatical to Central America.

The old pal never returned.

Rey, who had come to enjoy the fluid hours and working outdoors, was happy to inherit the business. Over time, the business had expanded from that of cleaning and caring for pools to the installation and repair of filtering equipment, heater upgrades, hot tub additions, and renovations. Wasn't long before young Rey had his contractor's license and was at the helm of two-ton excavators, digging holes in backyards from Burbank to Calabasas. From Rey's perspective, it was a boom business. He was a pool and spa designer and builder, living the dream in the San Fernando Valley, an area code boasting an average mean temperature of seventy-eight degrees and a minimum of three hundred days of sunshine per year. Swimming pools were the right of every Southern California homeowner. Backyard lagoons and the men who built them would always be in demand.

Or so Rey imagined.

In the Granada Hills home he had mortgaged to the hilt, Rey employed his own unique filing system. His bills were spread across the large dining room table he had made himself from Indian teak. Invoices from various lenders from subcontractors to power and gas to his local cable provider. Ordered from left to right: late, later, and latest. Rey's system was designed by himself and for himself. Much the way some think heavy books are too overwhelming to read, Rey viewed piles of unanswered paper as mountains so massive he couldn't possibly scale them. Thus, the system. Tiny bites of the elephant. He had initially employed the system to organize his jobs—from present to future—size to pay scale.

And that dining room table, built for the large family Rey had only dreamed of, seemed permanently employed as a flat-topped filing system, forever relegated to office furniture. If Rey didn't find a way to pay the bills that littered the table, he'd have to face a bankruptcy judge.

The air conditioner kicked on, sending a mild gust of cold air that made the bills ripple. It reminded Rey of the night not too long ago when he had received the phone call from a man named Greg Beem, who had identified himself as an old army pal of Danny's. Beem insisted that he and Rey had met, only Rey couldn't put a face to the name. There were condolences offered followed by thanks and a moment or so of small talk. Eventually, the conversation turned to the subject of shipping. Greg Beem, it appeared, had confused Rey with his older brother, the Long Beach mogul who specialized in refrigerated exports. Confusion led to Rey offering his assistance. In turn, Greg Beem promised the significant fee of $30,000. Enough money to clear a significant amount of paper from Rey's dining room table.

After Rey hung up, he had barely weighed the specter of illegality against the debt that threatened to destroy him. He wondered if, just maybe, he was getting a break for once.

"Less than twenty-four hours after the triple murder in Kern County, the FBI has thrown its hat into the investigative ring," said the Channel 2 news anchor. "Sources say that in the murder of television actress Pepper Ellis, her boyfriend, and a deputy, the FBI is on the lookout for this refrigerated long-haul truck…"

When Rey was home alone the TV was always switched on and tuned to a news channel, the volume leveled to act as background noise. So why Rey turned his attention to the news story was anybody's guess. On the living room flat-screen played the stop-framed video of the black tractor-trailer rig passing by the filling station just minutes after the murders. In what felt like a finger-snap later, the über-tanned news anchor had moved on to the next story about the record heat that was smothering Southern California.

Rey had a momentary thought of grabbing the DVR remote. If he had wanted, he could have reversed the broadcast and replayed the murder story about the actress he had never heard of. But that wasn't what had spiked his interest. It was the ghostly image of the black refrigerator truck that the FBI was searching for.

Greg Beem didn't come to mind at that exact moment as Greg Beem was already pretty much all Rey was thinking about. And how in the world he was going to manage the situation he had created. He was all done cursing his older brother. Though the anger remained just beneath the surface, pissing and moaning about a brother he couldn't control wasn't going to solve a damn thing. He had tilled his brain from every dark corner, searching for a palatable delay to offer Greg Beem. Nothing came. Zero.

He had even stopped by his neighborhood Catholic church—St. Euphrasia's—and lit candles for Danny, praying to the Lord for guidance out of the mess he'd made.

There was no overt connection between the TV news story about the FBI and Rey's problem with Greg Beem. It was something moving inside of him. A gut feeling? But instinct wasn't Rey's greatest asset. He had pretty much lost every bet he'd ever made—be it a horse race at Santa Anita, blackjack at the Rio in Las Vegas, or even when given a generous point spread on his beloved UCLA Bruins football team—Rey always seemed to be on the losing end.

At some point, Rey transferred his stare from the television screen to a photo collage hanging above an antique arts and crafts buffet table. The handmade frame built from tongue depressors and Elmer's glue had been a gift from Rey's live-in girlfriend, Mayako. It held a hodgepodge of maybe a hundred snapshots, each depicting a frozen moment in Danny Palomino's life: the father and son sharing moments from infancy to adulthood, Danny in a variety of colorful uniforms—school, Little League, AYSO, Scouts. The boy always showing off rows of youthfully perfect, pearly teeth with a mischievous look in his eyes. The photographs were wreathed around a larger Marine Corps graduation portrait of a nineteen-year-old Danny without the usual grin. In the photo Danny Palomino was square-shouldered, humble, and oh so proud.

"You're right," said Rey aloud. As if that portrait of Danny had made some kind of ghostly suggestion. He sought the cell phone that lived holstered to his hip and dialed 411. When the recording asked for the city and state, Rey said, "Los Angeles, California."

"Listing?" asked the information operator.

"I'd like the local number for the FBI."

"Connecting you with the number. Thanks for using Verizon Connect."

Then came a ring. Then another recording with menu options. Rey hated menu options over the phone. He, like most people, preferred speaking to human beings. The instant he called a number and got any kind of voice menu, he wanted to hang up out of sheer protest. And Rey nearly did with his call to the FBI. Then he heard an option that would allow him to speak with an operator. Rey pressed zero and waited as the line rang and rang and rang.

"FBI operator. May I help you?"

"Yes. My name is…Uh…I might have information about the three murders."

"Which three murders are those, sir?"

"Murders on the news. Just now. I forget where. Um…there was someone famous? I think?"

"Please hold."

Rey was left listening to a monophonic selection of pop hits from the 1980s. It was a long enough wait for him to wonder if the music was chosen demographically or, more likely, by someone within the national bureaucracy who was still a fan of Tears for Fears and Flock of Seagulls.

A voice broke in.

"This is Agent Dulaney Little," said the baritone, clearing his throat as if woken from a nap.

"Yeah. Hello. As I told the lady on the phone, I think I might know something about—"

"The Kern murders," said Dulaney. "Is that what you're talking about?"

"Not sure about where. There was a famous girl and a black reefer truck?"

"Yes. That's the one," said Dulaney, polite but fully aware that the odds of the call bearing actual investigative proof resided somewhere between slim and none. "First. May I have your name?"

Rey hesitated. He hadn't thought so far ahead that he'd have to give his identity.

"Yeah," said Rey. "My name is Rey Palomino."

"And where are you calling from?"

"I'm in Granada Hills. That's in California."

"Hey. I live in Reseda. We're practically neighbors."

Neighbors? Rey wondered. His brain scanned back through

whatever former client list he could assemble, searching for
Dulaney Little. Rey figured he must have sunk twenty-five swimming pools in Reseda. What were the odds that he had built a pool
for Special Agent Dulaney Little?

"I build pools. Lots of 'em in Reseda. Maybe I built yours."

"Easy answer," said Dulaney. "And that's no. We don't have a
pool. Would love a pool. But not on this year's salary."

"Maybe I can make you a deal," said Rey, instinctively in sales
mode.

"Not today, I'm afraid," said Dulaney. "Let's get back to why
you called. What do you have for the FBI?"

Once Rey gave up his address, driver's license, and social security number, Dulaney green-lit him to tell his tale. The story of
Rey's deceased son Danny. The contact made by Danny's former
Marine Corps acquaintance, a man going by the name of Greg
Beem. Rey's shipping connection with his brother. And his poor
excuse for nearly aiding and abetting the felonious crime of export
fraud—what else but the lousy damned economy?

All the while, Dulaney listened and responded with his most
professional affect. Flat. Nonjudgmental.

"So whadda you think?" asked Rey. "Could this be your guy?"

"If it connects up. But we won't know for sure until we get a
closer look. First thing I'm going to do is run the name you gave
me."

"Greg Beem?"

"See if there are any wants, warrants, suspicious associations.
Name sounds pretty common so we won't know anything until we
run 'em through a filter."

"Okay. How do we do that?"

"Not a 'we' thing," said Dulaney. "That's my job. Your job is to
be the contact. He's expecting you to call and tell him his products
will ship tomorrow."

"Right, right," said Rey. He hadn't thought any further ahead
than passing responsibility on to the FBI. "Can't you just listen
into my call to him and then trace him that way?"

"For that we would need a judge and warrants and more

evidence than, what is now, only a story told by you. And no offense, you're just a guy who dialed one-eight-hundred FBI."

"I understand," said Rey again. He should have known, having spent hours and hours using cable TV to fight his insomnia. His favorite channels were Discovery ID and A&E. His addiction: true crime shows.

"So here's what I suggest," continued Dulaney. "While we run this name through the grinder, you reach out to this Greg Beem fella. Tell him your brother is ready to receive his cargo tomorrow. Sometime around midday."

"Okay."

"Once he's out in the open, we won't need a warrant to pull him over, check out any suspicious cargo. If he's our guy, he's going down."

"And what about me?"

"Aside from the good citizen award? Whadda you want?"

Up to that point, Rey had thought little more than hoping the authorities were a spatula that could scrape him off a sticky hot plate. He twisted his head to look at that dining room table covered with unpaid bills.

"Could there be some kind of reward?" Rey listened to the crackle on the other end of the line. He could practically hear his credibility sink to the bottom of the FBI's informant list. "On second thought, no. Forget I said anything about a reward, okay?"

"Okay," said the government man, barely containing his sudden misgivings about Rey's motives and virtue. "Let's focus on what we're both going to do. And what's going to happen tomorrow."

"Okay. So all you need from me is a time and place for the meet."

"Time and place," repeated Dulaney. "But don't make it too early. My day to drive the kids to school."

"I hear that," said Rey.

16

Beemer flicked the gnat from his right ear, then leaned back into the window screen. He wanted to make certain he had overheard enough syllables of Rey Palomino's conversation with the FBI.

If he had been more emotionally chilled, Beemer would have been grateful for the luck of it all. To have stumbled up at the moment Rey had called the FBI. Proving that sometimes the difference between success and failure is merely the randomness of timing. But the steam under his shirt was already preventing calculated thought.

He crouched just beneath the sill of the powder room, its door wide open to Rey's den. The tile wainscoting of the bathroom acted like an acoustic funnel, directing pieces of Rey's voice through a double-hung window, permanently cracked open at the bottom for ventilation.

The quick Mexican meal hadn't settled well. After catching the news broadcast mid-enchiladas, Beemer had paid cash, guzzled the balance of his frozen concoction, and returned to the stolen Honda. That cream puff news reader had referenced the FBI's interest in the Kern murders. Beemer needed to postpone his much-required sleep, find his way to Granada Hills, force a face-to-face with Rey Palomino, and put the pool man back on his heels just to read him.

Beemer easily found the residence in the hillside development circa 1979. At first glance the Granada Hills neighborhood set north of the Ronald Reagan Freeway reminded him of scenes from movies like *Poltergeist* and *E.T.: the Extra Terrestrial.* Had he taken the opportunity to ask Rey, he would have discovered his memories to be quite accurate. Not only had both pictures been filmed on these very streets, but at the time, producer and director Steven Spielberg had chosen this particular suburb because he felt it best represented his idea of modern Americana.

Rey Palomino's house was a traditional split-level home fronting a sidewalk. Tudor-esque in design, only the stucco work looked dated, applied with a rough texture and painted a sandy vanilla color. Two large white birch trees in full leaf obscured some of the view from the street. There was landscape lighting, all of it low-voltage and dim. The nearest streetlamp was three properties to the east.

After parking the stolen Honda in the shadow of an overgrown pepper tree, Beemer set the brake and assessed the neighborhood for no less than fifteen minutes. He counted two dog walkers and a male jogger wearing a reflective vest and a headband bearing a blinking red safety light.

Rey's pickup truck was in his driveway, the bumper nearly touching the garage door, leaving room for another car to pull in behind it. Beemer presumed this was an accommodation for Rey's sometimes live-in girlfriend, Mayako, who appeared not to be home. Rey was probably alone. Or so Beemer hoped. Only by performing a brief recon could he be mostly certain. Beemer eased himself from the car, quietly closed the door, and made his way through the shrubbery along the property line. At the side of the house, there was a simple wooden gate that required nothing more than pulling a knotted piece of twine to release the latch. The hinges barely squeaked. There was no sign of a dog. The path alongside the house was a mix of dirt and pea gravel.

Had Beemer taken the time to assess the backyard, he would have been impressed at the beauty of it. A mix of exotic grasses, plant life, and custom stone hardscape framed an elevated swimming pool and deck, along which flowed a gentle waterfall. Paradise on a third of an acre. Beemer was counting on the sound of the waterfall to cover his footsteps when he rounded the corner near the powder room and heard the warble of Rey's television.

Beyond the powder room window was a covered patio with furniture built of weathered teak. Behind was a set of French doors, through which Beemer spied Rey standing over a large dining room table covered in short stacks of paper. For the longest time, Rey organized, then rearranged the different slips of paper. Beemer wondered if he had caught Rey prepping for the tax man. Then he observed the moment when Rey's attention was trapped by something on the TV. Whatever it was, Beemer couldn't see. Beemer was there when Rey addressed the portrait of his dead son, Danny. And when Rey withdrew his cell phone and dialed, Beemer returned to the corner spot where he'd heard the TV through the cracked powder room window. From there, he had heard most of Rey's side of the conversation. The sum of which was a wholesale betrayal. Beemer broke out in a sweat. As if every pore in his body opened a floodgate of perspiration. His clothes instantly dampened, trapping the moisture. The slope on the back of his neck turned into a slick. His fists were clenched.

The next five minutes of Beemer's life played like a home video across his inner eyelids.

It began with him rotating back around to the patio.

He hefted one of those heavy teak chairs and swung it through the French doors. He heard the sound of broken glass crunching under his feet. Rey, his legs stuck to the floor, stood frozen, saucer-eyed, too shocked to put up a fight. Beemer raised his pistol, sighted across the top of the barrel, and, without halting a step, quadruple-tapped his target. Four successive gunshots in one-point-five seconds, each bullet piercing Rey's skull before his knees could so much as buckle.

But that was just the initial fantasy—the preamble in his mind that Beemer needed to imagine the action prior to the actual execution. It was another training trick, a lesson learned from the private security firm that had recruited him upon his exit from the Marines. Some exit. The government contractors had immediately U-turned the young gun and returned him right back into the darker heart of Operation Iraqi Freedom.

Beemer forced himself to hit his own pause button. To breathe and see if he could ease his heart rate to an operational rhythm. Put a bloody cork in his inner idiot.

He had already erred that day. He'd let his impulses get on the wrong side of good tactical judgment. In doing so he had pulled the trigger and unnecessarily blown the face off that MF #1 down in Lynwood. A regrettable mistake.

Beemer, still crouched below the powder room window, labored over his breathing. Slow in and slow out. He felt his mobile phone vibrate against his thigh. He removed the phone from his cargo pocket. On the screen a familiar number was displayed. 818 area code. He retreated from his crouch below the window, slowly walking an arc up behind the swimming pool, careful to keep his silhouette against the thick landscaping.

"Hello?" he answered, his voice hanging barely above a whisper.

"It's Rey Palomino."

Beemer felt his ears burn as his blood pressure built behind his eye sockets.

"How's it going?" asked Beemer, finding some cool in his voice while slipping between the double trunk of a queen palm. From behind the fronds he had a clear view through the home's windows and those matching French doors. He watched Rey, padding the floor between his kitchen and den, pacing, cordless phone held to his ear. The pool man's obvious nerves reminded Beemer which one of them was the true predator.

"We're good," lied Rey. "Very good, in fact. I talked to my brother."

"You did?" inserted Beemer in an effort to prompt Rey into deeper untruths. Maybe there'd be more sustainable satisfaction in allowing Rey to pile up the lies before punching holes in his body with hot stuff.

"And like I said. We're good. For tomorrow," added Rey, as if he'd forgotten.

"For tomorrow? Sounds good."

Nearly all the lights in the house were ablaze. When Rey's natural anxiety sent him walking from room to room, Beemer found following him was like watching a caged game animal, turning in place or pawing the ground before the inevitable slaughter.

"Thought eleven in the morning would be good," continued Rey. "That way, wherever you're coming from, you won't have to fight rush-hour traffic."

"Thanks," said Beemer before his voice tripped over the puddle of saliva at the back of his throat. Beemer coughed out, "Thoughtful of you. Thanks."

"Least I could do after today," said Rey. "Oh. And my brother is very sorry about everything."

"Maybe I can meet him tomorrow?" asked Beemer.

"Sure you can. He'd like to meet you too."

It was a damned sweet sight. To actually observe someone as they lied to you. A man who had no inkling whatsoever that he was only moments from certain death. Like the time-honored military practice of "painting" with the point of a laser to guide a smart bomb up a target's ass.

"Do we need to go over the details?"

"Ten thousand cash. Twenty more when my product arrives at the destination."

"And my brother will provide all the documentation, paperwork. All that kinda stuff."

Rey had ceased his pacing, facing outward at the kitchen door, a single pane opposite the pool steps. Beemer instinctively receded to further obscure himself. He wasn't ready to kill Rey. Not just yet. He made a quick calculation, measuring the light in the kitchen against the low-voltage illumination in the backyard. Odds were strong that the pool man was gazing at his own reflection. Watching himself tell one untruth after another.

Beemer's silence seemed to spook Rey.

"Everything cool?" asked Rey. "Can barely hear you speaking."

"I'm, uh…" thought Beemer. "People around. Some kinda tea an' coffee place."

"Well, have a cup of joe for me," said Rey, stabbing at something glib, but falling well short on delivery. Beemer heard a quiver in Rey's voice. A sure sign of nerves? Or possibly an animal instinct informing the prey that the end was imminent.

"Everything okay with you?" asked Beemer, letting the pistol dangle in his grip, shaking loose the tension in his shoulder. He was going to let Rey hang up before his final approach.

Just like he'd already pictured it. *Teak chair through the window. Follow the breaking glass with two pairs of double taps.*

"Yeah. Sure. Gotta go, though. Got my girlfriend comin' home. See ya tomorrow?"

"No prob," said Beemer. "Looking forward to it."

What Beemer was looking forward to was taking out Rey Baby. The safety on his weapon was off. The gun was hot and ready go. But the rules of engagement had changed like the channels on Rey's big-screen television. Through the big rear window frames of the modern Tudor, Beemer watched a slight, middle-aged Japanese woman lead a coterie of tennis-togged housewives into the family room. Eight women in all, the sharp frequencies of their combined voices penetrating into the backyard like a flock of descending geese.

Beemer took three steps rearward and stuffed the pistol back into his belt. It was his first autonomic reaction since the flop sweat that had busted out and wet his clothes while eavesdropping under the powder room window.

The racket of Mayako's tennis crew sliding open the French doors blanketed Beemer's hasty exit. The rest was covered by the darkness, into which Beemer reluctantly disappeared.

New plans needed to be formed. Sleep would have to be temporarily damned. And the clock to 11:00 a.m. was already ticking.

17

Compton.

"Hell yeah, I saw him."

"So draw me a picture," said Lucky.

"You want me to *draw* you something? Serious?"

"With your words," explained Gonzo to the gangbanger Beemer had labeled MF #2. Detective Lopes had ID'd MF #2 as Tyrone Charles. Street name: Speedy. Soon after the youngest in that carload of burrito-eating Bloods had agreed to help the cops, the sheriff had traded texts with Speedy. Initially, Speedy wanted less than nothing to do with cops, especially the L.A. Sheriff's. He cited trust issues, claiming he possessed the scars to justify his reluctance. But then Gonzo had become a welcome addition. She was both LAPD *and* a woman. A phone call later, Gonzo had negotiated a location where Speedy would feel safe from arrest. It turned out that Tyrone had an older half sibling who served as a

Compton fireman stationed at the South Acacia firehouse. So, in a borrowed back corner of the massive garage, yards from the rear bumper of a neon yellow ladder unit, Speedy sat on a stacked pair of used truck tires. Gonzo was closest to him, interviewing him from a folding chair. Lopes and Bledsoe, whose puffed-up face was swathed in fine beads of sweat, were a few paces behind her. The big man needed a breeze to cool him down. The air in that corner of the building failed to circulate.

Lucky was leaning one shoulder against the concrete wall. Legs crossed. Fatigue beginning to set into his shoulders. He pinched the bridge of his nose with his thumb and forefinger.

"Like a white dude," said Speedy. "Tha's what he looked like."

"Got two white guys with me," said Gonzo. "He look like either of them?"

"Well, he wasn't no fat dude. Wasn't no skinhead neither." Speedy switched his eyes from Bledsoe to Lucky, who was withdrawing a bottle of Excedrin from his jeans pocket. Lucky shook the plastic container like a baby's rattle.

"Dark hair? Light hair?" asked Gonzo.

"Was dark brown. Maybe black. Short hair."

"Like a cop's hair?

"Not that short. You know. Just regular."

"Remember what he was wearing?"

"T-shirt. Some black pants." Speedy added, "Pants with the pockets on the legs. You know. Extra storage."

"Cargo pants?" asked Gonzo.

"Yeah. Tha's what they were. And new kicks."

"You remember that?"

"Yeah. Like runners, you know. Maybe blue. Guy likes to run, maybe."

"Jogging or running shoes. Blue. Anything else? Facial hair? Eye color?"

"Sunglasses. Like on *CSI*."

"Which one?" asked Lopes.

"Whadda you mean which one? The only one."

"There's three *CSI*s," added Bledsoe, smug grin spreading underneath his mustache.

"Miami, man," insisted Speedy. "The redhead motherfucker."

"Like aviator glasses," said Gonzo. She dipped into her jacket pocket and withdrew her personal pair of Ray Ban aviators.

"Yeah," said Speedy. "Like that."

"Anything else? Tattoos? Scars?"

Speedy wasn't listening to the questions, momentarily distracted by the Kern cop with the noisy Excedrin bottle. He observed Lucky shaking out twin tablets, popping them into his mouth with a single, expert dry swallow.

"Hey, man," said Speedy in Lucky's direction. "That shit's gonna eat up your stomach."

"Yeah?" asked Lucky. "Thanks for caring."

"Don't care for nothin'. Just sayin' a fact."

"You a doctor when you're not poppin' caps?" asked Lucky. "Maybe you attended med school between hits on the crack pipe?"

"I'm not a crackhead. But I did watch my momma chew her insides up from eatin' aspirins like they was Skittles."

"Important safety tip," said Lucky. "Believe the detective asked you a question."

"S'all I know. Asides from the motherfucker blowin' my homie's face off. Now what's his momma gonna do at the funeral? Can't even lookit him again!"

"Said you were tryin' to jack the truck," said Lucky. "Ever find out what was in it?"

"I tried lookin' but the back was all locked up."

"But you thought you knew," confirmed Gonzo.

"Yeah, we thought," said Speedy. "We thought it was all rib-eyes and shit. You know. Meat."

"Red meat," confirmed Gonzo.

"Hell yeah. Who don't like red meat?"

Lopes let out a laugh, joined briefly by Bledsoe, who was tired of leaking perspiration by the pint. He had already unbuttoned his shirt to his sternum, revealing a sweat-soaked wifebeater. When he was nearly finished rolling up the sleeves of his $19 J. C. Penney dress shirt, he hadn't quite noticed the silence.

But Gonzo had. In a matter of seconds she watched Speedy's all-too-comfy swag morph into sudden caution, then fear. His bulging eyes locked onto the extra-large sheriff's detective. Gonzo swiveled, tracking Speedy's stare to Bledsoe's fencepost of a fore-arm. Inked on vanilla white skin was the exact same image Gonzo had seen on Lucky's calf. A grim reaper holding a scythe in one hand, a pistol in the other. And a number. Bledsoe's was number forty-nine.

"Man, I know you!" said Speedy, on his feet, accusing finger pointing at Bledsoe. "I know all y'all!"

"No, no," calmed Gonzo. "You're talking to me, remember?"

"Fuck you and fuck them!" accused Speedy. "Them's all Len-nox motherfuckers!"

"Sit the hell down!" barked Lucky.

"You think *I'm* in a gang?" Speedy's angst meter was at the maximum. "Ain't no gang more evil than Lennox. They shoot a gangsta just because!"

"Nobody's getting shot," cautioned Gonzo. "We're just talking about what you saw—"

"I done. You tell my halfie I shook it loose."

"Look," said Bledsoe. "Rollin' down my sleeve. Pretend you didn't even see it."

Speedy cut left around Gonzo, head down and dead reckoning for the exit. Gonzo snagged him at the crook of his arm.

"Whoa, whoa!" said Gonzo. "C'mon. Don't just walk away—"

The thud of Lucky's left palm heel connecting with Speedy's ear had a slight, mid-pitch slap to it. The blow came moments after Speedy stuffed his hands in his pockets and set a course for the nearest exit. Lucky had two-stepped past both Lopes and Bledsoe and unleashed the meaty part of his hand on Speedy's head. The boy's knees buckled briefly before he slumped against the ladder truck. He instantly covered his head with his arms, expecting more blows to follow.

Gonzo set her feet and launched herself into Lucky. She locked her elbows and fired every pound of her six-foot frame squarely into the Kern cop, repelling him two steps backward. The rest was all reflex. Gonzo drew her pistol, snapped the safety off, and positioned herself. Knees bent, combat ready. Her Beretta thrust forward into Lucky's face.

Lucky slapped the gun to the side.

"Outta my way!"

"Stand down!" yelled Gonzo, retreating until she had Speedy safely pinned against the truck and herself between the unarmed gangster and the enraged cop. "Stand down or I'll put one through your face! I've got justification and I got witnesses."

Lopes knew exactly what she was talking about. He swung his gaze over the ladder truck to an open window, where the firehouse dining room overlooked the garage. Shadows of firemen had gathered, curious about the ruckus in the corner of their station house.

"I deserve some goddamn answers," breathed Lucky.

"Yes, you do," said Gonzo. "You've had a real bad day. But that's not my fault. And it's not this guy's fault either."

"You don't have the nuts."

"Neither will you if you don't back the hell off!" Gonzo lowered her aim to cover Lucky's crotch.

"Material witness to a capital crime," entered Lopes into the fray.

"You wanted him to talk to you and he talked," argued Gonzo. "If he wants to go now, then that's what he gets to do."

"Detective Gonzalez," warned Bledsoe, his voice taking on an officious, yet deadly, tone. His left hand was outstretched while his right was gripping the rubberized butt of his Glock, its muzzle non-threatening and aimed at the floor. "Listen to me. You have willfully placed yourself between county cops and a suspected felon. You have no jurisdiction. Strongly suggest you holster your weapon."

Gonzo nodded. With her free hand, she reached back and touched Speedy's ribcage. She could feel the gangbanger trembling, his bravado reduced to a case of the I'm-gonna-die shakes.

"You okay?" asked Gonzo. "Ready to go?"

She assumed the half squeak, half grunt she heard from Speedy was a noise to the affirmative. Grabbing a piece of his T-shirt, she began to drag him in the direction of the exit, all the while keeping herself and her 9mm between Lucky and his intended target.

The puffing from Lucky's cheeks appeared to deflate and his hands opened in sudden surrender. Next he gestured for Bledsoe to dial it back a notch. Lucky even forced a fake-assed smile.

"Know what?" said Lucky. "Actin' this way? I don't think you're gonna get that ride back to Pasadena."

"I'm all heartbroken," said Gonzo, backing away, each careful footfall one step closer to the street and a safe exit. Gonzo wheeled a one-eighty just in time to see Speedy dashing out the firehouse door, legs pumping, vanishing into the darkness.

Both Lopes and Bledsoe busted out some chuckles, then closed ranks around their brother-in-arms with back slaps and a huddle of hushed conversation.

Then it hit Gonzo while she was standing just beyond the station house door.

The interview with Speedy had for most investigative purposes ended. There was nary more information the gang member would have or could have been able to pass on to them. So why had Lucky pressed the issue with a nuclear outburst? Had he merely reached his emotional limit? Had frustration played its last card?

Or…

Was Lucky playing her? Was this his way of turning his lemons into lemonade? With that single hammering sock to Speedy's skull, Lucky had forced a reaction from Gonzo that would make it impossible for the partnership to carry on beyond that very moment. Hell. Gonzo had gone so far as to draw her weapon and threaten to kill a fellow police officer. The sum total was this: Sheriff's Deputy Lucky Dey from Kern Country had at last jettisoned his female LAPD chaperone.

Gonzo found her mobile phone and dialed up a cab ride back to Pasadena. Next, she speed-dialed her son, Travis. The eleven-year-old hadn't yet entered the stage of preadolescence when the odds of his answering a call from his mother was less than

30 percent. In fact, her one and only child took great care with responsibilities such as cleaning up after himself, completing his homework before any television, computer games, or Xbox, and keeping his cell phone charged and close.

Travis answered on the first ring.

"Hey, Mom."

"Hey, buddy. How's it goin'?"

"Nothin'."

"Didn't ask what you were doing? Asked how it's goin'?"

"Playin' *Madden*."

"Right. Okay. Tell Alice I'm on my way home. Might be an hour or so."

"Hey, Mom?"

"What?"

"Can you bring Taco Bell?"

"Didn't you eat?"

"Yeah, but—"

"But nothin'. Have some fruit."

"Awwwwww."

"See you when I get home. Love you."

"Mom?"

"Trav. I said fruit."

"I know. Just askin' if you're okay."

Gonzo exhaled deeply. There was never getting anything past Travis. The kid could read her like the large print on an eye chart.

"Just tired, buddy," said Gonzo. "Long day."

"But the day's over, right?"

"Yes," sighed Gonzo. "It's finally over."

18

Bel-Air.

The diagnosis was that Conrad Ellis suffered from an overly-busy mind. Thus the chronic insomnia. Since moving to Los Angeles ten years earlier, he had run through the gamut of possible cures. From reading to sound machines to soft music to warm baths. None seemed to tame his buzzing brain. There was, of course, medication. Pills. Conrad had tried those too. From over-the-counter remedies to prescription drugs with sleepy names like Lunesta and Ambien, Conrad had sampled them all. Either the meds didn't work or those that did left him lethargic and napping through half the work day. So Conrad gave up on the doctors and medical research and resorted to the tricks his father had used. A hard day's work followed by nights of banal television and whiskey, wearing paths in the rugs and floors of his home with his constant pacing. When sleep finally came it was a restorative surprise, only to be followed by successive nights of more insomniac wanderings.

Conrad recalled when he was a boy, stuffed into the corner of his tiny bedroom, window cracked so he could listen to Chicago's elevated trains as they rumbled across the skyline. And through his open door when the night grew silent, he would occasionally hear his father wandering from room to room, the sound of whiskey-soaked ice cubes tinkling in a water glass.

Conrad poured himself another serving of thirty-year-old Scottish single malt—so much better than the stuff his pop had drunk. The ice cubes crackled under the assault of the golden liquid. He lifted the diamond-cut tumbler and listened to the ice cubes plink inside the fine crystal. Was the sound any richer than that he recalled of his father's salve? Or was expensive whiskey just whiskey and Waterford glass just glass?

"Yeah, sure. Gimme that number," said Conrad, looking like a heftier version of Hugh Hefner in his silk pajamas, blinking Bluetooth stuck in his ear. "Don't text it to me. Just tell it."

As with most of Conrad's conversations, his assistant was listening in on the call. It was the assistant's job to write down the number and connect to the next call. That way, Conrad could continue his insomniac's march while keeping his hands free from touching a computer or a keypad that might carry germs. The scotch, he reasoned, was by its own alcoholic virtue, antibacterial.

"You said her name is Lilly?"

"Lilly Zoller," answered Garvin.

"And these are her personal numbers?"

"Home and cell. And you didn't get them from me."

"What else you got?" asked Conrad.

"Nothing new yet. I'll have a full report in your inbox by six o'clock a.m."

"I'll be up."

"How you holding up, sir?"

"Numb, I guess," said Conrad. "Dunno how I'm supposed to feel."

Conrad instinctively pressed the five key, the cue for his assistant, David Kang, to disconnect the call.

"Anything else, sir?" asked Kang.

"Yeah. Call that number."

"For Lilly Zoller?"

"Whatever her name is. Yeah."

Kang knew better than to remind his rest-ravaged boss of the time of day. Conrad could read a clock and really didn't give a rat's shit who he disturbed. Privately, Kang entertained his friends with stories of his boss's practice of dialing at late hours. He called it no-napping. And in Conrad's ten years as a producer-slash-motion-picture-financier, he had no-napped just about everybody. Movie stars, studio execs, directors. Even mayors and governors who had promised tax incentives in exchange for filming in their home zip codes. Conrad would no-nap them, grind out the best deal of the moment, and unapologetically move on to the next sleeping soul.

Kang prepared to no-nap Assistant US Attorney Lilly Zoller.

"Home or cell?" asked Kang.

"Flip a fuckin' coin."

The dog growled at the noise. But that was his job. Somewhere deep inside its mongrel DNA, there was a strip of code that demanded the feral creature protect the realm. In the case of the three-year-old rescue mutt, the realm was the two thousand square feet of a downtown Los Angeles loft, an architectural space softened with natural wood and corduroy-upholstered furniture. But in the monochrome of night, it was cast in grays and blues and the occasional flash of red from the lights outside.

Then came the noise again. Like a drill bit in the wall. Hollow. Reverberating. Danger. The dog's growl evolved to a bark. Its eyes practically glowed in the dark. There were times when Lilly liked that about her magic mutt. He was born with slightly bulging eyes, gray brown in color with girlish eyelashes. The dog's head would sometimes lift up from the bed covers, look from the floor to the ceiling, and, as if soaking up the reflection from all the ambient light, appear to be irradiated.

"Dingo. Shut up."

Pretty as the pup's eyes were, his bark could be sharp. A hatchet to the back of Lilly's skull. Something about the frequency. It got her right behind the ears. This time, it had woken her.

"Dingo!"

The dog's ears lowered. He spun a quick couple of revolutions and curled up at her feet. Lilly flipped her pillow to the cool side and rolled over, but before laying her head down again, she heard the sound, followed by a mild growl from Dingo.

"Ssshhhhh!"

She wanted to get an earful of the sound again. Then memory hooked in with the logic lobe of her brain. The loud drill-like interruption was the sound of her cell phone, still switched to vibrate after the party she had attended. The device was now buzzing across the top of her dining room table. The solid oak planks acted like a speaker's diaphragm, amplifying the smartphone's jitterbug into the sound of a full-blown invasion.

"Crap."

Lilly slid from the bed and trekked over to the dining table. She had half a mind to answer without so much as looking at the incoming number. Just press talk and unleash a blitzkrieg of expletives. Her other half thought she might want to check the caller's ID, then customize her curses for whichever legal idiot thought phoning the assistant US Attorney after midnight was a wise idea. A "damn 'em" if it was a wrong number unworthy of her wrath.

"Private fucking caller," read Lilly off her smartphone's screen. Then she clicked the green-lit button and spoke. "Whoever the hell this is, you're either drunk or stupid or too horny to exercise good flippin' judgment."

Most of her booty-buddies had the smarts to wait for Lilly to be the aggressor and dial them.

"Please hold for Conrad Ellis," said the strange voice.

Before Lilly could say "Conrad who?" the line clicked and the man introduced himself.

"Ms. Zoller?" asked Conrad in what was less a question and more a statement about the social order of things. "I'm Conrad Ellis. You might or might not have heard of me. I'm a motion picture producer. But most importantly, I'm the father of Pepper Ellis."

Still jarred from waking, Lilly's brain lagged. She was still trying to place the name of the caller when he'd dropped his famous daughter's name.

"Pepper Ellis?" asked Lilly. "Am I supposed to know you or her?"

"This is Lilly Zoller of the United States Attorney's office?"

"It is. How did you get my number?"

"I'm a simple man of power and means," said Conrad. "My daughter was everything to me."

"Your daughter, yes," said Lilly, finally catching up. "Your daughter is the murdered TV kid."

"She was seventeen and emancipated," said Conrad. "Emancipated not because she wanted to divorce her parents or anything—well, maybe her mother. Just saying she was her own person so she could legally work adult hours."

"I'm sorry." Lilly found command of her manners. "You must be devastated."

"Yes. I suppose. I'd like to know what you know."

"We've only just begun our investigation—"

"You know something. Or else you feds wouldn't have gotten involved. Now, I've already lived through the corn-fed runaround from the clowns up in Kern County."

"Well, it is their jurisdiction."

"Lilly? Can I call you that?" said Conrad. "I made my bones buying and selling Chicago real estate. That's Chicago, okay? Not much I don't know about how the Department of Justice operates, considering I've been investigated by them while at the same time I was their goddamn landlord. You hear me?"

Yes, Lilly could hear Conrad. The subtext being that he was connected and from Chicago. And nowhere in America did commerce and both local and federal politics intersect in such a sticky tangle. She needed to tread carefully because the man on the line had implied that either he or somebody he knew probably had the Attorney General's phone number on speed dial.

"I understand, Mr. Ellis. Would you like to come in and meet tomorrow? The afternoon? I'd be more than glad to show you what we have."

"Show me? Sure. But tell me now."

"Of course," said Lilly, knowing exactly how the obedience game was played. Keep the voice flat and without affect. Answer questions directly. Just not necessarily to the fullest extent. Appearing compliant was paramount when trying to keep a secret. And Lilly had a whopper.

"Our unsub," Lilly continued. "That's unknown subject—we believe he's driving a truck full of stolen biological materials. He was bound from Reno to Southern California when he crossed paths with the three victims."

"Biological? Like hazardous waste?"

"No, sir. Refrigerated blood products. Medical-use products."

"There an underground market for that?"

"We think possibly overseas. But that's still speculation. We need to stick with the facts of—"

"Why her, then?

"Her?" asked Lilly. "As in your daughter?"

"What did she have to do with any of it?"

"As far as we know, nothing more than impeding the perpetrator's path. Your daughter and her…companion…were in a traffic accident with the deceased sheriff's deputy, who was in the process of assisting your daughter when the murders occurred."

Lilly, who had stood in front of as many mirrors as judges, rehearsing arguments, learning to measure her own words and tone with precision, pleasured in listening to herself talk to the bereaved father. Sleep be damned. On the end of the line was an eight-hundred-pound gorilla she needed to tame. Her only concern was whether she had sounded too cold. As if she had been sitting at the boss's conference table, surrounded by other deputy US Attorneys, merely running off the deets of her case.

"So this…man," said Conrad. "He's of interest to the feds because he crossed a state line with a load of blood products?"

"He's of interest to us because he's a criminal. Because he's committed multiple offenses—"

"Because he murdered a pretty little TV actress."

"Sir?" asked Lilly. It was a stall. Was Conrad calling her out or just cutting to the chase?

"C'mon, Miss Zoller. Nobody likes headlines more than federal attorneys. If it ain't mob or politicians on the menu, what's tastier than celebrities?"

"Mr. Ellis. All due respect. Before this morning, I'd never even heard of your daughter."

"But you've heard of her now. You know she's getting more famous by the minute. You know she's got a popular TV show. Double the usual eyeballs for tonight's episode."

"She sounds very special, sir."

"Here's something you don't know. I gave that show to my little girl. Put up the money for the pilot and guaranteed the first twelve episodes on her perky pair of dimples."

"You produced the show for your daughter?"

"No. That woulda looked wrong," said Conrad, keeping a half step in front of her. "Not that anybody in Hollywood gives a shit about nepotism. For her, I guess. I wrote the check and watched her grow up on TV."

The man at the other end of the phone had just played his first note of melancholy. A tinge of regret had crept up on him. Lilly heard Conrad catch himself, inhale deeply, and exhale in an effort to gird his voice.

"You loved her very much," said Lilly between the man's grieving breaths. "I can't begin to imagine—"

"You're not anywhere on this," said Conrad. "If you were, you woulda said it already."

Lilly bit her lip. A habit leftover from her teenage years.

"Like I said, Mr. Ellis. We're just at the beginning but—"

"If I went to the press," said Conrad. "Put up some kinda big dollar reward, leading to the blah, blah, blah of it. You wouldn't object?"

"As a private citizen, you can do whatever you—"

"I can also take that money and promise to put it to work politically against you or your boss or anybody else who supports the local US Attorney's office if I discover you withholding information from me."

"I hear you," said Lilly. "I assure you that I hear you."

"That's the thing about money. Makes everybody listen," said Conrad. "So go and get your headlines. But you sure as hell better get a result that satisfies the victim."

"I assure you that my office will do everything in our power for your daughter."

"Not her!" barked Conrad. "My little girl's dead and there isn't a goddamn thing you can do for her. I'm the goddamn victim! You do this for me!"

Then the call was over. Conrad Ellis had hung up. Still, she left the phone stuck to her ear as she stood at her floor-to-ceiling windows, stark naked and staring out over the blue and red neon of the downtown Staples Center and the collection of theaters, clubs, and restaurants known as L.A. Live.

The heat of the day was still leaking from the scorched earth, rising in horizon-dissolving waves. The window radiated heat, making her skin tingle until it began to itch and bead with sweat. That was okay by her. She wouldn't be able to sleep until she showered again. There, under a lukewarm spray, she would war game whether or not to include Conrad Ellis in her circle of trust. Just moments before she had first drifted off to sleep there had been another call. There had been a tip from some pool contractor in Granada Hills. He'd told the FBI a believable tale about a nefarious shipping deal gone sideways. The pool contractor, who had been acting as some kind of middle man, claimed to be spooked and wanted to help the feds set up a sting. Dulaney had conceded to his boss that he'd initially put little faith in the caller's veracity. But after a few calls and some simple keystrokes through the

Department of Justice database, everything except the name of the perp had checked out.

Lilly emptied her hot water tank and still hadn't reached her verdict. That faceless man on the other end of the phone call had given her a good shake. There was some animal in his bark. Would Conrad Ellis really bite if she didn't play things his way? Of equal importance was what might happen if she broke FBI protocol and allowed the angry father in on the possible takedown plans that were still forming.

"Shit," she said aloud. "I gotta change my phone numbers."

19

Pasadena.

"Hey, Mom, guess what?"

Gonzo had barely crossed the threshold of her two-bedroom duplex when she heard Travis shouting over his Xbox.

"Hey, Trav. How are you? I'm fine, thanks," said Gonzo, preferring a gentler home landing than a verbal barrage of guess-whats from her eleven-year-old.

"Mom!" said the boy, undeterred, on his feet and greeting her where the front corridor met the dual kitchen-den. "Chaps scored another one."

"Oh, Christ. Killed another skunk?" Gonzo was getting a sudden case of heartburn at the mere thought of the oversized mutt having gutted another skunk. After the last one it had taken a month to get the stink out of the poor dog's fur.

"Huh uh," said Travis. "Chaps got another one of the crazy lady's chickens."

"Dammit, Chaps!" Gonzo dropped her Beretta into the quick safe she kept inside a decorative wicker basket and slammed the lid shut and locked. "Where is that stupid dog?"

"Not his fault. Chickens are just on the other side of the fence. She's supposed to keep 'em in a coop."

Only then did she catch the tension in Travis' young face. Nary a pimple yet, but full of nervous tics brought on by stress mixed with a blossoming anxiety disorder. Gonzo put her arms around the young beanpole, who was barely five inches short of her own six gangly feet.

"She doesn't have to keep 'em in a coop," said Gonzo, dropping her voice into a more calming frequency.

"But she does. I looked it up. City of Pasadena says chickens gotta be in a cage and not near a fence or where people sleep."

"You found that out?"

"It's called the internet, Mom." Travis spun and returned to his Xbox controller and bag of microwave popcorn.

"Did you eat dinner?"

"Pop-Tarts."

"Awesome," said Gonzo, choosing not to spark a fight with her precious child. "And did Chaps eat anything other than Mrs. Lorena's pet chicken?"

"He ate."

"You know she's gonna call animal control on us," said Gonzo. "But…at least when they come, we'll be armed with the law."

"And Mr. Kyle?" added the boy. "He sorta fixed the fence."

"What's sorta?"

"He put the old wheelbarrow in front of the hole."

"Well, good for Kyle," said Gonzo, referencing her tenant on the other side of their common wall. Kyle, sixty-two years old and closeted, was a gentle soul who worked in a small pet shop in nearby Altadena. The man kept mostly to himself, but when around was glad to train a watchful eye on Travis and clean up after Chaps as long as the pup wasn't harassing his house cats.

"Hey, Mom. Can we order a pizza?"

That was the last thing Gonzo remembered hearing. Her eyes must have been shut when the boy had made the junk food request. She was stretched across the couch, bottle of Gatorade stuck in the crook of her arm. Sometime while watching her boy battle computer-generated brain-chowing zombies, sleep had overtaken her. Had she snored? Who was there to hear her? Travis and the big mutt had long scuttled off to bed. Gonzo had been left to dream of nothing fanciful—not even able to escape her day handcuffed to the shaved-head hard-ass from Kern County.

She had dreamed that she had fallen asleep on the couch of her former Simi Valley house. The bigger one with the pool and the Suburban in the driveway. Only once she had climbed into the Suburban, day had flipped to night as if she had flipped a switch, and the interior of the Chevy Suburban looked an awful lot like a yellow cab. And there she was again, the dream having turned to a nightmare driven from recent memory. The cab was struck from behind. It spun across three rain-slicked lanes and impacted with the divider.

Then snap. Gonzo woke, her clenched jaw aching where it had once been wired and screwed in place. Yet despite the pain, she was as relieved as much by waking than the realization that the terrible memory was in the past. She was safe in the cozy South Pasadena duplex she had bought after getting out from under the anvil of her Simi Valley dream home.

In her half-dreamy haze she was able to settle herself by picturing the humble clapboard property much the way she had first seen it. Grandmotherly, with untended rose bushes and vines of blooming wisteria. And though the domicile dated back to the thirties, it was freshly painted in a rusty red with white shutters and an actual picket fence to match. The only downside was that the front door was a mere five paces from a street that served as an artery for commuter traffic. Hardly ideal. But once Gonzo had seen the knotty pine interior—all original—the manageable size, the smallish but private backyard, not to mention the attached rental property, the numbers added up.

The new home would also be four easy blocks from Travis's new school, Madison Prep, a specialty academy for children with both learning and developmental disabilities. The school was a godsend for Travis, who, without the special attention, would have drowned at his former alma mater, Simi Canyons. Nor would the boy be teased anymore about the facial tics over which he had zero control. That's because nearly every child at Madison Prep was a misfit in one way or another.

If only the tuition weren't so damned steep.

The gray light of dawn was just beginning to flood the small den. Gonzo's eyes tried and failed to focus on the old plaster ceiling stained latte brown by the chain-smoking former owner, a ninety-one-year-old great grandmother with an addict's affection for bourbon and unfiltered Camels. In the end, lung cancer hadn't laid a finger on her. But liver disease had.

Gonzo stretched and twisted. The sliding glass door a mere two feet from the top of her head led to a weedy backyard. What grass hadn't been torn up by the dog was either pee-stained or in tufts of Marathon choked with crabgrass. Again, Gonzo tried to twist her corneas into giving up some detail. But her vision was still cloudy from the Tylenol PM. She had gone for overkill with four caplets, double her usual dose.

"Why try?" she might've heard herself mumble, curling up around a velour pillow covered with dog hair. She let her eyes close and wondered if she'd get sucked back into that ugly dream. Nevertheless, she felt safe enough in her comfy little duplex.

Safe, she thought. *What in the world would her old friend, Ben the safety expert, think?*

Her mind drifted back to Simi Valley. To her wannabe romance with Ben Keller…or Ben Martin? What name was he going by now? It had been a few years since his world had invaded hers, leaving her near dead and petitioning the LAPD for lifetime disability.

"Cozy little getaway, Miss Lydia."

Yeah, she thought. But not so secure. Any moron could break in with a can opener and a pillow case.

"Sorry. But sometimes you gotta forgive a little breaking and entering as a last resort."

Last resort, my ass, she continued. There were far more lucrative houses to break into than Casa de Gonzalez. What was there to steal other than the Xbox, a couple of early-generation iPods, and a PC so slow that it considered a dial-up connection as pressing the speed limit?

"Lydia."

Lydia, schmydia. Ben never called her that. He used her nickname, Gonzo, just like everybody else who knew her more than a week.

Then why the hell is Dream Ben calling me Lydia?

It was as if the depth between her unconscious mind and her electrically charged waking state were thinner than a mosquito's skin. Gonzo snapped awake and flipped to her other side. And when she saw him her body gave a second jolt.

"You just woke. You're disoriented. So breathe and listen."

Lucky, appearing haggard with circles under his eyes, was comfortably seated in her antique rocking chair next to the fireplace. In his right hand was his untrained pistol.

"You—"

"Shut up and listen," snapped Lucky.

Gonzo's head swiveled, looking past the kitchen and down the tiny corridor. Empty.

"Your boy is still sleeping. As well he should," said Lucky. "Now, look at me and focus."

She focused all right, back to the badass model 1911 in Lucky's grip. An old-school handgun. .45 caliber. Heavy loads. Bullets guaranteed to drop whatever they struck.

"You took a sleep aid. So you were sleeping hard. I get this. Probably why you didn't answer my nine phone calls to your cell phone."

"I turned it—"

"Keep listening." Lucky leaned toward her. "I needed to talk to you. You wouldn't pick up your phone. So I did the next best thing, which was knock on your door. Which I did because your doorbell is hangin' by a dead wire out there. The reason why I'm in your house is because your queer granddad for a tenant let me round the back when I flashed him my badge. Yeah. I fudged the truth when I said I was your partner but, like I said, I had to talk to you. Are you getting all this?"

"Yeah." Gonzo nodded, her eyes still keeping tabs on where the muzzle of Lucky's gun was pointed.

"The gun? You're looking at my gun? Got that out because the last time you and I were face-to-face you had your nine-mil up in my face. You remember that or did you sleep that shit off too?"

"Coulda knocked on the glass."

"You need a coffee?"

"Why the fuck are you in my house?"

"I need your help."

"Right," said Gonzo, sitting up on the couch, pushing the hair out of her face. She swished her tongue inside her mouth. Dry. She nodded toward Lucky's pistol. "Can you put that away? 'Cause right now that's the only thing I can't deal with."

First he paused. Then came a simultaneous nod from Lucky as he eased to his feet and tucked the .45 into the holster clipped inside his waistband.

"I gotta make coffee," said Gonzo. "I can listen to your why-the-hell-you-broke-into-my-house excuse while I make coffee."

"Got any Benadryl?"

"Give yourself a rash from being an asshole?"

"Your dog. I got an allergy."

"Of course you do." Gonzo was already in the kitchen. She dug into a cabinet, shook a small bottle to see if there were pills inside, and then tossed it to the detective. "Still can't believe you're in my house. Jesus Christ!"

"Advil?"

There was a Costco-sized jug of ibuprofen against the back-splash. She tipped it over and rolled it across the counter to Lucky.

Lucky unscrewed the caps off each container, emptied a double dose of capsules into his palm, popped them into the back of his throat, and chased them with a couple of swigs from the spout over her sink.

"That skinny banger was right," said Gonzo. "That stuff's gonna eat holes in your stomach lining."

"Yeah, well, that string took us no place," said Lucky.

"Us?"

"One of my guys got a call from his connection with the feds. They think they're on to the perp. Got a takedown planned for around noon today."

Gonzo eyeballed a scoop of ground coffee, which she shook into a cone filter.

"Okay. So you're golden. Why come all the way out to Pasadena? Thought you could buy me breakfast?"

"I wanna be there. But everything about the takedown is under a shell of federal fucking silence."

"Here's an idea," spat Gonzo, her tongue sharpening with every waking second. "You got the deets on that FBI guy we stalked. Knock on his home address instead of mine."

"Yeah," said Lucky, his voice lowering to a growl. "You're close. But we both know he ain't gonna tell me shit. He is, though, gonna lead me to the takedown."

"Sounds like a sweet plan. What's keepin' you?"

"Can't really ID the guy, can I? I was creepin' his office while you were makin' the stall."

"Seriously?" Gonzo shook her head, switched off the hot water before the whistle woke the house, and began a slow pour. "Black man. Hundred-eighty pounds. Thirty-five to forty-five. Shaved head."

"Pretty stock description. Sounds like a lotta black dudes—"

"Not wearin' a suit and livin' in Reseda," said Gonzo, her voice elevating.

"Please," said Lucky, his voice a decibel above a whisper. "I can't afford another blind path here. All I need is the ID."

"So you want me to get in the car with you, drive all the way to Reseda just to point the man out."

"And quickly. We don't know if he's an up and at 'em kinda black dude."

"You should hear yourself."

"Coffee and go. C'mon."

"Absolutely not," said Gonzo, both hands braced on the old tile coping. "You want my help, then this is how it goes. I get a shower. I feed my son and walk him to school. Then we drive out to the Valley."

"And the feeb's already gone to work."

"So if he is, you can follow me back downtown and I'll ID him at his place of work. Far as I go. Take it or leave it."

Lucky didn't like the ultimatum. Fatigue was beginning to feel like an aggressor.

"Don't like my terms, then you can discuss it with my supervisor after I've filed my complaint against you for harassment, stalking, breaking and entering, brandishing a weapon on—"

"Fine. You win." Lucky surrendered and spun a frustrated one-eighty.

"And don't you even try to convince yourself that I'm doing this out of some kind of cop-to-sheriff's respect."

"God forbid."

"Doin' this because I feel sorry for you and your loss."

"Huh uh," snapped Lucky. "I don't need your pity."

"Yeah, you do," said Gonzo. "You got about an hour and a half. Crash on the couch, crash in your car. I really don't care."

Black coffee in hand, Gonzo shuffled off toward her bedroom and shut the door with a decisive *thump*.

Lilly Zoller slept five hours, woke, dialed before she got out of bed, and left a message for Conrad Ellis.

Conrad Ellis hadn't slept a wink. When Lilly called with the information about the when and where of the possible takedown, he was in the middle of a workout session with his personal trainer. He had told his assistant to tell all callers that Mr. Ellis was unavailable while he was getting down with some sweat therapy.

Once Conrad heard Lilly's message, he quickly passed the information on to Garvin Van Der Berk. Garvin, in turn, tapped out an encrypted email on his smartphone and hit send. He didn't need to wait for a response, certain the recipient would jettison whatever he was engaged in to meet him at 7:30 a.m. at Twain's coffee shop on Studio City's Ventura Boulevard.

"Eyes and ears?" asked Dave Wireman. "All he's looking for?"

"Presently," said Garvin. "Client's a grieving father who doesn't want to be left out of a possible arrest."

"So video too?"

"I would. But don't be obvious."

"No problem."

Self-defense expert and bodyguard, sometimes stuntman, unpublished writer, and most recently, wannabe actor, Dave Wireman was the ultimate hyphenate who had difficulty deciding what professions to put on his business cards. He had recently settled for just his name and contact information.

"Got some crumbs there," pointed Garvin at his buff friend.

Dave looked down and flicked the English muffin remnants off his one-size-too-small teal polo shirt.

"Damn," said Dave, noticing the butter stain. "Can take the slob out of the boy but not the boy out of the slob."

"Did you have an audition today?" joked Garvin.

"Naw. Have an appointment to see a stylist. See about cutting back all the silver in my hair."

"Thought that was your actor's calling card. The distinguished look."

"Thought so," said Dave. "But my commercial agent keeps getting calls to send me in on Viagra commercials."

Garvin laughed out loud.

"Not down with being the face of limp dickatosis?" asked Garvin.

"Not today. I'm your man," said Dave. "Want me to coordinate with my pals over in the PD?"

"No. Keep it black."

"Guns?"

"What for? You're an observer."

"Conrad Ellis, man. Client's a make or break guy in the biz. Ready to do him a solid if he needs a private resolution."

"One step at a time. Gave you the details. Shoot me updates on the half hour."

"Dunzo."

"I got the check."

The two men parted ways without a handshake. Garvin soon disappeared behind the tinted windows of his Range Rover. The door closed with a heavy thump and, in moments, he was headed back over the hill to his West Los Angeles office.

As was his custom, Dave had backed his late-model silver Lexus into a parking spot. This time it was behind the restaurant. Parking against a building like this usually provided a quick getaway, if needed. It also allowed Dave to pop his trunk lid and rummage under the custom-cut piece of Astroturf without concern that others could spy on the contents. This time it concealed him pulling on his Kevlar vest. Extra discreet and only three mils of thickness. He unpacked a brand-new polo shirt, tore off the tags, and pulled it over the vest. From a locked pelican case he chose a Sig-Saur 250, clipping it onto his belt. He then found a lightweight powder blue hoodie with UCLA embroidered in gold on either side of the zipper. It was 9:00 a.m. and already north of ninety degrees. Dave didn't care, though. He planned to spend most of the day in the air conditioning of his V8 Lexus. At the end of which would be ten crisp hundred-dollar bills in his wallet. All for observing the FBI takedown of some unsuspecting, murdering SOB.

While he was still at his open trunk, Dave decided to check his other wares. Three more handguns with ammo, all nine millimeters. Then hidden under an extra blanket in the deepest reaches, a military AR-15 assault rifle and a Heckler and Koch 416 A5, fully collapsible and recently greased-out after a test firing of five hundred rounds. Every square inch of the weaponry was perfectly legal for Dave. He recently leveraged his self-defense work into a Federal Firearms License in order to sell weapons to celebrity clients who didn't want to risk their left-leaning public posture to some tabloid reporting their patronizing a local gun shop.

Dave checked the video camera for battery power, lowered his trunk lid, then speed-dialed his number-one sidekick, Terrell.

"Yo, it's me. We're on. Comin' to get you in about twenty."

"Where we goin'?"

"Long Beach. Wanna suss out the topography before the feds lock themselves in."

"Twenty minutes. I'll be ready."

Tuesday

20

Reseda.

Reseda is a generally flat suburban landscape near the middle of the San Fernando Valley. The land had once been covered by thousands of acres of orange groves, but over time had evolved into a middle-class stronghold of postwar construction. Sidewalks flanked wide surface streets, all placed into an easily navigated grid of boulevards with easy freeway access.

The address Lucky was looking for held a smaller house on a wide corner lot that abutted the noisy 101. Towering above was a billboard advertising a Commerce casino, lasciviously depicting a stripperlicious blonde with a Kardashian-like body, winking at the camera, with a caption that read: Feeling Lucky?

"If there ever was a sign," said Gonzo from the back seat of Lucky's muscle sedan.

Lucky spun the car around and parked four doors north of the address. While he adjusted both of the side-view mirrors to better watch the blue and white stucco house, Gonzo twisted herself around to peer out the rear window. It was 9:13 a.m.

"Betcha twenty we're too late," said Lucky.

"Two cars in the driveway, one on the street," said Gonzo. "I'll take that bet."

"Give it thirty minutes and I'm gunning it back to downtown."

"Whatever," said Gonzo, getting comfortable. That back seat had saved her from riding shotgun all the way from South Pasadena. She had worried that her game face wouldn't hold. She was still feeling violated from the early-morning intrusion. Lucky had crossed so many lines with her in the last twenty-four hours that she had been mentally typing the official complaint since the previous night. After his uninvited entry into her house, she was now considering criminal charges to go along with the internal LAPD grievance.

But then there was that short drive to the drop-off line at Madison Prep. She had climbed into the back seat with Travis, having already served up one lie after the other to explain why the boy had woken to a strange man in the house.

While Gonzo showered, Travis had stumbled from his bedroom, jammies barely hanging on his skinny hips, rubbing his face, just to seek out his mother, whom he had last left dead asleep on the couch. The boy had been so startled when he discovered Lucky, fully reclined and snoring in the same exact pose he had last seen his mother, that he had let out a prepubescent scream that cut all the way through the hot water blast of Gonzo's bath. Gonzo had leaped into action, nearly slipping and crushing her own skull while extracting herself from the old tub. She quickly slung on her robe and rushed to her son's rescue, only to find Travis seated on the floor and giving Lucky a grand tour of his newest Xbox game.

Travis was just that way. Trusting. He possessed the kind of faith that led him to unthinkingly ask Lucky a question on that short drive to school.

"Who shot you in your head?"

Gonzo, at first surprised at the temerity of her boy's question, registered a slight tightening in Lucky's jawline.

"Travis," Gonzo cautioned.

"No, Mom. I know about bullet wounds. Seen all kinds of pictures and stuff online."

Lucky had unconsciously reached behind his head and scratched near the scalloped edges of his scar. Of course, Gonzo had noticed it the day prior, had cataloged it, but hadn't thought to ever ask him, considering she had spent most of the day looking for her way off the Lucky Dey crazy train.

"This your school right here?" Lucky had asked Travis.

"And that's my friend Albert!" Travis had pointed out, unbuckling before the car was even stopped, snagging his backpack, joyfully ready to start his school day.

Not another word about that curious scar three inches behind his right ear had been uttered during the ride out to the West Valley. While Lucky played talk radio roulette, never quite finding a show to hold his interest, Gonzo wrestled with that complaint she had begun to mentally compose.

"My guess is he's still home," said Gonzo, pointing a finger out the rear window of Lucky's Charger. "If that gray Taurus isn't what a fed drives, then I'm a Fox blonde with fake boobs."

Lucky released a brief chuckle. Gonzo could see the corner of his mouth curl. But her eyes couldn't help but stay affixed on the obvious scar.

"Sorry about what my kid said." Gonzo returned her gaze to Dulaney Little's Reseda house.

"Nothin' to be sorry about," said Lucky. "He's a cool kid."

"I meant the remark about the..." Gonzo found her words stuck in her mouth. So she just spit it all out. "About the obvious bullet wound behind your ear."

"So what about it?"

"Exactly," said Gonzo. "What about it?"

"Took one in the melon," said Lucky. "What else is there to say?"

"You survived? That you're some kind of miracle?"

"Ten percent of headshots are non-fatal."

"And ninety percent of them end up permanently disabled."

"Sometimes I wonder," said Lucky, leaving it right there. "Ten minutes and we're lookin' for this guy downtown."

"Where'd the bullet go?"

"What? After it entered my skull?" Lucky thought about his answer, glimpsing Gonzo in the rearview mirror.

"Still have screws in my jaw from a bunch of reconstructive surgeries," said Gonzo. "Bet you had a great plastics guy."

"No guy. No girl," said Lucky. "No surgery. Bullet's still in there."

Lucky gently rapped a knuckle above his right ear.

"No shit?"

"Swims in this little pocket of fluid between my frontal and temporal lobe."

"Was there trauma?"

"Whadda you think? Fuckin' twenty-five cal in my head? Induced coma. Buncha holes drilled in the cranium to release the pressure of the swelling."

"But everything else?"

"'Cept for the headaches? Like it never happened."

"How long ago?"

"Just before…" Lucky swallowed his words. Cleared his throat and readjusted the rearview mirror so he could see Gonzo's face. She wasn't looking at him. Her eyes were out the back window, still glued on the FBI man's house next to the freeway. The morning light, softened through the tinted rear window, cast a blue halo around Gonzo's frizzy hair.

"Around the same time," continued Lucky. "That I was foaming the runway for my brother. You know, up in Kern… Anyway. Me and Big Flip had just hooked up this honcho we were after. Walkin' him from his apartment and out to the car. Some dude. And, you know, like, I didn't see him. He just opens the manager's door, sticks out his pea shooter, and *pop-pop-pop*. Two in the haunch and one behind my ear. We go down. Bleds drops and turns the door into balsa wood. Dude in the apartment gets himself dead. Honcho's dead. I wake up in intensive care with a frickin' microwave antenna screwed to my skull. End of story."

"Good story," said Gonzo, realizing she was unconsciously looking for rationale to like the man. She had cut him slack the day before because he was grieving for his brother. But by 9:00 p.m. he had spent his cache of Gonzo's goodwill. He had already started at a deficit today, sinking even lower when he stirred her awake with the gun in his fist. Yet Gonzo was searching for something to care about beyond Lucky's obvious loss. Otherwise, she would grind over his behavior until it eventually morphed into words contained in a PPL complaint.

"Everybody said I'd set off the metal detectors," said Lucky. "Turned out to be a tub of bullshit."

"Too small, right?" said Gonzo on rhetorical remote. "Same with the screws in my face."

"Car accident?"

"Forgot my seat belt. Got tossed clear. Lucky to be alive."

"On the job?"

"Bone of contention when it came to disability," said Gonzo. "Union was on my side. But I still lost."

"Five minutes."

"Sure you stole the right address?"

Lucky remained silent on that one. Once again, fatigue was overwhelming him. His eyes, which he kept leveled on his right side-view mirror, kept creeping shut. Sleep was like a wave that would roll in, envelop him, then snap him awake seconds after he succumbed. It didn't help that prior to being awoken by his Kern County captain, he hadn't slept more than four hours a night for a week. The headaches had begun to border on migraines, leaving him too dizzy to catch more than an hour of slumber at a stretch. He'd been depleted before the madness had even begun. And now he was just fighting the inevitable. If he wasn't a cop he'd have gone trolling the nearest barrio for a few capsules of Dexedrine. Black Beauties. Military-grade stay-awakes.

Then came that damned jolt as his body forced him back to consciousness. He checked his watch to find he'd been sleeping for thirteen minutes.

"Time to go," croaked Lucky.

"Wait'll he gets in the car."

"Wait'll who…"

Lucky blinked and returned his focus back to his left side-view mirror. There, circling around to the driver's side of the new Taurus, was a black man in gray suit pants and a short-sleeved white shirt, cell phone glued to his ear. For all appearances, the man was in a hurry.

"Why didn't you tell me?" spat Lucky.

"Tell you what?" asked Gonzo. She knew he was depleted and needed sleep. Still, she couldn't keep the incredulity out of her voice. "That you were snoring so loud you couldn't hear me shout, 'THERE'S YOUR GUY!'"

21

My name is Dulaney Little. My name is Dulaney Little. My name is Dulaney Little.

Amongst close friends, it was no secret that Dulaney hated his birth name. For a child born with a speech impediment, spitting out two words as simple as his own name could sometimes be embarrassingly difficult. Just one L in a word could cause his tongue to inexplicably stick at the top of his soft pallet. But the prospect of following the first L with another within two syllables could be crippling, leaving an eight-year-old boy stricken, panicked, and secretly cursing his parents for naming him after a Dutch uncle he'd never even met.

Dulaney's middle-class mom and dad finally scraped up enough money to pay for a speech therapist. The daily exercises showed dividends in young Dulaney's grades and general deportment.

The wallflower who had spent his waking hours avoiding most social interaction bloomed and, eventually, even led his high school debate squad to the L.A. City finals. The cripple was cured but for the occasional stressful moment when he needed to blurt something out, usually his own name.

That morning Dulaney had set it all in motion. The late night tip had gone from improbable to promising. Dulaney followed by casting a net for an FBI tactical group to assist in the likely arrest of the Kern County murder suspect who had last been seen driving a black-on-black refrigerated semi. He'd also ordered up a helicopter team to secure the airspace over the takedown site.

The takedown site had yet to be confirmed. With every click of the minute hand, Dulaney started to worry. He had already swallowed three pressured phone calls from Lilly Zoller, a.k.a. the Mistress of the Bark. With each ring she was looking for the latest details on the coming event. Details that Dulaney would be short on until hearing from his source, Rey Palomino. Dulaney kicked himself that he hadn't set his alarm and driven up to Granada Hills to babysit the tipster. He had set far too much in motion based on a single informant. FBI practice was to stay glued to the informant throughout the setup. But family life sometimes had a way of throwing up roadblocks. Especially in the mornings when there were kids fighting, midday meals to be folded into insulated lunch boxes, and no damned skim milk in the house.

Finally, Rey Palomino called in with a breathless recitation of his minutes-old conversation with a former Iraq veteran with the so-called name of Greg Beem. The DOJ and Homeland databases had spit out over a hundred possible matches, two of whom were listed and accounted for as presently serving in the Middle East.

Dulaney jotted down every other word onto one of the neon yellow sticky notes his wife was accustomed to leaving around as honey-do reminders, grabbed his jacket and car keys, and hurried out the front door to his car. His first call was to the FBI tactical coordinator, who wouldn't necessarily recognize the caller ID. Stressed, but still trying to keep his emotions under the anxiety radar, Dulaney lapsed back into his third-grade body.

"It's Dulllllll…aney Llllll…little."

Dulaney's brain screamed at his tongue. He practically pressed the end button just from embarrassment. He caught his own breath, inhaled, released, and spoke again as if he were reading it from his own government-issued business card.

"Special Agent Dulaney Little."

With his tongue unstuck from the roof of his mouth, he passed on the pertinent details, tossed the phone on the passenger seat, started the Taurus, and backed out of the driveway. In an unusual display, he roared up his own street. He rationalized that the neighborhood kids were all in school, so speeding wasn't that big of a deal. Though upon reflection, he fully expected to get beaucoup phone messages from the nosy octogenarian three doors over. She missed no occurrence on their shared street. More times than he'd like to count, while Dulaney oh-so-patiently listened to her dispense neighborhood complaints, he'd been tempted to tell the old busybody that she would have been more comfortable working in the former East Berlin as a Stasi informant.

As for his speeding, Dulaney was only half correct.

Sure. The Stasi wannabe had noted Dulaney's accelerating Taurus. But she was more worked up over the strange Dodge Charger parked dead in front of her overgrown home. She had spent the better part of the last hour eyeing the occupants. A man in the front seat. Bald or with a shaved head. White, but maybe Hispanic. Possibly a gang member. And the rather tallish woman with a mop of black hair who kept twisting in the back seat, peeking her nose out the rear window. The nosy neighbor was fully prepared to dial 911 on the duo. But she was also convinced that LAPD dispatchers had been covertly developing a file on her copious calls to the emergency operators.

Then, just as her colored neighbor had sped his government car up the quiet street, the duo parked outside her property were quickly re-buckling their seat belts and gone before she could accurately recall the paint tint of the Dodge Charger.

* * *

Trent "Shorty" Reese was an out-of-work trucker with a blistering addiction to crystal meth. The former long hauler, who had
supported his Corona, California, family on a Teamster-protected
income, had turned to the pipe as a cheap but effective stimulant
when he needed the extra boost to get over the hump to his far-
off destinations. Over his most successful years, he had ingested
old-fashioned speed, legal amphetamines, and even snorted super
expensive cocaine. But Shorty didn't know the chemistry of crystal
meth. Nor did most other users. Crystal meth is quite possibly the
most addictive drug of all when considering the rewiring effects
on the part of the brain that produces the chemical dopamine. In
Shorty's case it all led to a quick skid downhill, arrests, divorce, and
the loss of both his union card and trucker's license.

When Shorty wasn't abusing the last of his familial rela-
tionships to get the coin to feed his out-of-control habit, he was
trolling internet bulletin boards for unlicensed short-haul gigs that
paid under-the-table cash.

It was one such job that had led Shorty to Burbank. It was
9:36 a.m.

"YO!" shouted Shorty. "ANYBODY 'ROUND HERE
LOOKIN' FOR A TRUCK DRIVER?"

He had followed the instructions the voice at the other end of
the pay phone had slowly and carefully recited. And though Shorty
wasn't more than ten minutes late, he was beginning to wonder if
he had blown his chance at a clean $200 cash. He turned a slow
circle on the weedy patch of concrete that fronted the old warehouse, shielded his eyes against the sun, and just as he was daring
himself to bang on the corrugated steel of the warehouse doors,
he heard the heavy *clank* of a lock being thrown. The big doors
squeaked like a million injured mice, then slid sideways.

"You the guy on the phone?" asked Shorty.

"You my truck driver?" said the squinting Beemer.

Shorty launched forward, right hand outstretched. But Beemer
held up his hands as if in surrender.

"Don't wanna shake my hand, dude," said Beemer. Sure

enough, his hands were sticky and brownish. "A little last-minute mechanicals."

"No problemo. I'm Shorty."

"Greg," said Beemer. "Wanna give me a hand? Kinda sticky."

With what strength he had left after the two years of meth abuse, Shorty assisted Beemer in sliding the rusty doors until both were wide open. Daylight filtered into the room through a blanket of micro-dust that seemed to stay forever suspended in the air.

"Well, ain't she pretty," said Shorty, catching his first glimpse of the black-on-black Peterbilt rig. Right next to it stood a generic white Freightliner semi-tractor and -trailer, also refrigerated. "Ice cream trucks, huh?"

"Without the ice cream," said Beemer. "Frozen meat products. Yum."

"You name it, I hauled it. So I don't care as long as the money's green."

"That's why you're my man," grinned Beemer. "Headin' down to a shipping yard at the Long Beach harbor. Hour-fifteen drive, tops."

"Happened to your other guy?"

"Food poisoning. Comin' out both ends," said Beemer, toweling the goo from his hands. "But you didn't hear that because my deal with the vendor is that just me and my partner were to get all this frozen shit to where it needs to be."

"Not USDA inspected, huh?"

"Don't know. Don't wanna know. My job and now your job is get it to Long Beach no later than noon. So whadda you say? Wanna saddle up?"

"No time like the here and now," said Shorty, who started walking toward the Freightliner.

"Huh uh," said Beemer. "I got the Freighty. You're in the Peter."

"The honey's for me?"

"Freighty's got a clutch I gotta baby some. Used to it, so you're gonna drive Black Beauty there. Okay by you?"

"You gonna pay me for drivin' her or am I gonna have to

pay you?" laughed Shorty, who was already beginning his walk-around.

"Hey," said Beemer, cutting toward the Freightliner. "Cab's up at the other end."

"Just doin' my standard trailer check."

"Not payin' you to impress me," chirped Beemer. "Payin' you to drive. Directions are already on the Garmin. I'll take up the rear. Now, let's get a move on."

"Sure, sure," said Shorty, sober and, for the moment, knowing which side of his bread was buttered. Then as he spun back toward the Peterbilt's cab, he sniffed at the air. "You smell that?"

"Been smellin' it all night."

"Fuel oil?"

"Think I'm the only underground hauler who uses this as a crash pad?" said Beemer. "Building reeked when we rolled open the doors. Poor dude musta sprung a leak."

"Must have," said Shorty, climbing up onto the black cab and trying on the big rig for size. He expertly adjusted the seat, ratcheting it closer to the pedals to accommodate his five-foot-five frame. He used to have lifts in his collection of fine urban cowboy boots. But Shorty had long since sold all eleven pairs to a vintage clothing store for less than a single C-note.

"Right behind you," said Beemer.

"I'll pull her out, then help you shut the doors, okay?"

"Naw. Let's leave 'em open. Let the joint air out."

Shorty nodded his approval of the plan, saluted his new boss, then pulled his door shut. Clutch, shift, first gear. The Peterbilt eased out of the warehouse like a giant Cadillac. *Wow*, thought Shorty. *What a honey of a truck.*

Greg Beem hadn't had much of a chance to clean up. He was splattered with globules of that sticky, smelly black and brown goo that, once congealed, stuck to his skin and clothing like tar. So as he eased the stolen Freightliner rig out of the warehouse, he was already skipping ahead four hours to the long, steamy shower with a big bar of soap and a one-gallon can of solvent. The night had been long without a lick of sleep. Thank goodness for that bottle of Ritalin he'd packed before leaving for Reno. Forty milligrams consumed every six hours provided plenty of pep for an adult male without ADHD. Though sleep still beckoned, it was going to have to wait just a little while longer.

At first, Beemer kept close to Shorty and the Peterbilt, following turn for turn as the for-hire driver wheeled the big rig onto the northbound Interstate 5 for the short jaunt to the west lanes of the 118. It wasn't the shortest route to Long Beach, but the simplest and cleanest in Beemer's view. Once they transitioned from the 118 to the southbound 405, it would be a straight forty-four-mile ride to Long Beach. The less complicated, the better. Especially after Beemer had caught his first glance at his hired gun, Shorty Reese. Beemer recognized the telltale signs of meth abuse the instant he laid eyes on the poor man. The gaunt scabby face and rotted teeth. Hollow, empty eyes.

Only when Beemer and his unwitting partner had taken to the road had the veteran given himself a chance to second-guess himself. The result of all his efforts of the last twelve hours were now in the unwitting hands of a broken-down meth head.

Berating himself wasn't going to get his frozen blood products overseas. The revised plan was this: the feds were on the lookout for a black refrigerator rig; that bastard, Rey-the-pool-prick, had tipped off the government and set up a place and time for Beemer's apprehension. The rest was simple. Give the feds what they're asking for: a big black fridge truck and a guy behind the wheel. By the time the government sorted through the error of its judgment and trust in the Granada Hills pool man, Beemer and his borrowed truck full of blood products would have crossed the border to Tijuana.

The transition from the westbound 118 freeway to the southern route of the 405 was a long, sweeping single-lane arc. Beemer could already see the heat waves distorting the horizon in a mirage effect. The disturbing image forced Beemer to reel in his focus back to the shiny, black beauty of a semi truck a mere eighth of a mile ahead. In less than ninety minutes he'd be green and on his way to San Diego.

With the 405 acting as his artery straight into the heart of

Long Beach, Beemer could back off a half click from the Peterbilt. He was just easing off the gas pedal when he heard an approaching whine. He instinctively checked his right side-view to glimpse a red spec in the parabolic mirror. No sooner had he heard and seen it than the spec appeared off his right fender—a vintage Porsche convertible at full throttle, its four-cylinder, 158-horsepower engine at maximum scream. The angle at which the old sports car shot out from off his starboard made it look as if a noisy red bug had just escaped from being crushed by the Freightliner's front wheel.

"Fuckin' asshole!" Beemer found himself saying aloud.

He had half a mind to dial the California Highway Patrol to report the dangerous son of a bitch. Just to keep the driver from wrecking and causing a traffic pileup that could put his just-revised plan at risk. Then again, phoning any authority could place himself and the newly stolen Freightliner on the police's radar.

"Didn't even get the license tag," Beemer reasoned with himself.

Soon, the near incident was shuffled to the back of Beemer's brain. He had quickly returned his fatigued resources to the moment and the matter at hand, which was safely trailing the black Peterbilt to Long Beach Harbor.

If only Beemer had seen the Porsche's vanity tag. Framed in a silly frame that read, "My other car is a pickup truck," the sunny California plate spelled out a simple but accurate moniker: POOLGUY.

"JEEEEE-SUS!"

Rey Palomino spilled out from the cab of his Toyota Tundra. How he landed on his feet was a miracle, considering the three-foot drop into fresh-tilled dirt that was fast turning to mud. It felt like his truck had been hit by a tsunami. But the reality was that, in his moment of panic, he'd backed up over a fire hydrant.

The morning had not gone according to plan and Rey was racking it up to a night without sleep. He had laid awake in front of the television, remote control in hand, constantly surfing for a program to take his mind off the situation he had placed himself in. Golf Channel, Discovery, Nat Geo, Cooking Channel, Tennis Channel, NFL Channel, ESPN, Bravo…None summoned sleep nor challenged his brain enough to dull the feeling that, by agreeing to use his brother's shipping enterprise to illegally disguise a truckload of undisclosed product as frozen vegetables, he had set events in motion that had led to the deaths of three young people.

After Rey's decision to phone the FBI, there had been three more phone conversations with Special Agent Dulaney Little. The first two came around 7:00 a.m., interrupting the über-tanned collection of morning news babes with their cleavage and giddy pre-packaged patter designed to jump-start the viewer's day with a dose of news and tease. Rey informed Agent Little that he hadn't yet heard from the man calling himself Greg Beem. Then by around 9:00 a.m., Rey had convinced himself that the whole deal was off—Greg Beem had thought better of the situation, spooked even, and moved on to some kind of plan B known only to him.

That hopeful bubble popped an instant later when Rey's cell phone chirped.

"Twelve o'clock, straight up," said Beemer over the phone without so much as a hello. "At your brother's depot. We finish this and we're square."

"Okay," said Rey.

"Repeat it back. Wanna make sure you heard me."

"Twelve o'clock. On the nose, right?" said Rey, practically busting into a cough, there was so much phlegm stuck in his gullet. "At my brother's place."

"Don't be late."

The entire call lasted less than ten seconds. Just the sound of Beemer's voice sent waves of fear pulsing the strands of Rey's nervous system. He looked at the clock, trying and failing to calculate the simplest of computations. The amount of time to get ready, drive south to Long Beach, and wait for the FBI to arrest the bad man and his illegal cargo. Yet while Rey continued to stare at the IKEA kitchen clock as if it were going to tell him what to do next, he was strangely stuck in time and unable to function. The fugue ended when his phone chirped again. Terrified that it was Beemer, Rey fumbled to check the incoming number and recognized it as a plumbing subcontractor with whom he had been trying to connect. He sent the call directly to voicemail and redialed the mobile number Special Agent Dulaney Little had left him.

The game was on. The FBI was in charge. So what the hell was that sour feeling he kept tasting at the back of his tongue?

Deciding he would rather wait for the final outcome in Long Beach, Rey grabbed his truck keys and hit the road without a shower, a swab of deodorant, or even brushing his teeth. The fast-food junkie had a favorite drive-thru in mind where he could get a breakfast muffin, French fries, and a tub of Diet Coke. That's when he saw the steeple. At the bottom of his street was a Catholic Church—St. Francis de Nomes—otherwise known as St. Franks to the neighborhood kids. Danny used to play in the parish's winter baseball league. And Rey would assist as coach.

The morning sun spiked through the church steeple. A question formed inside Rey. How long since he had confessed, lit a candle in Danny's memory, or even prayed to the God he claimed to put before all others? That's how Rey found himself wheeling his pickup into the parking lot, setting the brake, and dashing inside the church for a quick make-up moment with his Lord and Savior, Jesus Christ.

Rey recited three Hail Marys by rote along with the "Our Father" and lit nineteen candles for every year of Danny's short life, his hands shaking so badly that he had needed six wooden matches. There was no time to even take a moment to breathe it all in, calm his nerves, or find solace in the surroundings—the crisscrossing arches and the fourteen brilliantly lit, '60s-styled stained-glass windows. Rey hurried back out into the parking lot. He turned the engine over, dropped the transmission into reverse, twisted the wheel, and backed over the fire hydrant. The extreme high-pressure water fixture snapped clean off at the bolts and sent a geyser of high-pressure H_2O blasting into the pickup's undercarriage.

When the fire department rolled up, Rey was less chagrined

about his driving skills and more in a hurry to get the hell out of there. He handed over his driver's license and insurance info, claimed he had some important business with the FBI, then vanished back up the slope to his house. When the LAPD dispatched a radio unit to knock on Rey's door with a citation for leaving the scene of an accident, the kind tow driver assigned to impound the Tundra followed to return a kitchen-sized garbage bag full of personal items, including Rey's wallet. But after the uniformed officer received no answer at the door, he made a note that the garage was wide open and empty.

"Betcha he's drivin' his Porsche," said the tow driver.

"What? You know the guy?" the uniform asked.

"No. Just got his truck hooked up to my truck. Check out the license plate frame."

And there it was, the sibling to the license plate frame on Rey's vintage Porsche. It read, "My other car is a Porsche."

22

Long Beach.

Residents of Long Beach, like those of other seaside communities, were quick to grow tired of heat waves—even though the sunny days were usually accompanied by steady offshore breezes keeping the temperature about twenty degrees cooler than those oppressive heat indexes experienced forty miles inland.

"The locals are friggin' melting," said FBI Tactical Captain Zekemeyer, better known as Zeke to those in the bureau. "They can't take this shit."

"Aren't you local?" asked Dulaney.

"I live in Manhattan Beach," said Zeke. "But I'm from friggin' San Berdoo. And I got a long memory."

It was 10:35 a.m. Zeke had just walked Dulaney through the gauntlet he had set up to safely "corral" the suspect.

"See?" said Zeke. "Day one. They're all like, isn't it so nice and warm? Then come day two of this shit. All appreciation is gone and all the beachies can barely tolerate the heat. But they don't really complain because they know that any minute the ocean fan is gonna switch back on."

Zeke snapped his fingers. Dulaney was already laughing.

"Day three? Total meltdown. Everybody is bitching and crying about everything from global warming to why they hate their neighbor. Happens twice a summer and it's always a hoot."

"I live in Reseda," said Dulaney flatly, arriving at his Taurus, parked at the far edge of a Ralph's supermarket lot. He found himself looking at the palm trees that trimmed the property, wondering if he could see the fronds beginning to flap in the breeze—a sign that the heat wave was about to end.

"If it wasn't for the real estate boom," said Zeke, "I'd still be living in the IE. Me and my Suzy leveraged ourselves up and into a really sweet spot a block from the water. Best thing we ever did."

Like Dulaney really wanted to hear about all of Zeke's financial successes. He looked at his watch, noting that they were a notch more than an hour away from an arrest he hoped would go off without Murphy and his Law of Lousy Outcomes entering into the equation. For any success at all, the trucker they were so cautious about had to be the same suspect from the Kern County murder. On the drive to Long Beach, Dulaney had reminded himself that he hadn't yet met face-to-face with the informant, Rey Palomino. During the walk-through with Zeke he had received two calls from Rey, explaining something about a slight delay and a fire hydrant. *Just get your pool-constructing ass down to Long Beach so we can ID the perp.*

Thirty minutes later, Rey Palomino finally arrived, parking his vintage Porsche in the space next to Dulaney's Taurus. The pool contractor was a thorn bush of nerves, tongue-tripping so badly over his words that it made Dulaney feel almost omnipotent over his own buried impediment.

Dulaney tried to put Rey at ease, then requested he move his car halfway across the lot and to pretty please sit and wait on his trembling hands until the FBI decided where they wanted to perch

him. Rey, the good soldier, zipped his Porsche around the lot, settling on the idea of hogging a pair of spots to reduce the chance of
his recent paint job getting chipped or dinged. Rey stopped, killed
the engine, and set the brake.

"What's the difference between a porcupine and a Porsche?"
asked Dulaney, half to himself.

"I know this one but I forget," said Zeke.

"With a porcupine, the pricks are on the outside."

"That's it," Zeke chuckled.

"What do you want to do with him?"

"Let him chill until we need him."

"All right. What's next?"

"Brief review," said Zeke. "Because once we set the detour,
we're stuck with the plan."

"Think I got it," said Dulaney. "DWP trucks and sawhorses,
and orange cones set up the gauntlet. Traffic jam. Gives us time to
paint a target on the unsub. We take him in the intersection."

"So, you were paying attention," smiled Zeke.

"Just so you know, it was hard, considering all the scattered ass
walking in and out of Starbucks."

"All wearing their heat-wave gear." That smile had turned to a
wide grin. "And people complain about this weather?"

"Gotta make some calls."

"Radio?"

Dulaney reached into his back pocket and retrieved the small
walkie-talkie the tactical captain had loaned him.

"Okay," said Zeke. "Gonna check on my dispersion. Check
back in fifteen."

"I'll be right here in my air-conditioned office," joked Dulaney,
slapping the burning roof of his Taurus.

Dulaney thanked God the Freon was still circulating in the
sedan's air conditioner. Two seconds after he had turned the ignition key he experienced a refreshing blast of cold air. It wasn't even
11:00 a.m. yet and his body felt exhausted. That venti quad latte
he'd ordered at Starbucks hadn't given him the slightest boost.
He wondered if he had accidentally been slipped some dreaded

decaf. Then he wondered why the hell someone had even *invented* decaf—what was the goddamn point?

While Dulaney checked the digital clock on his dash, he reviewed Zeke's tactical plan. His initial reaction to the "gauntlet" approach was negative. Then once Zeke explained how his unit had been cut to a slim six tactical agents, understanding had begun to trump impatience.

The tac captain's first thought had been to take the suspect at the Palomino shipping facility. But without permission from the owner, who was said to be fishing in Cabo San Lucas, control of the facility couldn't fall to the feds without a court order. And there was too little time for that now.

Plan B involved mapping the two different routes to the site that trucks delivering cargo would be required to travel. By alerting the Department of Water and Power to investigate a potential water main leak, one trucking artery would be temporarily shut down, diverting all traffic through the southwest corner of downtown Long Beach. The slowdown would make it easier to both identify the truck driver and allow for a simple six-man assault. The unsub would be surprised. Handcuffed. Questioned. And processed at L.A. County Jail.

Then came the rapping on his car window. And because the knuckles landed only inches from his ear, it startled Dulaney so seriously he recoiled with comical bug eyes. He heard the cackles of laughter.

"Christ Almighty!" said Dulaney, rolling down the window.

"Should've seen yourself," said Lilly, still having a hard time getting her words out between the fits of laughter. "It's like your whole body just got tased."

"You did that right next to my ear."

"Note to self. Special Agent Dulaney Little scares like a little girl," laughed Lilly.

"What the hell are you doing down here?"

"You're not gonna invite me into your cool, cool car?"

Dulaney glanced at the empty passenger seat, as if he half-expected to find it occupied. Then he reached across and pushed the door open. Lilly waltzed around the front end of the Taurus, slid herself into the car, then smoothed out the wrinkles in her pencil skirt.

"Hot, hot, hot," she said.

"You're in my car," said Dulaney. "So, answer *my* question."

"Which question?"

"Why. Are. You. Here?"

"Supervising."

"What? You don't trust the Bureau to arrest one guy driving a refrigerator truck?"

"All the faith in the world," said Lilly. "Doesn't mean I can't come down to Long Beach and watch."

Crap, said Dulaney to himself, certain there was an angle on the case Lilly Zoller wasn't divulging. And since shit usually traveled downhill, if something were to go sideways, Dulaney was sure he would be the one to get smeared first.

"I call bullshit," said Dulaney.

"Call whatever you want," said Lilly. "You're assigned to the USAO, so whatever I say goes."

Dulaney let his eyes speak his insubordinate thoughts. He readjusted the air conditioning vents in order for the boss lady to get an equal share of the cold air.

"I'm warning you, DL, if you're trying to make my nipples hard I can bust you for harassment."

"Really?"

Lilly volleyed back with nothing but a wicked smile.

"Can I say something off the record?" asked Dulaney.

"Didn't know we were on the record," said Lilly. "But sure. What do you want to know?"

"Do you actually think that every guy in the downtown fed building wants to fuck you?"

Dulaney could tell the question pleased her by the way her eyes briefly widened.

"Only the black dudes," said Lilly, pushing the provocative envelope.

"Oh, man. Now who's harassing who?"

"So, tell me what's going on here," asked Lilly, shifting gears. "Gimme the deets. Leave nothing out."

In the heat of the chase, Gonzo had nearly forgotten to step out of the car. She'd had two opportunities earlier. At a Reseda Boulevard stoplight, only minutes after Lucky had begun to follow the FBI agent. And at the bottom of the freeway off-ramp that eventually emptied into the City of Long Beach. But by then, Gonzo was invested. Like any other cop, she wanted like hell to know what was going to happen next.

It was 11:28 a.m.

Lucky's Charger was parked in the alley next to a Radio Shack, partially obscured by a window repair truck strapped with slab-sized replacement panes. Gonzo, still in the back seat, had a semi-clear view of the Ralph's supermarket parking lot and Dulaney Little's Ford Taurus. She had observed the comings and goings of the uniformed tactical captain and the subsequent arrival of the petite, yet obviously confident, woman in the silk blouse and black pencil skirt. Gonzo could tell she wasn't a cop, nor FBI. Whoever the woman was, she was administrative...and in killer shape. Gonzo took a brief moment to imagine the lady's workout routine. She even went on her phone to tap out a personal reminder to renew her Krav Maga membership. Just glancing at the sharply drawn woman made Gonzo feel thick and out of shape.

Lucky flopped back into the driver's seat.

"You're still here?" he only semi-joked.

"Sticking it out to the arrest," said Gonzo. "Then you're driving me back to South Pas."

The bucket seat creaked as Lucky worked his way into the creases. Next, he unconsciously assisted his chin with extra force left and right to crack his vertebrae. The pops were violent and staccato like a quick volley of gunshots.

"Looks like a six-man tactical squad," said Lucky. "Two safety snipers setting up a crossfire. One on top of the parking garage over yonder. The other on the window cleaner cradle on the high-rise there. Other four are in vans flanking the intersection, so that's my guess for the takedown. Using some Water and Power detour two blocks over to create the squeeze play."

"Sounds to me like the feebs got this handled," said Gonzo.

Once again, Lucky didn't acknowledge her words. As if he were calculating his own federales equation.

"Clocked four unknown players," said Lucky. "Spinner in the black skirt—"

"Spinner? What's that?" Then Gonzo corrected herself. "Know what? Forget it. Don't wanna know."

"Definitely not packing."

"Really? How could you tell?" asked Gonzo with a rhetorical snippiness. There was only one place to hide a weapon in that woman's outfit.

"My guess she's the fuckin' US Attorney we missed yester-day—"

"Woman in the elevator!" said Gonzo, making the connection with the snap of her fingers. "She was so flirting with you, remember?"

"Yeah? Yesterday was such a blur, she coulda been blowing me and I wouldn't have…" Lucky stopped himself, knowing he had crossed the line. "Yeah. You get it."

"Who were the other unknowns?" asked Gonzo, switching gears.

"Middle of the Ralph's lot. One of your taco-lovin' brethren with decent taste in cars. Figure him for some kinda pool guy."

"Wow. Sheriff who's a racial profiler," sneered Gonzo. "Never saw that comin'."

"He's Hispanic. And the tag on his retro Porsche reads: 'Paul, double ocean, Lincoln, George—'"

"Pool guy. Got it. Whatever."

"Guy's a bag of ticks. Witness, informant, something."

"Moving on…" prompted Gonzo,

"Ten o'clock. Street parking. Lexus with a pair of muscle heads with Kevlar under their shirts. All eyeballs too. Not PD. Not federales. Private somethings. No clue why they're on the field of play."

"They with the perp, you think?"

"What for?" Lucky rubbed his face, screwing his fists into his eye sockets. "If they were with our bad guy both woulda gone rabbit by now. No. Interested party. Whatever. If they wanna tangle they'll be easy enough to dodge."

"Dodge?"

"Sorry. Tired," said Lucky, rolling down his window. "Just waitin' for the chopper."

Gonzo let loose a sigh. Yesterday morning she had been jacked up on visions of rotating off the street and into the LAPD flying corps. She could practically feel the controls in her hands. So, how the hell had the last twenty-four hours soured her mojo and made her feel that her air support dream was so far away? She peeked up at the sky, wondering what kind of bird the FBI was using to track the wanted man behind the wheel of the black refrigerator truck. Oh, what surprise the feds had for that SOB. She checked the time on her cell phone, then prayed the bastard was going to be on time. Assuming the arrest would be wrapped up by one, she'd have time to get home for a hardcore workout, a healthy meal with her boy, then homework for both mother and child. Travis with his schoolwork. And Mother Bear with her nose stuck in the *Los Angeles Law Enforcement Helicopter Training Manual.*

The LAPD's fleet of helicopters flew out of their own heliport based atop a parking structure in downtown Los Angeles. The FBI, though, were required to rent a hangar for their two Bell and Howell Nightstalker choppers. The part-time unit was based out of Van Nuys Airport, a geographic bull's-eye smack in the middle of the San Fernando Valley. So, it was pretty much luck that shortly after pilot Mike Lowe took to the air that FBI agent and designated observer Gerry Bland accidentally ID'd the black refrigerator truck.

Bland had been testing the gyroscopically stabilized field glasses and camera, capable of recording digital still images in high definition from a mile away. Soaring at five thousand feet, Bland was getting settled behind his electronic viewfinder, making certain he could accurately read license plate tags while detailing to Pilot Lowe how just once he'd like to use the advanced tech to peep on some of the prick teases who worked on the federal building's sixth floor. Bland had a connection in human resources who, for the simple price of copying him on every dirty photo, would gladly provide each and every necessary address.

"What's our truck?" Bland had asked.

"Black-on-black Peterbilt hauling a fridge trailer."

"Well, kiss my pale ass," Bland had said, eyes still stuck to the field glasses. "What are the chances we got two of the same semis?"

"I wouldn't put the odds too high. Mark the tags and call the chippies."

Chippies. A.k.a. the California Highway Patrol. Bland made the call over the Los Angeles Regional Tactical Communications System (LARTCS) and, quicker than he could say "Peeping Toms Anonymous," was piped into the local CHP dispatch center.

A northbound cop on a motorcycle interceptor, lurking for single-passenger drivers abusing the HOV lanes, got the order and changed direction at Howard Hughes Parkway. Less than a minute later, he had picked up on the target truck about where aircraft on approach to LAX belch trails of exhaust as they cross over the freeway. His instructions were strictly Do Not Approach (DNA), so he slipped behind the left rear axle of another long-haul truck with a refrigeration package—a dirty white Freightliner.

23

Beemer couldn't stop sweating. But it sure as hell wasn't because of the CHP officer gliding his Kawasaki off his left flank. If anything, Beemer was reassured. The bike chippy was using his stolen Freightliner to hide from the black Peterbilt, barely two hundred yards ahead. About every sixty seconds, the cop would peek out from behind Beemer's left bumper to catch a glimpse of the targeted semi rig. After, he would dip behind and slowly edge himself over until he confirmed his visual from the right-hand stripe. Then the chippy would repeat the moves, clueless that he was spitting close to Beemer and the second hot semi.

But why the sudden sweat? It wasn't the Ritalin. He had popped plenty of those without an extra beat of his heart. A virus, maybe? Or possibly a consequence of his predawn hours inhaling that toxic goo he had stirred until his rotator cuffs burned? He could still taste the chemicals on the back of his tongue.

His mind shot backwards to his grunt days in the Corps. Pouring diesel in a honey pot full of shit, setting it aflame, and swirling it with a heavy broomstick until the desert sky was filled with carbonized feces. For days he'd have that gack in his sinuses, smelling it with every intake of air into his lungs.

Was there any love left between Beemer and the Corps? Maybe in some deep moral fibers that still wanted to believe in something...anything. Beemer reminded himself that introspection was for bitches who drank designer vodka and the fags dumb enough to marry 'em. Marines solved their problems with a full clip and no regrets. Or so Sergeant Ronny Scipio had said in that nervy hour before the final assault on Fallujah. He'd been in the front passenger seat of the unit's Humvee. Beemer was behind the wheel, wad of bubblegum working between his molars, ready to plow into the mayhem and do some hella damage in the name of God, country, and his fellow Marines. He would have died that day for Sergeant Scipio or any one of his brothers in arms.

Familiar feelings of betrayal crept out of the dark places in Beemer's psyche and began to scratch at him. Like the first day of his court-martial. It was as if, on that cool morning in Charlotte, North Carolina, everybody in a uniform had locked arms in a conspiracy to lower the coffin lid and nail it shut with Beemer inside, leaving him to kick at the stuffing and run out of oxygen as they lowered him into the grave. A trap.

Beemer wondered if he was driving head-on into another kind of trap. Thus the flood of memories. And possibly the cause for a perspiration so heavy it dampened his clothes.

With permission from his client, Beemer's military-assigned attorney had placed Beem's entire mental health history into evidence. From boyhood through his brief incarceration. Each file proved consistent in diagnosis. The patient in question had a problem with impulse control induced by anger and/or severe anxiety, upon which critical thinking would take a back seat to negative action. The lawyer argued that the Corps had knowledge of Beemer's history and had still accepted him amongst their ranks, even placing him in combat.

In other words, why blame the jackass for braying? Or the snake for wriggling in the grass?

Yet acquittal still appeared unlikely. Then, on the afternoon the verdict was expected, Beemer was introduced to a government contractor who was known to hire directly from the Marines. In lieu of a court-martial, would Beemer be willing to accept a contracting job and return to Iraq?

A deal was struck.

Traveling at sixty-eight miles an hour, Beemer easily calculated that he would pull off at the Seventh Street exit in about ten minutes. It would be maybe another five minutes from the off-ramp to the Palomino shipping yard. He was so close. So very, very close.

Once Dulaney received word from the tactical commander that the probable target truck was en route, he exited his vehicle and crossed the hot parking lot to Rey's vintage Porsche. Only the pool man had slipped out of his convertible and into the air-conditioned supermarket to see if he could secure an iced coffee. Dulaney found Rey in line in the bakery section, a paper service ticket pinched between his fingers. An Indian woman in a maroon Ralph's apron who could barely see over the countertop called out Rey's number. She looked both left and right, called the number once more, then moved on to the next customer.

It was 11:46 a.m.

"He's early," said Dulaney, practically dragging Rey along.

Rey was hustled across a boulevard already choked with detoured vehicles, up a busy sidewalk, and through the doors of a three-story Sports Authority. They skipped the escalator and took the stairs. Rey was doing his best to keep up with the more athletic Dulaney. But that last half flight of stairs made his lungs scream for air.

"Don't have a coronary on me," said Dulaney.

"Out of shape," was all Rey could apologize between gasps for air.

"Good look from over here."

Dulaney led Rey through the hunting and fishing section to a broad span of tinted windows that offered a clean view of the intersection of Queens Avenue and Allen Street, a mere eighty yards away.

"Know how to use these?" asked Dulaney, producing a pair of small binoculars.

"Yeah, sure," said Rey, accepting the specs and bringing them up to his eyes. With his index finger, he rotated the focus wheel until the stoplight came into sharp relief.

"You think you can ID the guy from here?"

"You know, I never said I got a good look at him," said Rey.

"Better look than anybody else."

"S'pose so," said Rey. "He's gonna be comin' from which way?"

"This way. Dead on. Right between these two palm trees."

Rey lowered the glasses and surveyed the landscape. Three medium high-rises squared against a park, a supermarket, and a Chevron gas station, with the Long Beach Harbor beyond and all those container cranes checking off the horizon like long-necked waterfowl built out of Erector Sets. And there, three stories up and defended by a heavy pane of tinted glass, Rey found his nerves settling. He'd become oddly at ease. Feeling safe, even. Rey was in the cradle of the FBI, who in a matter of minutes would be arresting bad guy Greg Beem.

"So, whadda you guys use?" asked Rey.

"Use?" asked Dulaney. "Use for what?"

"Oh, sorry," said Rey, realizing he'd blurted the question without any context whatsoever. "When you...you know...take him away. Do you use regular handcuffs or those zip tie things I always see on TV?"

Dulaney smiled.

"Think regular old handcuffs will do in this situation," said the FBI agent. "But that's up to the tactical cappy." Dulaney pointed out the Long Beach city work van parked on Queens. "See that yellow van?"

"Yeah."

"When your man hits the stoplight, three guys in SWAT gear will pop out of there and—well, you can't see 'em from here—but just inside the office tower there are three more dudes. It'll be over in twenty seconds."

"And the lady in the black skirt?" asked Rey. "She's the one who offered the reward?"

"What reward?" asked Dulaney.

"For the guy who did the murders up north."

If Dulaney's head had been on a spindle, it would've spun.

"There's no reward," said Dulaney.

"Yeah, there is. Was on the morning show."

Dulaney didn't want to believe it. But the instant the word "reward" sprang from Rey's mouth, it stunk of Lilly. What did she know and why in Hades's name hadn't she told her FBI liaison?

"Don't know nothin' but we got a bad guy to ID," said Dulaney. "We're gonna stop the big rig. You're gonna ID him. Tac's gonna do their thing and we're all gonna get on with the weekend. How's that for a plan?"

"Yeah," said Rey, nodding enthusiastically. "Sounds fine by me."

24

Dave Wireman knew the moment was close. From where he'd parked his Lexus a half block away, he had been able to watch the federal unit set up their sting, cutting off one street and diverting traffic into a veritable gauntlet in order to capture the truck-driving killer. Eventually, as the tactical squad split into a pair of three-man teams flanking each side of the intersection, Dave sensed that direct action was mere minutes away.

"Stay with the car," said Dave.

"What do you think I been doin'?" said Terrell, his muscle-strung pal in the passenger seat.

"I'm gonna video from the high spot over there."

Terrell twisted to his right, looking across the small city park that covered an acre between the idling sedan and the Ralph's supermarket.

"The big hook thing over there?" asked Terrell.

"It's an anchor," said Dave.

"Real anchor?"

"Looks like a sculpture of an anchor," said Dave, popping his door open. "I'll climb up behind it. I should get an unobstructed view."

"Don't wanna get closer?" asked Terrell.

"Observe and report."

"I ever tell you that your shit's boring?"

"You gettin' paid?" smirked Dave, mockingly waiting for an answer. And when none came, he simply reached behind the seat to grab the video camera. He let the door swing shut with a luxury car *thunk*, then set a heading into the park toward a maritime sculpture seated atop a three-foot-high slab of gray concrete.

"Your shit's still dull," said Terrell, paying little mind to Dave's trajectory. Instead, he flipped his phone open and checked his Twitter statistics. He had fifty-three followers, down from fifty-five only two hours earlier.

The noon hour neared and Terrell's appetite was screaming to be quenched. He had pushed up the weight on his entire lifting circuit by 15 percent that morning. He had handled most of it without much strain. But that extra set of squats left his quads burning and his stomach set to full growl. There was a Panda Express across the street and four doors up. Terrell suddenly imagined himself waiting out the boring arrest with a take-out box of steaming kung pao chicken. The aroma would be heavenly while he stabbed at the food with a pair of chopsticks and, if luck were on Terrell's side, the Chinese concoction might even stink up Dave's car for a day or two. There was, though, the risk of residual heartburn. He usually quelled that particular side effect of HGH injections with both waking and bedtime doses of over-the-counter antacids. But in his morning haste, he'd forgotten his baggie of pills. Vitamins and supplements, mostly. All part of the bodybuilder's regimen for the ultimate physique.

The Panda called. And Terrell answered, extricating his aching muscles from Dave's Lexus, shutting the door without locking it, and then padding his way up the sidewalk, following his nose in the direction of the Chinese food franchise.

The closer Shorty got to Long Beach, the more the pipe called to him. With the Peterbilt practically on cruise control, it wouldn't have taken much to dip a couple fingers into his vest pocket, remove the three-inch glass tube, load the blackened tip with crystal meth pebbles, and put a flame to it. Yet there was another voice inside that begged him to resist. To prove he could finish one brief job without leaning on the drugs.

The Garmin GPS attached to the dash blinked and directed the veteran driver to the Seventh Street exit. He clutched, downshifted, and descended the ramp, found the light green, and swung south toward the harbor. Scrolling across the bottom of the screen was the destination reminder. Five more minutes to his destination. Five more minutes until Shorty finished the job. Five more minutes and he could steal a guilt-free hit on the pipe. Full load crank followed by a dopamine stupor.

About the time the drug fantasy was in full bloom, Shorty was turning the corner into the homestretch. But his windshield filled with orange signs and a portable lighted display electronically pointing the way to a detour. Beyond, he could see Department of Water and Power vehicles set up on a work site.

Shorty slowed the rig, downshifted once more, then expertly cranked the wheel east onto Queens Avenue. The traffic jam might as well have been a fist to the back of his skull. He instantly began to shake as minutes were added to his subconscious itinerary.

The silly little GPS device attempted to recalculate the new route, then begged Shorty to make a U-turn. Clearly, the device didn't have a clue whether Shorty was behind the wheel of a Prius or a Peterbilt. The Toyota advertised a turning radius of thirty-four feet while the semi would be lucky to carve a circle inside sixty feet.

"Please make the nearest U-turn," asked the electronic female voice.

"Can't you see I'm drivin' a fuckin' semi? Stupid twat!" spat Shorty.

Ahead. The stoplight at Allen Street. From green to yellow to red. Shorty braked the big fridge truck, clutched the gearbox into neutral, and, without thinking, fished into his vest pocket for his pipe. He tapped a small rock of crystal meth into the tip. As he searched for his disposable butane torch to spark a flame, he spotted the cop out of the corner of his eye. A man in black combat fatigues and a bulletproof vest, wielding an assault weapon, launched onto Shorty's front bumper and leveled the rifle at the window. Shorty heard muffled shouting from outside his window. There was another cop on the passenger running board, ready to open the door. At the same moment, there was a sharp rapping of a gun muzzle touching the glass of his driver's side window.

Shorty's initial instinct was to swallow the pipe. Just suck it into his mouth and chew the glass like it was candy, swallow, and damn the consequences to his colon.

Too bad for Shorty Reese. Because putting that meth pipe under the crush of his molars was the very last act of his pathetic, drug-addled life.

The fine black hairs on Rey's arms were at full attention, as if he had just grabbed both poles of a car battery. The electricity of the moment was more exhilarating than he could have imagined. Through that pair of FBI binoculars provided by Agent Dulaney, Rey had watched the entire scene at the intersection unfold. He couldn't believe that just yesterday he had been tangling with his sport-fishing big brother over a shipping gone wrong. Rey had feared for both his and his longtime girlfriend's lives. Then as he'd stood over a dining room table stacked with unpaid bills, he had found himself sinking ever deeper into a pit from which he may have never recovered.

But it was his dead son, Danny, whom Rey credited for reaching down and offering him a hand up. The news report about the murders in Kern County followed by his call to the FBI. And though it seemed to take days to get through the one sleepless night, Rey couldn't believe his good luck in going from criminal conspirator to assisting in the arrest of a suspect in a multiple murder. It was as if since Danny had been killed in Afghanistan, Rey had been on the lookout for something good to believe in. Little did he know that "the good" was within himself.

"Can you see the driver yet?" asked Dulaney.

Rey spun the focus wheel on the telephoto specs. The black rig was easing up to a stoplight turned red.

"There's some kind of reflection," said Rey. He anticipated the truck driver was just about to come into some recognizable detail when the windshield appeared to fill with sunlight. "And now I can't see anything."

Dulaney's eyes instantly tracked the sun, realizing the office building next door, with its windows polished to a mirror finish, was bouncing the high-noon rays directly onto the intersection.

"I don't have a positive yet," barked Dulaney into his radio. "We've got an obscured windshield."

"We can't hold the stoplight," squawked the tactical captain.

"Aw, hell…Move in. Arrest and hold," said Dulaney, snatching the field glasses from Rey.

Rey was disappointed. He had so wanted to witness the arrest. Without binoculars, he would miss it all. Later, Rey would realize, this was his moment. Because he was in the hunting and fishing section of the Long Beach Sports Authority, he instantly made a simple calculation. Within steps of the window, there must have been a display case filled with field glasses, plus rifles and spotting scopes. And, hell! Rey was with the FBI. Surely a salesperson wouldn't deny him a quick test-drive.

So, Rey wheeled a quick one-eighty, seeking out the nearest available salesperson to assist him in testing a telephoto device.

Rey's back was to the window.

Dulaney, meanwhile, watched through his own binoculars as the takedown unfolded. Six FBI tac cops, weapons raised, rushed the paused semi from both sides. One of the tac cops mounted the front bumper and leveled his weapon. Two more took position in the street while two others climbed onto the truck's footboards.

Then the image through Dulaney's specs suddenly blurred. As if, from the inside out, the black refrigerated Peterbilt were erasing itself.

25

"Stay in the damn car!" said Lucky. The words were meant to be his very last to Gonzo. And once his back was turned, he never expected to see her again.

"What do you think you're doing?" asked Gonzo, having barely enough air in her lungs to get the words out. She was launching herself into the passenger door, pushing it open, and finding her feet on the ground as fast as humanly possible. When she spun around to look over the roof of the Charger, Lucky was already striding across the street.

"Goddammit, stop!" shouted Gonzo, jamming her legs into chase mode. She nearly ate the asphalt as her boots slid underneath her. Lucky, though, was not running. He was well underway, walking at a sharp clip toward the intersection.

Having spotted the helicopter banking into a tight arc

overhead, Lucky took his cue. That's why, despite the oppressive heat, his window had been rolled down. He had been waiting for the sound of the rotors. He knew that there would be a black Peterbilt truck some fifteen hundred feet below the chopper. Lucky was on his feet before clocking the refrigerated rig coming from the west. But once he locked his eyeballs onto the chrome air horns atop the semi's cab, he ordered Gonzo to stay with the car and began angling for the intersection. Lucky's right hand instinctively reached backward, lifted his T-shirt to find the butt of his .45. By the time Gonzo dashed past Lucky and turned to block his path, the weapon was coolly hanging bootlegged next to his thigh.

"You're not gonna!" Gonzo shouted. Lucky merely sidestepped her and picked up his pace. Gonzo met him shoulder to shoulder. "You're exhausted and in grief. You are not thinking!"

And when Gonzo tried to circle around in front of him once more, Lucky just stiff-armed her and tried to spin her out of the way. Instead, Gonzo windmilled from her shoulder, slipped an elbow inside, and popped two open palm heels into his chest. Her intent was to shock the Kern cop out of his trance.

Lucky recoiled into a modified firing stance, pistol muzzle trained at Gonzo's face, his left hand reaching out in her direction.

"Move! Now!" barked Lucky.

"Gonna have to waste a bullet on me if you wanna shoot up an arrest scene."

"You stupid BITCH! GET THE FUCK—"

Lucky didn't hear the explosion as much as feel it. The shock wave hit his face like a hot blast slapping him at a thousand miles per hour. As he felt his weight thrown backwards, the crown of Gonzo's head thumped in his chest with an impact that felt like a ship's cannonball fired broadside.

Then Lucky blacked out.

The mixture had been the hardest part. There would be no ballparking the percentages. At least Beemer knew how to make the numbers work. Nine parts ammonium nitrate fertilizer to point-six parts fuel oil. Then stir, seal, and hope to hell gross fatigue hadn't affected his calculations.

The plan itself had formed quickly. No sooner had Beemer escaped the fast-evolving estrogen party at Rey Palomino's than his intent to harm suddenly materialized into a step-by-step plot. The result would be both a distraction to the feds from his truckload of blood money and would place the stink of suspicion on the hapless pool man. With only hours to accomplish the feat, it was imperative that he keep his anger and sense of betrayal suppressed just enough so his head remained clear and his actions concise.

Both the fertilizer and fuel oil could be procured either north at the southern end of the San Joaquin Valley or west in the agricultural belt located between the old California towns of Moorpark and Oxnard. The ammonium nitrate would be easy enough to ferret out of some farmer's storage shed, which was precisely what Beemer did. But fuel oil is usually in greater supply east of the Rockies, where it's used to heat homes. The veteran then remembered that fuel oil was also utilized to power smudge pots—or choofas—six-foot-tall orchard heaters used on freezing nights to keep frost from settling on the delicate buds of fruit trees.

So, Beemer had motored west and dumped the stolen Honda at a truck stop, where he promptly replaced it with the refrigerated Freightliner. He reckoned he had until daylight before some migrant strawberry picker discovered the driver's body in an irrigation ditch. Throat slit ear to ear. By then Beemer would have returned to his abandoned Burbank warehouse and begun his alchemy project.

Then it would be all about the size of the *pop*.

A fertilizer bomb—or ANFO bomb, in the parlance of the jackboots over at the Bureau of Alcohol, Tobacco, Firearms, and Explosives—was considered a threat to national security ever since Timothy McVeigh unleashed his hellish brand of patriotic revenge on the poor occupants of the Murrah Federal Building in Oklahoma City. Unfortunately, the chemical compost was popular with farmers and fuel oil heated half the homes in the American Midwest. So, as much as the government kept tabs on the sale of both fertilizer and fuel, they couldn't be quick enough on the uptake to stop a man who stole the components, mixed the brew, and lit the fuse within a matter of hours. By the time the feds sifted through the wreckage, Beemer figured his frozen blood products would have shipped out of the port at Mazatlan, Mexico. After that, he could hook up to the internet from just about anywhere in the world and find amusement in all the conspiracy theories trying to explain such a deadly attack.

Beemer had left the final cocktail to congeal inside three blue chemical barrels Gorilla-glued to the floor of the Peterbilt's refrigerator trailer. His muscles were so cold and fatigued from transferring all the blood product to the Freightliner that when it came time to fold the fertilizer in with the fuel oil—carefully counting each scoop from an old coffee can—his right arm shook almost uncontrollably, spilling the green ammonium pellets into the deep brown liquid. He mixed the final brew with an old broomstick and scraped the leftover brown goo off the bottom of his Nikes.

It was approximately around the time the chippy on the Kawasaki was using the old Freightliner for camouflage that the first tickle of doubt crossed Beemer's subcortex. The anger, which had taken second place to process, was barely warm on a mental back burner. Fear was now entering the equation.

Aw, fuck. What if the igniter didn't work?

The whole big bang relied on a crude firing circuit activated by a throwaway cell phone. Two battery wires were rerouted through a three-inch coil of monofilament wire wrapped around a handful of wooden match heads. The phone and the rest of the matches were in a dry plastic baggie suspended just beneath the surface of the ANFO gel. When Beemer dialed the number, the circuit would activate, igniting the matches and, theoretically, detonating instantly. The crude mobile apparatus was a favorite of Iraqi insurgents and their IEDs. But they were known to fail sometimes.

Yup. The *aw, fuck* moment Beemer had so earnestly crafted for Rey-the-FBI-loving-pool-man was residing on technology reserved for a bunch of towel-headed stone-tossers. Where was plan B if the baggie had sprung a leak and turned the exposed match heads into sulfuric mush?

There was no time for so much as a retreat. Beemer wheeled onto the Seventh Street off-ramp. His distance from the black Peterbilt was still about a quarter mile. Once he'd hit the first stoplight, the trailing motorcycle patrolman had surged around his left front bumper and roared off to tighten the leash on the target truck. Beemer flipped a coin in his head. It was a matter of chance whether or not the chippy would survive the next five minutes.

The DWP detour was a surprise, but not entirely unexpected. And before Beemer had even committed to the left turn onto Queens Avenue, he was able to glimpse the intersection a mere eighth of a mile to the east, where the FBI had surely set up its gauntlet. That's where he would have set up an ambush. Plenty of cover. A funnel of vehicles to slow traffic to an easy, manageable stroll. Perfect.

Beemer would have preferred to make a U-turn. But the Freightliner was barely able to negotiate a ninety-degree left. Two hundred feet beyond was an alleyway between a remodeled five-story office tower with a "now leasing" banner and a Bob's Big Boy franchise. Vehicles traveling from the opposite direction were few. The only obstacle was the five-yard-wide grass meridian that striped the middle of the boulevard.

Sure. Somebody might notice a big white tractor-trailer rig busting over a six-inch grassy patch. But the following explosion would likely distract and distort any memory. Plus, by the time everybody dug out, Beemer would be asleep with his arms wrapped around an empty bottle of south-of-the-border mescal.

The Freightliner's shocks compressed and the springs in the driver's bucket seat gnashed and bucked as Beemer wheeled the rig onto the meridian. He downshifted, gassed the diesel engine, and pointed the front end at the nearby alley. Next, he grabbed his iPhone. It was set for a one-touch speed dial. Like all violent actions, it all came down to a trigger moment. Shoot, don't shoot. Kill, don't kill. Beemer had never, ever flinched at such a crossroads.

He pressed the button. He heard the phone dial through the tiny speaker.

The starboard side of the Freightliner scraped the alley's cinderblock wall. A tighter fit than he had imagined. Nonetheless, the truck slid between the buildings. He popped the shifter out of gear, set the brake, and waited to feel the earth shake.

Nothing.

The only shaking Beemer detected was the shudder of the diesel engine begging for an ounce more of fuel.

Did I miss the pop?

Checking his side-view mirrors, he saw road, wall, palm trees, and meandering cars.

Beemer kicked the door open until it cracked the stucco side of the Bob's Big Boy. He slipped downward until he felt asphalt under his feet. A quick exam of his iPhone screen showed it fully engaged and connecting with the correct ten-digit number. And then, the message, "Cell signal fail."

Beemer prepared to hang up and redial, all the while gently picking up his pace alongside the Freightliner's refrigerated trailer.

He pressed End on the iPhone's touch screen and peeked his head out of the mouth of the alleyway. From his vantage point he could see the outline of the black Peterbilt, held up by the power of a red stoplight. Then in rushed three armed tactical cops hustling out of a storefront and across the sidewalk.

He looked to the iPhone screen, straightened his index finger, and carefully aimed at the redial function.

Beemer never got a second chance to press the button.

26

The destructive power of an ANFO bomb is not the resulting incendiary effect. There's a flash, but no fireball. The speed at which the ammonium nitrate and fuel oil combust is triple the rate of dynamite's, forming a catastrophic shock wave that turns tempered glass into popcorn and can easily rupture unprotected eardrums.

For those close enough to watch, the shock wave moves faster than the snap of a finger. Usually, it requires a slow-motion camera to capture such a rapid displacement of air. Only at a distance and in the cleanest of atmospheres can the naked eye witness the expanding bubble.

Pilot Mike Lowe missed it, instantly jockeying the stick to keep the helicopter from spinning out of orbit. But observer Gerry Bland had a clean view, catching the shock wave from the ignition's center and witnessing it spreading outward from the intersection, crashing into the buildings like a tsunami of angry air, following the path of least resistance down the boulevards and out to the ocean.

In later FBI reports, the observer would describe his overhead view of the bomb eruption like that of watching a flower bloom in one of those nature channel films on botany. Filmed in stop frame and sped up for effect. From a tiny bud to petals fully flexed in the near blink of an eye.

When the shock wave hit the helicopter, it instantly pushed the aircraft up another eighty feet. A lesser pilot might have panicked and overcorrected. But while Bland found his heart suddenly pressed up against his sternum, the expert jockey at the controls nosed the copter off the bubble as if surfing a wave while simultaneously keying his mic.

"Base. Be advised. We have a detonation of some kind of large explosive device…"

Lilly Zoller had to pee.

While seated in Dulaney's car, she cursed her tiny bladder for not being able to hold the gallons of water she consumed as part of her daily habit. Coupled with the diuretic nature of all that coffee she sucked back every dawn, she had become as used to holding her liquid as visiting the toilet. But the pressure in her abdomen was building. As much as she wanted to be present for the thrill of the takedown, she worried that her moment might be ruined by ill-timed cramping. She wrestled with herself. Go now? Go later? Finally, she chose to risk missing the climax, leaped from the car, and scuffled practically pigeon-toed straight for the green awnings of that nearby Starbucks, praying like hell the cafe's one bathroom wasn't occupied by a coffee-addicted new mother with a baby to change.

She later recalled reaching for the bathroom door handle at the exact second the lever turned in her hand without assistance. An overstuffed barista in a black apron that barely tied around her middle popped out of the unisex toilet.

"Excuse me," said the barista.

Lilly swallowed, concerned that in her step backward she might have leaked a cc or two of urine into her panties. She pulled the door closed behind her, twisted the lock, hiked up her skirt, and sat without regard.

The concussion from the ANFO bomb nearly knocked her off the commode. Acoustic shavings shook from the ceiling. Lilly's first inclination was that it was one of those local quakes that hit with little to no buildup, shaking the earth's surface with a singular merciless jolt, leaving most Angelenos momentarily breathless.

But locals didn't scream after such shocks. And that's just what Lilly heard from both patrons and employees in the shop, their shouts muffled by the bathroom door.

Lilly couldn't recall if she had even finished her business. She lowered her skirt and threw the door open. The Starbucks was fogged by concrete dust. Nearly all the glass from the windows was in piles of shards on the floor. Pedestrians with shirt fabric bunched over their faces scurried west while Lilly stepped onto the sidewalk, blinking to clear her contact lenses. Then her right heel sank into something soft. Fleshy, even. As if stepping on a sleeping dog. She half expected her own mutt, Dingo, to yelp and snap at her. Instead, she spun and looked down, discovering the face-down body of a muscled man, a piece of chrome sunk deep into the back of his skull, a barely eaten box of Panda Express kung pao chicken spilled next to him. The blood slick around him was ever-expanding like a deep red mu shu sauce.

"DULANEY!" Lilly shouted, twisting back toward the intersection.

That onshore sea breeze coastal residents had been waiting for began to show signs of life. As the airborne debris slowly dissolved, Lilly stood in slack-jawed wonder. Before her was a scene of urban destruction. Cars twisted and turned upside down. The sides of buildings looked sandblasted, most of them blown out and their veneers stripped of stucco and brick.

The intersection was flanked by stoplight standards, spun into industrial art. And ground zero, where there was once a shiny black

Peterbilt tractor-trailer rig, was now a depression in the asphalt. Not quite a hole. More like a fifteen-by-ten-meter footprint littered with various vehicle parts, none bigger than a toaster. The rest of the truck was gone or scattered amongst strips of skin and unidentifiable body parts.

"Jesus hell..." muttered Lilly.

Rey hadn't seen the explosion. While seeking a Sports Authority salesperson to loan him a pair of field specs, he had felt the shock wave hit him like a baseball bat across his shoulder blades, forcing him to his knees. This was followed by a hot wind and rain of tempered glass. Instantly, Rey felt a wasp-like sting on the back of his neck. He reached back and gently pinched a sliver of glass near his hairline, twisting it free then examining it on the tip of his index finger, the quick-drying blood acting like glue.

"Motherfucker!" cried Dulaney, his voice soaked in agony.

The call might as well have hooked Rey by the hypothalamus and reeled him forty feet across the floor to the injured FBI man. Dulaney was supine with his fingertips trembling near his bloody face. Tempered glass shards were nearly symmetrically embedded in his blue-black skin. Like raspberry rhinestones.

"Can you see?" asked Rey.

"I don't know..." Dulaney painfully blinked. "Yeah. Yeah, I kinda think I can. Think the binoculars..."

"They're right here. What about 'em?"

"Saved my eyes."

"'Kay. But don't move. Your face."

"Wrong with my face?"

"Glass in it."

"Right, right," said Dulaney. "Did you see it?"

"Did I see what?"

"Bomb."

"No. Felt it, though. Where'd it come from?"

"Truck."

"What truck?"

"Our truck…Your bad guy…is a terrorist."

Terrorist? Rey couldn't process it. Instructions were traveling across his mental news ticker: get cell phone; dial 911.

Rey stood, fumbled around his pocket for his cell phone, and pressed the number nine. While his phone speed-dialed, he finally gave a look outside the evaporated window. The destruction was awe-inspiring in its efficiency. A single bomb had, in a matter of moments, rearranged the urban and seaside paradise into a scene usually reserved for Rey's extra-wide TV screen. He could have been staring out over the streets of Baghdad or Kabul. And the sounds too. A cacophony of car and fire alarms intermingled with the growing wail of fire and police sirens.

"Holy shit," Rey said of the scene. "What have I done?"

The way Dave Wireman figured it, the blast wave must have carried him twenty feet in the air. One moment he was adjusting his video camera from his perch atop the maritime statue, the next he was reeling backwards. And he remembered every millimeter of the ride, which ended with him landing squarely on his back in a soft patch of Bermuda grass. Dave felt the gas escape his lungs and the temporary paralysis as the proverbial wind was knocked out of him. He rolled to his side, wheezed for oxygen, and was on his feet with a rather speedy grace. He scooped up the video camera without checking to see if it had survived the impact and hauled tail back toward his parked Lexus.

It was all such a damned blur. A soundless scurry into the driver's seat. Though his hands were vibrating, he didn't hear the jangle of his keys or the sound of the eight-cylinder engine catching. It was half feel for the private eye, half instinct. Whatever had just happened, whatever he had just borne witness to, was way bigger than the job he had signed up for. The last thing he cared to be was a public witness to an obvious terror attack on American real estate.

"Shit, shit, shit, shit," he kept saying over and over like a Hindu mantra. Only he couldn't make out his own freaking words.

And Terrell? Dave Wireman didn't even think to ask himself or any other horrified passerby where he might be. He merely jacked the luxury car into gear, swung the steering wheel into U-turn mode, and threaded his way onto a side street.

Dave began laying on his horn to urge curious pedestrians, running either to or from ground zero, to get out of his way. That was when he first noticed something else that was wrong. He could hear nothing. Not the sound blasting from behind his grill or the screams coming from the anguished faces he was trying so hard not to run down.

With a quick adjustment of his rearview mirror, Dave saw blood trickling from both his ears. A sure-assed sign that his eardrums had ruptured.

"Shit, shit, shit!" he screamed, only registering the vibration of his curses inside his cranium. "I'm fucking deaf!"

Dave needed a doctor. A hospital. And an emergency room to fix him. But the hospitals would be overrun with victims. There would be cops and questions about who he was, what he was doing at the crime scene, and who he was working for. Screw that. His ears could wait. He would drive back to L.A. In forty minutes he could be at Cedars Sinai Medical Center in Beverly Hills. By then he would have a story to explain his bloody condition.

So Dave drove, wrestling with his brain in his own sad silence. And while he wondered if he would ever be able to listen to his Steely Dan records again, his cell phone rang and rang and rang and rang…

After leaving three messages in three minutes on Dave Wireman's voicemail, a frustrated Garvin Van Der Berk spun his cell phone across his desktop while unmuting the sound on his television. As was his habit while working alone in his two-room art deco West Hollywood office suite, he kept his TV on and tuned to one of the national finance channels. He would tell clients that the constant background chatter was just him keeping an eye on the markets. That he had investments to monitor. If that were only half true.

There had indeed been a time when the high-profile private eye was a player with a sturdy financial portfolio built from profits and insider stock tips from grateful clients. But one of those customers was invested heavily with Bernard Madoff, the famed New York master of the Ponzi scheme. Garvin was kissed into the deal and, within three years, had moved all his liquid assets into the doomed fund. Adding to his further bad luck, he had signed his final divorce agreement only months before the Ponzi scheme's bubble had burst so publicly. His wife got the hard assets—house, cars, and the condo in Palm Desert—while Garvin had hung on to the investment portfolio. Oops.

Nearly all that Garvin had left was his name, the private detective shingle, and his image as La La Land's super-successful private detective to the stars.

Thus the television served more as something to keep him company during the long hours slogging through the piles of unglamorous reading that his job required.

In the twenty-four-hour news cycle, reports of violent events usually begin with a trickle from one source, which expands to a slow stream and eventually unplugs into an avalanche of coverage with very little detail. The bomb blast in Long Beach seemed to blitzkrieg onto local and national stations in a matter of seconds. News anchors scrambled for information while traffic helicopters were rerouted from freeway tie-ups to cover the expanding smoke cloud just off the harbor.

Garvin had left his desk and was retrieving a reduced-calorie grape Gatorade from his mini fridge disguised as a retro wall safe when he heard the breathless news voice talking about some kind of large explosion in Long Beach. Why Garvin checked his watch, he didn't know. It was eleven minutes after noon.

There were a thousand logical reasons why there could be some kind of fiery conflagration in Long Beach, he reasoned. First of all, it was possible the report of the location was erroneous. There was a large petroleum refinery south of the city and just to the north were acres and acres of natural gas wells. The most likely explanation was that there had been some sort of industrial accident. And if that wasn't it, there were the millions of tons in cars and trucks that maneuvered through the vicinity daily. The harbor itself served as the busiest port in the entire United States. Even before 9/11, authorities had warned that it was only a matter of time before terrorists used a shipping container to deliver a bomb to American shores.

With that, Garvin gazed across his corridor-like office to the television screen. Without his glasses, he had trouble focusing more than five feet away. On top of that, the late morning sun had hit its peak, blasting off the solar panels mounted like sentries on the roof of the design gallery next door. Garvin reset the vertical blinds until the glare was redirected to his wall of fame—a space dedicated and chockablock with framed five-by-seven photos of grinning Garvin arm in arm with every celebrity he had ever worked for.

Garvin broke the safety cap on the Gatorade, coated his throat with grape goodness, then returned his specs to his face. There was a live helicopter image of downtown Long Beach bordered in an array of up-to-the-minute market figures. The camera, optically zoomed from three thousand feet above, scoured the post-explosion geography—the overturned cars and gashed hunks of steel surrounding a smoking gouge in the earth.

"Son of a bitch..." said Garvin to nobody but himself before rushing to his computer and googling the address he had received from Conrad Ellis. In a matter of seconds, a satellite map appeared. As the image crystallized and zeroed in on the intersection, all doubt was vanquished. Whatever event had shaken the attention of the cable news world was somehow connected to the murder of young Nickelodeon actress Pepper Ellis.

"Damn, damn, damn."

Garvin picked up his cell phone and, once again, dialed Dave Wireman.

27

Victims of the blast were split between Long Beach Memorial and St. Mary's Medical Center, which was a mere three city blocks from ground zero. Triage teams of nurses and doctors, designated by post-9/11 preparedness, leaped into the messy job of separating the medically savable from those most likely to succumb to their injuries.

St. Mary's, the smaller of the two hospitals, was overrun. While the emergency room was choked with bleeding victims surrounded by a growing corps of medical personnel, the lobby was repurposed for triage. Those without life-threatening issues were shunted into the first- and second-floor corridors, where they were left unattended, waiting on gurneys and rollaway beds parked flush against the walls.

"Screw this," said Gonzo. "I'm good to go home."

But in looking at her, Lucky didn't think so. She had been lying flat on her back for an hour, neck in a foam cervical immobilizer. Lucky hadn't left her side, pulling a medical waste bin from a bathroom to serve as a short stool next to the gurney on which the EMTs had carefully placed her. A triage nurse had assigned her to the survivor column and gladly accepted Lucky's offer to act as a medical assistant. So he wheeled his temporary partner into an open slot between a unisex restroom and an elevator bank.

"Neck compressions," said Lucky. "Let's not forget the concussion."

"So what? I have a sore neck. And you don't know I have a concussion."

"You were out for a good five minutes. Call it a qualified guess."

Somewhere underneath her skin Gonzo knew she needed an MRI of her neck—that her gray matter had received a serious shake when the top of her head had connected with Lucky's sternum.

"How's your chest?"

"Sore. But I can breathe."

"You should get an X-ray."

"Think I'm at the back of the line."

Lucky couldn't have been more understated. A cracked breastbone wasn't anywhere near the same zip code as the ailments suffered by the casualties surrounding him. In any case, the treatment would be little more than rest and a two-week course of anti-inflammatories.

Still, his skull felt like it was going to split open without a strong dose of caffeine and Excedrin. As an excuse, he offered to find Gonzo a bag of ice for the lump on her scalp.

"Gonna find the cafeteria," said Lucky. "Be back in a minute."

"Hey," said Gonzo once Lucky's back was to her. She waited for him to turn around and face her. The question was nagging her. "All along. Were we chasing a terrorist?"

"Dunno. I was just lookin' for the guy that popped my little brother."

"But the terrorist thing. That would explain the FBI, right?"

"Got a few questions too," said Lucky. "Lemme go get you that ice first."

Questions demanding answers that would surely come about as quickly as sucking cement through a straw. Or so decided Lucky. That's because the feds were in charge. And they shared information like a wolf shares his kill.

The hospital cafeteria shared the basement with the radiology and imaging department. Windowless and painted saffron and pale gray in an effort to lighten up its submarine-like atmosphere, it was strangely occupied by a growing contingent of news and media personnel forbidden by the hospital from interviewing patients until they'd been cleared.

Lucky asked the cashier for a pair of plastic bags and placed one inside the other as he cut the line to the soda dispenser. But when Lucky depressed the lever to release an expected torrent of cubed ice, the motor whined and produced nothing but an annoying noise.

He wanted to complain.

And not just about the empty ice maker. His mind flooded with grievances. Free-associating from Filipino nurses to unrelenting gasoline prices to physicians who think because they graduated from med school they have a right to talk to you like you're a moron.

"Is this broken or—"

"Comin' with more buckets," said one of the undocumented cafeteria Oompa Loompas. "Ice very soon."

"How soon?"

"Coming soon."

"Might've exhausted his command of the language," said the man at Lucky's three o'clock.

Lucky agreed with a nod, then grumbled out of the side of his mouth. "Lowered expectations. The key to us all getting along."

"Doncha know it, brother."

Lucky glimpsed at the man, expecting some blue-collar video jockey who worked for one of the local news stations. Instead, he was nearly alarmed to see a haggard fellow with bloody gauze glued to half his face, an arm hanging limp from a denim jacket, and a bloody right knee showing through a pair of dirty dungarees.

"Shouldn't you be in line to see a doctor?"

"Hell yeah," said Beemer, clueless as to whom he was addressing. "But looks like my injuries are the survivable type so they stuck me in a wheelchair and left me this."

Beemer held up his own bag for ice, only most of it had melted into a dirty soup.

"I gotcha," said Lucky. "But aren't you afraid you're gonna lose your spot in the patient queue?"

"Screw that," said Beemer. "I'm gettin' more ice and walkin' out. Nothin' I got can't be fixed by a Korean doc with a needle and thread."

Lucky regarded the man.

"Yeah, I know," said Beemer. "Looks like I got into somethin' outside a bar. But no. Turned the corner and whammo."

"The blast wave?"

"Goddamn Bob's Big Boy fell on me."

"Bob's—"

"You know. That fat boy holding the hamburger."

Lucky rewound his memory to his counterclockwise loop around ground zero. He recalled seeing the Bob's Big Boy diner. He'd gotten a noseful of some kind of bread baking. Sweet. He'd questioned if he was hungry enough to stop and eat something just moments before pushing on with his reconnaissance.

"One second I'm walkin'," continued Beemer. "And the next this big plastic statue drops me. Next thing I know I'm in an ambulance comin' here."

"Did you see the explosion?"

Beemer shook his head. "But somebody here said it was a terrorist thing," added Beemer. "Suicide bomb. That right?"

Lucky showed no response. It was a mystery to him why the murdering SOB had blown himself and Lord knows how many others to unholy hell. But then again he had stopped questioning the motives swimming inside the minds of criminals after the little sister of a gunned-down Grape Street Crip drove her Mercury

Sable through a bus stop crowded with what she thought were Compton Bloods. Instead, they were part of a high school Christmas choir on their way home from a middle school performance in Baldwin Hills.

"Can you believe that shit? Here? In America?" asked Beemer.

A thin streak of blood trickled down Beemer's arm, across the inside of his left wrist and his circled tattoo, spiraled around his thumb, built up into a gravity drop, then splatted onto the floor.

"Might be better off hangin' around," said Lucky, gesturing to the man's obvious injuries. "Seein' a real doctor."

"Thanks. But all I need right now is some more ice."

"Hope you leave your name with the cops. 'Cause they're gonna need to talk to you," said Lucky. "You were there. You're a witness."

"You work for the hospital?"

"Deputy sheriff. Kern County."

"Sure, I know Kern. Kinda far from home, aren't ya?"

"Long story."

"Listen," pleaded Beemer. "I didn't see nothin' but Bob's Big Ass droppin' on me."

"That's what you think, but you never know," said Lucky. "All I'm sayin' is that you should stick around to—"

"Know what I am?" said Beemer, leaning in closer to Lucky, his voice dipping into a hush. "I'm a truck driver who's behind on his child support. So it's my lousy luck I get wrong-turned into a traffic jam. If I hadn't gotten out to check my tail lights…"

"I'm sure whoever you're haulin' for will understand—"

"Dude. Thanks for the advice. But I got an old Freightliner fulla frozen peas and maybe an hour left of fuel before it all turns to guacamole."

"The load ain't covered by insurance?"

"Sure as shit it is. But my salary? Not a chance."

Lucky scanned across Beemer's eyes, looking for dilated pupils behind the dangling strands of sweaty hair. But the redness from bloodshot hours of driving gave away nothing.

"Where's your destination?"

"San Diego."

From his breast pocket, Lucky produced a business card and a ballpoint pen with the phone number of a Bakersfield taxi service silk-screened on the barrel.

"Name, address, and contact info," suggested Lucky. "I'll pass it on to the FBI in case they need another witness."

Beemer bent over and scribbled a bogus name, address, email, and telephone number.

"There you go," said Beemer, handing the card back to Lucky. "Got one for me?"

"You want a card?"

"In case I remember something," said Beemer. "Oh, wait. Maybe I should just call the FBI? Or do I call the local cops? Like Long Beach PD?"

"Never hurts to call everybody," said Lucky, fishing for another Kern County Sheriff's business card. The acceptance of which was interrupted by the crashing of a bus tub full of ice being dumped into the soda machine.

"Finally!" said Beemer, who was quick to refill his plastic bag. "Nice meeting you…"

"Detective Dey," said Lucky. "It's on the card."

"Right. Cool. Thanks."

Beemer raised his bag of ice in a farewell salute, stepped out of the cashier's line, and slipped away.

Lucky released a few half gallons of fresh ice into his plastic bags, twisted the tops into knots, then made his way out of the cafeteria. Yet something nagged at him about that five-minute encounter with the wounded stranger. He recalled some advice his training officer had drilled into him during his first weeks at Lennox. All cops are installed with a bullshit detector. Trust it with your life.

Lucky's bullshit detector was pinging.

Not necessarily an unusual occurrence. Lucky had pegged the truck driver as a drug user of some kind. Probably holding.

The average Joe with a Ziploc full of weed usually tripped Lucky's alarm the moment he discovered Lucky had a sheriff's shield in his back pocket.

Lucky was gassed. Operating on empty. He needed to get the ice back to Gonzo, arrange her return to Pasadena and her boy, Travis, then begin his way back to Kern County, where he'd have to face the dreadful tragedy of burying his little brother.

28

Beemer was so spooked by his run-in with the Kern deputy, he decided to forgo the elevator and take the stairs back to the first floor. Descending them made his right knee want to bellow in pain. Beemer's dust-up with that Bob's Big Boy statue had dislocated his patella, exposing what little meniscus tissue he had left to excruciating punishment with every simple step. But he couldn't stop thinking of the cop from Kern fucking County.

He was plenty familiar with the counties of California—particularly Kern—because when plotting his route from Reno to Long Beach, he'd planned to spend a significant number of predawn hours cruising the back highways of Mono, Inyo, and then Kern County. Precisely the same real estate where he'd been delayed by a flipped Porsche SUV and a ready Eddie deputy who'd innocently asked the truck driver for assistance.

His exhausted brain reeled. He knew that both the LAPD and FBI had been on to him. That they'd been hooked into him by Danny Palomino's asshole dad. He'd seen the trap, drawn them all together, and unleashed hell upon them. But how in Moses does a deputy sheriff from bumfuck Kern County make it into the mix so damned quickly? Was it because he'd killed a cop? He decided it didn't matter—everyone probably thinks he evaporated himself with two hundred pounds of ANFO.

The past two hours might have been the most excruciating of Beemer's thirty years. From the few minutes following his abandonment of the Freightliner truck and from every step he traveled eastward in hope that he could trigger his fertilizer bomb, to the breathless moments he'd traded post-apocalyptic small talk with a Kern County Sheriff's deputy. Every second of it had been more emotionally hellish than all his days fighting Middle Eastern insurgents.

The explosion itself had been shock enough to the system. The blast wave had caught him by surprise, sending him hurtling backward into the comical figure of Bob's Big Boy. In an effort to protect his eyes from the debris, he'd twisted his neck hard to his left, not realizing how close he'd been standing next to the rough stucco exterior walls of the restaurant. He could only imagine the skid mark his torn flesh had left behind.

Though he didn't recall it, Beemer's knee must have also contacted the same surface, tearing a credit card–sized hole in his jeans and forcing his kneecap to rotate out of joint. Once he'd come to his senses—Lord knows how many clock-turns after the detonation—he was already being attended to by an off-duty paramedic who, moments earlier, had been mulling over the decision to order the Super Big Boy Combo for lunch or the huevos rancheros as a second breakfast.

The twisted irony that the man who'd concocted and set off the devastating bomb would be one of the very first to be rescued by EMTs was lost on both men.

Before Beemer had wits enough to protest, he'd already been strapped to a stretcher, loaded into an ambulance, and delivered to St. Mary's Medical Center. Before long he was just waiting for the most inconspicuous moment to get up and walk out of the hospital. He knew the Freightliner, if still undiscovered, would be operating on little fuel—its precious cargo in danger of spoiling if left unattended for much longer.

Beemer was easily able to pocket vials of both the anesthetic numbing agent Lidocaine and the narcotic pain reliever Demerol along with a few disposable hypodermics to manage his pain. His one error was the detour to the cafeteria to refill his melted bag of ice. But that had been all he could imagine would assist in relieving the aching his neck had suffered from tangling with Bob's Big Boy and his platter full of plastic burgers.

On the hellish mile-and-a-half walk back to the scene of the crime, Beemer had to slip into an alleyway and behind a dumpster twice to jam a fresh needle full of Lidocaine under his crooked kneecap. He calculated that the needles must be missing the proper nerve or else the horrible pain would've subsided to a dull ache. Instead, with every flex it raged like there was boiling grease in the joint. Beemer would have to rely on his post-military experience. He'd been inches from being court-martialed out of the service. But then he'd been resurrected as a private operator and re-immersed in a training regimen culled from the Navy SEALS. He'd learned to bury his pain and push his body to greater levels of endurance. So what was a sharp pain in the knee compared to nearly six months of swallowing shit on the Navy's Coronado Island?

As he neared ground zero it appeared that chance was once again working in Beemer's favor. The federal crime scene perimeter stopped a mere block from where he'd abandoned the Freightliner. However, he'd been dangerously mistaken as to how much diesel fuel he had left in the reserve tank. When exactly the engine had gagged and stalled was unknown to Beemer. And though the hood was still hot, so was the midday sun at its 2:00 p.m. apex in the sky. Thank the devil for the backup battery.

The semi's refrigeration unit hummed, working overtime in the summer heat. Soon, the battery would be sucked dry if Beemer didn't get on the hoof to the nearest filling station. That's when Beemer reached deep to squeeze the *mean*. One of his trainers had once whispered the secret to him. When a certain kind of man felt his last ounce of will was exhausted and hope had been reduced to a pinprick of dimming light, that was the time to grab ahold of his own testicles and crush 'em until he found the stuff that made him mean. There, in that place of excruciating pain, only the toughest of soldiers could find his final reserves. Screw the knee. Screw the pain beneath his skull.

With that—along with every wincing step—Beemer allowed his brain to flood.

Every bully he'd ever encountered.

The men who'd questioned his manhood.

The women who'd spurned his amorous affections.

Authorities he'd never respected.

The foster mother who'd molested him.

The government that had abandoned him.

The savior the chaplain claimed had died for him.

Each memory flashed in Beemer's brain in high-def—the faces a live-action kabuki show of emotional insults. And from the images a warmth began to spill from his core, creeping into his extremities until the spasms in his neck eased and his right knee found four more inches of flex.

Gas can in hand, Beemer completed his four-block trek to a Chevron gas station, where he paid cash for two gallons of diesel. All the while, his jaw was so clenched, testing the tensile strength of the enamel covering his molars, that when the cashier asked which pump to switch on, Beemer answered by holding up three bloody fingers.

"Hey, man," expressed the cashier. "Were you there? Did you see the bomb happen?"

Beemer just shook his head tersely, swept the change off the counter, and returned to his task.

The gas can filled in a matter of seconds. Then as Beemer was screwing the cap firmly into place, his ears picked up the sound of a throaty four-cylinder engine in low gear, slow-turning into the filling station and stopping at the opposite bank of pumps. It was a vintage Porsche convertible. Out of which stepped none other than Rey Palomino.

Beemer stood at a frozen distance, involuntarily observing the pool man shove his credit card into the pump, punch up a billing zip code, and insert the nozzle into the Porsche's gas receptacle. It would have been nothing for Beemer to cross the five yards, douse the pool man in diesel, and scratch a match. The fire and screams that would surely follow would provide distraction enough for Beemer to hobble away with minimum notice. Then again any violent deviation from plan B could set off a new string of dominoes with no way to tell where or how they would land.

Yet the venom stirred inside Beemer. And as much as the *mean* was enough to quell the anguish in his knee, the malice inspired by the sudden proximity to Rey Palomino could've killed more pain than an acre of heroin poppies in full bloom.

Obscured by the gas pumps, Beemer watched the pool man top off the tank of his hobby car, sink the nozzle back into the cradle, and disregard the display when it offered to print him a receipt. Then Rey flopped back behind the wheel and seconds later was back on the boulevard, wind busting through his hair as if he'd just spent another day visiting the beach.

Because he had a new plan, Beemer was sanguine enough to shuffle off in the opposite direction, trudging the four blocks back to the old Freightliner.

Once back in the driver's saddle, he meant to point the stolen rust bucket south, cross the border at Tijuana, then last-leg it to the shipping yards of Mazatlan. With his blood cargo finally on its way to a North African port, Beemer could choose his next move. Maybe time off to heal at a Central American surf resort. Or he could quietly reinsert himself into Los Angeles, where he would be free to stalk and kill the betrayer, Rey Palomino, at his leisure.

With a gas can brimming with enough diesel to revive the dying reefer truck, Beemer set a course back to the alley where his cargo awaited. He wouldn't have had an inkling if his pain receptors were still switched to positive. The warmth he'd felt in his extremities had advanced into a glandular-born numbing agent. *Mother nature, man. She mixes a motherfucker of a pain-killin' cocktail.*

When he turned the corner into the alley, Beemer was again encouraged to hear the whine of the Freighty's compressors fueled by a healthy battery. He set the gas can on the ground then prepped his wracked body for a climb into the semi's cab, where he recalled the fuel lock lever sat near the hood release.

But his foot slipped on the first step, before he even had a handhold. Gravity did the rest, sending the vet backward and into a puddle of syrup. A warm and viscous goo that had greased the bottom of Beemer's Nikes now seeped into his pants up his backside. His first thought was that he'd slid on some used cooking oil the restaurant cooks had surreptitiously dumped in the alley instead of disposing of it properly through city recycling services.

A second assault by that fat-ass Bob.

However, after boiling up thousands of servings of fries and chicken wings, old cooking product smelled. The gunk that had Beemer crawling back to his feet was sticky and had a sweet odor on par with something more sugary.

Corn syrup?

Beemer examined his hands. Through the tiny bits of dirt and black asphalt, the sticky stuff was a somewhat cloudy yellowish-green. Like snot from an allergy-prone whale.

Animal byproduct?

What made Beemer wonder if the gunk was some kind of mammal extract was little more than gut fear. He lifted his gaze from his hands to the trailer's steel door. The thermal barriers dripped with the very same swill he'd fallen into. His blood product! *Aw, fuck!*

Not only was Beemer's cargo melting before his own eyes, but clearly some of the packaging had been compromised. The alley was slowly flooding with a mix of spun blood and human plasma. And under the blaze of the late afternoon sun, the goo was quickly congealing with the tar in the alley's asphalt, bubbling itself into a hot, black, useless slick.

Beemer swung around to the rear of the trailer, lifted the latch, and swung it outward. The insulated door squeaked and swung wide, clanging against the façade of the office building.

He didn't even need to feel for the light switch. His nose told him everything. What had smelled almost sweet and sugary in the hot air of the alley was a pungent fist to the face once Beemer saw the utter failure of the old Freightliner's refrigeration system. The trek for the diesel had proved utterly useless. Despite the truck's relatively new batteries and that the compressor's motor was obviously still engaged, a catastrophic malfunction had occurred, leading to the coagulated mess that lay before him. The best Beemer could calculate was that the meltdown had begun some hours earlier. Possibly before even arriving in Long Beach.

By the stench alone, Beemer could tell the spoilage was complete. A total loss. All efforts from Reno to Long Beach—not to mention the hiccup in Kern County—had been for naught.

Instead of turning from the stench, Beemer forced himself to breathe it in as if he wanted to remember the smell of such a massive personal failure on a cellular level. And with each subsequent whiff, Beemer purposefully allowed his dangerous inner friend to pry the lid off the hatch that kept him at bay. Something in him knew that before he could move on to plan C or D, the idiot would need some time outside himself to rant and rage…and kill Rey Palomino.

29

Bel-Air.

"It's a simple question," said Conrad, the ends of his words clipped as tight as his fingernails. "What the hell does any of this shit have to do with my dead baby girl?"

Conrad Ellis loathed hearing his own voice rise above more than the average decibel. Most in his employ knew this as a fact of working life, doing their level best to keep their master happy and emotionally sated. So at the sound of his bark, his kitchen staff froze, pressed themselves against whatever stainless-steel appliance they were scrubbing, and hoped to hell for calmer tones.

"I'm beside myself with abject wonder!" shouted Conrad. "How does this go from you—the feds—being after some guy who'd ripped off some blood bank in Reno? You said it was all set to arrest him. Yeah? That's what you said. So how the hell does this turn into him blowing himself to bits along with half of Long Beach?"

From his Bel-Air veranda, overlooking the gardenia-flanked brick steps that led down to his tennis court, Conrad squinted through his sunglasses at the sun as if to dare it to make him sweat. He was feeling a hint of perspiration between his Bluetooth headset and his ear. He wondered how much buildup of fluid it would take to short out the made-in-China electronics.

"The TV? You know what it is, yeah? Every goddamn news channel says it's a terrorist attack. That America is, once again, under siege from a bunch of Middle Eastern cave monkeys. So I ask you once again. What the Christ does this have to do with Pepper Ellis?"

The child's real name was Dorothy. Dorothy after his mother. Jane was the middle name, chosen by his estranged wife for no other reason than she thought it linked such an old-fashioned first name with the last name of Ellis in a nicely metered way.

Dorothy Jane Ellis.

But Conrad never called her Dorothy or Dot. From day one he'd nicknamed his only child as Pepper. While his missus recovered from an emergency caesarian delivery, the OB had sent the father off with the baby girl as she was properly washed and weighed and fitted with a tiny pink beanie. During the inoculation process, little Dorothy cried so hard that every millimeter of her skin turned bright red. Like a jalapeño pepper. The name stuck like fly paper.

Conrad later divested himself of his billion-dollar real estate investments, divorced his wayward plastic-surgery-addicted wife, and relocated himself and seven-year-old Pepper to the warm confines of Los Angeles. He soon discovered that by heavily investing in entertainment companies, an instant but shallow social life formed. Thus began his battle as a germophobe. Not that Conrad found showbiz types to be infested with dangerous bacteria. The inhabitants of the dream factory were, in fact, quite hygienic compared to the average Midwesterner with whom he'd grown up trading spit and bare knuckles.

Inherently, showbiz people were a bunch of liars and old-fashioned street-cheats.

Somewhere in Conrad's super nimble brain, he'd made a sub-primal connection between dishonesty and microbial filth. The association stuck and Conrad Ellis became a near shut-in with a psychotic aversion to the unseen organisms that grow and thrive in humanity's Petri dish.

Any thoughts of leaving Southern California for cleaner climates were vanquished by the idea that Pepper would be crushed to lose her school chums, her active social life, and proximity to an acting career. So while Conrad suffered with his advancing phobia, he began taking larger financial positions in Disney and Viacom, the owner of all things Nickelodeon. Soon, cuddly little Pepper Ellis was guest-acting on sitcoms like *Hannah Montana* and *The Suite Life of Zack and Cody*. Eventually, she landed her very own weekly series aimed at the constant flood of preteen girls connected to homes with basic cable.

Blessed with her mother's features—strawberry-blonde hair, Icelandic cheekbones, perfecto-porcelain skin, a constellation of freckles, and a set of preternaturally pillowed lips—combined with her daddy's killer acuity—Pepper Ellis, Conrad's precocious baby girl, eventually became a bona fide TV star.

"I'm famous now, Daddy," she'd declared only last Christmas.

"Famous enough to get into trouble," her daddy had warned her.

"Oh, you know I'm too smart for that."

Yes. Pepper was bright as hell. But still young and vulnerable enough to be swayed by the world that was just beginning to align at her feet. Drugs were Conrad's biggest fear. And sex. Since setting up business in Tinseltown, he'd had plenty of young and spectacular flesh sent to his door. Each a wannabe star. He'd ask them to shower before he'd ever allow them to touch him, observing and instructing the women as they washed. The routine became its own form of personal gratification for Conrad. After, as he tried in vain to sleep, he'd think of his little girl and wonder what made her different from the high-priced harlots who'd lined up to service him. Certainly not intelligence, considering the education of some of his *guests*. One particular knockout had even confessed to

Conrad that despite her master's degree in biochemistry, her face and body were better suited for the three F s of Hollywood: fun, fame, and fucking.

But who could have predicted the kind of danger that happened upon Pepper Ellis and her ne'er-do-well boyfriend on that lonely Kern County two-lane?

"I'm waiting for an answer," said Conrad.

"And I'm saying I don't know yet, Mr. Ellis," Lilly clearly answered from the other end of the cellular phone conversation. "It's going to take God knows how long to sort through all this. I'm about to be at the center of a massive multi-agency investigation. And without yet knowing the identity of the bomber—"

"Bomber, maybe. But murderer, yes. Of my daughter, if you recall. Unless by happenstance a terrorist attack occurred at the exact same place at the exact same time you said the FBI was going to take down my daughter's killer?"

"Did I give you information of a place and time of an arrest? Yes. As a courtesy? Yes. But we were going by one source. A source we don't know much about. A source who, for all we understand, might've been working with the terrorist himself."

"So you are saying my Pepper was killed by a *terrorist?*"

"I'm saying she's not the only one," impressed Lilly with a firm tone. "I've been looking at a dead FBI team in pieces and, possibly, twenty or forty more. So, Mr. Ellis, I kindly ask you to let me do my job and trust that I will clue you in whenever and wherever I can."

"Because I'm the father of the victim?" pressed Conrad. "Or because you know what I can do for you—or against you—in the future?"

"Because you figured out how to hound me in my condo at 2:00 a.m.," cheered Lilly in a moment of pitch-perfect politics. "And any man with that kind of resolve deserves both my respect and response."

Conrad found himself nodding.

"Good enough," he said. "For now. We'll talk soon, yes?"

He didn't wait for her to answer, merely clicking off the call and filling his lungs with the aroma of the blooming gardenias. The air was as sweet as expected. But little did it salve either his aching heart or the part of him that naturally distrusted lawyers.

For Lilly Zoller, being in the spotlight was closer to a craving than a gift. She worked as hard on her outward appearance as she did her intellect and verbal acuity. She yearned for both men and women to be as intoxicated by the content of the words flowing from her collagen-enhanced lips as by her timed entrance into a room. Her goal was always to enter every major encounter with style then leave her audience in awe. And though she understood the watermark was pretty much humanly unattainable, it was a bar she stubbornly refused to lower.

That was until the son of a bitch she'd planned to arrest had blown himself and a good portion of Long Beach into microscopic bits of human DNA.

Lilly had used the call with Conrad Ellis to momentarily excuse herself from the interrogation. She even lied to the Homeland Security liaison, claiming the caller was actually her boss in Washington, Deputy Attorney General Lawrence Knockburn. She'd needed a moment to compose herself before she'd returned to her debriefing.

"I'd like to get back to where we left off," said Mark Stubbitz, the Los Angeles–based Homeland Security liaison. Stubbitz was former FBI but looked more like a trainee out of college. Short hair, acne that hadn't yet receded, and a piercing need to know.

"Certainly," said Lilly, returning to her seat in the Long Beach Arena's mezzanine. Row FF, seat 8. Homeland Security had borrowed the shabby old hockey-arena-turned-function-hall as a space to perform triage on the crime scene. The floor of the building was already being striped with masking tape into a grid that would soon be filled with evidence from the blast.

As Lilly's eyes wandered the upper tiers where she was seated, there appeared to be other debriefings taking place. One per section. She guessed that once Stubbitz was done with her, she'd move on to the next section for an interrogation by another agency.

"This unsub and the US Attorney's office interest in him," said Stubbitz.

"Unofficial," corrected Lilly. "This moved quickly. It didn't go beyond me."

"So you were tipped to the blood bank robbery in Reno," said Stubbitz. "You see that the same perp is involved in the Kern County murders—"

"That's a bit backwards," said Lilly. "Agent Little—

"Dulaney Little," confirmed Stubbitz.

"Yes. If I recall correctly, Dulaney Little brought the incident in Kern County to my attention," fibbed Lilly, shading responsibility for the operation away from her office. She didn't know what Dulaney would say. She had morbidly assumed that he was one of the FBI men obliterated in the blast, making it that much easier to throw his possibly dead, disarticulated body under the proverbial bus. "One of the victims was an actress on some show I'm not familiar with. But Dulaney was. He has kids, so—"

"So he was the one interested in the murder."

"Curious, I think, is more accurate. Somehow he'd put the interstate thing together on his own."

"Would you know why he chose to keep his information to himself and investigate instead of handing off to the L.A. Bureau?"

"Slow week in the US Attorney's office?" mused Lilly, a bit too glibly considering the circumstances. "Dulaney was assigned to the entire floor. I can't say what the other prosecutors had him doing."

"But you authorized his investigation?" pressed Stubbitz.

"I did."

"Why?"

"My guess is that Dulaney felt things were moving too quickly for a hand-off to the Westwood feebs. In no time he'd been hooked in with the witness. There was going to be some kind of shipping transaction. I told him to go with it."

"Sounds like more than 'go with it,'" said Stubbitz. "I mean, you were here for the bust."

"So what if I was?"

"That's awful involved for a US Attorney."

"You stationed here?"

"In L.A.? I'm from here. Pomona."

"So you've noticed that it's hot."

"I've noticed."

"Friday? A chance to get out of downtown and check out a few hours of action in Long Beach?"

"You're saying that the reason we found you at the crime scene was because of the weather?" Any attempt for Stubbitz to keep incredulity from creeping into his voice failed.

Lilly leaned forward in her stadium chair. It creaked loudly as if begging to be replaced.

"As far as I know, *nobody* knew what was going to happen down here. Not Agent Little. Not anyone on the arrest detail. And certainly not me."

"So it was just pure coincidence that when the terrorist detonated the bomb, you just happened to be in the bathroom inside Starbucks?"

"Told you. I had to pee."

Stubbitz three-counted as he stared her down. Lilly met his stare with equal weight.

"Since the bomb went off, have you had any contact with Agent Dulaney Little?" asked Stubbitz.

"No."

"Texts? Emails?"

"No."

"You last saw him speaking with the witness?"

"Yes."

"Do you recall the witness's name?"

"Jay? Clay? I'm not sure."

"Hey, Ron?" shouted Stubbitz, his voice echoing over the arena. "You got a name on that witness?"

"The Porsche guy?" shouted the Homeland Security agent from two sections over. "Rey Palomino."

"That's it," confirmed Lilly.

"We have a line on him yet?" shouted Stubbitz.

"Yeah," shouted the other agent. "We found 'em at home. Bureau is sitting on him 'til they get an Identi-Kit over there. Should have a picture within the hour."

"Terrorist motherfucker's in a billion bits so we still don't know what he looks like," said Stubbitz.

"Anything else for me?" asked Lilly.

"Not just now," said Stubbitz. "But hold tight. We got ATF on the way in. And I reckon we're gonna want to get a location map so you can put a timeline to your movements. Then maybe we'll cut you loose. Maybe we won't."

"I understand," said Lilly, playing the part of the reliable team-mate. She was relatively certain she wouldn't be in any trouble for shading the truth of her connection to the crime. Surely the more the government would dig up on the mysterious suicide bomber, the further away Lilly's tangential involvement would appear. If anything, she'd most likely end up with a lasting measure of credit for being the federal prosecutor who was inches away from collaring the SOB before he'd acted so violently against the public at large.

"We'd really appreciate it you stay off TV before all agencies have debriefed you," said Stubbitz.

Television. Yes. The nexus of Hollywood and terror-ism hadn't yet struck Lilly. TV would be suckling at the teat of the twisted tale for months on end. How the interstate hunt for the killer of a popular young actress morphed into one of the nastiest acts of terrorism in US history. It was ripe and juicy and came with career-making legs that could run for years.

A thin smile appeared on Lilly's lips. One she covered with a shaky index finger, feigning the slightest hint of post-traumatic stress.

"No problem," said Lilly, forcing the corners of her mouth downward in an attempt to appear somber.

But beneath Lilly's skin, she was vibrating with the lust of possibility. If she worked the next forty-eight hours in the right sequence, she could emerge a star, playing the part of a real-life heroine in constant demand for her expert commentary at every network with a news division. Followed by a rich publishing deal, professional speaking fees, and anything else fame could conjure.

The bloody winning ticket for a deputy US Attorney.

For Lilly, the sky was never the limit. Hers was the furthest reaches of her unbridled ambition.

30

Pasadena.

"Cool, Mom! You're home!" exclaimed young Travis. Though the boy's excitement was limited by his perch on the couch, Xbox controller glued to his fingers much like his eyes were to the TV screen.

Gonzo eased into the duplex, her neck elongated by a precautionary cervical collar.

"Lord, what happened to you?" said Kyle, the neighborly tenant who'd been plenty happy to look after Travis for the afternoon. He had the corners of a large jigsaw puzzle nearly assembled. The affable old gent, soft in both the middle and thighs, had entertained the oft-generational delusion that the eleven-year-old might actually engage in an analog challenge.

"Better than it looks," said Gonzo, dropping her purse to the floor with a thud. She was still waiting for her boy to notice. She briefly considered standing tall over Travis until he finally deigned to look at her. The plastic collar would've given him a surefire charge. Thus Gonzo thought better of it. Travis had been through enough emotional trauma after her near-death cab wreck only two years earlier. She'd spent months in rehab, including weeks in a similar medieval-looking device.

Gonzo sat at the kitchen table and looked over Kyle's complicated jigsaw puzzle. The photo he was attempting to assemble was an intricate depiction of the Sistine Chapel Ceiling. Gonzo groaned on the inside.

At the sound of her ripping the Velcro fasteners on her collar, Lucky made his presence known.

"Hey. That's a lousy idea," observed Lucky, having followed Gonzo into the house at her invitation. He'd half thought of dropping her at the curb and starting the drive back north, but fatigue—not to mention some measure of remorse for having dragged the LAPD detective into his forty-eight-hour sinkhole—had lured him through the doorway.

"Just needed it for the ride home," said Gonzo. "Now that I'm here…"

"It's the Luck-man!" said Travis, suddenly quick to ignore his Xbox. The boy still hadn't so much as glanced at his mother, but showed immediate interest in the man he'd only met that very morning.

"Hey there, Travis," said Lucky, then offering a nod to Kyle. "How are you…Aw, man. Sorry, but I forgot your name."

"Kyle," said the neighbor.

"That's right," said Lucky, tapping his skull with his forefinger.

"Is Lucky staying for dinner?" asked Travis.

"Up to Lucky," said Gonzo. "As long as he doesn't expect me to cook."

"Pizza!" burst Travis.

"Sorry," said Gonzo, smirking at Lucky. "In Travis's universe, pizza is its own food group, along with Taco Bell and cold cereal."

"Works for me," said Lucky without really mulling it over. All he knew for sure was that he didn't much look forward to climbing into his car for a long drive with only himself as company. His brother and only living relative was dead. For the first time in his life, Lucky feared loneliness.

"Before Detective Dey agrees to sharing," said Gonzo. "You better tell him what kind of pizza you like."

"Sausage, onions, and stinky cheese!" said Travis.

"Stinky cheese?" asked Lucky.

"The blue crumbly kind," added Gonzo.

"Oh," nodded Lucky. "I guess that means you get your own pizza."

"My mom likes it too."

Gonzo raised her hand. "Guilty as charged."

"Then bring on the blue cheese," challenged Lucky. "As long as you don't mind if I order plain pepperoni for myself."

"Proves it," said Gonzo. "PD cops are more adventurous than sheriffs. At least in the epicurean way."

"And thus endeth the argument," joked Lucky, revealing a rare show of teeth. The grieving detective's skin crinkled at the corners of his eyes as he gave up a smile.

Travis hopped behind the family computer and ordered via the local pizzeria's website. And while waiting for delivery, the threesome pulled chairs up to the dining room table and joined Kyle in puzzling together the tiny jigsaw pieces.

The familial-like moment wasn't lost on Gonzo. For a while, it went a hell of a lot further in easing her neck pain than her Advil and Aleve cocktail. By the time the pizza had been consumed and Kyle had retired to his own address, Gonzo's fridge had been picked clean of beer. When she'd suggested that she and Lucky upgrade to rum and coke, Travis had trundled off to bed. The fan the boy employed to both cool and calm him through the nights was switched on to high, reverberating through the duplex with a consistent drone.

"Stick with me," said Lucky, his body sunk deep into the couch. "Think I'm somewhere between dead tired and way too drunk to drive."

"Like I'd let you drive," said Gonzo, her back flat on the floor, pillow under her head, her feet propped on the couch's corduroy arm.

"So if I got up to go…you'd stop me?"

"Too comfortable," said Gonzo. "Maybe I'd try and trip you."

"Wouldn't be hard."

They both laughed until their voices trailed with ease. She could've easily closed her eyes and counted up the hours that had passed since she'd stepped in front of the Kern detective hell-bent for leather on gunning down the Peterbilt's driver. With a little more effort, she could have pictured how things might have gone down had Lucky had his way. The FBI tactical squad having secured their truck-driving suspect—possibly even lifting the handcuffed bastard off the pavement—taken by surprise when the head-shaved cop squared up to them. Nobody would have expected the pistol—the old-school model 1911 .45—let alone to see the weapon speak so efficiently. Two loud pops dead in the center of the bad guy's ten-ring. The double heart shot would've caused the target's face to contort and knees to give out instantly. Like the storied moment when Jack Ruby plugged Lee Harvey Oswald in the basement garage of the Dallas PD. The Kern County killer would've been dead. End of story.

Instead there came that hellish explosion and subsequent, memory-rearranging blast wave. From thereon everything seemed to change. Most of Gonzo's growing tally of complaints about Lucky, though not erased, were seriously mitigated. Maybe because the ugly chase to find the truck was over? Or was it because her assignment to assist the renegade deputy was near its end? Or even because she knew that Lucky's pain over the loss of his brother was so piqued he was willing to sacrifice himself and his career to put a deserved bullet inside the murderer?

Do I feel sorry for him? she asked herself. *Or do I just feel for him?*

Gonzo was too tired to decide.

"I have one request," she said without a flicker of forethought. "That you shower before bed."

"You're saying I smell?"

"I'm saying I'd rather you smelled like soap."

With one eye open, Lucky stole a look at her. She was smirking again, as if she carried a secret.

"What about the boy?" asked Lucky.

"With the fan on, it'll take an earthquake to wake him." Gonzo used her toes to stroke Lucky's hairline. The stubble from where he buzzed it tickled.

"And I thought you didn't like me," said Lucky after an exhale.

"And you thought I played for the other team," said Gonzo.

"Crossed my mind."

"Well, I don't," said Gonzo, a little throaty. "And for the record, I haven't decided if I like you or not."

"Fair enough."

Gonzo gathered up the usual guest stack: a clean towel, facecloth, and a new bar of Ivory soap. Then after voluntarily tossing Lucky's clothes in the washing machine, she joined him in her small shower. What began with giggles and goosebumps and giddy anticipation turned into a wordless conversation. After the unlikely duo washed each other in somber, ritualistic strokes, they slipped between a pair of laundered sheets and generated streams of clean perspiration. From the first squeak of the shower faucet to the last drop of sexual sweat, the carnal act lasted barely an hour before both Gonzo and Lucky fell asleep in a tangle of hair and legs.

It was 9:53 p.m.

31

Long Beach.

Dulaney woke up screaming.

He'd had an awful nightmare.

He'd been standing at that same floor-to-ceiling pane of insulating tempered glass. But this time he was without binoculars to protect his eyeballs. Instead, his hands were pressed against the massive sheet of glass as if pushing against it would prevent it from exploding into a million shards. The scene beyond was precisely the same. The traffic jam. The black Peterbilt semi. The FBI tactical squad, moving in two-by-two formation to take down the truck driver. That and he could see the faces of all the other players on the field. The casual passersby. The parking meter attendant. He was even able to spot a stranger, standing atop a park statue that looked like a huge anchor, home video camera held out in front of him.

"Who the hell is that?" asked Dulaney in his dream.

"Who's who?" asked Lilly, who, in the dream, was ten steps behind him, dressed in body-hugging sweats, working up some personal steam on one of the showroom's elliptical trainers.

"The guy with the video camera? Do we know him?"

"This is your takedown. It's all on you and the Bureau."

The giant pane of glass began to rattle and vibrate. So Dulaney braced harder, splaying his fingers to their fullest as if his two hammy hands could prevent the oncoming blast wave from penetrating the air-conditioned second floor of Sports Authority.

"Need. More. Morphine," said Dulaney, finally awake, but finding that speaking made his lips hurt. So he tried to puff a word at a time, putting a little extra air behind each syllable. His eyes were desperate to find some kind of focal point beyond the constant dull blur. He semi-recalled a barely intelligible neurologist urging him not to worry—his eyesight would most likely return to normal strength within a week. The same with his memory and cognition. Such was often the case with intracranial injuries. But Dulaney had no idea what the hell had happened to him.

His skin burned. The sting was excruciating. From his ankles to his forehead, he'd been penetrated by a thousand tiny specks of sharp glass. The blast wave had both shattered the massive window and propelled tiny shards through Dulaney's garb, symmetrically lodging in his skin from head to toe. Some of the larger pieces of glass were easily removed by an emergency room intern with a flashlight and tweezers. The rest were best left to remain embedded until Dulaney's body naturally rejected the micro-bits as if it were sweating out a toxin.

Until that day came, Dulaney would feel as if he'd suffered third-degree burns the length of his body.

The shadow of a nurse entered Dulaney's cloudy field of view. He couldn't tell much more than she was a female of color. Filipino or Indian, he guessed.

"You in pain?" asked the nurse.

"More...morphine," said Dulaney.

"Not morphine," said the nurse. "But we're using very strong painkiller."

"More. Please."

"Too much of a good thing—"

"Need. Lilly."

"Is Lilly your wife? A sister?"

"Lilly…Zoller…Attorney."

"Will your lawyer recognize you? Or have you remembered who you are?"

In the chaos following the explosion, between the EMTs, hospital staff and emergency volunteers, Dulaney's ID was either lost or stolen. For the nearly eight hours he drifted between consciousness and searing pain, Dulaney remained a John Doe.

"F…B…I…" puffed Dulaney.

"Are you FBI? Or is this Lilly person FBI?" probed the nurse.

"White. Male. American. Marine. Danny. Palomino."

"Wait. Lemme write all this down."

"Tattoo. Anarchy."

Dulaney's brain was flooding with words. Recollections. He was remembering the five-minute walk from the Ralph's parking lot to the Sports Authority. Rey Palomino was alongside him step for step. During which Dulaney realized he'd missed some background. It'd only been a matter of hours since Rey had made contact with the FBI, volunteering to assist in the apprehension of the man he only knew as an acquaintance of his deceased son.

"Okay. You said Danny…?" asked the nurse, who stood at a dry-erase board.

"Palomino."

"Like the horse."

"Marine."

"Got that."

"Tattoo. Red A. Circle. 'Round it."

The pool man had never gotten much of a look at the perp. His only crystalline memory was of a tattoo on the inside of Beemer's left wrist. The capital letter A with a red circle drawn around it. Rey Palomino had mistaken it for a reference to *The Scarlet Letter*. But Dulaney knew better, cataloging the marking as the universal sign for…

"Anarchy."

"Right. Yes. I've written here," said the nurse. "Who should I tell? Do you have family?"

"Lilly. Zoller."

"Yes. Her. Who is she again?"

"United. States. Attorney."

It was as if the evening breeze that Gonzo depended on to cool her duplex had taken a vacation. For better than a week a sticky hot stillness had overtaken the neighborhood and, more importantly, Gonzo's bedroom, waking her shortly after midnight. She'd shifted her position in the bed, making more room for herself and Lucky, then tried to fall back asleep to the leftover smell of soap and sex. Instead, her sore neck made nearly every reclined position impossible. So she found a fresh T-shirt, slipped it on, and shut the door to her tiny bathroom before flipping on the light. She temporarily squinted while attempting to examine herself in the mirror. She noticed that the pillow crease lines striping her cheeks matched the same red color in her eyes. She ran the cold water for a moment, splashed a bit of it on her face, towel-dried, then rummaged for an old prescription of Soma, a muscle relaxant she sometimes took when the permanent screws in her jaw aggravated the surrounding nerves. She found the bottle. Though it was sadly empty.

Gonzo washed back two ibuprofen by drinking directly from the faucet and crept back into bed, taking extra caution not to wake her guest. She propped a few pillows against the headboard and tried to decide between the book on her nightstand and the television remote. It was a coin flip in her head that she kept on delay as she rewound the last forty-eight hours over again and again. How had she gone from such utter loathing for a fellow cop to inviting him into her bed? *Weak, weak, weak.*

She kept hearing the phrase mercy sex rattling in her skull. If such were true, which of them was the gifted screw-ee? It'd been well over eight months since Gonzo'd swapped spit, let alone orgasms, with anyone. The most recent was an old high school boyfriend who'd long ago set up shop as a heart surgeon in Seattle. He'd somehow caught up with Gonzo's involvement in the Simi Valley safety expert case—the one ending in the near-tragic attack on Gonzo and her handcuffed prisoner as they raced down a rainy San Fernando Valley freeway. The former flame successfully stalked her on Facebook, rekindled some days-gone-by interest via email and instant messages and the occasional Skype chat, then two romantic visits later, the pair hooked up in a suite at the Langham. Afterwards the bastard weirdly confessed to being unhappily married with two needy children. The man hadn't so much as wrapped up his confessional soliloquy when Gonzo was slipping back into her panties and looking for the fastest exit. When he physically attempted to prevent her from leaving, Gonzo had dropped him to the floor with a quick strike to his nose. She could still feel the cartilage cracking under the heel of her palm. His knees buckled and he flopped next to the bed, bleeding over his naked self and cursing her with the worst of words: fucking cunt-bitch-whore.

Another in a long list of bad decisions she'd have to live with. But then she'd return home to Travis, her one and only true care, and the sole male deserving her unconditional affection.

As for Lucky? All that Gonzo knew about him was how much she didn't know. He'd lost his brother to a terrorist. Or so said every talking head on every television news channel. She'd forgotten the mental coin flip and, without a conscious decision, had picked up the remote control out of habit and flicked on CNN. She let the mute button cut the sound to zero. Then between reading the constant scroll at the bottom of the screen and matching the stories to the flash of images, she would glance left and use the flickering light to survey the landscape of Lucky's naked body, as if it would give her some answers.

Out of the corner of her eye, Gonzo spied the FBI rendering of the suspected terrorist. It was the classic Identi-Kit picture. Black and white. The large sunglasses pictured left little room for facial features. Gonzo's instant reaction was that there were two million men in Southern California alone who would easily match the description of the suicide terrorist. But then came a second image on the TV. It was a sketch of a man's left arm with a medium-sized tattoo on the wrist. The tattoo was a distinct letter A with a circle drawn around it.

Gonzo didn't need to imagine the crime scene. Every five minutes, the network would cut to a high-definition camera they'd mounted atop a Long Beach high-rise. It was already permanently pointed into the hole left by the bomb. The entire scene was lit by massive banks of lights, each hung from one of six industrial cranes. Gonzo pictured one of the many inspectors, picking over her assigned block of the grid for evidence of bomb or body parts, eventually stumbling over a torn piece of skin with the bomber's tattoo on it. Would it be a "bingo" moment or would the discovery bring a sickly bit of lunch up with it?

"What's the news?" groaned Lucky.

Before he'd even finished his sentence, Gonzo had pressed the off button on the remote. The TV blanked back to black. Her motherly instinct was to assist Lucky's fractured soul in catching up on some much-needed sleep.

"Didn't have to do that," said Lucky.

"Sssshhh. Just go back to sleep." Gonzo gently combed his hair with her fingertips.

"What'd the news say?" Lucky's eyes were open and fixed on the empty television screen.

"Nothing new."

Lucky rolled to his left and twisted his head until his eyes were full of her.

"*I* should be sleeping?" asked Lucky. "What about you?"

"Needed a coupla Advil. Was letting the TV do the rest."

"Closet insomniac."

"I usually go for a book but something made me wanna see what's what in the world."

"You look good in the middle of the night."

Gonzo just shook her head then gifted him back the tiniest of smiles. She gestured with her chin toward the other end of the bed.

"I gotta ask," began Gonzo. "The one tat."

"Mine?" Lucky turned his foot counterclockwise, as if he needed to see his own ink.

"Lotta talk about the Reapers. But you know. Just talk. What's it really mean?"

"Means there's guys out there who are there for me. Anytime. Anyplace. All I gotta do is call."

"Like *Ghostbusters*," joked Gonzo.

"Somethin' like that."

"They all outta Lennox?"

"Current and former. Yeah."

"And is it true you gotta make a kill before you get inked?"

"Why the sudden interest in cop ink?" shifted Lucky. "PD envy? You got any?"

"Ink?" asked Gonzo, shaking her head. "Used to think I might get somethin' here—you know—across my abdomen to hide my stretch marks, but..."

"But..."

"But once I realized I couldn't get somethin' as cool as a Reaper tat..." She capped her joke off with a smirk.

"Seriously," said Lucky. "What would you get? One tattoo. Just for you. What?"

"I've thought about that so many times." Gonzo chuckled at herself. "What would I get? But then it's more like I know what I *wouldn't* get."

"Like?"

"Tramp stamp. Like a butterfly or a heart above my ass."

"'Cause it's such a great ass. Wouldn't want anything taking away from that."

"Thanks..." she said dismissively. "Moving on. Okay. So what else wouldn't I get?" Gonzo's eyes swirled, as if searching her brain for bad tattoo images. They came in a flood. "Ring of barbed wire above the bicep. That one's too stupid for words. Chinese symbol on the back of my neck. Little red heart right here." With that, Gonzo touched her index finger an inch inside her hip bone.

"Where?" Lucky rolled onto his stomach, trying to get a better angle.

"There," she repeated with her index finger.

Lucky found her hip bone with his lips.

"Right there?" he asked.

"Little to the left, I think," giggled Gonzo.

"What else?" asked Lucky between sexy nuzzles.

"Well, definitely not a butt-ugly Reaper-with-a-gun tat *any-where* on my body…"

"Definitely."

"Oh. Nothing creepy like an anarchy A in a bloody circle."

Lucky froze. Did he hear her correctly?

"Well, don't stop now," said Gonzo.

"What'd you say about anarchy?"

"Was talking about a tat. You know. Capital A in a red circle."

"Yeah, but why *that* one?"

"I dunno. 'Cause it was on TV?"

Lucky sat up and showed her his face. It was as if he were a question mark afraid of the answer.

"The suicide bomber," continued Gonzo. "They showed it with the FBI Identi-Kit rendering."

"The tat."

"Distinguishing mark on his—"

"Inside left wrist?"

"Yeah…"

A hand went to Lucky's head. He first rubbed his face and then the stubble on his scalp. Worry began to leak from every pore.

"You sure that's what they said?" asked Lucky. "You didn't dream it?"

"Just ten minutes ago. Before you woke up."

"I think I met him."

"Who? The suicide bomber?"

"Not suicide. I met him after."

"After what?"

"Whadda you think after?"

It was as if gravity had hit Gonzo like a fifty-pound brain freeze.

"I need to make a call," said Lucky, spinning out of her bed and into his denim pants with remarkable alacrity.

"You need to call the FBI."

"Reapers first. Then everybody else."

Gonzo already felt as if she were ten steps behind. Lucky appeared to have accelerated from zero to a thousand miles per hour in a matter of seconds—dressing, holstering his pistol, and lacing up his shoes. Gonzo was still organizing her thoughts around the entire situation and what to do with Travis when she realized that Lucky was mere moments away from leaving without her. That's when she snatched Lucky's car keys from her bureau top and angled out of the bedroom. He half-chased her, nearly spilling to the floor as he hopped on one foot while pulling on his other shoe. Gonzo calmly speed-dialed her neighbor Kyle, instructed him to please finish off his night's sleep on her couch, then spun about to face her houseguest, pointing his car keys at him.

"Whether you like it or not, I'm your partner on this," she affirmed. "I'm with you until the books close on this thing or I get orders to cut you loose."

"On one condition," said the Kern cop.

"Gotta hear it first," she said, arms folding across her chest.

"You put on some goddamn panties and move."

As it was, Gonzo was well aware of her half-nakedness. And in the moment she couldn't have given ten rips. She leveled both eyes onto an imaginary spot on the man's forehead, let her gaze linger long enough to be certain he felt her incredulous stare, then thumped her bare feet back to the bedroom to find some cop-appropriate garb.

Lucky hadn't expected her to keep the car keys.

Once the situation with Travis was squared away, Gonzo climbed behind the wheel of Lucky's Charger and turned over the throaty engine. Her argument was simple enough. Lucky needed to burn up the cell towers between his Reaper pals and the FBI while somebody else's hands were on the wheel.

Only Lucky never phoned the FBI. While Gonzo carefully busted through every red traffic light between her duplex and the Pasadena freeway, Lucky woke up Bledsoe, verbally walked the big man to the nearest empty pad of paper, and performed a machine-gun reportage of his day, from picking up his LAPD escort at her Pasadena domicile to the moment he'd learned of the terrorist's distinguishing tattoo. In turn, it was Bledsoe's chore to pass the information on to the authorities without the feds, in turn, throwing a chop-block on Lucky and Gonzo's westward trajectory. Their target was the northern San Fernando Valley suburb of Granada Hills. There they expected to find the home of pool contractor and eyewitness Rey Palomino. Lucky's pal Lopes provided the address while watching the continuous loop of "live shots" from TV news puppets lined up on the sidewalk outside Rey's house.

Lopes's simple directions to the "pool dude's casa" were little more than "go west 'til you smell all the TV gasbags on the dude's lawn, then north 'til you step in their bullshit."

Thank goodness for GPS. The smartphone app blinked green and, second by second, counted down the distance to the Granada Hills address. Gonzo slowly lowered the accelerator, keeping the speedometer floating near ninety miles per hour as she split the lines of the HOV carpool lane. The traffic they streaked past paid little notice. It was past midnight on a Friday. And the flashing blue and red lights that pulsed from behind the Charger's grill could've told any kind of short story. Drug bust. Officer needs assistance. Or plain-clothed cop wants to get home before his wife figures that he'd dipped his wick into some local brown sugar before high-ballin' it home to her and their sleeping kids in Simi Valley.

Road noise crept up from the asphalt to the tires, transferring through to the torsion bar and into the steering column. The sweet vibration reminded Gonzo of the feel encountered when gripping the stick of a helicopter in flight. The training choppers she'd worked out in were especially sensitive, teaching new pilots to rely on their senses as much as the aircraft's instruments. Gonzo craved the airborne sensation and the lift provided by every thump of the rotors.

Then again, as cop moments go, she wouldn't have traded her current spot for just about anything. She was smack in the center of something significant. Life changing, even. Yet she hadn't a glimmer just how those changes would manifest themselves.

Gonzo forgot if she'd ever actually asked Lucky if he had some sort plan for when he finally arrived at Palomino's house. Or if she'd already been able to assume that his plan was as unformed as wet papier-mâché.

"It's going to be a mob scene," she recalled saying. "Cops. Feds. He's the one man who can put a face to the worst terrorist act on US soil since 9/11."

"Those your words? Or a Fox News alert?"

"Just tellin' you that we've stepped into something massive. Bigger than your brother. Bigger than any Reaper-payback street shit you've cooked up in your head."

"Noted."

"Lucky?"

But Lucky's phone buzzed. It was Bledsoe passing along that powers in the Department of Homeland Security were ordering the unlikely duo to peel the Charger off at the nearest freeway exit, where they were to park and wait for the feds to pick them up for an immediate debrief. So important was the directive that DHS did not want to risk any kind of detour or fender bender.

"Feds say jump and expect us to drop our pants before our feet hit the ground," moaned Lucky.

"So we didn't get the order," braved Gonzo. "Not directly."

"I was on this motherfucker before the feds were. The PD. Everybody. Nobody's gonna pull me off again."

"Nobody?"

"Not even you."

For the briefest second Gonzo took her eyes off the freeway to glance at Lucky. His voice told her he was as serious as a heart attack. But she needed to get a look at his eyes to underline his full intent.

"Yeah, I meant what I said," said Lucky, meeting her flickering gaze. "No more stunts like you pulled in Long Beach. There's no more getting between me and however this ends."

She could've argued. Even briefly wrestled with her conscience over his sudden and intractable stance. Instead, she bit her tongue and kept her foot on the accelerator. The immediate future was a blank slate. How history would record their actions in the next two hours was a total and complete unknown.

32

Malibu.

While much of America, especially those living in Southern California, were hooked to their televisions in hopes of hearing just one more nugget on the terrorist attack in Long Beach, Garvin Van Der Berk was thanking his lucky stars. For a month he'd been attempting to corner a stalker who'd been harassing a celebrity client. The pervert had been successfully trailing the famous model all over the hemisphere, edging closer and closer to the object of his obsession all while cleverly avoiding local authorities and a chorus line of ineffective restraining orders. The model's hedge-fund-honcho boyfriend, exhausted from living under constant precaution and sharing his house with a woman who was quickly slipping into becoming a beautiful nobody afraid of her own shadow, had at last pulled the trigger. He quietly hired the famed private detective to deliver a "gift basket" to the stalker.

Garvin's secret sub-specialty was a cash business. And because it involved the illegal use of force and he risked a mandatory prison sentence, he employed zero contractors whatsoever. All he required was a bit of planning, sixty seconds of alone time with his target, a stun gun, and a retractable steel baton. Stalkers, who nearly always lived alone, would answer their doors to a bearded white man in thick glasses wearing a gas company work shirt. They'd find a stun gun driven into their ribs. The next thing they knew, they'd be prostrate on the floor inside their own threshold with a fistful of gauze stuffed into their perverted pie-holes. Maybe they'd hear the *snap-click* of the baton locking into position a split second before their left kneecaps shattered from the impact of heavy steel on bone. The bearded man would kneel, whisper the name of the current woman who kindled the stalker's obsession, and vanish.

Garvin's sideline gig had a remarkable success rate. Stalkers were loath to call the police, terrified any investigation would lead to the dirty truth about their favorite pastime. And by the time the stalker rehabbed from a premature knee replacement, his mojo for that one famous feline had usually waned to something close to nil.

For over three months, Garvin had been having unusual difficulty hand-delivering the gift basket from the model's boyfriend. Though the stalker in question kept a small apartment near Malibu's Latigo shores neighborhood, he rarely seemed to sleep there. His job as a traveling nurse kept him moving from city to city, filling in wherever there was a health care shortfall.

But thanks to some luck and an act of domestic terrorism, Garvin's stalker decided to spend his evening noshing on takeout Chinese while staying plugged into the breaking news story of the year. Garvin had clocked the locale and timed his approach. With the hour closing on midnight, the hillside apartment complex appeared as if it and most of its occupants had buttoned up for the night. Marine fog was forming around the outdoor lights, a certain sign that the high barometric pressure was beginning a retreat and the heat wave would soon be abated. The windows of his borrowed Land Cruiser were wide open and his ears tuned to his surroundings. Between the beats of the distant waves crashing and the crisp air filtering through his nostrils, Garvin wondered why he'd never thought to buy in Malibu.

Get out of the car, he thought. *Crush this guy's kneecap, whisper the model's name, and get the hell back to Culver City.*

Then his cell phone trilled.

Instinctively, he let his eyes swivel to the screen. Not that he was going to answer. He'd waited too long to deliver the gift basket. Nobody but nobody could get him to pick up a call. But there it was. Conrad Ellis. That ten-digit number that had become so familiar in the past forty-eight hours. Plus, it was the Conrad Ellis witching hour. The beginning of that very time of day Conrad would force his will on whomever he could convince to pick up the telephone. And that was most people.

"Conrad," said Garvin into his phone, clipped and hoping a blistering moment of genius would materialize in the form of words to convince Pepper Ellis's pop that it'd be worth waiting for Garvin to call him back.

"Granada Hills," said Conrad. "Do you know where that is?"

"Listen, Connie—"

"You do or you don't know Granada Hills?"

"I know where it is," conceded Garvin, any moment of genius passing him by. "It's in the North Valley. Why?"

"Because that's where the pool man lives."

"What pool man?" asked Garvin, certain the old man was two drinks past his limit. He tried to listen for the telltale sound of ice tinkling inside a scotch tumbler.

"That witness who knows the man that killed my Pepper."

Garvin recalled the sound bite. Somewhere within the swamp of information choking the last half of the daily news cycle he might have heard a thing or two about a man who had identified the murderer-cum-suicide-bomber.

"What about him, sir?" asked Garvin.

"I want to talk to him," said Conrad.

"Of course." Garvin agreed, but was still confused.

"Tonight."

"You're not serious."

"Have you ever known me to bullshit?"

"If he's a witness, I'm sure the authorities have him on lock-down."

"They do," said Garvin. "Watching it right now on TV. He's inside his house under police protection."

"Okay. Just like I said."

"Like I said, Garvin," said Conrad. "I want to talk to him. Not tomorrow. Not after he's got himself a lawyer and is booked on every TV show from here to bumfuck."

"Conrad—"

"I'm gonna pay him to tell me what he knows. And you're gonna make that deal tonight."

"But you said the authorities—"

"I have someone inside the government. She's my next call. I'm going to have her foam the runway."

"So you want me to drive up to Granada Hills and offer this pool man money?"

"Fifty grand—cash—if he gets in your car and you drive him to my house."

"Wow," Garvin heard himself saying aloud.

"I know it's a lot," said Conrad. "But it's worth it to me to hear what he knows. In person. Before the rest of the world gets it for free."

Garvin's eyes squeezed shut. It wasn't his job to question the motives or judgment of his clients. His chore was always the same. Make the client's wish—no matter how difficult or misguided— come true.

He checked the digital clock on his dashboard. 12:05 a.m. Garvin flicked one last glance at the stalker's window. The light hadn't yet been extinguished. He put the odds at better than two to one that the stalker would be asleep within ninety minutes. Garvin quickly calculated he'd have no more than five hours to return and deliver his gift basket.

"Yes, sir," Garvin heard himself saying. "I'm already on my way."

His headlights scraped the hillside topography of Malibu scrub brush and eucalyptus trees as he U-turned the Land Cruiser and pointed it back toward Pacific Coast Highway. He figured his drive to Granada Hills would last roughly forty minutes. Plenty of cushion. And time enough to roust Dave Wireman out of whatever drunken hole he'd crawled into.

It was about the time Mark Stubbitz was wondering where he'd last set down his skinny can of sugar-free Red Bull that he'd gotten pulled into a run-through of all the gathered video from the crime scene. A collection of portable computers and laptops had been assembled on a folding buffet table just twenty paces from the southern entrance to the Long Beach Arena's floor. Chairs were pulled up and portions of all the camera feeds were re-reviewed by Stubbitz and the four other assigned DHS investigators. In total, there were forty-three different recordings. From low-quality retail store security footage to a high-resolution weather video recorded by an ocean-aimed camera perched high above the Bank of America building.

Of particular interest was an unidentified white male who drove a silver Lexus. On seventeen of the camera feeds, the unknown subject could be viewed crossing the park and climbing onto the nautical sculpture centerpiece. Once set, the unsub produced what appeared to be a video camera and aimed it directly at the intersection where, moments later, the black Peterbilt refrigerator truck disintegrated in the massive explosion. Six feeds showed six different angles of the unsub tumbling from his perch. He was then seen retrieving his camera. More cameras captured the unsub as he limped hurriedly back to his Lexus and rushed from the crime scene.

"Can we get a tag on the vehicle?" asked Stubbitz.

"Uploaded everything to Quantico," said the tech. "They're working on it right now."

"And the guy he rode in with?" asked Stubbitz, referring to the black man who, moments before the detonation, could be seen exiting the Lexus, patronizing a nearby Panda Express, only to be flattened by the hurtling debris.

"Sorting through the DBs," answered an unshaven investigator. "Not the only dead black guy recovered."

"Need IDs," demanded Stubbitz. "Bet a sushi dinner the guy with the camera's got a stake in this."

"What if I don't like sushi?" asked the lone female on the team. Blonde, short, and broad in her gray-on-gray pantsuit.

"I'll buy you Happy Meals for a month," said Stubbitz. "But I need names, people. Names. Names. Names."

Big Dave Wireman thought he was going to have a heart attack. In the hours after the Long Beach bombing, he'd done everything but pop Xanax to try to calm his pulse rate.

He'd first noted the compound racing of his own heart while speeding back toward the San Fernando Valley. Ever since he'd picked himself up off the park grass, found the video camera, and hustled back to his car, Dave had been trying to replay the episode in his mind. He'd left Terrell in the Lexus and climbed atop the sculpture, zooming the camera until the black Peterbilt rig filled the video frame. Then BOOM! It all felt so surreal to Dave that somewhere near Inglewood he'd briefly pulled off the freeway to check the replay on his camera. That's when he noticed that his body was shaking. Not from nerves but from the excess pounding coming from his chest cavity.

The video playback confirmed it hadn't been a bad dream. He'd witnessed the event. One second the Peterbilt was in his camera sights. The next it had vanished into dust, with the little Sony Handycam dutifully remaining in record mode until Dave had exited the freeway to check the camera.

"Jesus," he'd recorded himself saying the second before switching to playback mode.

And not until Dave had wound the video forward and back had he even noticed that Terrell wasn't in the back seat. Another "Jesus" escaped his lips as he wondered aloud where the hell the muscle head had disappeared to. Then came a quick "screw 'im" from Dave. There was no way on earth he was whipping his car around and returning to Long Beach. Terrell was a grown man. If he were still alive and wounded, there'd be little if anything Dave could do for him—even less if he were dead.

Dave wasn't adept at dealing with big issues. So he stuffed the ugly thought along with the video camera into a protective case and, once again, sped north with every intention of handing the video to Garvin as soon as he'd attended to his damaged eardrums. He'd changed his mind about seeking help at Cedars Sinai. Instead he went to a less public urgent care facility in the Valley, where he was examined and prescribed both an oral antibiotic and ear drops. His hearing had been cut in half and was accompanied by a high-frequency buzz. Hopefully, it was temporary. Not that it bothered him nearly as much as the creeping feeling that he'd stepped in something outside his pay grade. He was plagued by a flop sweat nearly every time he rewound his memory back to the Friday noon hour.

Then there was the news. First over the AM radio of his Lexus, then on the big-screen TV that took up most of the living room wall of his apartment: Muslim terrorists had struck the Port of Long Beach. As local and national news organizations rolled out their pundits and pre-produced terrorism packages, Dave Wireman tried like hell to square what he was hearing over his television with the silly morning assignment he'd been handed by the famed private detective. On one hand, an attack by Islamic fundamentalists on America's most significant western port had long been predicted by everyone from the president of the United States to the International Longshore and Warehouse Union, whose reps were seeking greater safeguards for their members. On the other hand, Garvin had hired Dave to videotape the FBI takedown of some murder suspect for a big-dollar client.

Or was that just a ruse?

Dave Wireman needed time to think. And for that he needed distraction and noise other than the nattering talking heads on his TV or the double-jackhammers busting through the concrete sidewalk right outside his apartment window. A dark movie theater on a hot afternoon seemed like a calming idea for both his mind and his palpitating heart. From his one-bedroom NoHo apartment, he could walk the two short blocks to the air-conditioned multiplex just down the street. He first locked the video camera and the information it contained inside the five-hundred-pound gun safe he kept hidden behind a pair of overcoats in his closet.

The movie unspooled.

Dave Wireman kept one hand on his large Sprite, the other in his bag of buttered popcorn, and between gulps and loud mouthfuls he'd perform ten-second checks of his heart rate by pressing a knuckle up against his carotid artery. Not before the credit roll of the first feature did the thumping diminish to south of one hundred beats per minute. Dave asked for another go-around as he squeezed a fiver into the palm of one of the ushers assigned to clean up the theater.

With the second viewing of the movie, Dave didn't watch the picture as much as he let it distract him from his swelling paranoia that Garvin had set him up as some kind of patsy. *But for what?* he asked himself before answering, *The patsy never knows he's the patsy until he's either dead or in jail.*

That was about the time Dave Wireman decided not to contact Garvin. Instead, he'd watch the news unfold and patiently wait for Garvin to find him—a call that didn't come until some time after midnight. Dave woke to his cell phone vibrating across his coffee table, which was littered with empty Corona bottles. He could feel that he was still half drunk when the first words wouldn't quite roll off his tongue.

"Dave Wireman," he answered.

"It's Garvin. We gotta catch up."

"Time is it?"

"Don't matter. I've got another job for you. Two hours, tops, but Big Daddy is still paying your day rate."

"It's a new day?"

"Exactly," said Garvin. "Heading your way from Malibu. Meet on the way to Granada Hills."

"What's there?"

"A guy we need to deliver a message to."

For the briefest moment, Dave didn't recall the issue he had with Garvin, where he'd spent the past six hours, or the thousand conspiracy theories he'd hatched while sitting in that air-conditioned movie house. He merely responded according to the question.

"Roscoe and the San Diego," said Dave. "7-Eleven there."

"Near the brewery, right?"

"Right there. Fifteen minutes?"

After Garvin hung up, Dave rolled onto his back, finding the TV remote poking him in the kidney. He reflexively removed the offending device and unmuted the TV. The Fox News channel punched him in the eardrums with its breaking news theme. With that, the day came flooding back to the wannabe actor in a rush of unwanted memories.

"Fuck me," Dave said aloud.

33

Inglewood.

What am I doing? he asked himself. *Turning chicken shit into chicken salad, you idiot.*

That very same idiot had already chewed on the inside of Beemer's cheek until it bled. Beemer had to listen to him, considering he'd loosened the screws to the idiot's hatch. He was still planning to feed the idiot by consuming the life of one Rey Palomino.

But first things first.

The lights of surrounding Inglewood barely cut through to the blackened dirt roads and man-made canyons of the historic oil field. Beemer had dispensed with cutting through the locks on the chain-link fence. Instead he employed a couple of the Freightliner's remaining assets. Power and g-forces. At an opportune moment, Beemer extinguished the semi's lights, veered off La Cienega

Boulevard, and plowed through a cyclone fence topped with razor wire. When the dust settled and he was certain his act of trespassing had gone unnoticed, he'd set the parking brake on a fifteen-degree uphill slope and gone about the task of unloading his former million-dollar load.

He hefted the last few cartons of thawed plasma and carried them to the tail of the reefer trailer. He tossed each onto a growing pile of cardboard and leaking plastic IV bags. He punctuated the chore by discarding the worn pair of woolen gloves that he had found in the rusty refrigerator truck. The next order of business would be to find a convenient place to switch out the faulty Freightliner for a tractor-trailer rig that was less likely to fail him.

The chore itself proved therapeutic. Exhausted as Beemer was, the activity required an unthinking peace within which he found the space to cement a new direction. With a replacement truck, the entrepreneur could set a course for either Phoenix or Albuquerque. There were blood banks there. Equally as remote as the Reno warehouse and ripe for the taking. In a quiet corner of Beemer's brain, he painted a new scenario that had him crossing the border with a spanking fresh trailer full of frozen plasma. His UAE middleman would only suffer a delivery delay of barely one week.

He was back on track—with just a brief detour to Granada Hills. A forty-five-minute drive. The old Freightliner behaved downright giddy to drive with its trailer swept clean of cargo.

Next, Beemer readied his equipment, which included the field dressing of both his sawed-off pump shotgun and pistol. The chore was easily completed in the skinny sleeper space behind the Freightliner's seats. With a visit to a CVS Pharmacy he was able to buy a neoprene knee stabilizer. It was painful enough to bring tears when he finally slipped the device onto his leg. But it was worth it to save the last few cc's of numbing agent. He washed back a double dose of ibuprofen with a liter of orange Gatorade, reclined in the sleeper compartment, and let the hum of the unworthy refrigeration compressor lull him into a much-needed nap.

The alarm on Beemer's phone woke him at 11:00 p.m.

Fifteen minutes later he'd found a place to set the brake on the reefer truck—a darkened grade school parking lot five hundred yards downhill from Rey Palomino's home. From the residential street below Rey's, Beemer could see the unearthly glow from all the TV news crews in the midst of a variety of live shots.

He considered turning around. Driving south. But he didn't. Instead, he slung the shotgun under his jean jacket, stuck the pistol in his waistband, and began a gimpy hike up the sidewalk-tilted grade. Concerned that his pronounced limp made him stand out a bit too much, Beemer turned his attention to a yappy Yorkshire terrier that was patrolling its territory, a corner lot trimmed with a decrepit wooden fence laced with blooming bougainvillea. Without much effort, Beemer kicked the rotted slats until a hole formed and then coaxed the friendly Yorkie into his gloved hands. All Beemer needed then was a leash. A short length of low-voltage lighting wire torn from the earth proved suitable. And in a matter of moments, Beemer and his limp were transformed from the proverbial turd in the punch bowl to just another neighbor out to walk his loyal pup.

"Need to get you a new name," whispered Beemer to the Yorkie. "How about I call you Duke, after my old dog? You like that? You wanna be called the Dukester?"

From the breadth of the glow Beemer had seen from below Rey's property, he'd miscalculated the size of the news crew. He'd figured three, maybe four, news trucks and possibly a total of twenty or so news producers and technicians. But the trucks themselves added up to eleven in all, their microwave masts cranked so high into the air they looked like sailing vessels run aground on the curb. That and there was more than double the amount of crew he had anticipated, not to mention the four LAPD units that had been assigned to protect both Rey and his neighbors from overzealous journalists.

Adding to the spectators at the scene were the front-yard gawkers who'd come out of their houses in hopes of getting an update on the terror attack or maybe catching an eyeful of one of the many news Barbies assigned to serve up-to-the-minute reportage to TV audiences all over the world.

Beemer, playing the part of a curious dog walker, nudged one of the beefy electricians between lighting adjustments.

"After midnight," said Beemer. "Isn't the local news over?"

"Yeah," said the electrician. "But there's crews here from as far away as Australia. After we go dark we rent 'em equipment packages."

"No shit?" said Beemer.

"Even charge 'em for the microwave, satellite uplink," said the electrician, rubbing his pigskin gloves over his stubble. "Union got us a deal that makes out-of-town networks pay us time and a half. See over there," pointed the electrician. "Other side of the mailbox. Dark-skinned Bollywood-lookin' slice of ass?"

"India?" asked Beemer.

"Al Jazeera," said the electrician. "Big news over there when it's America who gets bombed, eh?"

Beemer just nodded his agreement while taking a half step back into the shadows. With his lousy luck, the Al Jazeera crew could've easily contained survivors from a reverse IED attack he'd both plotted and engineered in 2006. Paid for by a foreign contractor, Beemer and his team of talented former military misfits stole Iraqi ordinance and wired them to appear like the work of insurgent commandos, only to scare the bejesus out of foreign correspondents who opposed the coalition. Some journalists were killed. A few more were maimed for life. Beemer rationalized that getting themselves hurt or dead served the bunch of propaganda-swilling word-hacks right for forcing their beaks into a conflict about which few of them understood, let alone could report on accurately.

"Cute pup," said the electrician.

"That's Duke," said Beemer.

"Yorkie, huh?"

"What's that?"

"Duke. Yorkshire terrier. Good dogs?"

"My roommate's," shaded Beemer. "I'm just trying to put some points on the board."

"I hear that," said the electrician.

"Lemme ask you something," said Beemer. "You're, like, what? Electricians union?"

"IATSE."

"Right, right. So the guys who drive the vans? They with you? Or's that a Teamster thing?"

"Local news gets a waiver. We're all IA," said the electrician. "Which means everybody drives but the cookie."

"Cookie?"

"News wench. On-camera. Like your Bollywood girl over there."

"The women don't drive?"

"Guy cookies too. They don't drive either. All of 'em are a buncha divas."

Beemer forced a guffaw. While he pretended to be looking up and down the line of lighting rigs bathing a variety of male and female news cookies, he was performing a more accurate mental headcount. Twelve, maybe thirteen, on-camera Barbies and Kens. Triple that in camera crew and drivers. Six uniformed LAPD cops either patrolling the nearby lawns or flanking the front door to Rey Baby's house.

Then there was the man himself. Rey. Hiding behind the shut curtains and blinds of his house. Every window was covered, yet most of the house lights remained on. Rey had to be inside, visited by Lord knows how many federales. Beemer carefully gauged the shadows in the house. Most were faint, changing the direction of a light or momentarily diminishing the cast on a window. None, though, were distinguishable but for assisting Beemer in the most general guesswork. Three, maybe four, people.

Family? Law enforcement? Armed or otherwise? The obvious risk of any violent approach would be described best as suicide. It wasn't too late to walk the little dog back to its home and call it a night. Leave Rey Baby to rest in the brain's bargain bin. But that would mean Rey Palomino would have to share a mental prison cell with the idiot. And Beemer sincerely doubted one could survive with the other.

Rey was close. Only yards away from Beemer, separated only

by the obvious and tired obstacles. The last lament simmering inside of Beemer was why, only twenty-four hours earlier, he hadn't damned the silly estrogen party brought on by Rey's girlfriend, crossed the threshold, and blown the bastard's head off.

But as far as Beemer was concerned, history had a sick sense of irony. Here he was, a full turn of the earth since his last bite at the apple. And so much had happened. Beemer could still smell the fuel oil on his fingers and, if he closed his eyes, he could imagine the sweet remnants of spent nitrate in the air following the spectacular detonation. The variety of video angles of the blast had already made it onto the web and Beemer's smartphone.

"Can you believe that shit?" asked the electrician.

"No," said Beemer. "Maybe that's why I keep lookin' at it."

"On that little screen? That ain't nothin'. I got bomb shots in HD on the truck."

Beemer gave a glance upward at the beefy electrician. The gaze that returned was piercing and without a lick of mystery. It was an invitation to more than a view of some high-def footage of Beemer's bomb blast. The big man was casting a line for some quickie inside-the-news-van sex.

"No shit?" said Beemer, choosing to etch a smile over his repulsion. Gay or not, opportunity had just knocked. And the rest of his plan formed in microseconds.

"No shit," answered the electrician.

"Well, then," said Beemer. "Show me the way."

For Rey Palomino, all the sudden attention was anything but welcome. Yet beneath the facade of his compliant federal witness character, he felt the spotlight was deserved. After all, he'd let the devil in. Rey had agreed to act as the smuggling agent in exchange for paying down a dining room table overloaded with overdue debts.

But that wasn't the story he'd told the FBI.

Once he'd decided to turn over the murderer to the authorities, Rey giddily played the good guy. Rationalized his stake in the event. Even accepted kudos from the EMTs who'd come to rescue Special Agent Dulaney Little. Deep down, though, he knew he was a key witness to a history-making crime. That every federal cop from coast to coast was going to want to speak to him. So it wasn't so much that he'd fled the crime scene in his antique Porsche. He'd just wanted a little time to himself before the FBI caught up with him. Rey had no clue that once it became public there was a witness who had actually been involved with the terrorist, the world would arrive on his doorstep with microwave antennas, blazing-hot TV lights, and interview requests. The women had such breathtakingly perfect teeth that, had they not been wearing designer suits and holding microphones festooned with TV channel logos, he might've guessed they were former Miss America candidates.

The FBI had requested that Rey conduct no interviews until they'd finished with their own due diligence. And though he was not under arrest or suspicion of anything, they'd still asked him if he wanted to call or engage an attorney.

Rey had answered no.

Outside, the lights from the TV crews lit up the windows like the unfiltered desert sun. He'd had to close the windows, shutter or curtain them, and crank up the air conditioning. Investigators from the FBI, Homeland Security, Long Beach and Los Angeles PD, L.A. County Sheriff's, ATF, and the Port Authority had shown up with the promise of untold debriefs to come. By 11:00 p.m., having been awake for nearly thirty-six hours, Rey's eyes were so heavy and his thoughts so jumbled, he'd begged for the interrogations to be continued the next day. He was left with three ATF sentries in the house and more LAPD cops outside. The intent was both to keep their witness safe and from hopping in his antique Porsche and buzzing off to points unknown.

Instead of retiring to his bedroom, Rey planted himself in his living room Barcalounger. He tilted himself to a first class–styled recline of about forty-five degrees, thumbed the remote around the satellite's news channels, and watched his day repeat as if told from fifty different points of view. On occasion, the picture would cut to a live shot from outside his house where one of those toothy reporters would regurgitate the thoughts some other talking head had uttered only five minutes prior.

"You awake?" asked the tiptoeing ATF agent.

Rey twisted his neck. It was the shorter of the trio. A pint-sized agent of thirty years with a Navy haircut, wearing a Kevlar vest printed with ATF in neon yellow.

"Who wants to know?" asked Rey.

"Someone who works with Special Agent Dulaney Little," said the small ATF man.

"What the hell?" Rey muted the television and held out his hand for the agent's cell phone.

"Just lemme know when you're done with it 'cause the battery's almost dunzo."

"Hello?" Rey said into the phone.

"Mr. Palomino?" said the feminine voice. "My name is Lilly Zoller. I'm an assistant United States Attorney. I believe we were introduced this morning down in Long Beach. You know. Before things turned upside down."

"Okay," said Rey, not even trying to remember her. His mind was somewhere between mush and rice pudding.

"I know you've been speaking to just about everyone from Justice," said Lilly. "I want to know if you've made any arrangements for interviews outside of law enforcement."

"Nothin' yet," said Rey. "Everybody suggested I wait on that, which is fine by me because I'm just a little overwhelmed by—"

"I'll get right to it," interrupted Lilly. "I'm sure by now you know how this all began. There was a heist of some frozen blood product in Reno. Then on the way to shipping it somewhere, the man you met killed a young couple and a police officer up in Kern County."

"Heard somethin' like that."

"One of the victims in Kern was a young actress," continued Lilly. "Pepper Ellis. Have you ever heard of her?"

"No. Don't think so," said Rey, still inhaling in half breaths as he waited for the other shoe to drop.

"The victim's father is a man named Conrad Ellis. She was his only daughter and he's quite distraught."

"Okay."

"Conrad Ellis is a friend of mine. And he asked me to phone you and ask if you'd make some time to speak with him privately about what you know."

"Talk to the girl's dad?"

"Exactly," said Lilly. "Off the record. Just a private meeting between you and the grieving father."

"Sure, okay," stammered Rey. "I could do it, I guess. But why's he wanna talk to me?"

"Can I be frank with you, Mr. Palomino?"

"It's Rey. And yeah, sure."

"Rey. Yes," she began. "Conrad Ellis is a man of significant wealth and power. And I learned a long time ago that men with money and juice have their own way of doing things. This, I assume, is Conrad's way of grieving. Only he doesn't want to read about it in the news or hear from the FBI. He just wants to know what you know."

Rey had met plenty of rich people, having built a number of backyard pools for them. So, yes. Folks with money could be pretty damned peculiar. Still, the request sounded strange until Lilly added a dollar sign.

"Conrad Ellis, of course, is willing to pay for your time," she said. "Now. As a government official, I can't negotiate a fee for you. I can only make the introduction. But as we speak there's a man named Garvin Van Der Berk on his way to your home. Conrad tells me he's authorized this man to both negotiate an acceptable cash payment along with providing you transportation to and from Mr. Ellis's Bel-Air home."

"I'm sorry," said Rey. "I'm tired. Did you say they wanna drive me to and from Bel-Air?"

"Garvin Van Der Berk. You should tell your keepers to expect him."

"Right. Okay. And what's your name again?"

"I'm Lilly. I work with Dulaney."

"Yeah. How is he?"

"Dulaney? I haven't seen him. But I'm told he's resting okay."

"You know, I was with him when it happened. You know. The explosion."

"We were all there," said Lilly. "Remember. Garvin Van Der Berk."

34

Sunland.

As it stretches east, Interstate 210 is comprised of eight lanes that nearly reach from Los Angeles to Palm Springs. But for the final eleven miles of its westerly route, the traffic artery jogs north along the edge of the Angeles National Forest. Mountains rise up on both sides and for a while those omnipresent city lights disappear. This was one of Gonzo's favorite ribbons of Southern California blacktop. The roadway was rarely crowded. It turned gently through the low-lying hills of scrub and oaks with a gentle rise and fall. Late at night, driving it at any speed was a little slice of peacefulness.

Gonzo had let the Charger's speed creep up to just shy of one hundred mph when, as they crested over a rise, distant brake lights flared. The cars ahead were all, in choreographed unison, braking in a hurry.

"Ah, shit," said Gonzo.

Lucky sat up in his seat, trying to see beyond the cars to the cause of the midnight traffic jam. A quarter mile beyond, a tanker truck carrying fresh whole milk had somehow jackknifed and tripped on its side, splashing the freeway with twenty thousand gallons of pasteurized whiteness.

In her rearview mirror, Gonzo saw a pair of CHP cruisers descending on the accident scene, their lighting arrays swirling red and blue. The cruisers rocketed down the road's shoulder, trailed by two fire trucks and a mobile EMT unit.

"Follow 'em," said Lucky.

Gonzo was already on board. She wheeled the Charger hard right until she felt gravel under the front wheels, then squeezed the Dodge between the stalled traffic and the guardrail. The amount of dust kicked up by the heavy-duty tires of the fire vehicles made for a sandy brown fog, reducing visibility to barely three car lengths.

"Keep up, keep up!" urged Lucky.

"What does it look like I'm—"

"Watch it!"

Lucky needn't have shouted. Gonzo's right foot was already navigating from the gas to the brake pedal, forcing it down with every fast-twitch fiber south of her pelvis.

The wheels on the Charger locked up. The vehicle slid, fish-tailing slightly to the right. But not slowing in time to keep from impaling the brain trust in the unregistered Volvo wagon who'd snap-decided to sneak up the road shoulder. The impact spun both cars into the guardrail, pinning one to the other. Dirt billowed and settled in a spray.

All forward momentum was, in a matter of seconds, retarded by a pair of cars in a messy roadside tangle.

"What's your name?" asked Beemer, following closely as the beef-cake electrician led him to the news truck.

"I could tell ya," said the electrician. "But names kinda take the spark out of it, dontcha think?"

"See whatcha mean," said Beemer, playing along. He'd assumed the hairy ape was the kind of gay man who enjoyed frequenting public restrooms for anonymous sexual encounters.

"This one here," said the electrician, stopping at the right rear bumper of a white and maroon van festooned with all the de rigueur equipment for delivering up-to-the-second news video to an info-hungry public.

"You stay there, Dukester." Beemer carefully knotted the Yorkie's lead to a nearby street sign.

The electrician held the door for the stranger, half grin creasing through his beard. Beemer stepped up, instantly assessing the space. His eyes landed on an Indian-bred uplink operator.

"Break time," said the electrician, gesturing with a head feint toward the open door. The uplink operator gave Beemer a cursory once-over, unable to disguise his disgust. The electrician gave a low chuckle then leaned forward to whisper in Beemer's ear. "Union seniority has its privileges."

Beemer felt the man's big arm around his shoulder, helping him squeeze left so the uplink operator could slip past.

"Don't go," said an apologetic Beemer to the uplink operator.

"Huh uh," said the electrician. "Three's a crowd and I don't take my blow jobs with curry powder."

The uplink operator wanted to wince.

"Now, that's just mean," said Beemer, edging to his right and blocking the uplink operator's immediate exit. Beemer reached around, shut the door, and latched it.

"Seriously, dude," said the electrician. "Benji here's straighter than a honeymoon dick."

Beemer gave up a surprised laugh. "That's one I haven't heard," he said, slipping the .40-cal out from his waistband, placing the muzzle up against the uplink operator's skull, shielding against unwanted blood spray with his left palm, and squeezing off a single shot. *Bam!* Poor Benji's motor was cut and he dropped.

"OW!" shouted the electrician in a completely involuntary utterance. Before he heard the shot he felt the shock in the air and the fine spray of death against his face. Instinct repelled him backwards, tripping over his supersized flip-flops before he crashed to the deck.

The rest had already played out in Beemer's head. All that was left were two more pulls on the trigger. He stepped forward, fired a shot that first passed through the electrician's palm, held out in an impotent defensive pose. The projectile tumbled and lodged in the electrician's neck. The third and final shot was a coup de grâce to the victim's forehead.

Each report from the pistol offered little echo, unusual for a small space, but not beyond Beemer's expectations. When he was prepping for the IED attack on journalists, he'd learned all about TV trucks and the acoustic deadening with which the interiors were normally equipped. The vans essentially served as portable sound studios for the Kens and Barbies of cable news, allowing for both video editing and audio recording on four sturdy wheels.

Nobody heard the shots.

Brimmed by a wave of inner cool, Beemer eased up to the cab and surveyed the exterior landscape, glad to discover the keys to the vehicle were dangling from the ignition.

Next he needed to find the switch to lower the microwave mast. Then he would be obstacle-free to engage his flavor of the moment: Rey Palomino.

Headlights splashed the side-view mirror as a car slow-rolled past on the left. Beemer automatically flicked his eyes toward it, then went back to looking for the mast mechanism. But he found himself doing a double take. The taillights of a silver Lexus flared as the sedan slowed to barely a half mile per hour.

Spook school had taught him to trust the hairs on the backs of his neck and arms. That sometimes an extra glance or double take was a sub-neural recollection. Somewhere, somehow he'd seen the car before. But where and why it would matter to him in the middle of hijacking a news van was a mystery.

The mechanism that controlled the hydraulic servos that raised and lowered the mast had a yellow face, pan and tilt buttons for the microwave dish, and a big red stop and start button for safety's sake. Beemer quickly forgot about the silver Lexus and began figuring out how to lower the hundred-plus-foot telescoping arm.

"Shit! Shit! Shit! Shit! Shit! Shit!"

Lucky punctuated his machine-gun outburst with an equal number of left fists into the Dodge Charger's roof.

Gonzo, roughed up from the collision, both hands gripped at ten and two on the steering wheel, felt the sting of a split lip.

"Airbags," she spit, almost resigned to the fact that some cops didn't like the idea of anything impeding their escape from a wrecked vehicle to continue a chase. "You disabled the fucking airbags!"

"'Course I did," said Lucky, quickly giving up on his side of the car. "My door's jammed. We're out your side."

He was already climbing over the console, forcing Gonzo to shove herself into the driver's door. It swung wide with a loud, uncharacteristic squeak. Once past her, Lucky circled to the front end of the Charger. Under the right fender was bad news. The wheel was bent and nearly folded under the axle. He grit his teeth, kicked at the bent tire, then took four long strides to the trunk, popped the lid, and removed a pair of bulletproof vests. He tossed one at Gonzo while slinging on a Remington pump shotgun with a ballistic bandoleer full of twelve-gauge ammo.

The Kevlar vest lay at Gonzo's feet.

"If you don't wanna come," said Lucky, "by all means, stick around and trade insurance info with Gary Numbfuck."

Gary Numbfuck—a.k.a. the bushy gray-haired driver of the Volvo with the inebriated air of a relation to actor Gary Busey— was slow to exit from his vehicle. And when he finally stood before them, he was quick to lay blame on Gonzo.

"What the crap?" said the Volvo driver, his unbelted cargo shorts barely hanging on to his hips. "You don't look where you're goin'?"

"Where we're goin'?" said Lucky. "See those cops and fire units go by?"

"Maybe I did. Maybe I didn't," said the Volvo driver. "But I'm not talkin' to you. I'm talkin' to the bitch who was behind the wheel—"

Lucky one-arm-racked a shotgun shell into the pump action's chamber. That distinctive sound was enough to stop any drunk from running his mouth.

"Straight up, dipshit," said Lucky. "Your car drivable?"

Did he hear the question? The Volvo driver's eyes were still fixed on the shotgun.

"Your car!" barked Gonzo. "Can you drive it?"

"Want me to move it?" asked the Volvo driver, his attitude reversed into compliance mode.

"Requisitioned by the LAPD," said Gonzo, dusting off the bulletproof vest and marching past him.

"Requi-what?" asked the Volvo driver.

"Wait for the tow," said Lucky, stuffing a business card in the Volvo driver's aloha shirt. "Lemme know where my car lands."

With that, Lucky folded himself into the passenger seat of the Swedish-made wagon, slamming the door shut with a heavy clank. Gonzo hit the gas and the Volvo's wheels spun and spit gravel.

35

North Hills.

Obediently, Dave Wireman had unplugged himself from his dark apartment, started up his silver Lexus, and cut northwest across the central San Fernando Valley. Surface streets delivered him to the meeting point, a 7-Eleven convenience mart at the bottom of the 405's Nordhoff exit. Garvin Van Der Berk was waiting for him, sipping a forty-four-ounce Big Gulp cocktail of Diet Coke and super-caffeinated Mountain Dew. The private eye was nearly unrecognizable in his faded denim, baseball cap, and gray L.A. Dodgers jersey. The two men conferred briefly, decided Dave would drive to the Granada Hills address, then both embarked in the Lexus for the ten-minute midnight cruise.

On the drive from NoHo, Dave had decided to play things close to his vest. Keep his own counsel. Wait for Garvin to ask questions concerning the morning events in Long Beach. Leave it to the boss to inquire about the videotape he'd asked Dave to record.

But once again, Conrad Ellis was all Garvin had on his mind. The detective took the entire short drive to bring Dave up to speed on Conrad's newest request. They were to offer some witness named Palomino stacks of cash to entice him into a late-night interview with the eccentric mogul. Pieces of the story began to string together for Dave. The man he was supposed to have videotaped getting arrested was, in fact, some kind of terrorist who'd set off a suicide fertilizer bomb in downtown Long Beach. This Palomino guy was someone who could actually put a face to the obliterated bad guy.

And Conrad Ellis wanted to have a chat with him.

Upon arrival at the scene, Dave, an Angeleno who'd seen all kinds of news sieges in his years, was still surprised by the level of attention this witness was receiving. The eleven news trucks and accompanying civilian and police cars occupied most of the curb space. The peaceful hillside neighborhood was lit up with the flat white glare of television lights. Video cameras were mounted on tripods like turreted machine guns, each and every lens aimed at a home that could easily be described as a classic slice of American pie.

Instead of seeking a legal place to park the Lexus, Dave decided it was late enough that nobody would give a rip if he blocked the driveway of the home directly across the street from the Palomino home. Garvin had already instructed Dave to remain with the car while he made the cash appeal to the witness. If Mr. Palomino agreed to the terms, Garvin would call Dave and ask him to pull the car into the drive, thus shortening the distance the witness would have to walk in front of the cameras.

"Stay off your phone, okay?" reminded Garvin as he stepped out onto the asphalt.

"Gotcha, boss," said Dave, deciding to dispense with the air conditioning and roll down all four windows.

The air remained still and without a hint of breeze. When he hit the switch to retract the moonroof, Dave hoped that when he looked upward the leaves from the tremendous overhanging pepper trees would show signs of moving air.

Reserve Police Officer Tanner Cooley would have preferred his usual volunteer duty—patrolling the hot spots of the Valley in a radio unit. The mix of summer, an unusually high heat index, and the first night of the weekend usually guaranteed plenty of action for the LAPD hobby cops. That and veteran street cops were perfectly happy to leave much of the gun-chasing to the part-timers and volunteers.

In the wake of the morning's terrorist attack in Long Beach, he and the other reservists were called in and pooled for random assignment. Too bad for Officer Tanner Cooley, he'd been assigned to babysit a bunch of news jockeys in Granada Hills. Not that he was feeling sorry for himself. His full-time job as a regional manager for a national fast-food chain provided him with a recession-proof job. Profits were up along with waistlines. The numbers in Tanner's life had been treating him well.

And Tanner loved numbers.

He was an accounts whiz at his job. He could recite by memory the box scores and stat curves for the current season of his beloved San Diego Padres. And before he'd let his boots touch the pavement on those nights he worked as a volunteer cop, he'd commit to memory the license tags of recently stolen cars.

What made the license plate on the silver Lexus so beguiling to Officer Cooley was that he hadn't read it on a hot list. It had come over the computer system from Homeland Security as a vehicle possibly used to assist the suicide bomber in the Long Beach bombing. DHS had also noted it was not yet releasing the identity of the suspect.

7SKD872.

Officer Cooley could have eased from his corner post on Rey Palomino's front lawn over to his cruiser, called up the DHS alert on the MDT screen, and double-checked the digits. But one thing Tanner Cooley trusted was his keen mind for sequencing. Words. Symbols. Numbers.

He keyed the shoulder mic Velcroed near his collarbone and radio'd his partner for the night, a four-year LAPD veteran he'd only just met at the shift change. Ninety-five feet away, she was short and solid, severely featured with sandy-blonde hair pulled into a bun tighter than a Russian ballerina's. And when Tanner had casually asked her for a first name, she had tersely answered, "Officer."

"Officer Cerrano?" said Cooley. "Need to talk to you about that silver Lexus that pulled up."

"One of the occupants is with me now," she responded. "US Attorney's office cleared him. He's expected."

Cooley paused, quickly glancing back to the vehicle and its driver concealed behind a tinted windshield.

"The tags and the make," said Cooley into his radio. "They're a match for a DHS warrant."

"Copy that. Wanna double-check the warrant?"

"Don't need to."

"In fact, you do need to because I said so."

"Tellin' you it's on the sheet."

"Yo, hobby cop," said Officer Cerrano. "Double-check the tags and then get back to me."

Cooley tracked the veteran officer escorting an older man in a Dodgers jersey across the lawn to the front door of the Palomino home. His orders from the officer in charge were to revisit the DHS warrant. But Cooley had already done as much in his own mental memory banks. The numbers in his brain didn't lie.

Cooley's legs moved at an uncorrupted gait as he angled his approach on the Lexus from the driver's blind side. His shoulders swiveled left as his right hand came to rest on the grip of his service pistol. He'd yet to unholster the weapon in his reservist career. Was this going to be the moment? The Lexus's windows were rolled completely open. The driver appeared preoccupied with trolling the stations of his satellite radio. Cooley felt the pistol skin from its resting place, clear past his hip, and find its practiced position at the point of both his outstretched arms. He sighted down the top of the pistol's slide, aiming at the driver's collar bone.

"Both hands on the steering wheel! Now!" barked Cooley, making sure his hips and feet were locked underneath him. "C'mon, lemme see 'em!"

Officer Eugenia Cerrano had barely rapped her knuckles on the front door when the Baldwin latch turned and the door swung inward to reveal a thick ATF agent with a pair of wire-rimmed readers pinching the end of his nose.

"Hi," said the private eye. "I'm Garvin Van Der Berk. I believe I'm expected."

"Yeah," said the ATF agent. "Rey's in the den watching TV."

"So he's good?" asked Officer Cerrano.

"Yeah. He's expected—"

The ATF agent's head unconsciously tilted twenty degrees upward. This is when the lady cop saw the bright flash of light in the reflection of his glasses. The last thing she heard was the roar of an accelerating engine.

Garvin, on the other hand, had twisted around far enough to see what was coming. Behind the headlights and the muscle of an engine was one of those television trucks, bucking down the bricked footpath as it picked up speed. Hard-wired walkway lamps, each with its own pool of decorative light, were mowed over one by one by the truck's bumpers in splashes of sparks and firecracker pops. Sod was spit into the air as the yawning bumper bore down on the front door like a charging water buffalo.

Meanwhile, the trio on the stoop barely moved, as escape was futile.

36

Granada Hills.

As a matter of convenience, Beemer hated seat belts. When under a hail of insurgent gunfire, having to get out from behind a seat belt was a secondary concern. He would, however, concede their necessity and, in his present circumstance, could actually appreciate that he was securely lashed in by a three-point harness to the news van's driver's seat.

Operating the vehicle was easy enough. Once the microwave mast had been lowered, the engine started up on the first turn of the key. Then without much notice, he had slipped the van away from the curb and down the residential street, where, at the nearest intersection, he was able to make a slow U-turn before the start of his accelerated run. The automatic transmission shifted seamlessly and, for a microsecond, he lamented all the clutching and shifting he'd endured over the past few days behind the wheel of those two rigs.

Ahead and to the left was the pool man's suburban haven, still under the glare of all those television lights. With all the other news vans and police vehicles taking up curb space, Beemer's only angle of attack would be to cut across the short ramp into the driveway. He worried that, when airborne, the news van would lose its trajectory toward the welcoming double doors that fronted the residence. He tightened his grip on the steering wheel.

He'd done this before. Only it was in a heavy Humvee and the target address was built from little more than unreinforced block and mortar. American construction codes were far more rigorous than those found in Fallujah. Especially so in California, where earthquakes were a constant threat. Bearing walls. Rebar in every foundation. Even steel I-beam reinforcements were now part of some Los Angeles County residential construction formulas.

The news van bottomed out on the soft sod of Rey's lawn. The shock absorbers responded by bouncing the chassis back upward. For the briefest nanosecond, Beemer imagined those adorable walkway lamps as runway lights, guiding him to a bull's-eye of a landing.

The entry to the home was framed by a pair of heavy wooden posts bracing a large, shingled gable. On the crossbeam were three words in crude tile mosaic. The obvious work of the child who'd once lived there. *Home. Sweet. Home.*

There were three figures at the doorway. An unknown male just inside the threshold. A uniformed woman cop. And some older joker in a gray visitor's baseball jersey. All appeared to have been swallowed by the news van the moment it impacted the structure. The van itself appeared to slip perfectly between the posts, almost like a torpedo striking a battleship just below the waterline. All but for the lowered microwave mast, which splintered the gable in two, retarding the van from completely disappearing into the home.

To protect himself from wooden beams penetrating the front windshield, Beemer had wisely ducked at the first contact, releasing the steering wheel and becoming a mere passenger on his own death ride. Equipment sparked and popped as the van spiraled a quarter turn clockwise before coming to rest fifteen feet inside the entry. His fingers found the button to release the seat belt and he struggled to find a footing in the twisted cab. The safety glass windshield had peeled away, making a convenient escape hatch.

Instantly, a figure appeared before him—diminutive, chiseled, and wearing an ATF bulletproof vest. Unprepared for attack. Beemer lifted his pistol and quickly double-tapped the ATF agent with two slugs in the face. The body fell forward, dead before it hit the floor.

To his right Beemer heard the voice of a man barking into a radio. A mayday call. ATF agent needs assistance. With adrenaline giving him an appreciated boost, Beemer trotted down the corridor to the open kitchen. The ATF agent with the radio had barely gotten off a barstool and was amidst losing his balance when Beemer fired three quick shots, each missing high and right. As if the ATF agent had his shoes tied together, he thumped to the floor behind a brown suede sofa. Beemer readjusted his aim, calculated his angle, then popped off three more rounds. The bullets cut right through the cushions and struck home. The ATF agent screamed in pain, cursing the floor. "Fuck, fuck, fuck, fuck, fuck…"

Beemer flipped a chair to the left of the couch to potentially draw the downed agent's fire, then circled quickly to the right. He found the agent bleeding, prone, and working to wield his pistol left-handed. The fed never saw Beemer again, nor heard or felt the single and final slug he took to the back of his skull.

A figure flashed in front of Beemer, eyes as wide as silver dollars. Rey!

The pool man had none of the pretend cool of a federal agent. No gun. No intent to stand and fight. Rey's flight response was in full sail, practically peeling the screen door off as he bolted for the open space of his backyard.

Beemer leveled, panned, and unleashed the rest of his clip. The tempered glass of the floor-to-ceiling windows shattered in a hail of jagged pebbles, redirecting the bullets away from the target.

Beemer trotted, cutting off the angle toward Rey as he tried to shuck a fresh clip into the pistol. He didn't see the ring of brick coping that edged the barbeque patio. His right toe caught and, before he could process the error, he found himself planted face-first in a bed of flowering azaleas. *Aw, fuck.*

When he scrambled to his feet, Beemer had lost the gun in the bush branches and fresh-tilled soil. He heard Rey breathing hard, gasping for air.

"HEEEELLLLLPPPP!" Rey screamed. At the top of his lung capacity there was an asthmatic squeak. He was squared up with Beemer, unsure whether to break right or left. Then when he saw his assailant's distinct gimp, he swiveled his hips to the right and started what he thought was a swift move toward the side gate.

Beemer lunged, snagged the collar of Rey's T-shirt, and reversed the pool man's momentum. Rey found himself yanked, spun around, and oddly airborne. He shut his eyes, expecting to feel his shoulder connecting with the stone hardscape. Instead he felt the slap of water, enveloping and smothering him in a shock of cold.

Instinct.

Were Rey's body to have landed on concrete, his torso would have compressed and expanded with a sudden intake of air. But water is another matter. The instant Rey's skin turned wet, his mouth closed along with his sinus passages, defending his lungs from sudden suffocation. He struggled to right himself back to the surface so he could breathe.

Beemer didn't wait for Rey to catch a breath. He was on top of him before the pool man could figure up from down. Between the flailing arms and the wild kicks for life, Beemer kept his grip on the back of Rey's neck, plus a handful of his shirt. He briefly wondered how many seconds Danny's old man would be able to struggle before letting go and sucking in a lungful of chlorinated H_2O.

Forty-five, forty-six, forty-seven, forty-eight…

The water around Beemer eventually showed less churn as Rey began to succumb. His struggle for life on earth was about to be abandoned. *This is what happens, Rey Baby. This is what assholes like you get for fucking up my plans!*

As the clock to Rey Palomino's life counted down to zero, there was a second ticking timer at the back of Beemer's skull that was screaming. It was an internal stopwatch that had been running from the second he'd jumped the curb in the news van to that very moment he was in the pool, drowning Rey Palomino. Any second and cops would be pouring into the yard.

But Rey wasn't dead yet. Not for certain. So what if the man was limp in his arms? It had barely been a minute. There was no guarantee he wouldn't breathe again. After all, Rey was in the pool business. For all Beemer knew, the man had gills.

As if taking orders from his drill sergeant self, Beemer found himself releasing Rey. He used his near-dead arms to extract himself from the pool and began his pre-planned exit.

But not before one last look back. Into the pool. If there was a body in there, Beemer couldn't see it. That had to mean Rey had swallowed a lungful of pool water, lost buoyancy, and sunk.

So Beemer ran. Downhill.

What had appeared to be a suicide run had more in kind with a quick execution hit with a backdoor escape. Beemer had never expected to exit the way he'd entered. His preordained path was always through the house, over the back fence, then downhill to the waiting Freightliner. So at the moment more cops arrived and brave news crews began making their way inside Casa Palomino, Beemer was already vaulting over the rear fence and threading through the darkness of Rey's backyard neighbor's overgrown yard. Through an unlocked gate he was on a sidewalk fronting another street—a sixty-second trot to his idling reefer truck.

"You're fuckin' lost!"

"No shit, Sherlock!" spat back Gonzo, cranking the old Volvo into a squeaky residential U-turn. She could've kicked herself for leaving her phone behind in Lucky's car. And with it, the GPS app that had been guiding them to Rey Palomino's home.

Lucky's cell was dead and they were driving blind up and down the sloping streets of Granada Hills with only prayer and hope for navigation.

"Saw a Circle K back near the freeway," said Lucky. "I'll use the pay phone to call Bleds."

"Jasper or Casper Place," said Gonzo. "I remember keying the address. All I gotta see—"

"So you're gonna keep drivin' up and down 'til you get lucky?"

"Already got Lucky—pun intended." Gonzo hoped to lighten the mood, if even by the slightest margin.

"You wanna head back downhill?"

"Sure," said Gonzo, beginning to execute a three-point turn. The brakes of the Volvo chattered as she turned into a gated access drive to a county water-treatment plant. She shoved the balky gearshift into reverse and was pressing on the gas when—

"Wait!" cautioned Lucky, whose window suddenly turned white from the glare of headlights.

Gonzo touched the brakes, waiting for the vehicle to pass. The roadway underneath quaked as a tractor-trailer rumbled by.

Then Lucky became transfixed, as if watching a prehistoric beast.

"Freightliner fulla frozen peas..." recited Lucky in a ghostly monotone.

"What?"

"That was a reefer truck," said Lucky.

"Yeah? So what?"

"Freightliner, right?"

"I didn't notice."

"I did."

"So what about it?"

"Follow it."

"Why?"

"Just do it!"

The Volvo reversed back onto the blacktop, then continued down the slope some two hundred yards behind the semi.

"You wanna tell—"

"Guy I met in the hospital," interrupted Lucky. "Tattoo guy. Said he was haulin' frozen peas with a Freightliner."

"And that's what's in front of us?"

"Yup."

"Could be just another refrigerated truck fulla who knows what."

"We've been drivin' around here for twenty minutes. You seen a supermarket? Any place you'd expect to see a fridge truck makin' deliveries?"

Gonzo didn't need to answer. She already knew she was going to follow the rig because, once again, she was caught up in Lucky's orbit. Though driving the car, she was still his willing passenger.

"How far we gonna take this?" she asked, simply wanting Lucky to measure the depth of his hunch.

"As far as it goes," he answered cryptically.

Wednesday

37

Azusa.

Beemer's senses were heightened thanks to the adrenaline. From his nearly frostbit fingertips to his displaced kneecap to the retinas in his eyeballs, his nerves were at full attention. And it felt absolutely awesome.

Possibly because his senses were so acute he paid more than a passing interest to the battered station wagon making a three-point turn before falling into what appeared to be a locked-in tail position. As Beemer maneuvered the big rig across the freeway overpass and onto the eastbound on-ramp, the station wagon kept pace, never leaving his wake. In his side-view mirrors, he could easily make out the silhouette of the vehicle. It looked like an older model. But for the moment, the make eluded him. A question mark that would keep him perplexed for miles.

For sleep's sake, Beemer had plotted a two-piece trip east. The first leg was to travel the 118 to the 210 East until he reached Interstate 15. From there, he needed to hold off resting his lids for only another two and a half hours until he reached the state line at Primm, Nevada. Once there, he could park and abandon the old Freighty amongst all the other long haulers and steal twelve hours of sleep in a blacked-out casino hotel room before waking to a bargain breakfast and plotting his next move to either Phoenix or Albuquerque.

The moonless blanket of black sky appeared suspended above the freeway, separated by the atmospheric glow of a million tiny sources of light. From streetlamps and surging beams from cars, to the porch lights that adorned nearly every suburban tract home, the night in Los Angeles and its outlying sister cities was rarely and truly dark. It was closer to shades of gray, trapped by a faint and moist layer that penetrates nearly fifty miles inland from the ocean. With the marine layer came a coolness that teased a coming end to the suffocating heat wave.

For nearly an hour, both the semi and Volvo wagon drove in interlocked tandem, always due east and within the speed limit.

Gonzo felt it was a risk. That with every mile she put between herself and Granada Hills there would come an eventual disappointment. That ahead of her, squarely between the Volvo's dim headlights, was just another reefer rig on its way to an early-morning delivery. There was relief in the thought. Following a blind lead, though frustrating, would nearly always result in zero danger. Her mind even wandered to the eventual aftermath of her three days with Lucky. Aside from all the red tape and reports and explaining her way out of all the broken protocols, she was still concerned about Lucky. Emotions were suddenly in play. Plenty of conflict interrupted by a surprise moment of intimacy. All that and the poor wrecked Kern County deputy hadn't yet had a day to bury his baby brother.

Lucky rolled down his window and let the air buffet him. Gonzo equalized the Volvo's cabin, cracking her window and glancing over at her would-be partner. His face was stony. *A flaw*, she thought. Her guess was that, as a generality, Lucky was unreadable to a fault. Probably impossible in a relationship built on a traditional courtship, let alone convenience. *Relationship? Jesus. What am I thinking?*

"We're at an eighth of a tank," said Gonzo.

"Maybe that's his plan," said Lucky. "Run us 'til we hit fumes."

"If he has a plan," said Gonzo. "Assuming he's our guy or even knows we're tailing him."

Lucky didn't answer. He was all in with the pursuit of the dirty Freightliner and its phantom driver. The duo had already discussed the options. Neither had a working phone to call and request backup. Without an official vehicle, there was no siren or flashing lights to safely alert the truck driver to pull over. And while on the freeway, any attempt to flag down or overtake the rig would be both dangerous and irresponsible as hell.

It was like playing chicken with fuel. Whose reservoir would be first to run dry? Lucky was putting his money on the Freightliner despite its twin hundred-gallon gas tanks. Shit for odds.

Mile after mile, the tandem dance continued past what appeared to be endless real estate consisting of little more than freeway-convenient car dealerships, fast food restaurants, big box stores like Walmart and Home Depot, and finally a massive Miller beer brewing and bottling factory. Steam spewed from the stacks and, for a two-minute stretch, filled the car with the sweet smell of cooked hops and barley.

"So I kinda noticed something," said Lucky, briefly stepping out from behind the monotony.

"Noticed?" asked Gonzo.

"Next to your bed. Binders and shit. Flight manuals."

"Oh, that." Gonzo cleared her throat. It was dry and she could've used a liter of water. Her skin felt brittle. "I'm training to fly helos."

"Air Support?"

"Yup."

"Always wanted to do a ride-along with those boys," said Lucky. "What's it like up there?"

It wasn't the first time a fellow officer had asked her the

question. Her standard retort was to glibly quip about giving her a better view of the questioner's bald spot or spying on his or her naked rooftop liaisons with confidential informants. It was harmless, classic cop trash talk.

"Peaceful…" answered Gonzo. "Dreamy…"

"Must feel like you're above it all," said Lucky. "The blood, the concrete. All the shit."

Gonzo merely nodded her agreement.

"I can see the attraction—" said Lucky, cutting his own thought off at the precise moment Gonzo eased off the accelerator.

The brake lights on the semi rig were flaring and the blinking indicators signaled that the truck was preparing to exit the freeway at Azusa Boulevard.

"You familiar with the area?" asked Lucky.

"Everything from A to Z in the USA," said Gonzo.

"What?" Lucky's voice sharpened.

"Just somethin' I heard once. Azusa. Everything from A to Z in the—"

"I heard it the first time."

"All I know about this place. Been a long time since I've been this far east—"

"Signal."

The stoplight at the bottom of the off-ramp was quickly turning from yellow to red. The big rig was already steaming to the left. Gonzo stomped on the gas and surged into the intersection just barely ahead of the cross traffic. The Volvo's wheels chirped loudly against the asphalt and its top-heavy frame made it feel as if it were inches from a rollover.

Lucky said nothing.

"Well," began Gonzo. "If he didn't know we were behind him, he probably does now."

"No sense keeping a passive distance. Keep us tight."

The heavy Volvo, picking up speed, closed the gap to the rumbling reefer rig to thirty yards. Despite the hour and nearly nonexistent traffic, the truck driver appeared careful to keep his speed under the posted thirty-five miles per hour.

"Where do we think he's going?" asked Gonzo.

"Someplace isolated," said Lucky, barely above a whisper. "Someplace where he can kill us."

The GPS app on Beemer's phone showed that, after two miles of suburban sprawl Azusa Boulevard slowly snaked its way into the heart of the San Gabriel Mountains, leading to a pair of public reservoirs. It was a safe call that after 2:00 a.m. traffic would be next to negligible.

All the while, the stalking station wagon and its two occupants remained in Beemer's mirrors. Who they were didn't so much matter as what was soon going to happen to them. One thing for certain, the pair were neither cops nor feds. In the miles they'd rolled off since Granada Hills, there'd been one chance after the next to bring in the squad cars and helicopters. Beemer reasoned they were most likely thieves or private military contractors who must have been trailing him.

The highway rode a low valley as the high desert mountains lifted on both sides. Beemer checked his speed. Twenty-eight miles an hour. A glacial pace. But sufficient enough to move his slowly evolving plot to an eventual resolution. He only needed to keep control of his patience. It was just another detour. After which he could continue crawling toward Stateline. And once there, some overdue damn slumber.

The Freightliner's headlights ignited a sign reading "Bridge— 200 yards." Precisely the kind of landmark Beemer was hoping for. With the reservoir stretching out to the north, he checked his side-view mirror once more, then downshifted. He let the gears slow the heavy load, finally braking the big rig to a stop once his rear wheels had crossed the 120-foot span.

Neutral. The old Freightliner's diesel engine coughed, spit some smoke, then found a breathable mix of fuel and air. To Beemer's ears, it sounded like a giant alley cat with sleep apnea. A deep purr, smooth silence, hacking, an inhalation. Then the cycle would start again with another deep purr.

Not once, though, did Beemer take his eyes off his mirrors. He watched the Volvo roll to a stall with its rusty front end just inches from the bridge. As if a strange mechanical instinct prevented the vehicle from crossing. The driver, Beemer concluded, was a tall female with a spray of unkempt hair. African American or Hispanic. Confident posture. In the passenger seat, a hairless male, either bald or shaven. A common feature of civilians, PDs, and the military.

Beemer had half a mind to swing out of the tractor rig's cab and empty his first clip on the station wagon just to see how the unknown duo would react. Whatever their response, it would be informative. But not necessarily the most efficient at neutralizing the threat. Better to lie in wait. Force the faceless foe to make a move.

The semi-auto shotgun was on the seat next to Beemer. On his lap, the .40-cal pistol. He slipped two spare eighteen-round magazines in the left cargo pocket of his shorts.

"Okay, sports fans," said Beemer to nobody in particular. "Waiting on y'all."

A chill crept over Gonzo. It meandered up her spine to the top of her skull, then repeated in such a way that she had to shake it off.

"Christ, what's he waiting for?"

"For us to make a move," reckoned Lucky.

Gonzo checked the dashboard clock. 2:17 a.m. By her count they'd been parked at the bridge for almost five minutes. And nothing whatsoever had changed. The dirty white Freightliner, rear safety flashers still blinking at a rate close to sixty heartbeats per minute, stayed immobile in the Volvo's high beams.

Outside both windows, rising above the idling engines, she could hear the sound of water churning over rocks as the reservoir released its nightly irrigation quota. The air above it cooled, reaching like wet tentacles into the car.

"Okay," began Lucky. "We go right and left. Start at the back and hug the trailer 'til we make the cab."

"What happens then?"

"He won't wait that long. He'll pick a side and try to take one of us out with his first clip. Incumbent on the other of us to charge hard, flank from the other side, and take him down."

"Dontcha think he knows that?"

"I don't know what he knows."

"You knew he was leading us here. You knew he'd make us wait to make a move."

Lucky cracked his door, but waited for her to follow his lead. Gonzo swallowed. The dryness in her throat stung. She tried to hock up some spit for some vocal lubrication. Next, she rechecked her pistol to make certain there was a cartridge in the chamber, then began her move from the wagon.

They stepped into the Volvo's headlights, casting long shadows all the way to the hillside beyond.

He sees us now, said Gonzo to herself. *He knows this is the moment. This man whose name we don't even know.*

With a simple hand gesture, Lucky signaled for Gonzo to widen the gap between them. So she eased to her left and into the empty oncoming traffic lane. Lucky hugged the bridge railing, his forward momentum deliberate and unrushed. His .45 in a combat grip, muzzle twenty degrees shy of level.

And Gonzo was with him. Step for step. It felt like an academy moment. An exercise in how to approach a suspect. Right out of the field combat textbook. But all the while, Gonzo was aware of a simple fact. In her career, she could count on one hand the number of times she'd unholstered her weapon in the line of duty. The last time was when she'd stuck it in Lucky's face to protect that skinny Blood he'd wanted to beat the tar out of.

Would you have really shot him, Lyd?

She wanted to kick herself for letting her focus wander if even for a microsecond. As Gonzo continued to advance from the left, the white Freightliner began to loom like a dirty, gargantuan icebox that had been tipped onto its side. The angle of the dormant truck blocked the cast of the Volvo's headlights from illuminating the cab. The windows appeared black and impenetrable. What Gonzo would've paid for air support and that 1.6-kilowatt Nightsun spot-light. The thirty million candlepowers produced enough juice to ignite a bathroom through a keyhole. Even the most dangerous of subjects felt their testicles shrink when struck by the helo's beam.

In her periphery, Gonzo saw Lucky nearly disappear from sight as he slipped to the right side of the trailer assembly. Through the undercarriage she could still see his shadow inching closer to the cab. Twice as close as her. So with her gun sights fixed on the driver's door of the truck, she trotted and cut the distance in half, fully prepared to unleash every round in her magazine.

"OUT OF THE TRUCK WITH YOUR FACE ON THE GROUND!" shouted Lucky from the other side.

"YOU GOT HIM?" yelled Gonzo.

"DOOR OPEN, SHOW YOUR HANDS!" barked Lucky.

Gonzo first squatted, peering underneath the truck to see if she could glimpse a man climbing down on the opposite side. Instead, she saw nothing. Nary a shadow or a shift in light.

"TELL ME WHAT YOU GOT, LUCK."

Gonzo rotated left, crossing right foot over left in a sidestep that she hadn't performed since her days at the academy. She kept dipping into quick crouches, seeking to locate Lucky or the perp beyond the silhouettes of axles and tires. She was no longer fixed on the blackened windows of the big rig, let alone the darkened trap between the cab and the refrigerator unit. She missed the first move from a shape atop the trailer. The outline of a man lifting to a one-kneed stance, barely formed against the moonless sky. The image was so amorphous and unexpected that Gonzo's brain receptors couldn't trigger her defenses fast enough to save her life.

That's when she saw the muzzle flash.

The bridge had seemed as good a place as any. As Beemer had led the unknown duo in the Volvo wagon into the desert mountains of Azusa, he had observed that the somewhat level stretch alongside the reservoir gave him the best vantage point to see any cars that might come along. He set the parking brake on the far side of the bridge, took a minute or so to measure the threat in the station wagon, then climbed through the sleeper cab to the window hidden between the cab and the trailer. The hinge that louvered the rectangular pane of safety glass was easily dislodged with a couple of heavy kicks. It swung inward far enough for Beemer to squeeze himself out of the cab without so much as opening a door.

Despite the cargo trailer being empty, the faulty compressor continued to run and vibrate, the exhaust resulting in a cooling mist, making for a wet climb up to the roof of the trailer. Once there, Beemer edged around the failed cooling unit. Then, on his stomach, he wormed his way to the end.

He didn't dare peek over the edge, exposing himself to the Volvo's high beams. He flipped over and lay flat on his back and utterly motionless, letting his ears gather the necessary information for his immediate survival.

Again, Beemer concluded that the duo couldn't be law enforcement. There was no backup. No helicopter in the sky. Which brought up the question of private contractors. But he couldn't imagine who would have hired them. The government? That poorly secured blood bank in Reno? Hardly. More than likely, Rey was dead. But he had relatives—including a sibling who owned the Long Beach shipping enterprise. Could Rey Palomino's brother be a guy connected to the mob? Or even one of the international drug cartels? Such was the scenario Beemer settled on. Though it wouldn't change his tack. Whether the duo in the Volvo was a mob hit team or merely a pair of hijackers, the sum of their actions was about to result in them getting themselves very dead.

Beyond the vibrations from the compressor and the white noise from the river, Beemer listened for the station wagon's doors to swing open. Both doors were audible, but the driver's door made a distinct squeak at its tensile. Next came the footfalls, relatively noiseless but for the occasional crunch against gravel. In stereo. The heavier steps were to Beemer's left. He made the easy assumption that those shoes belonged to the male. The lighter crunches were to his right and further away.

Women were generally smaller in scale. Sometimes slower yet

more difficult targets to strike with a bullet. Beemer had chosen his first target. He only needed his ears to guide him, tracking her ever-fainter steps as he gingerly rolled to his stomach and shimmied. Inches at a time. Angling closer to the aluminum stripe riveted to the edge of the trailer's roof.

Then came the shouts:

"OUT OF THE TRUCK WITH YOUR FACE ON THE GROUND!"

"YOU GOT HIM?"

"DOOR OPEN, SHOW YOUR HANDS!"

Mystery solved. Only cops or feds would bark those kinds of orders. But without the usual backup? There should've been a cavalcade of black-and-whites descending. Beemer could've taken the moment to double-check his six. Re-sweep the landscape for bogies. The sky for an incoming chopper. Only he sensed a slight measure of advantage. While the advancing tag team traded shouts, potentially distracting each other, Beemer listened to his primal drive. He rolled right, rose to one knee, and used the compressor unit as partial cover. What followed was as practiced as table manners. Rise, set the muzzle on the target, adjust for downward elevation. And three quick squeezes.

The muzzle flash was blinding.

Against the black night, only the first shot felt true. The recoil and resets and subsequent microsecond trigger pulls seemed slightly out of rhythm. The usual solution was to take a breath and send another trifecta of hot shit into the target.

But then Beemer felt the sting of sheet metal splinters. Sparks. He was enveloped in a cacophony of gunshots. Large handgun caliber, he guessed. The bullets that didn't send sizzles into the compressor scored through the atmosphere, leaving high-pitched whistles in their wake.

Beemer lurched hard to his left, slapping the top of the trailer with a thud. Another miscalculation. He'd left himself no room to decelerate. And within the blink of an eye he experienced nothing but air underneath him, the heavy pull of gravity, followed by the inevitable bone-crunching collision with the road.

Then came the blackout. As if the master breaker box had thrown a switch. His eyes would eventually open. And when they did, Beemer would find himself staring at a moonless sky, clueless as to how long he'd lost the tick-tick-tick of his internal clock. And his gun.

The slide of Lucky's .45 snapped open, signaling that he'd clipped out of ammunition. He thumbed the release button, ejecting his empty magazine downward. He was already running and felt the spent magazine drop on the asphalt, kick off his shoe, and sail under the truck. Lucky hadn't aimed at the assailant. When he'd heard the reports of shots fired in Gonzo's direction, he'd back-pedaled and held his pistol high over his head, unleashing his entire clip across the roof of the trailer. The angle was all wrong, though. From his position so close to the rig he had no visual on the shooter. The most he could hope to accomplish was to retard the sudden barrage and race to his fallen partner.

He jacked a spare magazine into the pistol, rounded the grill of the Freightliner, and saw her. Prostrate on the ground like a wounded animal already struggling to right herself. Her weapon impotent and out of reach.

The first bullet had struck Gonzo center mass. Dead in her chest. And though the impact was easily absorbed by the Kevlar vest, she still felt as if she'd been kicked by a mule.

She hadn't a clue why she'd lost her grip on the gun. It flipped away from her like a fish. Her instinct was to chase it and snatch it back into her hand on the first bounce. Only her nerves were lying to her brain. Nowhere in her conscious self did she know the second bullet had cut right through her elbow. The joint shattered in an instant, the muscles contracting and releasing at practically the speed of light, involuntarily tossing the pistol away.

Gonzo had spun, catching the third slug in the crease between her butt cheek and her hamstring. It cut her wheels and sent her crashing face-first to the pavement. In the scattered moments after, she wondered if it was blood she tasted in her mouth or the flavor of residual road oil.

Only one leg wanted to function. And she still couldn't manage anything with her right arm. Useless. As if she'd left it attached to the steering wheel of the Volvo. She heard footsteps. Heavy shoes slapping at the pavement, closing with every quickened stride. She felt Lucky sliding down to her side.

"Where you hit?"

"I dunno," said Gonzo. If she'd had time to think, she might've been able to assess her wounds. "Think everywhere."

Lucky positioned himself on the ground between the rig and Gonzo, reloaded .45 outstretched, sweeping all eighteen wheels of the Freightliner.

"Did you get him?" She twisted on her left hip, the pain reaching every nerve ending. She slumped.

"Unknown," said Lucky. "Can you move?"

"If I could do you think I'd be like this?"

"Right."

Lucky slid behind her without ever letting the barrel of his pistol leave the big rig.

"Can you sit up?" asked Lucky.

Gonzo didn't answer as much as command herself to roll the opposite way and utilize every strand of her abdominals to bend at the waist. It was then she got her first look at her right elbow and her dangling forearm.

"Fuck. My arm."

Lucky hoisted her without warning, grappling her around her chest until he'd begun to drag her backwards. Away from the semi. Inching toward the drainage ditch just beyond the road's shoulder. All the while, his pistol still stretched out defensively. Prepared to unleash hell.

"Where the hell is he?" breathed Gonzo.

A shadow crossed. So quickly it was like a camera shutter flipping open and closed. A mechanical eye blink. The figure passed in front of the Volvo's headlights, momentarily paralyzing both Lucky and Gonzo.

The Volvo's engine suddenly roared. The timing belt's slippage made a piercing sound that cut through the air. The wagon's almost bald tires chirped against the pavement in a sudden surge forward on a doubtless path. The beams bucked at the first acceleration, then zeroed in on the struggling duo.

Compelled by instinct, Gonzo planted her good leg into the ground and tried to stand, only to have Lucky spin her away from the surging Volvo. Gonzo hit the pavement again, this time six feet closer to the ditch, but hardly clear of the Volvo's closing bumper.

Then she heard the scream.

The sound began low in Lucky's diaphragm. A guttural foulness that built into a banshee howl. He charged the rushing station wagon, the Colt pistol as his leading edge, spitting heavy lead.

The left headlight sparked and died, turning the oncoming wagon into a three-thousand-pound one-eyed beast. Three more bullets slapped the windshield. Cracks in the automotive glass spidered all the way to the rubber molding.

As for Lucky, he was beyond thinking. He had a picture of Beemer in his mind. Despite the headlight's glare, the Kern detective etched himself an image of the nemesis behind the wheel of the oncoming Volvo. A grinning joker, hell-bent on painting chaos wherever he went.

The Volvo closed. Impact was imminent. But Lucky wasn't going to die on the grill of a late-model station wagon. He leaped forward, laid himself out horizontally, and met the rushing vehicle at the damaged windshield. The weakened glass gave way, inverted under the combined Gs of his weight and the vehicle's speed, and collapsed inward in a crush of glass, metal, and tangled bodies.

Gonzo used her shoulder to throw herself left, avoiding the Volvo by mere inches. The station wagon blew past her in a rush of wind and exhaust, pitching over the shoulder and eventually coming to rest after digging through twenty feet of soft ditch.

The Volvo's horn sounded, stuck on a single obnoxious note.

The adrenaline feeding Gonzo's muscles lifted her onto her one strong leg. She was able to skip-limp without falling over to her pistol, which still lay on the pavement, hammer cocked, safety engaged. She ignored her dangling forearm, gripped the gun with her left hand, then returned her attention to the finished Volvo that lay steaming in the ditch.

"LUCKY!" she shouted. "I'M COMIN', AWRIGHT?"

She held the pistol forward, nearly sideways for balance, and continued to step-shuffle closer—then closer again—to the ditched car.

"YOU HEAR ME, LUCK? HANG ON!"

Gonzo approached from the passenger's side. The taillights, stuck in full-braking flare, brightly ignited her anguished face. Her back teeth were set, molar to molar. On full lock-jawed grind. She leaned her shoulder against the side panels for balance and bounced herself down to the rear door latch. The door popped open easily and downhill gravity did the rest. The interior dome light glowed dull and yellow.

Muzzle first, Gonzo expected to see a bloody mess. Instead, she found windshield bits, a mangle of interior plastics, and Lucky.

"Jesus…" she said, suddenly hacking up the spit caught in her throat.

The man, who only hours ago had shared both her bed and sweat, was twisted around between the front and rear seats. Lucky's clothes were either roughed up or shredded by the glass. His limbs appeared askew, no longer ergonomically intact. His exposed skin was scored and bleeding. Gonzo read his breathing. Short and labored, hampered by Lord knows how many broken ribs.

As a traffic cop she'd seen this enough times. Yet it was what she couldn't see that usually killed the accident victims. Internal bleeding.

"Lucky…"

One of the man's eyes cracked open amidst his badly lacerated face. His lips barely moved.

"Don't let him…" whispered Lucky.

That's when it registered to Gonzo that the driver's seat was empty and that damned squeaky door was wide open.

Gonzo pushed herself out of the vehicle, spun around the

door, and fell headlong into the dry ditch. Her forehead struck sand. But her left hand never let go of her 9mm. She threw her shoulder forward, placed the gun where she could retrieve it, and effectively performed a single one-armed pushup until she could find a purchase. Then she rose, pulling herself up over the Volvo's right fender.

That's when she saw him.

Downriver. Stumbling along the rocky bank was the distant figure of the bad man, unsteady yet progressing in full retreat. The lone headlight of the ditched Volvo painted him in a flat and distant hue. Getting further away with every second.

She lifted the pistol, rested it on the angled hood, and tried to focus through the steam that misted from the ruptured radiator.

The right-handed cop had to switch off the safety with her teeth. The lever clicked and left her with the bitter taste of gunmetal and blood. Gonzo sighted the weapon, closing her left eye and sticking her chin into her left shoulder. The dimming figure bobbed in her line of sight as he climbed up and down the heavy boulders at the edge of the rushing spill-off.

She remembered her very first academy shooting lesson. She let the voice of the range instructor whisper to her inner ear. Inhale. Exhale. Hold. Squeeze.

Bam! The pistol bucked in her hand. The muzzle flared with a white-hot powder burn against the blackness and disappeared in time for Gonzo to see the nameless bad man twitch and pitch sideways into the rushing water. The body slapped the water and was carried away in less than a heartbeat. Gone.

"I GOT HIM!" shouted Gonzo, echoing her inner voice. "YOU HEAR ME, LUCKY? I GOT HIM!

"LUCKY? LUCKY!"

Epilogue

Santa Monica Mountains.

The memorial service for Pepper Ellis was scheduled for a cooler Saturday afternoon at Bel-Air Presbyterian. Only the weathermen were wrong. The high-pressure bubble that had settled over Southern California, inviting more than a week of fire-breathing temperatures, had promised to dissolve. But overnight, it had returned to muscular form, shocking the experts and placing pressure, once again, on the already distressed power grid.

The Mulholland Drive church, perched on five acres of prime real estate, was known as much for its multimillion-dollar views of the over-baked San Fernando Valley as it was as the favorite Sunday respite for former president Ronald Reagan and his wife, Nancy. The house of worship with a capacity of sixteen hundred was overstuffed with mourners, well-wishers, and deal-makers who were paganly using the sad event to make their presence known. It appeared that practically overnight the precocious seventeen-year-old Pepper had transformed from a kiddie-cable up-and-comer to nearly a household name.

To make the event feel even more crowded, news networks, looking to maximize viewership, sent anchors and news trucks to cover the memorial.

"Nothing like a little blonde TV star as icing on the cake to a terrorist story," confided Lilly Zoller to her date, Graham McDonald, the assistant-US-Attorney-pal-slash-booty-buddy. Luckily for McDonald, the Attorney General had sent a number of his best lawyers to Los Angeles to ride in a close herd on the continuing terror investigations.

Lilly had respectfully accepted Conrad Ellis's invitation to attend his daughter's memorial. She'd chosen to sit in a back pew, on the aisle, just in case she needed a quick escape. For days her cell phone had been buzzing with interview requests fielded by her new agent.

"Before me," whispered Graham, "you didn't know who Pepper Ellis was."

"Don't sound so smug. It's not attractive."

Lilly surveyed the room. Never had she seen so many good-looking people dressed in designer black. All members of the Hollywood club. Showbiz insiders. With Conrad Ellis as an ally, who knows? Lilly might get beyond the invited guest stage and gain full membership.

The altar was adorned with large high-resolution photos mounted on easels set amongst impressive sprays of white roses. Each image appeared to have been chosen by the PR folks hired by the network's executives. Pepper Ellis would be remembered more as how she had lived as an actress and less than as a daughter.

Conrad ambled before the front pews, greeting the elite mourners with a gloved hand.

"I hear he's a germophobe," whispered Graham.

The man could wear a body condom for all Lilly cared. After all, he was the grieving father and could do exactly as he pleased.

"You *are* gonna introduce me," Graham stated.

"*I* haven't even met him yet," said Lilly. "At least not in person."

"So it's only been phone sex so far?"

Graham's joke didn't land well with Lilly, who flicked him a distasteful sneer.

"Shame on you. It's a memorial—"

"Okay. My bad," said Graham without even trying to sound remorseful. "Just wanna be able to tell my daughter I met Pepper's dad."

A cell phone whistled. Lilly instantly recognized the sound as her own ringtone, embarrassed that she'd forgotten to set it on vibrate. She dug into her voluminous black Marc Jacobs bag and retrieved the offending device.

"Fuck me," said Lilly, rereading the memo in hopes that she'd gotten it wrong the first time.

"You gonna share?" whispered Graham.

"Deputy AG just touched down at LAX. Wants to meet up in Glendora." Lilly glanced up from her phone. "Where the hell's Glendora?"

"Thought you were from here."

"Just 'cause somebody's from Disneyland doesn't mean they can pinpoint every pimple on Goofy's ass."

The text on Lilly's phone revealed an inconvenient meeting time.

"Jesus. I'm gonna have to go," said Lilly.

"Swell," said Graham, clearly and coldly disappointed. "So I'm not gonna meet Pepper's dad."

"Stick around for all I care," spat Lilly. "Maybe you can get an autograph."

Rey never had a chance to thank the police officer who'd rescued him from his pool. The most he ever learned was that a lone cop, following Beemer's trail of mayhem through the house and into the backyard, had mistakenly flipped on the colored pool and landscape lights. Upon sighting Rey laying motionless at the bottom of the shallow end, the former lifeguard had jumped in and begun lifesaving measures. The first thing Rey recalled was waking up coughing. As if recovering from a nightmare only to find out the lung he was gagging up was his own waterlogged organ. He laid sideways on the stone hardscape, convulsing as he involuntarily expelled those last deadly drops of chlorinated water. He recalled seeing a thinnish black man in a dripping, navy blue uniform, pointing around the backyard as if directing traffic. But Rey never saw his face nor got his name or badge number.

Chalk that up to another regret.

After an ambulance ride and a brief stint in the emergency room, Rey was released with a prescription for an albuterol inhaler and a follow-up appointment with his family physician.

When he called Mayako to ask her for a ride home from the hospital, his query had gone straight through to voicemail—her habit when she didn't want to talk to him. So he called a cab with plans to pay the driver once he'd returned to his Granada Hills home. But upon arrival he found his suburban refuge had been taped off as a federal crime scene. A faceless fed paid the fare and ordered up a car to take Rey to a hotel near the Bob Hope Airport. Rey remained there under twenty-four hour-guard for six days and nights in a suite without a working telephone. He never left his room. Not a soul came to visit him. Not Mayako. Not his brother, Heber. Still, he questioned no authority, never asked to retain a lawyer, and appeared content to rack up a huge room service and in-room movie bill that the government obligingly paid.

All the while, Rey waited for somebody—anybody at all— to appear at the door with some kind of recording device. The government would clearly need a statement from him. A from-beginning-to-end recitation of events from Rey's point of view. After all, he was a significant cog in the news event of the year. Domestic terrorism. America had been attacked from within. For God's sake, it was still not just the lead story in every news broadcast, but a bloody mystery all over the globe.

Who was Greg Beem? And why did he do it?

As far as the outside world was concerned, Greg had blown

himself to kingdom come in Long Beach. A suicide bomber of domestic proportion. Yet Rey knew different. The man called Greg Beem had paid a visit to the pool man a mere thirteen hours after the catastrophic event in Long Beach. He'd killed seven more in Granada Hills, tried for an eighth with Rey Palomino, then escaped over the fence into the neighbor's yard.

Rey mentally prepared for his interrogation by the FBI.

He couldn't identify the man who tried to drown him as Greg Beem for certain. It had been dark. A night full of waiting followed by an oh-so-sudden case of shock and awe. But he had no doubts it was him.

"Who else could it have been?" Beemer would say aloud to himself.

On the seventh day, a different yet equally faceless fed informed Rey that it was safe for him to return to his Granada Hills home. He was given a ride, dropped off on the residential street that fronted his house, and bid goodbye.

The news vehicles were all gone, including the van that had been turned into a deadly projectile. What had once been a welcoming front entry was now a gaping torpedo hole. The face of the injury was masked with heavy-ply plastic sheeting stapled haphazardly into place. Had it rained once, disaster would have been imminent. The sheeting would have acted as a funnel, flooding his home and causing untold damage. Rey gave thanks for the dry weather that had come with the unrelenting heat.

The spare key to the deadbolt on the laundry room door was hidden inside a faux river rock, tucked neatly into the real stones lining the gravel walk that stretched along the west side of the house. Rey entered his home, fully expecting it to smell as if the air molecules hadn't moved in a week. Instead, he discovered the central air was blowing full tilt. The pleasant surprise was followed by a brief tightening in his chest. Had the air conditioning been running nonstop for the entire week? He imagined a massive uptick in his electricity usage. The next bill would be huge. Strangely, this led Rey to his dining room table, which, despite the sustained tidal wave of destruction, appeared to have been barely touched. Those neat stacks of accounts payable remained intact, ordered precisely as Rey could best remember them. No blood had been spilled on them. No stray bullets had disturbed a single past due sheet.

"Do you want to come in here, Mr. Palomino?"

The voice startled Rey. It had a baritone quality. Deep and penetrating. The pool man twisted ninety-five degrees to his right to find a gray-suited man seated on a nearby sofa. He stood, revealing the sizeable frame of a former basketball player and a curly shock of white hair.

"Scared the shit outta me," said Rey.

"Apologies," said the gray-suited man. "Nobody told you I was going to be here?"

"Nobody," said Rey. "Who are you?"

"Just a government lawyer," said the gray-suited man, showing both his palms. "Pull up a seat. Let's talk."

"So it's gonna be you?"

"Excuse me?"

"I've been waiting," said Rey. "For my, you know. Debrief, I guess? Nobody's talked to me yet."

"And more importantly," added the gray-suited man. "You haven't talked to anybody else."

"Exactly."

"Very good. Then this shouldn't take long."

"The interview?"

"We don't want to interview you, Rey. Can I call you Rey?"

"Sure...Why don't you want to interview me? I mean, I haven't talked to anybody yet."

"Which is just the way we want to keep it." The gray-suited man sat on the sofa and, with his fingertips, swiveled a short stack of documents to face his host.

"What's that?"

"NDA," said the gray-suited man. "Non-disclosure agreement."

"What's that?"

"Contract between you and the federal government. In it you

agree not to discuss any details or events of and relating to the man you know as Greg Beem."

Rey brought his hands to the sides of his head. His unmanicured fingernails massaged his temples.

"Talk to nobody?" asked Rey. "About anything?"

"Of and relating to—"

"I heard that part," said Rey. "You know, I may not have finished college but—"

"Twenty-two units at College of the Canyons," said the gray-suited man. "Is that not finishing or not starting?"

"You know my college stats?"

"We know a lot about you, Rey. We know you have outstanding debts and some accounts payable adding up to a pretty penny."

Rey glanced back at his dining room table covered in bills. All those neat stacks. Had the man in the gray suit—or his minions, for that matter—rummaged through every red letter of his lousy finances?

"My business is my business," said Rey, hoping to find some depth in his own vocal cords.

"FBI Special Agent Dulaney Little? You remember him?"

"Yes. How is he?"

"Recovering nicely. At least as far as I know. Why I mention him is for this reason alone. He says that you'd inquired about a possible reward."

Rey suddenly felt flush with embarrassment. His ears, he was certain, were turning beet red. After all that had transpired, the significant tally of the dead, Rey felt sickened at his own greed. The loss he'd suffered when Danny had died had been compounded fiftyfold. Because of Greg Beem—and the complicity of one Granada Hills pool contractor—families all over Southern California were grieving over their own dead sons, daughters, mothers, and fathers.

"I wasn't really serious—"

"There is a reward," said the gray-suited man. "And the check is right here in my pocket."

"A government reward?"

"No. Third party. But I'm authorized to hand it to you. But only once you've signed the NDA."

"What if I don't want the reward?"

"Take the money. Pay off your debts. Treat your girlfriend to a vacation in Hawaii."

Rey, who'd been plotting his words—his thorough and complete recitation of his involvement in the new crime of the century—found himself stuck on pause.

"Questions?" asked the gray-suited man. "Because after you sign this it's locked lips and riding off into the sunset."

"If I don't sign…" began Rey.

"More than you can imagine," said the uninvited guest.

And Rey had imagined plenty. Federal prison, for one. Intent to violate Lord knows how many export laws. Conspiracy to receive stolen property. Of course, then there's accessory to mass murder. If Rey didn't sign, it would quickly become the Granada Hills Pool Man versus the United States Government of Kiss Your Ass Goodbye.

"One last question," said Rey. "How much is the reward?"

The gray-suited man grinned broadly. "You gotta gimme your signature to find out."

During the short hours when Gonzo could find sleep, she had dreamed of flying helicopters. Then she'd wake up to find her right arm angled in place by a fiberglass cast. The four temporary pins used to set her artificial right elbow extended two inches beyond both sides of her arm, tearing holes in her bed sheets.

As for painkillers, Gonzo wasn't a fan of anything harder than the most basic anti-inflammatories. She'd woken every hour or so, soaked in perspiration from the pain that radiated deep into her shoulder and neck. The throbbing was often so intense it made the tiny chunk of muscle carved out of her glutes by that third bullet feel like little more than a sore hamstring.

"Sorry, Lydia. But until you're totally rehabbed, we can't even consider you continuing with helo training."

If there was a silver lining in Gonzo getting shot in the line of duty, it was her LAPD union rep calling to inform her that her next petition for permanent disability retirement would be nothing short of a slam dunk.

"Only I don't want to retire anymore. I want to fly Air Support."

Against doctors' orders, Gonzo had been driving ever since the day after her surgery. She would drop off Travis at Madison Prep, then point herself east until she arrived in Glendora at Foothill Presbyterian Hospital. Once there, she'd play temporary nursemaid to Lucky and his laundry list of injuries. In addition to the litany of broken bones, the Kern cop suffered a number of internal complications, including a torn spleen, severe liver and intestinal bruising, and two punctures to his left lung. To keep him immobile, the docs kept the deputy narced on morphine derivatives, dripped into his veins along with bags of sustaining fluids replaced on the hour.

When Lucky was awake, Gonzo was at his side with a book or the TV remote. And when he slept, she'd escape to the rehab unit for a little work on her new elbow.

Not once, though, had Gonzo been ordered to the Glendora hospital. When the directive to attend the federal debrief landed in her voicemail box, she didn't volunteer that she'd already planned to spend her day at the locale. She dutifully replied in the affirmative via both email and text, shuffled Travis off to school, and continued on with her new routine.

Oddly, the meeting would be held in Glendora. Probably because the feds felt they'd needed to include Detective Lucky Dey in the meeting.

Maybe someone should've told Los Feebos that Lucky spends most of his day comatose on Demerol.

For the debrief, the hospital moved Lucky out of the room he was sharing with a pneumonia-fighting octogenarian and into a single-bed unit with a view of the freeway. Gonzo supervised the transfer, hovering like a mother hen. And once the nursing staff ran down their list, checking every IV line, drainage port, and electronic monitoring connection, the all-clear was given.

Deputy Attorney General Lawrence Knockburn entered the hospital room no differently than he would a White House soirée. He swept in and turned in place until he found a hand to shake.

"Larry Knockburn," said the deputy AG, hand stuck out toward Gonzo.

Gonzo, parked in her usual spot off Lucky's left ear, pushed to her feet. She offered her left hand.

"Detective Lydia Gonzalez."

"You're the other cop," said Knockburn. "LAPD, right?"

"That's correct."

"I'm with the Department of Justice," said Knockburn. "Deputy AG of the United States. And this, I presume, is Detective Dey."

Lilly Zoller, still decked out in her funeral black, had followed Knockburn into the hospital room. Gonzo quickly recognized the lawyer from both their elevator tête-a-tête and from Long Beach, only moments before the big bad boom that had tragically transformed so many lives.

"Hi. Lilly Zoller," she introduced herself.

"Lydia," replied Gonzo with a nod.

"Is he awake?" asked Knockburn.

Gonzo bent down to Lucky's ear and whispered. His face, despite the reduced swelling, was still discolored beyond human recognition. Speech of any kind was going to be painful. Yet Lucky's lips moved and his eyes fluttered open.

"He's good to go," said Gonzo.

The deputy AG, who appeared round and Sicilian from head to toe, unbuttoned his jacket and pulled up a chair. Lilly shut the door until it clicked, but remained standing on her stacked heels.

"This shouldn't take long," said Knockburn. "We just need to go over a few investigative facts."

"This is it?" asked Gonzo.

"You were expecting?" asked Knockburn.

"Detectives," said Gonzo. "Federal investigators. Not lawyers."

"Detectives dig up the facts," said Knockburn. "Lawyers try the facts."

"We haven't been officially interviewed yet. Or interfaced with any of our immediate superiors," said Gonzo. "I've made notes but haven't had a chance to file any kind of substantive report, so…"

"But you've had conversations. Over the phone…"

"Sure. With my immediate boss. But Lucky, he hasn't had any chance to download—"

"So consider this as something preemptive," interrupted Knockburn. "A way of cutting to the chase, so to speak."

"Okay."

"I want to talk about your alleged attacker."

"Greg Beem," confirmed Gonzo.

"The Long Beach bomber," added Knockburn. "Now, as far as the government knows, he died in the explosion. So how do we know that was him you followed to…"

"Azusa," finished Lilly.

"Right, Azusa," said Knockburn. "Did either of you make an ID?"

"Not exactly."

"You did or you didn't."

"Lucky…I mean, Detective Dey here. He identified a refrigerated truck in Granada Hills. A white Freightliner. We followed it out this way."

"Based on what intel?"

"Detective Dey encountered a man of the same description in the Long Beach hospital *after* the bomb."

"So Detective Dey ID'd him?"

"ID'd the truck. The bomber said it was a Freightliner full of frozen peas. Right, Luck?"

Lucky gave the slightest painful nod.

"The trailer that was recovered was empty," said Lilly. "No frozen blood or peas."

"Once again," said Knockburn. "Was there ever a positive ID?"

"He drove. We followed," said Gonzo. "Until he led us to a place where he could engage us."

"But you don't know who he was," confirmed Knockburn. "Yes. There was a gunfight. Yes. You both sustained injuries—"

"I shot him."

"So you say. But there's no body. No evidence whatsoever."

"What about the timeline?" asked Gonzo. "We picked up the Freightliner minutes after the attack in Granada Hills."

"Yes, you did. But once again. There's no witness that can place the bomber there either."

"C'mon. It can't be a coincidence!"

"Here's a scenario," said Knockburn. "You pick up a suspicious refrigerator rig. You follow it. The rig's driver, who might've just been hauling Lord knows what kind of drug contraband, gets a little jiggy. Drives you to some out-of-the-way place. Gunfight breaks out. You both sustain injuries and here we are."

"That's not what happened," said Gonzo.

"But could it have happened that way?"

"I don't think it did—"

"But could it have?"

Lucky pursed his lips and moaned. It sounded horribly painful. All the way from his bone marrow. Though the sound itself was wordless, nobody had trouble reading Lucky's intent as pure protest.

"Hard for you to swallow? Sure. I understand," said Knockburn. "But the government feels that it's best for everybody to accept the facts that the same man who stole a truckload of frozen blood also murdered Detective Dey's brother and two others in Kern County. In doing so, he sucked local, state, and federal agencies into his orbit. Once everybody was in his web? Kaboom. Blows himself and everybody within shouting distance to kingdom come."

"And everything else?" asked Gonzo, not trying to bury her incredulity.

"World is full of mysteries," said Knockburn. "Some questions are meant to remain unanswered."

"…get the fuck out," groaned Lucky, his words followed by a tumult of painful coughs.

"I'm here as a courtesy, Detective," said Knockburn. "I'm here to save you further pain and trouble if, for some unintelligent reason, you or Ms. Gonzalez choose to pursue those unanswered questions."

"What you're saying is the government won't help us?" asked Gonzo.

"I'm saying that the government is going to close this case as quickly as humanly possible. Still, after an event as big as this, there will always be talk. Crackpot conspiracy theories. You know what I'm talking about. Do us all a favor and don't add your voices."

Lucky's body shook with anger, damning all pain that came with it. He was moving his lips but didn't make sound enough for anybody to hear. Gonzo leaned in again, her ear inches from Lucky's mouth.

"He says all he wants is to bury his brother."

Knockburn nodded, stood, and decided not to offer his hand in goodbye.

"I hope you both recover very soon," said Knockburn. "Have a nice day."

The deputy attorney general gave a confident smile then made his exit, leaving Lilly to linger behind if only for a moment.

"I remember you both," said Lilly without a trace of her usual fake ebullience. "We were all stuck in that stupid elevator."

"And?" asked Gonzo, wondering what the hell Lilly's observation had to do with the price of tea in China.

Lilly merely shrugged the shoulders of her Helmut Lang jacket and followed in the wake left by her boss.

"Who is it?" asked Conrad Ellis. He hadn't recognized the number on his cell phone and, based on that singular fact, would normally have let the call go through to voicemail. But maybe, having just interred his daughter's ashes into a Forest Lawn crypt, he wasn't ready to be totally alone with himself.

"It's Lilly," said the voice. "Lilly Zoller."

"Oh, yes. I missed you at the funeral."

"I was there for most of the service. It was really quite beautiful."

"What do you want?" asked the mogul from the back of his limousine. He'd already peeled off his jacket and tie and was set to apply antibacterial gel to his exposed skin.

"I want to give you a couple of names."

"What names and why?"

"Cops," said Lilly. "They have an interesting story to tell you. About your daughter."

"Do they know something I don't?"

"They know what they know. But I think the three of you might be able to help each other."

"Okay."

"Write this down. LAPD Detective Lydia Gonzalez. And Kern County Deputy Lucky Dey."

"Lucky Dey? That's his name?"

"I'll text you their digits."

"Then what?"

"Then you do whatever you have to do," said Lilly. "Gotta go now. Bye."

Acknowledgments

Though I'm usually by myself when I write, I'm never alone. I'm very grateful for the following people, without whom I wouldn't have a clue how to put one foot in front of the other.

To start, my dearest wife, Karen—a.k.a. the War Department. She's the font from which most in my world springs.

My reps, Alan Wertheimer and Valarie Phillips. You are incredible resources in my life. But more importantly, you are my friends. So, God bless you and thank you.

Robert and Michelle Tepper. You know who you are and what you mean to me and my family.

Jeanne Bowerman and J. T. Ellison. You inspire, advise, and listen. A powerful hat trick.

Carrie Herbertson, Candy Dooley, and Noreen and Ivan Green. Your eyes and ears are invaluable.

Aidyl Gonzalez-Serricchio and Fred Serricchio. What you mean to my family is without measure. You've changed all our lives.

And last, but hardly least, Henry and Kate. I love you. You are the reason I breathe.

About the Author

Doug cut his teeth writing movies like *Die Hard 2, Bad Boys,* and *Hostage* until sharp enough to pen the Lucky Dey crime thriller series. He lives in Southern California with his wife, two children, and three mutts.

You can learn more about Doug at www.dougrichardson.com and drop him a line at bydougrich@dougrichardson.com. You can also follow him at www.facebook.com/bydougrichardson, on Twitter @byDougRich, and on Instagram @bydougrich.

99 PERCENT KILL

1

Hollywood, California.

It was so much easier than the old days. Back then, it was closer to a fifty-fifty deal. Half of the investment came from the sheer force of Herm's personality, the other half in pure sweat equity. Herm was fast closing on sixty years old, practically ancient in the flesh game. And with no retirement plan but for the slivers of cash he could stow in his City National Bank safe deposit box, the former pimp was all about less talk and a high-efficiency system for identifying the most commercial girl.

"Just look into the camera and speak your name," said Herm flatly, but in his naturally resonant voice. It was meant to sound as if he'd performed video auditions tens of thousands of times instead of only a few hundred.

"Sandy Smithers," said the candidate through an artificially bright smile.

"That your real name?"

That's when the actress wannabe revealed a sheepish gleam. Innocent. Marketable.

"Stage name," she said. "Do you need my birth name?"

"No," said Herm, interjecting a little of the old charm along with a shiny grill of fine dental work as a pearly contrast to his near-perfect complexion of eggshell-brown skin. "As long as it's the same name on your headshot."

"Oh, good," said the girl, twisting from side to side on the pivoting stool. A sure sign of her nerves.

A pair of umbrella lights on aluminum stands cast a couple hundred watts of soft light onto the subject. The rest of the candlepower bounced off the Sheetrock walls to be absorbed by some low-pile industrial-grade carpet. The videographer's kit looked professional enough and cost Herm less than thirty bucks on Craigslist. Add to that the rental of the fifteen-by-fifteen audition space and advertisements in *Backstage*, and Herm's total monthly investment clocked in at just north of three bills.

"Is this good like this?" asked Sandy, crossing her legs in order to show off her toned stems.

"That's totally fine," said Herm, flicking his eyes up to check the image on the tiny monitor screen instead of actually looking at the subject.

In his bad old days, Herm would have rejected Sandy the moment she'd uttered her stage name. *Sandy Smithers.* Sure, it had a nice double-S sibilance and rolled smoothly and memorably over both the tongue and eyeballs. Just way back then the right girl would've been two to four years younger with an invented stage moniker chock-full of starry ambition.

Like Ashley Apples.

Herm suddenly found himself repeating the name—if only just in his head—freely allowing it to ricochet between his temples as he adjusted the video camera lens, pushing the frame until it was hugging Sandy's curves as tight as her peekaboo blouse.

"Now, I'd like you to please twist yourself about a quarter turn counterclockwise," said Herm.

"That'd be this way, right? Little bit to my left?"

"That's good right there."

"Keep smiling?"

"Probably don't have to tell you that," said Herm.

Little Ashley Apples.

Herm had met the fourteen-year-old in a Sunset Boulevard coffee shop. He could tell from the instant he saw her that she was ripe. As brand spanking new as a shiny penny fresh off the assembly line at the US Mint. She was just off the Greyhound bus and sharing a four-top booth with her hot pink rolling suitcase. And where was she originally from? Was it Washington State or Idaho? Near Spokane came to mind. Man, she was something to remember. A once-every-ten-years find. Herm remembered all the ones who ticked off his top boxes. They were the unicorns. The perfect perfects. Produced by none other than the hand of God for man's earthly consumption. And, if the stars and planets aligned, for Herm's personal profit.

"Do you have something for me to read or do you want me to do a monologue?" asked Sandy, beginning to wonder how long Herm was going to let his video camera linger on her.

"Car commercial," said Herm. "Clients are going for a certain look."

"Any particular kind?" asked the wannabe. "I can do other looks."

"I'll bet you can," said Herm, reverse-zooming the video lens back to the widest angle. "But, hey. Why mess with perfection?"

The actress giggled a little too easily. More tease than surprise. A sure sign she was accustomed to attention.

"Any piercings or tattoos?" he asked.

"Excuse me?"

"Might be some bikini work. Both the agency and automaker are European. I expect the ad will air somewhere overseas."

"Can't they just airbrush out a tattoo?"

"Airbrushing's for still pictures. Digital film is way more expensive," said Herm, easily spilling a little showbiz factoid in the name of veracity. His. Proving that a little truth could go a long way.

"Oh."

"Gotta ask. On the agency casting form."

Herm picked up a clipboard and flipped over the first page to show her. Never mind that it was little more than a copy of an actual casting form he'd printed off the Net. He'd been using the same dog-eared sheet for two years already.

"I have two tiny bits of body art," said Sandy. She twisted at the waist and used a hot pink fingernail to pinpoint the first. "One on my shoulder here. And another cute one in kinda, you know… private place."

"So, pink's your color?" weathered Herm, shifting gears and, more importantly, not taking her bait. His game required a professional demeanor. Non-threatening. Entirely devoid of malevolence. That was his job in the food chain.

"I do like pink," answered the girl, revealing a trace of Dixie in her voice. "What about you? You like girls who like pink?"

I just can't get enough of pink.

At least, that's what little Ashley Apples had said to him back in the day.

I like me lotsa pink and just a little bit of gray.

With that, Ashley would gently rub her knuckles up against Herm's spiky salt-and-pepper sideburns, grown just long enough to appear retro, à la some kind of seventies rock star. He'd been about forty years old back then. Ripped like a gym monkey and full of Southern California vitality. Yet the gray around his temples gave him a distinguished streak. When some men of a certain age were spending hundreds of dollars in salon chairs, dyeing their years into blonde or brown submission, Herm found wearing his forties like a badge made the teen girls he hunted feel that much safer in his care. Funny, he used to think. These young women whom he'd chosen to pluck from the runaway tree had all arrived in L.A. with a trunk full of parent issues. Abused. Already halfway down the trail to a future heroin, meth, or crack addiction. Yet it was a daddy sort of lover they still so desired. And hell if Herm wasn't going to be there to provide for them.

I like pink all right. But Herman Bland needs him some green. You wanna help him with that?

And rare was the girl who said no to Herm. At least, not the girls from the bad ol' days.

Why the crap do things gotta be so different today?

"Okay. I think we're good to go," said the finely aged man behind the camera.

"That's it?" asked Sandy, hoping to have been given more opportunity to shine for the lens.

"All I need," said Herm, giving a final once-over to her model consent form. "Now, is this your home phone number or a cell?"

"Cell."

Check one.

"And do you live in town?"

"You mean, here in LA?"

"Exactly."

"Hollywood. Well, I think it's Hollywood. Or is it just East Hollywood?"

"Roommates?"

"Two. I'm sorry. But what does that—"

"Not the best part of town. My guess is you're new to La La Land."

"La La Land?"

"L.A. Hollywood. Tinseltown," explained Herm, his voice reaching down for the tonal mellifluence that lent him such gravitas. His height, smooth yet ethnically confusing pallor, and easy grace reminded many of famed character actor Morgan Freeman. A comparison he used to his advantage.

"You guessed that I was new to California?" she asked.

Check two.

"Good you don't live alone," added Herm.

"That's what my dad always says."

"Might need to travel for the job. That a problem?"

"I love to travel. Where?"

Check three.

"Undetermined. These things change a lot. One day they're shooting the spot in Cancún. The next at an airplane hangar in Lancaster."

"Where's Lancaster?"

"Don't worry. No place you wanna go unless they're paying you."

"Good. 'Cause I really need the money right now."

"Don't we all need the money?" smiled Herm as a way of wrapping up the audition. "Thanks for coming by. If there's a callback, I've got your number."

"Don't call us. We'll call you," joked Sandy. "But I couldn't call you anyway cuzza I don't have your number."

Herm released a polite but still fraudulent chuckle, slipped his six-foot-four frame past the umbrella lamps, and opened the door. Sandy said a faint goodbye, eventually disappearing down a long barren corridor with identical thresholds. It resembled a veterinary clinic more than a commercial casting operation renting audition space by the hour. Once the wannabe had vanished down the stairs, Herm swept his eyes over to the petite young woman in a pair of size-zero Daisy Dukes and bright red lipstick. She was seated in one of two folding chairs that flanked an Arrowhead water cooler.

She was no unicorn. For that matter, neither was Sandy Smithers. But either—given the right circumstance—would still be worth some coin.

"Are you Bristol?" asked Herm.

"I am," said the girl, springing to her feet.

"Well, come on in and let's get you on video."

2

Van Nuys, California.

Lucky Dey loathed stakeouts.

Aside from his longstanding opinion that it was a waste of his time, he had spent enough hours with his ass wearing holes in car upholstery that he'd come to the conclusion that it was also an utter flush-hole of taxpayers' resources. He imagined the cumulative hours of his life lost on what he'd come to call *watch and rots.* He'd imagined the same for other L.A. County sheriff's detectives, then applied salaries, union-negotiated overtime payments, plus the required contributions to each and every health and pension plan. It was a boondoggle, in his undervalued opinion. When cops could have been spending their on-duty time trying to solve actual crime cases, chasing gangbangers with guns, or even the general minding of the public safety, they were often assigned the life-sucking task of watching some empty doorway and cataloguing every innocuous matter of a suspect's comings and goings. Sure, it might possibly, maybe, or eventually lead to a real live hook. But Lucky rued the man hours that would be saved if assistant DAs and the judges who signed warrants would reach into their pants, rediscover their testicles, and allow smart cops to bust down those empty doors and sort out the bad guys from good guys.

What made this Monday stakeout different was that instead of grinding over the waste of his precious time, Lucky was left to ponder the ungodly emptiness that had haunted him from the moment he had woken from his dreamless sleep. Distraction was his only relief from the nearly constant detachment he felt from the human race.

It was December in L.A. and unseasonably cold. Lucky's habit on stakeouts was to leave his car windows rolled down in order to utilize his ears as part of the surveillance. Hearing was key. Be it the throaty fingerprint of a car engine or identifying the direction of gunfire. But the bitter air outside made all those metal pins screwed into his bones just ache, convincing the Los Angeles native to keep the tinted windows at full mast and utilize the late-morning sun to warm the borrowed, mid-nineties model Crown Victoria. It surely wasn't the stealthiest of vehicles. The old Ford reeked of cop car, complete with the hand-operated spotlight mounted just above the driver's side-view mirror. The car was beat to hell, a patchwork of Bondo body repair and primer gray, blending well into the Van Nuys neighborhood that mixed small industry and lower-middle-class single-family homes.

The Crown Vic was parked with its back end up against a Circle K. Lucky, sucking on a forty-four-ounce cocktail of Diet Coke and Mountain Dew, checked the Breitling watch that had belonged to his deceased younger brother, Tony. It ticked in tight Swiss circles, the only survivor of the upturned car fire that had consumed its previous owner.

It was 9:49 a.m.

The Ukrainian bastard Lucky was waiting on should have shown by now. The cop yawned. His eyes autonomically slammed shut as if to demand a power nap just before he forced his lids back open after a bone-shaking sneeze. The ensuing spew left fine speckles on his rearview mirror. With no tissues to clean the misty mess, he tried utilizing the cuff of his jacket, only to leave a horizontal smear across his own blue-eyed reflection. Still, his view was clean enough to chart the deep creases on a face that was less than classic good looks and more akin to a buzzed-cut cage fighter who'd taken one too many cracks to the nose. Considering all the punishment, Lucky was sometimes shocked he could still breathe through his oft rerouted nasal passages.

Personal distractions aside, now was not the time for messing up. He had to get this done and move on to the next item on his never-ending list of duties.

Finally, he spotted the man.

He was hard to miss in the bright yellow Bug. The little damned intel Lucky had was the man's name. Benjamin Anton Kuzmanov. And that nearly everybody, including his employees, five children by three different mothers, and two ex-wives, called him Kuz. The report also expressed that Kuz could best be found driving a newly leased VW Beetle between the hours of 8:00 a.m. and noon on most weekdays. That's when he would leave his fabricating plant for a late-morning meal at Beeps Diner, a local fast-food landmark. Guaranteed, Lucky's female source had claimed. The man apparently couldn't go a weekday without his Beeps' Big Pastrami Breakfast.

The restaurant, famously trimmed in hot pink and turquoise, sat on the northeast corner of a busy boulevard, across which Lucky dodged a variety of cars, their horns sounding like noisy geese chased by a bird dog wanting to play. Lucky ignored the shouts from the annoyed driver of a Wonder Bread truck. The words weren't in a language he could recognize, but they fit well with the middle-fingered gesture the driver used to punctuate his angry, anti-pedestrian tirade.

As the sticky soles of Lucky's boots landed on the opposite curb, he re-directed himself to cut off his target before the man could reach the restaurant's entrance. Lucky was reaching around to retrieve something tucked into the small of his back when he spoke the man's name simply and clearly.

"Benjamin Kuzmanov?" announced Lucky, only to discover his voice swallowed by a cargo jet taking flight at the nearly next-door Van Nuys Airport. So, Lucky waited for a count of three, then elevated his volume with a simple, sharply enunciated, "Kuz!"

The runty man in question glanced over the top of his sunglasses, gathered in the visage of the buzz-cut cop in boots and Ray-Ban aviators, and reversed his direction with a burst of purse-thief speed.

"STOP!" shouted Lucky.

Son of a bitch.

Before the cop even realized it, he was in a race, chasing the runty rabbit between parked cars and into four lanes of morning traffic. Lucky recalled hearing squealing tires coupled with relief that the sound of high-pitched friction on asphalt wasn't followed by the telltale *whump* of metal crunching metal.

Twenty yards ahead, all Lucky could see were those short damned legs cranking at what felt like double his own pace, a jean jacket flapping, and dark hair trailing as the man called Kuz cut behind the filling station and right-turned himself into the side yard of a transmission repair shop.

Why the hell am I chasing this fucker? thought Lucky.

Once in the yard, Lucky glimpsed the man vaulting over a wooden fence. Disappearing in a flash of curled black hair and denim. Lucky suddenly imagined himself in pursuit of some kind of former Soviet gymnast.

It was as Lucky hoisted himself over the fence that he felt the first significant spike of Monday's pain. A wincing jolt that radiated all the way through his limbs to his fingertips. Yet he continued the pursuit. Keeping his feet underneath him. Driving with his legs and arms down an overgrown back alley that reeked of week-old fry oil before he plowed into an eight-foot-high vertical stretch of chain-link. Lucky climbed as if on autopilot. Got purchase with his feet, but got hung up when trying to sling his body over the top. A rogue wire had punctured through his Wranglers at mid-calf.

"Shit-fuck!" Lucky barked before landing on what felt and smelled like fresh-pressed asphalt.

He spun, scanning for the rat-faced runt he was already blaming for ruining a new pair of dungarees. The radiating pain, though, that was all on Lucky with an extra special mention to the team of docs that had pieced him back together with steel sutures and what must have been yards of orthopedic-grade titanium. The rest of the blame was reserved for an evil former Marine named Greg Beem, who, by some miracle, had survived a car wreck, a bullet to the back, and a rushing river that should have drowned him.

The Ukrainian was dashing across the fresh pavement without an ounce of slowing down. Just beyond was a pair of enormous airplane hangars. Big white elephants set atop an ocean of black asphalt. The short bastard had put some stretch in the distance between himself and Lucky. The running little prick was smaller, faster, and unfortunately blessed with a far more efficient pulmonary output.

That and you're goddamned outta shape, Luck.

A lime green SUV swept wide around the southernmost hangar, cutting off Kuz's angle and forcing him to downshift his stubby legs and make a ninety-degree turn. As he pivoted, his suede deck shoes lost traction, nearly sending him to the tarmac. Then, in no time, his arms were pumping again and his speed was back.

But he didn't see Lucky's fence post of a forearm.

The clothesline move employed by the air-sucking cop instantly turned Ben Kuzmanov from a free-runner into a doorstop. As his back landed on the asphalt, all air left him in a single exhale. Those superior lungs emptied, leaving the small man wheezing for oxygen.

"You're okay, ya dumb runt," insisted Lucky. "Just got the wind knocked outta ya."

Kuz could only offer the slightest up-and-down nod of his chin, acknowledging Lucky while trying like hell to force his diaphragm to re-expand.

"Now, yes or no?" asked Lucky, astride his captive. "Are you Ben Kuzmanov?"

The tires of that green SUV chirped, driver and passenger doors jackknifing open.

"Yes or no?" demanded Lucky, his right fist unconsciously balled, knuckles pale and prepped to pummel.

"Yeah…" coughed the runner, palms open and pleading surrender.

This is when Lucky, in the most accustomed of rituals, reached around to the small of his back to where so many cops stowed guns or handcuffs or both. Instead, he withdrew a short stack of papers, folded in thirds and sealed, then dropped it on the runner's chest.

"You've been served, shit-wad," spat Lucky.

"Whoa…wait…" hacked Kuz, still seeking inflation to his lungs. Despite the lack of air behind them, his words were clear yet thickly coated with a Russian accent. "I'm getting sued? You're a fucking process server?"

"Got sweat in your ears?"

"Thought you were a cop!"

"I *am* a goddamn cop!" barked Lucky. "Just not today."

"So, you're a cop?" interjected the heftier of the two Lockheed Martin security officers who'd taken up trained positions at ten and two o'clock. Their uniform shirts were the same shade of green as their SUV with brass badges so shiny the sun was glinting off them. Both men were armed, hands placed on the butts of their unskinned weapons.

"L.A. County," said Lucky, finally catching his own breath. "Dude hopped your fence. I'm just the pursuer."

"He's a fucking process server!" said Kuz, finding his feet and dusting off his khakis with the process papers.

"So, which is it?" asked the security officer. "Cop or process server?"

"Both," said Lucky, fending off their looks with a shrug. "So what? Never heard of moonlighting?"

"That means you're *both* trespassing on private property," said the security officer. "Gonna have to ask you to please get in the vehicle."

"How's this?" offered Lucky, snagging his prize by the back of the collar and jerking him as if setting a hook. "I turn around and drag runt-turd's ass back over the fence and we forget this ever happened?"

"If you're really with the sheriff's," said the security officer, "then you should understand protocols."

"We really gonna do it this way?" asked Lucky.

"Lockheed's a government contractor," said the security officer. "Homeland Security writes our rule book. Now, please? Get in the truck."

Though Lucky shook his head in disbelief, he quickly relented for no reason other than he'd ridden down such a road way too many times before. Whether it was the Feebs or just some bullshit jurisdictional beef between county deputies and the jack-booted LAPD, it was sometimes more efficient—let alone easier on the personnel dossier—to acquiesce and let the bureaucrats have their petty procedures.

As Lucky started toward the back of the SUV, the runty runner's tony deck shoes seemed to be stuck in the asphalt. So, Lucky popped him in the back of the head with an open hand.

"The both of us means me *and* you," reminded Lucky.

"I have a business to get back to," demanded Kuz in a practiced protest that Lucky wrote off as that of a habitual shirker of responsibility. "Asshole. You should've left me to my breakfast."

"Next time, don't run, Mr. Kuz."

"Not Kuz. Cooooooz. You hear the 'ooooo' sound? Kuz. That's how you say my name."

"Get in the truck, Kuuuuuuz, before I hang you up and use you for a piñata."

Join Doug's mailing list
for sneak previews, exclusive content, and
news on the release of the latest Lucky Dey thriller.

Visit www.eepurl.com/cRe5-v